D.E. CIOLAK

Edge Of Time

Eternal Chaos Series

First published by D.E. Ciolak 2026

First Edition Published by D.E.Ciolak on Amazon London, England

Cover Design by D.E.Ciolak

First edition

ISBN (paperback): 978-1-0369-5236-5
ISBN (hardcover): 9798250361095

Editing by Wendy Buckle

This book was professionally typeset on Reedsy.
Find out more at reedsy.com

To my family, friends and partner who supported my dreams.
Thank you so much.

Eatera
Belldale
Eclia
Geuchun
West Kingdom
Relin
Upira
Nahrius
Thehill
Yalan
The Elmwater
Icelands
Sebraycia
Keolin
North Kingdom
East Kingdom
Jutaes
Uzaemura
Karue
Quiet
Woods
Naikaterra
Eswos
South Kingdom
Strauzifeth
Keennaes
Braqora
Qeyekar
Acrar

Contents

By D.E. Ciolak

The Eternal Chaos Series

Serenade of Shadows

About the book

This book contains explicit and dark content including gore, death, explicit sexual content, violence, mentions of torture, explicit language, struggles with self-worth, and implications of suicide. Readers are advised to approach the text with caution.

The hourglass had been flipped.

Chapter 1

"Catch me if you can!" I laugh, racing through fields of golden wheat ready to be harvested. The summer sun sinks behind thick pine trees, warning us that night is coming.

Dirt crunches beneath my boots as the flowery dress mother put me in brushes against long stalks. I hear panting behind me. My heartbeat quickens, adrenaline and excitement flooding my veins as I nearly get caught.

I inhale fresh forest air, letting it sink into my aching bones. Summer in Upira is unlike anything I've experienced. No other season compares. The world takes on a different face, one where everything seems peaceful and balanced. There's no threat of elven soldiers appearing to slaughter us for the simple sin of being human. Summer gives us long days and brief nights so we can stop dreaming and finally live our deepest fantasies of freedom.

I sprint from the farming field into greenery where insects come alive, their sounds creating an evening symphony.

"Got you!" A pair of hands wraps around my waist, and I tumble onto grass, laughing.

"Let go! Please, Issac, I cannot bear being tickled!" I plead, giggling as my hands scramble to push the boy away, but he doesn't listen. Instead, a playful smile stretches across his lips as his pale fingers continue the torture.

"No! This will teach you never to run from me." He chuckles, pulling me closer whilst ignoring my struggles. "You can't escape me, Thea. I'll always catch you." His crimson eyes glint with mischief, warming my entire being.

I blink, smiling, and when my eyes open, the scenery transforms completely. No tall trees, no golden sunbeams, no green fields stretching endlessly. Instead, I find myself kneeling in mud. Or perhaps blood?

Quickly, I scramble away, but there's nowhere to run, nowhere to hide. My heart races as questions flood my mind. Only then does the manor appear, Aagon's vicious laughter echoing through silence as he severs Theo's tongue. Alea's limp body rests at the stair's base, and Issac. Oh, Issac.

He stands inches away, cold eyes completely opposite to his warm laughter. One hand grips my shoulder, knuckles white, whilst the other holds something against my core.

I glance down slowly, vision blurring, and then I see it. A blood spike piercing my chest. The laughter grows louder as tears roll down my cheeks onto his hand. His jaw clenches, then relaxes.

"No, no, no, no." I repeat, shaky hands rising towards his stoic face. "Please, Issac, it's me." But he doesn't react or respond. Instead, he holds my gaze with the same blank expression, as though I'm nobody but another person to eliminate.

I feel my heart shattering. Not because his blood spike threatens it, but because I've lost him. Again. After months of effort, I've lost him. As if everything I've done means nothing. Like the nights we shared discussing our childhood and the missed past don't matter.

In Issac's eyes, I am his greatest enemy, his tormentor and sweet release. If he kills me, he's fulfilled his duty and can finally be free.

A cry slips past my lips, sounding like my heart's been ripped out and trampled on. Every inch of my body aches. Everyone I care about is gone.

Issac leans towards my ear, his touch burning my skin as his grip tightens. "I hope you know no peace, Althea. That not even in hell will they applaud what you've done to us."

I wake gasping for air, my body trembling so violently I crash onto the floor in a foetal position, unable to stop crying. Everything hurts. From my pulsing head to my racing heartbeat. With each breath, I feel it fracture, flesh strings holding it together snapping, making me bleed internally.

I'm unsure how long I remain like this, haunted by recent events and past choices, before someone appears. They lift me from the floor and guide me towards the hammock. I let my head fall onto their knees, feeling their hands brush along my back. A gesture I didn't realise I needed until now.

"Shh, I'm here. You're okay, we're okay, Thea." Desily's tired voice reaches my ears, her warm brown eyes filled with concern.

Another sob pushes from my stomach's pit, nearly making me vomit. "It hurts, Des. It hurts so fucking much."

I feel her arms encircle me, rocking us back and forth in an attempt to calm me. "I know, I know, and I'm sorry, but there's nothing I can do." She whispers into my hair, waiting for this horrible moment to pass.

The nightmares have haunted me since we left the manor

and boarded Graham's ship sailing towards Sebraycia. Since then, I cannot bring myself to sleep, tormented by awful images of everyone dying.

They begin lightly, with some past memory, then twist into reality. Most nights, I see Issac. The expression on his face after Theo commanded him to seize me. How helpless and apologetic he seemed before coldness wrapped his mind in a murderous haze. It's the reminder that I've lost him, that I've no idea how to get him back.

If it isn't Issac, it's Lisa and her beloved visiting occasionally. Images of their murder replay endlessly until I cannot bear the guilt anymore, but ultimately it always returns to that awful moment.

The moment Theo was forced to command Issac to catch me regardless of consequences, then having his tongue severed. Alea's lifeless body beside me as I tried to determine if she was alive. Lathai revealing himself as Aagon, laughing at how gullible I was, how trusting I'd become.

I never should have let this happen. If only I'd refused his help then, none of this would have occurred, none of them would be hurt. But I was desperate, craving connection with somebody since I haven't received it in ages. I surrendered to Lathai's kindness as it was the first time I'd felt seen and assured I won't be alone forever. How foolish.

Time passes before I calm down, Desily beside me throughout the entire panic attack. She's here often, accompanying me after nightmares. During the day, she busies herself checking on me, but there's nothing she can do. Nothing to heal, as the psychological damage inflicted upon me is the only thing she cannot mend. So I watch her sit helplessly, trying not to fall apart at our state.

She's exhausted, I know it. Between tending to Alea and healing Theo's wound, she's overwhelmed. I feel like a burden, always needing her beside me at moments like this. There are far more important matters, like keeping Issac asleep so he doesn't try killing me.

Gods, this is dreadful.

"Are you okay?" She questions without breaking the embrace, her fitted leather jerkin with small metal shoulder plates pressing against my arm. I nod in response, blinking away stray tears. "I've got to check on Theo. I'm almost finished patching his tongue."

As it turns out, her power has limits. It's easy stitching skin together when there's something to start with, but growing body parts from scratch? No. She tries harder than anyone could, knowing it's our only hope of getting Issac back. Of getting me back.

Fuck, I'm a mess.

"Thank you," I whisper, pulling away. A sad smile tugs at her lips before she rises from the hammock and strolls towards the door, boots making soft thuds against old wooden planks.

"I can bring you some herbs?"

"No." I answer too harshly, causing her to flinch. Quickly, I force a smile. "I'll be fine."

She nods and leaves, abandoning me with torturous thoughts. I cannot take her herbs knowing others need them more. Besides, I deserve this. How could I sleep peacefully when Theo cannot speak anymore? When Alea was so traumatised she couldn't talk for days? When they've lost their home, belongings, family? I'm the reason for it all and must repent for those sins.

I move towards the corner chair in this spacious room. It's not my first time aboard a ship, but it's the first of this size. As it turns out, Theo has many things to show off. The most stunning now in ruins.

My throat tightens. Guilt crawls from the void in my heart. I've been useless lately. With only one idea of where we should flee, I cannot think of anything else. Instead, I spend days sitting at the ship's end, staring at the vast sea, hoping it would calm me and provide much-needed strength for when we arrive in Sebraycia.

I slip into warmer clothes that Theo's soldiers had stashed for sudden trips. Most are dead now, but not all. Whoever managed to escape found themselves either at the ship or somewhere in Eswos awaiting news from their Lord. They have no home, nowhere to go. All thanks to me.

Footsteps above inform me that Desily and Alea have left to visit Theo. She's been doing better lately, talking more, but refusing to discuss what happened between her and Lathai. Not even Des knows. A mystery to us all. I suspect it's a feeling of shame at not protecting her home, at letting herself be captured and used as leverage. I understand her, and if I could, I would take that pain away. She's not to blame.

I sit before a mirror, braiding my hair into two plaits. My fingers brush along long strands, separating knots. I've looked worse, far worse, with dark circles beneath my eyes, but I've never felt this horrible. It's as if someone extinguished the fire inside me, and I cannot relight it. Is there any hope? Anything at all?

"Get a grip. We need to focus on the mission now that Aagon has revealed himself." I flinch, dropping the nearby brush. Jino's voice becomes living proof that I'm not dreaming, that

there's no turning back. And I hate that more than ever.

She hasn't spoken much since that day, barely muttering words about how sly the man was in deceiving her. She never sounds worried or apologetic about what happened, instead focusing on the mission at hand. I hate her.

"Feeling mutual, girl. Now get a hold of yourself and stay alert. Aagon might be slowed down, but he knows your plans. He'll follow, so be prepared." Her voice rumbles inside my skull.

"Has it ever occurred to you that I don't want any of this? That maybe, just maybe, I care more about my friends than your stupid conflict?" I snap back, finishing the braid and walking towards the door. Her laughter rings inside my head, causing me to stop, fingers gripping the cold brass doorknob.

"Has it occurred to you that if we don't stop him, there'll be nothing to save?" I purse my lips, refusing to admit she might be right. I know she's not responsible for what happened, yet simultaneously, she's responsible for everything.

"And who's going to stop you, Jino?" I dare to ask the question that's been bothering me for ages. It's one thing to get rid of Aagon, but another to get rid of her. The mission has always been to stop them both, but somehow lately it feels more like stopping Aagon rather than taking them both. Jino is equally as bad as him, that I know for sure.

Lathai deceived me because of her. Elven army pursued me because of her. Theo and Alea lost their home, and Isaac is again a puppet. All because of her. Because they hate each other so passionately they'd rather see the world burn than cease existing. For that, I despise her.

"I guess you better get to work then, girl." She chuckles and my blood runs cold. *"Trust me, Althea, if I wanted to I'd find my way out, but for now I shall provide aid to make sure that*

bastard is dead."

"Why should I believe you? What makes you better than him?" I ask, awaiting her answer. Perhaps I'm being deceived by her the same way Lisa was by Wyrran, the same way Lathai fell for whatever Aagon promised him.

"Who said you should believe me?" She snorts, the sound vibrating uncomfortably through my bones. *"Besides, I am better than him. Your friends are still alive, aren't they? I haven't harmed them in any way."* Her point is difficult to argue against. Although I know her powers are limited by my sheer will, Jino never asks something impossible of me. She just points me towards the easiest direction of getting her out of my body and into the world. Something I will never allow.

Neither of them should roam free, yet Aagon succeeded, taking over Lathai's body and pulling the strings. Fortunately, we have time. He's not fully out yet.

I step outside. A sudden ocean breeze blows stray hair strands from my face. Blue water stretches beyond the horizon, past the place we called home until recently. I hear silent seagulls flying overhead, their low, piercing calls slicing through harsh winds. As we near Sebraycia, the temperature begins dropping.

A couple of soldiers pass, nodding formal greetings before continuing their tasks. Some knights on this ship are the same people I saved in the manor. Their wounds long healed, thanks to Desily, but their eyes empty of gratitude. No one here knows what lies ahead, not even Jino.

I take my usual seat at the ship's stern, eyes fixed on murky waters, watching waves crash against polished wood. I wonder if Lathai is doing okay, if he regrets betraying and deceiving us all. If he misses our shared moments, and if his heart breaks at the thought that nothing will ever be the same.

A larger part of me knows he's horrible for what he's done, but then I remember I'm no better. I can relate to him in ways nobody can, being spoken to by Jino constantly, disrupted when I wish to be alone. It's never easy dealing with this solo, making decisions based on my own views. But then I had Desily, Theo, Alea and Issac. They opened my eyes, showed me I don't have to be alone, that some burdens rest on their shoulders too.

Lathai didn't have that. He had nobody, despite his calls for help and perhaps that's what drove him mad. Gods, if only I'd spoken to him more often, perhaps we'd still be fine, we'd still be friends.

"Thea?" I twist around, noticing Alea standing behind me. Her face paler than usual, eyes lacking the fire and confidence I always admired. She gestures towards the free space beside me, and I scoot over, wood creaking under our combined weight.

I might not want to face anyone out of shame, but I cannot avoid them forever. The last thing I want is for them to think I've developed deep-rooted hatred over what happened with Issac. I haven't. I couldn't. I tried.

"How is Theo?" I question, keeping my eyes on swaying waves, unable to look at Alea's smooth cheeks longer than I deserve.

She sighs, tucking knees beneath her chin. "Better, much better. We're trying to think of ways to communicate other than writing. Our sign language isn't in the best shape." I nod, gears in my head already working, wondering if they have bookshops in Yalan.

I've only been there once, and honestly barely remember anything. It was too cold to venture anywhere, too dangerous with monsters hiding behind snow piles. I asked around about Issac and left as soon as possible, travelling to warmer parts of the world.

"How are you doing?" She asks, and I tense. I'm sure Desily told her about my nightmares, not to mention the man locked below deck in a deep sleep. She must think I'm mad, broken. And perhaps she's right.

"Just fine." I lie through gritted teeth, her gaze burning holes in my body as though she has power to set me aflame. I know she doesn't buy it. The muffled sigh escaping past her chapped lips. But she doesn't press for truth. Instead, she remains quiet, fiddling with her scarf's hem, her bright and composed eyes now clouded with worry.

I swallow hard, praying she gets called to work, that someone would end this torture, but nothing happens. Alea's restlessness reaches me as she shifts side to side, stopping herself from asking a question that has her fidgeting.

"What?" I finally snap, turning to face her.

She licks her bottom lip, eyes fixed on scratched wooden floorboards. I don't know what has her so agitated, but I'm losing patience and the solitude I hoped for. "Have you," she pauses, exhaling pent-up emotions, "thought about him much?"

I flinch, the sting in my core reminding me of something I'm trying desperately to forget. Alea's eyes meet mine, bottom lip trapped between her teeth as she gnaws at it, awaiting my answer.

It's not Issac she wonders about. Everyone here knows I

cannot stop passing by his locked cabin, worried he might wake when nobody is watching. There's another person on her mind. One I try so hard to justify and remember as good. As someone who helped me reach Karul safely, held me when I cried, shared laughter in our campfire's warmth. Lathai.

Of course I think of him, or what became of him, or how I let that happen. The fact I let him kiss me and didn't see through his lies. A person I considered a friend, someone I was ready to die for. It hurts. Every memory of him hurts so badly that I've pushed it into my brain's far corner and even despite that it often finds its way out. The times I see him most are during my nightmares, but even then he isn't himself. It is Aagon who's haunting me, not Lathai, I remind myself. He will always be amongst the people I've let down.

"I think of him." She admits after a long pause, and I stare silently, the worn bone horn hanging on the wall behind her catching my eye momentarily. "Part of me hating him for what he's done to Theo."

"It wasn't him." I cut in, something in me still defending the same man who destroyed our home, hopes, and dreams.

Alea smiles sadly, eyes as dark as the depths of the sea. "I know." She admits softly, her face turning towards the water. "Part of me feels sorry for him. For what Aagon did to him, because I know he put him through hell and no one was there to pull him out. Sometimes I wonder if it's the same for you."

A tear rolls down my cheek, but I wipe it away before she notices my weakness. I have no right to shed tears for him, yet I do. More often than I'd like to admit. It's wrong on so many levels.

I get up from the floor and walk away without a word,

leaving her alone. The lump in my throat grows. I try swallowing it down, but guilt laughs in my face, and so does Aagon's memory. The ground beneath my feet disappears bit by bit, air becomes so dense I struggle to breathe properly, but I make it to my room. Only then do I let myself come undone.

The sins I've committed weigh heavy on my shoulders, crushing me beneath their weight. I've lost everything and everyone in a foolish attempt to have it all. Taking away Issac and Lathai was the only way to remind me I'm not living a dream but a nightmare. We all are.

Chapter 2

One hundred and seven. There are exactly one hundred and seven cracks in the wooden panels on my ceiling. Three hundred and twenty-four if you count the walls and the floor. If you were to add each and every hole I have spotted so far, it would make four hundred and fifty-three imperfections I have spent my time searching for. That is the exact number, and I know it because in the past few nights I have done nothing else but count and recount the cracks. Looking for ones my eyes could have missed. Forcing myself to stay awake so that I do not have to dream.

After the conversation with Alea, I have successfully managed to avoid both her and Desily for the next couple of days. Only sneaking out of the room during nighttime to have my usual stroll along the boat leading straight to Issac's cabin below the deck. His door always shut tight with a golden lock only Theo has a key to.

They know I would never ask him to open it. Too scared to face the man who lost his tongue trying to protect me. Thanks should be in order, but I am afraid, petrified even of the way he will look at me.

What could it be? Disappointment? Hurt? Betrayal? Fury?

Fuck, do I even want to find out?

I push the palms of my hands into my eye sockets. The relief of having my eyelids shut washes over me. I need sleep. The exhaustion is catching up with me, and soon it could turn dangerous. Yet I refuse. Sleeping means dreaming, and dreaming means nightmares. Memories I want to forget.

Since we have left Eswos, I have thought of ways to have a peaceful rest, one of them being stopping my heart so I can die only for a few minutes or hours and pretend like I do not exist, like I have paid my dues. But that is what cowards do. I have too much to think about to just take my life away like it means nothing. People died for it and I don't deserve to treat it so lightly anymore.

Desily would be devastated, disappointed if I ever did that. She has offered help so many times only to be turned down. I cannot find a shortcut. I have to keep going. There is no other way.

I jump off the hammock and reach for the bag Desily had packed for me, anything dear to my life stashed away like a pile of gold. The letters, the books, the journal, the map we have drawn. I have it all, and from time to time I revisit it just to make sure I made the right decision sending us to Sebraycia. I glance at the book with a mysterious message hidden behind a sheet of paper, my interest piqued for a moment. I'm still wondering just who exactly I.E was and why they've been searching for the source of magic, but my brain is quick to remind me that I shall not dream. That mysteries and secrets are not my priority but the safety of our people is. I cannot afford another slip-up, not with our troops falling to barely twenty people.

Tonight, however, it is not the plans I want to study but the unread letters Theo gifted me shortly after our conversation in the office. He did not tell me who they belonged to, nor did he spare me a single glance before shoving them in my palm and leaving. It did not bother me. These letters were just a way for me to remain sane, and that I did.

The only time I have experienced happiness was upon reading new entries. Whoever this person was, whatever Lord Graham did to them resonated with me on a deeper level. It felt like I was learning more about his methods, his tortures, and part of me hoped I would find a way to help Issac. If that person went through the same thing he did, maybe, just maybe, I would be able to find a way out and get him back. Foolish thinking, but truth be told, it kept the dim flame of hope lit inside my chest. I have to try.

My fingers brush against the rough parchment and the words written in haste. I am not sure if I read everything in order, but so far the letters given by Theo seem newer, fresher, with the ink barely smudged or rubbed off with time. These surely were at least fifty years old, as Theo described in them was only forty. It seems like a lot, but in elven years that is practically adolescence.

It is funny to think that both Issac and I are only ten years older than him. Either of us should be long dead yet still alive. In another lifetime we would have never met, perhaps never became friends, and I would never cause him so much pain. But in this reality, I brought him nothing but misery.

I shake my head and dive into the first letter of the night, carefully reading the words to not miss any important information, something of help. I barely notice when night shifts into day, too trapped by the horror stories passed down onto the dirtied paper.

"Thea?" I blink rapidly as the door slams open. Desily standing in the arch, dressed in a winter coat. "You are awake. Great."

"Good morning to you too." She walks inside, ignoring the mess scattered around me. "Something wrong?"

Her eyebrows are furrowed when she scans my features. "When was the last time you slept?"

I gather the letters into my bag and chuck it under the desk swiftly, ignoring her burning gaze. If I answer, she'll worry, and that is the last thing I want. She needs to focus on Theo, on Alea, Issac, and the still wounded soldiers. Not me. Not right now. "I had a nap," I lie, putting my hair into a braid. "Now tell me, is everything all right?"

She looks me over, suspicion clear in her eyes, but after a moment her shoulders drop. She's finally resigned herself to my refusal, and for that I'm thankful. "Nothing important, just wanted to inform you we will be in Sebraycia tomorrow morning."

"Already?" I ask, spinning around to face her. I have almost forgotten this trip was not just to torture my tired mind but actually to find the paper with Jino's ritual written on it. So much time has passed I started to believe they sent me here only to make sure I remembered everything that happened that night with great detail. Because of that, I have not studied the map and our plans nearly as many times as I hoped to.

Right after boarding the ship, I promised Desily to change our journey, knowing that Lathai planned this whole thing. He knew our next move, our every pit stop, and we had to work around that. Sebraycia was not that big a continent, but precautions had to be taken. So the second night after

I woke up from a nightmare, I spent the remaining hours drawing out our plans. The thought of running into him has my skin crawling.

"Yes?" She answers, confused at my reaction. "Are you sure you are all right?"

"I am fine, Des, really." I know that I will get dragged to hell for the lies I keep telling my friends, but it is the only way to keep them safe. If I have to withstand the pressure of holding my thoughts to myself, even if it is slowly eating me from the inside, so be it. They have endured enough.

"Right, well, Theo wants to see you. He asked about the plans you have made for us." She adds, and I feel the colour draining from my face, the walls getting closer and the cracks I have counted repeatedly getting bigger, waiting to swallow me whole.

I look over at the bag and search for the piece of paper I sketched. The roads I picked for our travels, the monsters I made sure we avoid, the villages I chose to trust. It is all here, right in my hands.

"Can you not give it to him?" I whisper, scanning the map and making sure it is perfect. When the three of us used to study in the library, I listened to Lathai explaining why he chose certain routes. To him, speed mattered most. To me, the safety of our companions was priority, so I searched the depths of my mind to create the safest, most perfect route of all time leading us straight to Yalan.

Lathai aimed to land in Keolin, a small city south of Yalan, and then walk the rest of the journey on foot. I, however, picked a piece of land closest to Eswos. South-East shore where we would begin our journey through the woods straight to the small village called Thehil, and from there

Yalan will be reachable within a day's walk.

Yes, Lathai's route was foolproof, having many villages on the way, but we opted for monsters to lurk around given how inhabited those areas were. My route had barely any witnesses around, and perhaps fewer monsters given they were drawn towards magical folk in hopes of getting an early dinner. We should be safe, or so I tell myself, looking over at the map.

"You cannot hide from him forever, you know?" Des stands behind me, her hand resting on my shoulder in reassurance, and the weight I have been carrying lifts with the gentle squeeze she gives me. "He does not hate you."

"How do you know?" I scoff, folding the paper neatly into a square.

"Because none of us do, Thea. As much as you believe it, we do not blame you for anything." With that, she sends a half-smile my way in the reflection of the mirror sat before me and leaves the cabin, knowing I would go without further protests.

My heart aches a little at her words, relief and forgiveness trying to push past the guilt, but I shut it off. Not yet. I cannot let myself think they actually moved past everything so quickly. I have not, so why should they?

I reread through the papers for the rest of the day, making sure I have not missed anything of importance. If something is to be changed I am sure to write it down in Lord Graham's journal. Once again, I recount our steps and the journey ahead. Everything should go as planned. That is only if we avoid getting into trouble, and the issue is we have trouble in our hands.

The thought of Issac breaking free and chasing after me

through the snowy tundra has my skin crawling. To think we spent nights in each other's company not long ago.

Around lunchtime, Alea pops in, setting a tray full of food on my desk, sparing me a worried glance before she leaves. I am too focused on making sure everything goes well that I forget to eat altogether.

By the time my stomach rumbles and I decide to take a bite out of whatever stew they cooked today, the food is cold and the outside seems darker. Well, that is my cue, I guess. Time to see Theo.

My legs shake as I take slow steps to the top of the moving ship. The cold gust of wind becomes the least of my worries as I shiver, reaching the top of the staircase. There is nobody around except for a single guard patrolling the vast waters in case another ship comes into view. He nods in my direction, and I smile, ignoring the fact I am wearing nothing except for the dragon scale chest plate, a simple white shirt, and a pair of leather trousers.

Despite the weather, my skin burns. Droplets of sweat taint my shaky hands. Explaining our mission is not my biggest worry. It is the way Theo might look at me that has me in a choke hold. The last time our eyes locked was right before we boarded this ship, and even then he seemed mournful. After all, I cost him everything.

My lips purse into a thin line as I slowly knock at the thick wood separating our worlds. I hear shuffling from the other side, heavy footsteps nearing, and I still. The door cracks open, and from behind it comes the frame of a man I know all too well, yet not at all.

His onyx eyes appear tainted with lack of sleep, but the

usual spark upon seeing me dances somewhere between the shadows. The long scar across his eyebrow glares at me in a mocking manner, as if to remind me that I have caused him more trouble than necessary.

"Hi," I whisper, clutching the papers closer to my chest as if they are going to protect me from the emotional damage I am about to endure. Theo smiles, his hand gesturing for me to come inside, and I follow. The warmth of his cabin instantly wraps around me.

The inside of his room is far more spacious than mine. With a double bed, a desk, and a huge chest full of weapons and whatnot, I feel envious. At least he still has something to his name, unlike the rest of the people.

I take a seat on the chair and neatly place the papers in front of us. Theo stands right behind me, his hand gripping onto the railing of the chair, making me feel uneasy. Is it really all right to just talk? To just pretend like we have not escaped a massacre and abandoned everyone else with it?

A sheet of paper slides to my right, and I snatch it. *'So, what's the plan?'*

I turn to look at Theo once again. He has a gentle smile on his lips, his eyes awaiting my answer. Fuck, what have I done?

I swallow hard, remembering he cannot talk. That he is now forced to communicate through written notes that some might read and some might discard. I have taken away one thing from him that really mattered. His voice. If only Desily could help him, if only there was a way.

My lip quivers, and I turn around, releasing a suppressed exhale. I cannot do this. I have to get this done and leave.

I walk him through the map, explaining each and every

detail. The roads we would have to stay on, the forests we would have to hide in, the villages we would trade in, and he listens. He listens without making a noise, not a single movement made in the next ten minutes of me rambling.

For a moment, I imagine he is someone else. Desily, perhaps. As I show him the map. I point out the time it would take us to arrive in Yalan as well as the possible obstacles in our way, most of them unlikely to happen but still. Finally, after getting to the part where we reach the capital, Theo slides another note, and I read it.

'Sounds pretty good. I trust you.'

I meet his eyes, searching for the lie written on the paper reflecting in them, but there is nothing except honesty and kindness. I shake my head in refusal. This is not right. I do not deserve this.

"How? How can you trust me after what I have done?" My voice shakes as I turn to the side to fully face him. The man studies me for a second, confusion painted all over his stare. After a silent moment passes, he scribbles something down and hands me yet another note.

'Do you believe I am mad at you for what happened?' I nod back, handing him the note only to get it back within seconds. *'I am not.'*

"I do not understand! How can you not be?" I protest, throwing my hands in the air, tears forming in my eyes despite the fight I put against it. "I have taken everything from you, from Alea! For fuck's sake, you do not even have a home!"

Theo grabs me by the shoulders, and only then do I note the wetness of my cheeks, the shakiness of my shoulders. A sob rolls out of my tongue before any words can as I stare at him, waiting for some kind of reaction.

Yet he remains still. Sadness clouds his eyes as he scans my face. Then I feel his shaky finger point at my chest, then turn to his before he extends two fingers, placing them on top of his other hand, and then forming a circle. "What?"

He does it again, but I stare at him in confusion, trying to calm my racing heart. I'm sure he's trying to communicate with me through sign language but my head hurts, my eyes are blurry and his hands are shaky. I am in no state to decipher his words even if I've studied sign language for years. With a roll of his eyes, Theo grabs onto the pen and paper, writing something down before shoving it at my chest.

I read the words aloud. "Home is where *WE* are. Not in the manor, not anywhere else, but by each other's side." I stare at him as he does the gesture again, finishing the last written sentence in a whisper. "We are family."

Forgiveness should not be handed out so lightly, especially not in my case, yet Theo does it with such ease that I cannot help but let the walls around my heart crumble. Brick by brick, the rays of light shine at the cracks in my heart, filling them up with hope, lifting me up from the bottomless pit of darkness I let myself fall into in the previous days.

I wipe the tears from my cheeks and grab Theo by his hands. "I am so sorry. I am sorry for everything that happened, and I do not expect you to fully forgive me for losing everything you worked so hard on."

He shakes his head and writes for a moment, leaving me to slowly calm down from the storm that took over my heart. I want to believe he moved past everything, but losing Issac and the ability to talk must have taken a toll on him. At least on me it did.

When the pen drops, I grab onto the note and read through the neatly written lines of words he cannot express.

'I knew from the day Issac told me about you the danger that might follow. I knew I might get hurt, we might, since the day I let you stay in the manor, so don't go blaming yourself for the unfortunate events that followed. If I can, I'll share this burden alongside you. After all, my people died, and not only that, but I've cost you someone important. It should be me asking for forgiveness, Thea, not you, so I am truly sorry.'

"You mean Issac?" He nods, and I half-smile. Of course he blames himself as well. Issac is his best friend, a brother perhaps, and to command him to take away his free will like his father once had must have been brutal, heartbreaking even. Not once had I considered that he might be carrying a burden himself, one that might feel heavier than mine. "Theo, I do not hate you for that. You had no other option. Alea was in danger."

I wait a second for him to write a response. *'It seems wrong to pick between my happiness and yours. It should have never happened.'* He shrugs, and I waste no time wrapping my arms around his neck to bring him into an embrace.

For a moment, I await his hands at my shoulders, shoving me away as far as possible, but that never comes. Instead, he brings me closer, his face hidden in the crook of my neck. I slide my fingers through his rough, black strands of hair, whispering quietly. "I do not hate you. I never could. You did what you had to, and we will work it out together."

He nods slowly before pulling away, a final note written down before we move past this and confirm the plans I originally came to him with. *'If you forgive me, I forgive you. We stick together.'*

That we will do, for sure.

After spending a couple more hours in Theo's company, going over the map and the things we have been through so far, I find myself strolling through the empty deck. Before leaving his cabin, the man had forced me to take one of his jackets despite my protests.

Perhaps he was right. I needed it more than I thought as the cold air shakes me to the core, my feet shuffling through the wood in the opposite direction of my room. Tonight I do not feel like locking myself up with the demons residing inside my head. I cannot, not anymore. With Theo's words circling around my mind, I find more courage to push past the guilt and shame and get to work. If I stay like this, Aagon will never be defeated, Jino will forever be trapped inside my body, and every human on this planet will remain a slave for as long as they believe they are helpless.

I come to a halt in front of a reinforced door, one that is meant to hold prisoners locked up for a period of time, and slide down against its frame until I am sat staring at the worn out wood at the depths of the deck. A quiet whistle of the wind rushes past the wooden beams, dancing around to the melody of the unfamiliar waters.

"I wonder what we would be doing right now. Arguing, I bet." A chuckle pushes from the depths of my throat, my head resting against the rough wood. In that moment, I let myself imagine that Issac can hear me, that he is not on the other side locked up and under magical herbs keeping him sedated. Just for a split second, the world around me falls quiet, the horrors of the night releasing their tight grasp around my neck. "I have spoken to Theo. He is doing all right. So are Alea and Desily. Well, as much as any of us can.

I wish I could ask how you are doing, but I know you would hate for me to speak to you. When you wake up, you are going to hate being in my presence."

Sadness clutches onto my heart, and I try hard to push the tears away. I have cried enough. Let the rest of today be peaceful.

The moment Issac wakes up tomorrow, I know the gentle look he has given me over the months will be gone. I will not be able to hold a simple conversation with that man, let alone be in his presence. From tomorrow, Issac will return to the person I first met in the manor. Somebody who thought I had ruined his world. But this time it will be true.

Oh gods, do I have the strength to pull through again? Do I have enough time to pull him out of the darkness before it is too late?

"I know you warned me about this, warned me about what falling for you could mean, but it is too late, I am afraid." I pull the jacket closer, keeping the warmth of my body trapped inside the thick material. "I will not leave you, though. As I promised, I will stick around no matter what. I am right here, Issac."

My words get carried away by the wind into the darkness as I stare at the half open doors leading outside, waiting for an answer. It does not come. I know it will not. But I let myself dream. In my head, Issac will wake up without the effect Theo's command had on him. He will ask me if everything is all right, and I will come undone, letting him see the burden I have carried over the weeks. Then we will mourn the people lost in the battle and talk about the journey and perhaps laugh a little about how we escaped death once again. In this dream, I am not destined to be on the run from him of all people, but rather spend my waking days in his presence.

Our fate is not what has been written from the beginning of time but rather what we make of it here and now, and that is why I let myself dream as I drift away. For the first time in a long time, there are no nightmares to wake me up. I find the biggest comfort in a place where I should not let my guard down, next to one of the monsters chasing after me in the real world, and that sums me up as a person.

Chapter 3

ISSAC

Clicking. Sharp fingers snap beside my ear, jolting me from unconsciousness. I surge upward, but heavy metal bites into my wrists, dragging my body back onto the cold floor. I wrench against the restraints, primal urgency clawing through my chest, but the chains hold fast.

I blink through the haze, vision swimming as candlelight flickers across my face. Where am I? What is happening?

"Can you hear me?" Someone's voice reaches my ears and I try to reply, but the dryness in my mouth stops me from doing so.

My throat feels like a fucking sandpaper, every swallow agony. The thirst claws at my insides as if I had nothing but a bag of sand for three days straight. Every muscle screams, my skull's ready to explode, but nothing compares to this desperate craving for water.

The liquid hits my lips. I gulp greedily, feeling the cool water flood my throat. Life seeps back into my withered cells, transforming me from wasteland to something that might survive.

After a moment passes and everything settles, I finally recognise the person standing before me. "Alea."

"Hello, Issac." She nods and takes a step back. My eyebrows furrow in confusion when I try lifting my hand only to be stopped by heavy metal keeping my wrists bound together. Why am I restrained? Where the hell are we? "I know you're confused. After all, we've given you the potion to keep you under until we reach Sebraycia, and now that we have—"

"Alea, what's going on? Take these off of me." I demand, pulling onto the metal cuffs holding me in place. I remember the day Theo's father had made them like it was yesterday. The scorching metal poured over my skin, melting into the shape of my hands so that if I decide to disobey, they can lock me up. We've never needed to used them, not until now.

My fingers wiggle inside the metal, but I cannot do much more. Someone would have to cut my hands off for me to gain freedom, or use the key, but I doubt they'll do that since they've put them on. I stare at Alea, anger bubbling underneath my skin as she remains silent, her gaze avoiding mine.

Have I done something to them? No, that's not possible. If I had, I'd wake up in a cell inside the manor, but we are on what looks like one of Graham's ships. Right, she said we've reached Sebraycia. Why are we here?

A sudden flash of memories has me wincing in pain as everything falls into place. The attack on the manor. My rushed departure from the grounds towards the first spotted enemy. Journey through the woods and back, finding Lisa dead, alongside her a man.

Fuck, I was too late. Why was I too late?

Kill her. A voice I know all to well echoes inside my head making me cringe.

Another memory pushes through. This time I see monsters swarming my soldiers from every side. They've all died, and I barely managed to escape. Something told me to go back to the manor, that's why I came, but upon my arrival Lisa was dead. Was she not the one calling for me?

Wyrran's stupid face appears in front of my eyes and I grimace. Someone sold us out and that's how he managed to get past all the guards placed throughout the woods. Not only that, he made it to the manor. He was searching for something. No, someone.

Capture her, alive or dead. I grind my teeth together so hard I'm sure I hear a crack.

An image of teary eyes grasps onto my heart, dragging and dragging, pulling the flesh off the organ until it's bleeding everywhere. My mouth goes dry once again, every inch of my body shaking.

I fought him. I almost won, but I left. Why the fuck did I leave?

Capture her...don't kill her...

Strands of ginger hair cloud my head, the intoxicating scent of vanilla and cinnamon wrapping me up. Those tear-filled eyes appear again in front of my vision, pleading words escaping soft, cherry lips. Althea Starbane. I left because of her.

Whatever pain I'd felt moments ago is nothing compared to what I feel right now as pure fury and hatred overtakes all common sense, telling me to find her. It's what Theo told me to do before—

"Where is Theo?" I huff out, my breaths becoming uneven.

"Waiting outside. We weren't sure who should come get

you since Theo—" She cuts herself off, pondering for a moment if the piece of information she's holding onto is worth telling.

Did Althea hurt him? No, there was someone else. Something else happened before I blacked out and woke up on this bloody ship.

It hits me all of a sudden. Lathai. He was there holding Theo and Alea hostage. Althea was talking to him, pleading to release them, but it was too late. It wasn't Lathai after all.

I tug on the chains with all my strength, screaming at the top of my lungs. He was right under my fucking nose since the beginning and I let him in, I let him destroy everything. I should've seen through his schemes. A part of me knew something was off, but I decided to trust him. Why the fuck would I do that? I should've killed him the moment he stepped into the manor, yet I didn't. I didn't because of her.

"Where is she?!" I scream, the wood where the ring holds the chains in place slowly peeling away.

"Issac, stop!" Alea rushes to my side, but it's no use. Theo's command echoes around my head, reminding me that I have to obey. I have to capture Althea Starbane.

'I command you to capture her no matter what, Issac, but you cannot kill her' is what he told me. Is what I need to do before I go insane. My skin's already on fire from the fight I've been putting up to break free, from the anger I'm holding against her. She's the reason why we are in this mess, why I'm so fucked up and why I cannot get away.

I yank once more, the sound of the wood breaking bouncing off the nearly empty room. Alea stares at me in fear before making a run for the door, but I am faster, pushing her out of the way and finally making it outside.

The gust of cold wind pinches my cheeks red. White landscape stretching before my eyes is almost blinding and I stand in place trying to readjust. We're in Sebraycia, that much I've gathered, but why? Why here out of all places? Though a voice in my head tells me I know the answer, nothing actually pushes forward. Are my memories erased, twisted? Is there a reason why we aren't at the manor?

"Stop him!" Alea's voice rings behind me and I snap back into reality, running across the ship, avoiding all the soldiers that should be listening to me.

Just as I'm about to make my way towards the upper deck, a wooden pole appears out of nowhere, knocking me down to the floor. I gasp for air, the instinct to access my magic tugging at my core, but the cuffs around my hands remain, whether I like it or not.

"Now, now, Issac. No need to run. You might slip and fall." Desily's silhouette steps into view and I groan. Fuck, I forgot about her.

"Piss off before I help you."

She chuckles, slowly crouching down to look over my frame. "In that state, I doubt you'll be able to do much, honey." Her condescending tone makes me want to launch myself at her neck and strangle the fairy with the cuffs, only to prove the point, but I don't. She's not my priority.

"Where is she, Desily?" I bark at her, trying to get up, but Desily has her wooden pole digging into my abdomen. I can't do shit.

"I know how eager you are to see her, but a simple hello would be nice." She giggles once more and I roll my eyes. Foolish of me to ask her anything about Althea since the two of them are joined at the hip. Desily would rather die than sell her best friend out to me. If only she could see how dangerous Althea truly is. How destructive and lethal that girl can be.

A surge of adrenaline has my muscles working as I pull my legs up, wrapping them around the wooden pole and crushing it in half. Desily steps back, half shocked, half impressed, and I take it as my opportunity to run as far as possible. They can try stopping me, but there is only one person whose commands I will listen to.

I sprint to the bridge connecting the ship with the land. Someone screams after me, but I ignore it. I've got a mission to fulfil.

A few more steps, and I come to a halt upon seeing the familiar figure before me right at the end of the bridge. "Theo."

The man stares at me with sadness in his eyes, emotions I cannot read as he slowly walks in my direction. All the voices inside my head go silent, and for a split moment it's just me and him. The person I am bound to listen to.

His hand lands on my shoulder, a strange sensation taking over a portion of my brain before he pulls me into a hug. "Are you all right? What is happening?"

"He cannot tell you. At least not the way you'd like to hear it." Alea steps to the side, her lips pursed into a thin line. Something tells me it will be a while before we leave.

I scan the inside of the cabin. It's as homely as it can get when travelling across the sea. There have been a few occasions where I had to go on a small trip down south of Karul using this type of travel, but the memory is a distant whisper in the back of my mind.

Theo, or should I say, Alea, completed the puzzle inside my head. Although most of it makes sense, the majority doesn't. Like the fact that according to her, me and Thea were close. Closer than I'd ever let it happen.

A part of me nags that I should be up and searching for her, but the man sat in front of me says otherwise. His pleading eyes beg me to remain seated and so I obey. There is no way of stopping me anymore. Now that Theo's unable to speak, I am forced to complete his last wish before Aagon took his freedom away.

All because of her.

"Issac, I know you won't listen to me, but you have to understand. Theo had no choice. The command he gave you was Aagon's, not his."

I scoff, crossing my arms on my chest. "Good."

"Good?" She winces, confusion swirling in her mousy voice.

"At least someone had the guts to do what neither of you could. She needs to be gone." I lean back against the chair, waiting for their protests, but neither talks. Not that Theo can, for which I'll be sure to kill Aagon in a thousand different ways. He had no fucking right, and although I stand by my words, I don't agree with the fact he was the one to task me with such a mission. That at the end of the day, I am doing his bidding. Fuck, if only things went differently.

"You wouldn't have said that a month ago." Alea stares down at her knotted fingers, shadows of pitifulness hanging off her tired eyelids.

"Well, that was a month ago. Today is now, so?" I shrug, turning my attention to Theo, whose eyes have been fixated on the window behind his sister.

"A month ago you would've killed anyone who dared to hurt her, including yourself." She counters suddenly, and I exhale deeply, getting up from the chair. Ever since they've told me about how close me and Thea had gotten over the past months she stayed, a feeling of dread and anguish washes over me at the forgotten memories. I try to fight it, to push it so far away that those memories stay exactly what they're meant to be. Recollections. But the harder I try, the more it hurts. For some strange reason I remember the attack, Lisa's death, every failure—but nothing about Althea beyond anger? It's like my mind's only keeping memories that will further fuel my anger.

"Fine! I won't hurt her, but that doesn't mean I like her. As requested per our Lord, I am to catch her no matter what, so that I should do." The bargaining chip had been thrown. Perhaps that will make them remove these cuffs from my hands.

Alea turns to Theo, her eyes waiting for confirmation, and when he finally nods, she cracks a smile. The first one I've seen since she woke me up.

"That's fine, but since she's already here, that means you are to make sure she doesn't get kidnapped or hurt, right?" A cocky smirk spreads across her lips, and I stare in disbelief. "According to what Theo asked of you, she needs to be caught but not killed, so if someone tries to take her away, you'll stop that."

I scoff, biting the inside of my cheek. I see, so they've decided to take a different approach, twisting their own words so that I won't accidentally kill her or let her get killed. Smart, truly admirable. "I guess I'll do just that."

"Perf—"

"But don't think for one second I'll be nice about it. She's ruined our lives, my life, and the lives of everyone inside the manor. I will make sure her life is just as miserable as ours."

I move towards the door, ignoring the shocked looks on their faces. Just as I reach for the door, Alea's voice catches me off guard once again. "Those were the exact same words you said months ago before ultimately falling for her."

Screw them both.

ALTHEA

A cloud of cold mist rushes past my lips as I unload one of the rucksacks from the ship. Not long ago, Alea had woken up Issac, and from the alarming sounds heard from a great distance, I knew it didn't go well. I tried to occupy my mind with other tasks, but my eyes always drifted towards the ship, hoping I'd catch a glimpse of him.

I got woken up in the morning by one of the soldiers when he stumbled across me cuddled up by the reinforced doors.

Embarrassment couldn't catch me fast enough as I rushed towards my room where Desily and Alea already awaited my arrival. Neither of them aware of my whereabouts. They told me to refrain from making any type of contact with Issac, even if it was just a smile, unsure of what could happen. I wanted to protest, but a part of me knew if I tried, it could get ugly, so I left it in their hands.

"It's so pretty here." Desily's voice catches me off guard, the sound of her footsteps pushing past the thick layers of snow echoing through the empty pine forest.

"You've never been?" I ask, turning to look at the tall mountain peaks staring at us from every direction. Sebraycia is not for the weak. If you hate cold and long, vigorous walks, then you've got nothing to look for here.

"No, never been outside of Eswos." She admits, smiling as her eyes take in the mesmerising view. "My sister would've loved this."

I nod, letting my muscles relax, the harsh air biting at my exposed skin. Perhaps it's the first time in a while that I actually feel so alive. Sebraycia might be one of the purest countries, its white look so captivating it makes you want to stay a while longer and stare into nothingness for as long as possible.

Tall pine trees surround us from everywhere, and behind them lays the outline of the mountain peaks. The snowfall here is so thick that one misstep means getting buried under. I shiver, pulling my jacket closer. It's not even the nothingness that's bad here. It's the never-ending cold wind biting at your legs, your exposed cheeks and nose. Breathing feels like pushing tiny needles down your throat. Winter in Sebraycia is much different to the one anywhere else in the world. If you as much as forget your gloves or scarf for this country's weather you will die. It's as simple as it sounds.

Winter is also the only season they have here. Perhaps that's why the people of this land are so calm and collected. How can you hate the outside if the world around them is nothing but blank and they're the only colour in it?

"How did it go?" I clear my throat and begin walking towards the ship where a few more sacks wait to be moved.

Desily stills for a moment, her full lips sealed before she reluctantly gives her answer. "It was... something."

"Something?" I cock my brow at her. She scratches the back of her head and jogs to match my pace.

"Well, he didn't murder you, so I call it a win."

"Des." I plead before stopping at the foot of the bridge. "Is he, well, all right?"

"As all right as one can be. Theo and Alea went to have a talk with him. Hopefully it will bring some memories back." Doubt that. The Issac I'd met almost a year ago knew who I was, but our history was strands of twisted memories he tried so hard to leave untouched.

It took me ages before making progress. To be honest, I'm not sure how I got through, but I did. Perhaps I can do it again, but time is on our arseholes. With the threat of Aagon showing up at any moment, followed by Wyrran's army, we are at the edge of time. Time I cannot spare anymore to save him and the future I had dreamt of.

Half an hour passes before we manage to get everything off the ship. Most of the soldiers are coming with us, whilst the rest agreed to work as a decoy and sail towards Keolin. I've tried to stop them, clearly lost the fight, and had to swallow the sour taste of guilt as I watched them get ready to leave. If Aagon finds them, they will die. There is no doubt. And I'll be left living with that grief for the rest of my life.

Why does everyone want to die for me so badly? Why do they choose their own limited life over mine? Putting faith into a girl that barely knows what she's doing, fuck. I guess I owe them to take this as seriously as I can for the sacrifices made, otherwise they'll catch me in the afterlife and make sure even there I won't know peace.

"When is our first stop?" Desily steps closer and I pull the map from my pocket, looking it over for the upcoming three-week journey.

"Just before those high peaks." I point to the giant, snow-covered mountains. If it was any other land, the journey might've been far shorter, but we are fighting against snow drifts and unknown monsters. "Tomorrow we will have to get past the crevice and should reach the Elmwater Moun—"

"She's the one leading us to Yalan?" The sound of the voice well known to my body has me straightening my back.

The world around me falls quiet. Even if it already was, I don't hear the sound of the crashing waves or the quiet calls of the birds above us. I don't even hear my own heartbeat as my head slowly turns, the hair on my body standing up, my skin covered in goosebumps.

Issac is a few metres away, his face twisted in a grimace as he stares back at me. The well-known hatred reflecting in his red eyes. I take in the image of him as if seven years had passed instead of few weeks. He's still the same, with his black, wavy hair, and the freckles scattered around the palish face. I would've gotten fooled if I didn't know any better. Right here, right now, he's the Issac I gave my heart to, the person I let inside my soul and let explore the darkest, deepest corners of my mind. The same man who told me about his haunted past, and then cuddled me to sleep in his arms.

But he's not the same. There is no love or kindness in his eyes, but the same exact coldness I got welcomed with when I first reached the manor. For a split second, I let the world shatter as the memory of his apologetic face rushes into my mind just before it's gone.

"Thea was originally the person that came up with the plan. It was her, Desily, and Lathai who worked on it. Later on, you joined them." Alea explains as if Issac has amnesia. I stay still, holding his gaze and hoping, praying that a part of him might recognise the devotion in my eyes. Foolishly so.

"Should've known she would be the one working with that traitor." He scoffs, and I hate the sting his words give me. It's like I'm wearing a mask, playing pretend just for the sake of us all.

"I didn't know." Words leave my mouth before I can stop myself, Issac catches onto them and immediately narrows his eyes.

"Funny you didn't know, but he was by your side the whole time. Not only that, but you've vouched for him, didn't you? How do I know you're not lying?" He spits and takes a step forward, but Theo's grip on his shoulder stops him in his tracks.

I curl my fingers into a fist, squeezing as hard as possible because this fight with Issac is not the one I've grown to love. There is no playfulness and understanding, but hatred and pent-up anger. So much fucking anger.

Besides, I know he's right. The things he's saying, no matter how hurtful, are true because those are the same things I've told myself over the past few days. The difference is, I was too afraid to voice them, but Issac isn't. He never was.

"I've changed our journey completely, and do you really believe for a second I'd risk everyone's life here just for fun? That I'd drag them across the continent for some twisted fantasy?" From my previous battles against Issac, I learned one thing only. You can only win if you've managed to make his sins greater than your own. If you can shine a bit of hope on yourself, he just might believe you.

"I do." He spits back, his jaw ticking as he chews on the next words. "You've done it before, haven't you? In Naikaterra to that human family, in Karul whilst we searched for Lathai, and now in our manor, our home we've let you stay at."

I wince, the pain almost unbearable. I take it back. This Issac is far worse than the one I'd met before for one simple reason. He knows too much about me and is willing to use it as a weapon to crush me under his shoe. I know him, I know Theo won't let him hurt me, so he will do it in a way he knows best. With his words, because if there is anyone out there who knows me better than myself, it's him.

"Pipe down, Issac. It wasn't her fault. None of us knew, not even you, and you've spent as much time with Lathai as any of us. As a general, it's a shame to miss something so simple like that, is it not?" Desily's words are soaked with venom even I don't dare to acknowledge. Of course, she doesn't hate Issac, but the man standing in front of us is nothing but a shell of who he truly is.

I try not to hate him either, even if he makes me wish I could drown in the cold seas and disappear from this planet.

Issac kisses his teeth and turns around, not sparing a single glance towards us. That's the argument finished. Perhaps I'd be useful if I could ignite the fire for those arguments with him like I'd had before. But it's hard, impossible almost, when each time I look his way I see someone who devoted themselves to searching the world for me.

Alea shuffles towards Desily, letting the fairy wrap her in a tight hug as I'm approached by Theo, a note written in his hand.

'We've tried talking to him. However, he's adamant he doesn't remember anything about the time you two shared. His memory is very selective. I'm sorry, but on the bright side, we've convinced him to protect you instead of trying to hurt you.'

"What?" I stare between Alea and Theo, waiting for either of them to give me more context. What exactly do they mean by Issac protecting me? The shitshow we've just had should be enough proof that the man wants nothing to do with me. Probably doesn't want to be anywhere near me, so what are they talking about?

Alea snatches the note and skims over the lines before releasing a tired sigh. "I told him that his mission was to capture you, and since we've sort of done that, he needs to make sure you don't run away."

"I beg your pardon?" I turn to Desily, who replies with a confused shrug.

"I'm sorry, Thea. It was the only way. Issac will be your personal guard."

I'm sure my jaw hits the floor as I gape at the three of them. I'd wanted him close by, and I guess my wish was granted. I've got my very own, exclusive guard from hell. A demon on my shoulder, one might say, as I am sure Issac will do anything in his power to inflict as much suffering on me as possible. Well, that's what you get for wishing for something. Can't have it all since a balance must always be met.

Chapter 4

Our first day in Sebraycia was disastrous. We'd barely made it into the forest when the sky turned grey and a snowstorm hit us from out of nowhere. For the remainder of the day, the convoy of fifteen people had to hide in a nearby cave and wait for the weather to subside. On the bright side, there was enough room to fit everyone and start a campfire to keep us warm. On the bad side, Issac was looming around me. A disturbing thought in the back of your mind you try to push away, but it always returns.

I thought about what Alea said, how they'd changed his mind from trying to hurt me to keeping me safe instead. Sure, it sounds better, but that doesn't turn my life into something pleasant. If anything, it makes it worse. I'm constantly reminded that the man I fell for is inches away, but I can't touch him, can't tell him what's been bothering me and get lost in his kisses. Instead, I have to settle for murderous glares and his keen eye should I try to run away. Which, of course, won't happen.

Still, a feeling of dread latches onto my chest as I think of all the possibilities of what might come should I separate from the group. Issac might be content with the fact I'm peacefully resting alongside everyone, my presence keeping him at bay, but what would he do if I had to leave? Would he try bringing me back by force even if it meant breaking every bone in my body? Would he hurt me just for fun and out of spite for things I haven't done? I don't wish to find out.

I stare into the flames of the campfire, unable to join everyone in their sleep. I had my night of rest. The only time I was granted the opportunity to escape the nightmares. But that's long gone. I'm sure if I were to fall asleep, I'd wake in a blink and cause everyone else to follow suit. I can't do that. They don't deserve to lose their sleep over me and worry about things only I should bear.

As quietly as possible, I push off the ground and walk around people scattered across the cave to reach the entrance. The snowstorm still causes chaos outside, bending trees. Hopefully it'll go away soon. Otherwise, we might face our first obstacle.

"Trying to run away already?" I wince, spinning around on my heels, the dagger I've tucked away in my trousers ready in my sweaty palm.

I've become paranoid. Understandable when Aagon could be days, hours, minutes, or even seconds away. Not to mention, I fear he has some connection to my mind. The memory of a vision I had when Lathai went missing bothers me to this day. Jino won't tell me anything, so I'm left fending for myself. Once again, I can't share the deepest secrets with anyone except for the man in front of me.

"What do you want? Am I not allowed to have some alone time anymore?" I hiss, tucking the dagger further into my sleeve. I don't trust Issac. At least not this version of him.

He's proven before that if he wants to, he can hurt me despite what Theo told him. After all, the memories Lord Graham pushed inside his mind do play a nasty trick on him.

"No, you are not." He barks back, pushing off the stone wall and slowly walking in my direction. The heavy cuffs obstructing him from using magic aren't a reassuring sight. Part of me feels sorry. They're clearly custom-made, a story Issac never got to tell but has to parade in now. Yet at the same time, if they weren't there, who knows what he might do? I hold my ground, my chin raised high as I await his first blow. "If you have not forgotten, I have to monitor you, much to my displeasure."

"The displeasure is all mine," I sneer back.

"Well, at least one thing is clear between us. Would hate to see you care about me when I know it is all a lie." My brows furrow. It's as we thought. His memories are jumbled with whatever sick things Theo's father told him. Although the things we did still exist, they're nothing more than a whisper in his mind, clouded over with the generated hatred towards me.

"It was not a lie, and I still do." I whisper, which has him stopping in his tracks. Issac watches me attentively as if I'm about to slip on my own words and laugh in his face, revealing it was just a joke. "Do you really not remember anything?"

"No, and perhaps that is for the better. Whatever you did to me is thankfully gone because I would have hated to stick around somebody like you." There it is. The first blade sliding between my ribs. But I keep up the façade, smiling as if nothing happened. As if I don't wish to cover my ears and wallow in silence.

"What is it exactly that I am, Issac?" I inch closer, my skin burning with desperate need to touch him, but I know better than to taunt a wounded animal. He looks me up and down with such disgust it makes my stomach churn, a sneer twisting his features before the words roll off his tongue.

"A curse." The word hits me, and I feel my breath catch. He takes a step closer, his voice dropping to a venomous whisper. "You're a walking plague that infects everything it touches. A disease that spreads misery wherever it goes."

I stare at him, my heart fracturing with each word, but he isn't finished. The cruel satisfaction in his crimson eyes tells me he's just getting started.

"You want to know what you are? You're the reason people die. You're the shadow that follows good people until they break. You're every nightmare, every scream in the dark, every moment of pure terror when someone realises they trusted the wrong person." His voice grows colder, more calculating. "You're not a nuisance, Thea. You're not even a misfortune. You're a catastrophe in human form, and everyone would be better off if you'd never been born."

The words land. Each one more devastating than the last. My vision blurs as tears threaten to spill, but I refuse to give him the satisfaction. My hands shake at my sides, and I can feel my magic responding to my emotional turmoil, sparks of heat flickering beneath my skin.

"The funniest part?" He continues, circling me. "You actually believe people care about you. You think your little friends back there give a damn about your wellbeing when really, they're just waiting for the right moment to be free of you. Do you think any of them would choose you if it came down to it?"

A broken sound escapes my throat, somewhere between a gasp and a sob. "Stop."

"No, I don't think I will." His smile is cruel, predatory. "Because this is the truth you've been running from your entire pathetic existence. You're alone, Thea. You've always been alone, and you'll die alone, because that's what monsters like you deserve."

The mask I've been wearing shatters completely. I can't piece it back together this time. The fragments are too small, too sharp, cutting into my soul as they fall. My bottom lip trembles violently, and the tears I've been holding back spill over, tracking down my cheeks.

"You think I don't see it?" He leans closer, his voice barely audible but sharp enough to slice through steel. "The way you look at me when you think I'm not watching? The way you still hope, even after everything? It's pathetic. Whatever delusion you've built about us, about what we were, it was never real. I could never love something like you."

The final words hit me. My knees nearly buckle, and for a moment I think I might collapse right there in the snow. The pain is so acute, so all-consuming, that I forget how to breathe. This is worse than any physical torture. This is the complete annihilation of hope.

I stare at him, unable to answer, the truth in his words, twisted and cruel as they are, piercing my heart with ruthless accuracy. If I'd known this was the person I could have met all those years ago before he gradually opened his heart, I would never have tried so hard to find his whereabouts. The old me surely would have crumbled into pieces, but the current me is left with nothing but the dying embers of hope still trying to keep me sane.

Issac watches my breakdown with something that might be satisfaction, but then his expression shifts. For just a moment, I see horror flash across his features, as if he's waking up from a nightmare and realising what he's done. The realisation of his words makes him stumble backwards, his eyes searching mine with something that looks almost like regret.

It's almost as if he regrets every syllable that came out of his mouth, as if my reaction didn't give him the satisfaction he thought it would. As if seeing me break this completely was never what he actually wanted.

But the damage is done. The words hang between us, and no amount of regret can take them back.

I hurry past him before he changes his mind and make it to the campfire, where I spend the rest of the night staring at the dancing flames. I replay the memories of us together in my head until it hurts to think, until I believe there's something redeemable in him. Every now and then, I glance at the entrance expecting him to show up, but Issac never returns. Not a single sound made inside the cave even as the world around me screams.

***

"How long is left?" Desily shivers at my side, her furry boots vanishing under the tall snow banks as we move through the forest, hoping to make it near the mountains by tomorrow. We've been on foot for nearly two weeks now, some days gone without an ounce of sleep.

"Haven't you asked that already, like twenty minutes ago?" Alea chirps in, her heavy breaths a sign of how worn out she is from dragging her small silhouette through the snow. We're all tired, to say the least. Ever since the snow storm, we've done nothing but walk, trying to make up for the time lost while we waited for it to pass. For the record, it wasn't my idea. It was Issac who forced everyone to get up at the crack of dawn and marched us out into the wilderness knowing I got little to no sleep. We haven't looked at each other since that awful conversation, but somehow I still feel his presence despite the absence of his gaze.

"I did, I think. I don't know!" Desily throws her arms in the air, a fake cry coming out of her mouth. "Everything here is so fucking white that I can't think straight."

"Agreed," murmured one of the guards at the front. I never paid them much attention, most wearing helmets to hide their identity, but in these conditions all of us are forced into winter jackets and thick scarfs.

My interest piqued as I look at his white, matted locks tied into a ponytail. His skin is a darker shade of golden brown with white spots here and there. He must have just reached his adulthood, the seriousness and formal fashion in which other knights move absent. I wonder how long ago he joined Issac's ranks, and if they gave him proper training to manage against the violent magic Aagon uses.

His head turns to the side, as if feeling my curious eyes, and I note the distinct feature which makes him different from me. Pointy ears. He shoots me a half-smile, a silver ring pulling on his bottom lip, before he turns away.

"Sorry, I'm not sure if I'm allowed to talk. Everyone here is so dull." He whispers so that only I can hear, which pulls a giggle out of me.

"Well, they have a reason to be." I answer, speeding up

my movements so that I can walk next to him. Would it be wrong to try and find out more about him, even if in the future it might cost him his life?

"Yeah, I heard. I mean, I wasn't there. That day they kept me posted at the port tending to the ship." He shrugs, and I smile. He's still a child at heart, but something made him join the army. Be it his skills or sad past, either way he's here now, which somehow worries me more than it should. A child shouldn't throw themselves into war, not like Issac and I had to. He should be out there, spending time with his family and friends, chasing dreams instead of enemies and long-lost rituals.

"Soldier Erdove, less talking, more walking. We're in enemy territory. Keep your eyes and ears open." Like a bad neighbour, Issac's annoying voice reaches the two of us, making my ears turn red almost as if I got scolded alongside the young elf. I turn around, sparing him a single glare, which, of course, does nothing but make me angrier. Fuck this. Time for payback.

"I'm Thea, and you are?" The boy looks around, unsure if he should answer. I smirk, patting him on the shoulder. "Oh, don't worry, he has no real power here. I'm in charge of this mission. He's just a tag-along."

I don't have to turn around to feel Issac's furious eyes burning holes into my head to know that I've pissed him off. Good. Well deserved for everything he said yesterday.

"You're Althea, right? The one in possession of Jinoros's spirit?" I nod, and he smiles, flashing a set of pearly whites right at me. "I'm Ryo Erdove."

"Nice to meet you." I extend my hand, and he shakes it. A white spot covering the whole of his knuckles gets my attention.

"This? It's vitiligo. Quite a rare condition, but I guess I'm special."

"And young." I point out, and he laughs, rubbing his neck. It's strange to say, but he reminds me a lot of how Issac used to be when we were younger. Carefree and curious about the world. Nothing like who he is right now, far too reserved and an arsehole.

Ryo and I talk for a while, forgetting about the snow and the journey as we tell each other about our lives. He reluctantly reveals that he joined the ranks after being saved by Theo's knights during one of the monster raids, and I tell him a bit about my life.

He listens attentively, and questions me every now and then. I answer truthfully, telling him about the monsters I'd fought, the lands I've travelled through when searching for Issac, the people I've met. For once, just once in my life, someone is interested in getting to know me and my life, not the immortality or the hardships.

"What was Eswos like a hundred years ago? I must have been eight, so I barely remember anything." I look ahead of us, a distant memory of my mother and father bringing us over to the fairy land dragging out from the back of my head.

"It was beautiful, just as it is today." I tell him, a smile creeping onto my lips. "Although, back then everything seemed more alive. The trees danced as we passed them, the wind whispered secrets into your ear, and at night," I get closer, lowering my voice, "I swear you could hear the flap of dragon wings just above the mountains."

"You're lying!" His mouth hangs open, and I giggle. What

had happened a hundred years ago is a mystery and a blur in my mind. Gods know if what I heard was true. It was the only thing keeping me company whilst I waited for a certain someone to turn up at my porch.

A scoff reaches me from behind, my head twisting. "Something funny, Issac?"

The man shrugs, a constrained frown plastered on his smug face. "There's nothing funny, just the fact that he's got you figured out ahead of time. At least it might save his life."

My lips purse, annoyance prickling at my skin as I stare at him before suddenly stopping. Issac follows suit, and so does Ryo, unaware of our bitter history. How I wish he could have met his superior when he was actually nice. "What's that supposed to mean? When have I lied to you?"

An annoyed sigh pushes past his lips as if I'd asked him to do the most mundane task. "Should I start naming everything aloud, or would you rather I submit you a list?"

"One thing. Do go on. Name one thing I've lied about." I snort, putting my arms on my hips.

His gaze narrows as he holds my stare. I swear, for a second there he looks ready to launch himself at me, before his mouth suddenly opens. "On the day of the ambush, did you not promise to keep everyone safe?"

My expression falls. I stare at him in utter shock. How does he—I thought everything we did together was forgotten, but it seems Issac can pick and choose his memories at will, especially the ones that might throw me off.

Silence falls between us. He knows his words worked, and I know they were true. I did promise to keep people at the manor safe, but I failed, causing nearly most of them to be killed either by the monsters or Wyrran's soldiers. It might be the only time I failed to hold my word, and fuck does it hurt.

Issac's triumphing face rubs salt into invisible wounds, and all the sadness I've stored inside my heart vanishes as anger spreads through my core.

I cut the distance between us in two strokes, my fingers curled into fists at my sides. "How about the lies you tell?"

He scoffs. "What lies?"

"You love to hold me up to high standards like I'm some sort of fucking saint, but when it comes to you, everything is fair game." My finger pokes his chest, but he doesn't budge, doesn't even flinch as I continue. "Issac can go and kill everybody, lie about whatever his heart desires, and have zero consequences because who should care about you when I exist, right? Put all the blame on me like I asked for any of this."

Silence settles between us, like freshly fallen snow nobody dares to disturb, but deep down they want to mess it up, to imprint a part of themselves into the stillness. I know I want to say more even though I shouldn't, things we've already resolved long ago, but if he's willing to bring up my mistakes, why shouldn't I?

Issac's eyes narrow into slits, his tongue brushing against the top row of teeth. There are a million things hidden behind his tempestuous eyes, half of which I'm sure he's itching to say, but none come out because if either of us speaks, all hell will break loose.

The sound of Ryo's feet shuffling behind us brings me back to reality, and I pull away from Issac to notice everyone had stopped walking. Their concerned looks snap me out of whatever it was Issac had put me into. Perhaps I'm frustrated over the fact that nobody here can say anything to him, and once again the responsibility of making him a better person falls onto me. The first time around I wanted it, until I didn't. There's only so much hurt one can handle, and Issac has an abundance of it at his disposal. A bow with unlimited supply of arrows. Either way, their expectations are set high on somebody who can't meet them, yet again.

"Is everything all right?" Desily shouts from the side, her eyes searching mine for an answer which I'm unable to give. Admitting defeat to her is acknowledging failure to myself, and I won't give up, not yet.

"Yeah, sorry, let us keep going." I look around, sending an apologetic smile before turning to Issac. His expression remains as wrathful as when I left him. Great to know he doesn't give two shits about what people think about him. After all, it's my reputation on the line, not his, once again proving my point.

Out of nowhere, a sound of whooshing reaches my ears, like thin cloth in the wind accompanied by soft whispers of cries. My brows furrow, searching around for the culprit but finding nothing.

The sky had already begun turning darker, a few stars peeking from behind the cotton clouds. I wonder if we're going to make it to our next stop before sundown, but that thought is interrupted as something rushes past my ear. "What was tha—"

My head turns, time slowing down as Issac's gaze locks with mine. Just then, for a split second, I see the hesitation in his eyes. The moment that could save or doom my life. It's that exact moment he fights against himself, against his very own nature, and decides to discard his own views. His handcuffed palms push me backward with so much force I can't find any balance and fall to the ground.

I watch as he lands on top of me, the contact I've craved ever since we left the manor finally there, but not in the way I want it. It's enough to satisfy my heart, but not the starved body.

"Watch out!" Someone screams, and then I see it. The figure of a woman as if she's made of glass charging past us, her sharp nails cutting through air in the spot where I stood mere seconds ago. If Issac hadn't pushed me out of the way, I'd be sliced to pieces. But he did, even if it cost him his pride, even if he hesitated for far too long. He did.

I wiggle around, an attempt to push him off myself, but he doesn't move. Doesn't say anything as his body shakes, muscles tensing, eyes tightly shut. I scream his name, bang my fists on his chest with no answer. What the fuck is he doing?

"Issac, get off me!" The sound of swords being unsheathed reaches my ears, and I stare to the side, urgency tugging at my legs to go and help without success. Issac is like a boulder. Heavy and floor-bound. Whatever's going on inside his head might cost us our lives, and I'm not willing to get blamed for yet another death, the list growing higher. "Ryo!"

The young boy snaps his attention back to me immediately, clocking on what I need him to do. My arm wiggles out from below Issac, and he grabs onto it, sliding me out. "Thanks."

"Anytime." He winks, and I smile before turning to check on Issac.

My heart squeezes. His eyes are full of confusion and pleading as if he wants me to stay down, as if he regrets letting me go. For a moment I let myself believe these feelings are true. That perhaps there's some part of him that won't allow anything bad to happen to me. But that thought vanishes. He's not doing this because he cares, but because he has orders to. I'm not a bystander watching the battle inside his mind unfold, but the catalyst of the conflict between what's considered right and wrong.

"Let's go." I rush Ryo towards the commotion, and we leave. A feeling of betrayal and guilt tags behind me when I abandon Issac. I know even with the cuffs he's capable of handling himself, so why does it feel so wrong to leave?

Before reaching the soldiers who swing their swords around in the air in hopes of hitting the strange monster, I tap into my magic. It's the first time since we left the manor, but somehow I'm not uncertain. The familiar feeling of warmth prickling my fingertips just as the flow appears in my vision, passing by everyone gathered here. It never ceases to amaze me. The fact we're all connected at the end of the day, how sad no one else can appreciate the beauty.

Ryo pulls a few crystals from his satchel, a purple and green aura wrapping his body. I know he'll have some protection and strength, but is it really enough for a young boy?

Around me, a few other soldiers follow his lead along with Theo and Alea, who are to my right. Desily is right at the front, her daggers held in front of her face as she scans the area around us.

"What the hell is that thing?" She shouts, ducking as the woman charges at her.

I watch her float around, almost as if she's carried by the wind, an evil grin spread across her face before a laugh slips past her thin lips. There must be something I've read about this, an important piece of information tucked away in the back of my mind.

The woman passes through the thick layers of snow, only to reappear below someone in a blink of an eye. Her long, white hair swaying to the side just as her nails cut through the air, a low hum escaping her mouth. "A snow wisp!"

Everyone stares at me, half confused, half spooked. It's not common to come across them, but we've established long ago that in my company anything is possible. Many monsters who are either extinct or rare to spot are drawn towards my magic, and that would put everyone here in danger. Good thing they have someone who travelled across many lands in the past hundred years and read every book that could be of help.

"Get out of the way. You won't cut it!" I scream, running towards the front where the wisp had grasped onto one of the soldiers. *"Ignite."* The fire burns the atmospheric ghost, scaring her away and giving the soldier time to flee.

"Thea, what do we do?!" Des shouts from the side, and I look around to find the wisp. If I remember correctly the only thing that can destroy them is fire. Lucky for us, I've got plenty of it.

"Go, run towards safety! I'll kill it."

"But you-"

"Go!" Without sparing them a glance, my feet take me towards the woman who tries going for others, but I cut her off, fire pouring out of my palms to trap her in between.

She stares at me, hatred swirling inside her white eyes before she flies up. I scan the area. There are too many places for her to hide in, and night is approaching fast. I've got a couple more minutes before things could go bad for everyone.

"*Shield*," I murmur, moving forward, my shoe slipping into the puddle of water the fire had left. Great. Now I'll have to sit barefoot at the campfire waiting for them to dry.

The whooshing sounds behind me, and I duck in time to avoid the wisp's wrath from ripping me to shreds. Her scream nearly causes me to go deaf, but I react faster than she can think of her next attack. "Orbis!" The blue ball charges at her, and she makes an effort to try and escape, but I don't give her that chance. Fire follows her, constantly being on her arse, but the wisp is in her territory, avoiding getting burned just as I'm about to get her. Fuck this. I might attract more monsters, but it'll give me time to run before they get here. I pray that everyone else is long gone before muttering the next words. "*Explodeo*."

With a snap of my fingers, the ball bursts, swallowing the wisp in its flames. She cries again, her body melting away, and I exhale. This was far too close, but luckily I thought every possibility through. If there's a chance we might be in danger, I'll put myself out there first, because I can't afford these people to risk their lives for me indefinitely. Too much was lost in recent times, and these people have someone to go back to. I don't, not right now at least.

I brush my hands on the fur jacket and turn around. The forest has wrapped itself in a blanket of shadows, not a single sound made when all of a sudden—

"Holy shit." There, in the dim light, I spot them. A dozen wisps flying out from behind the tall pine trees, snow hills, and boulders. All looking right at me.

Chapter 5

My body had never felt such an adrenaline rush. Perhaps once during the fight with ghouls, but this time it's different. There's no going home, no proper rest after a battle. If I get hurt, it could slow us down, and that's the last thing we need. So I run as far as I can, holding up the shield with whatever magic is at my disposal, my brain working overtime with all the thinking I'm doing. I have to take them all down. Otherwise, they'll just follow me until I reach everyone else, and that might jeopardise the whole mission.

"Shit!" I stop running and turn around. One idea. A dangerous one. It pops into my head.

The wisps are metres away, their blank stares drilling into mine. I note how some are smiling whilst the rest wallow ever so quietly. I might join them soon, both crying and laughing hysterically as I pray that somebody finds me after what I'm about to do. Let's hope the snow isn't thick enough to hide me behind its cover.

ISSAC

I don't know who drags me to my feet. I think I see a glimpse of Theo's black hair before it's gone. My head hurts like I've had it banged against a brick wall for at least six hours straight. Every inch of my body is aflame, making me wish I could shed skin. I grimace as another memory rushes to my brain, hurting every bone, every muscle, every vein inside me.

A girl hidden in the shadows, an irritated smirk tugging on her lips as she eyes me from the other side of a counter. I'm talking to her. She's listening. Perhaps we're arguing, but it's hard to tell when nothing can get past the ringing echo surrounding my head. She's dressed in a long white dress, the material perfectly wrapped around her toned body. I inch closer. She stares at me with desire sparkling in her eyes.

"What do you want, Issac?" What do I want? Her. I want every inch of her by my side. I want to see the hope and joy in her gaze, the way her brows furrow whenever I say something possibly offensive, and the way her body jolts with need when I'm near her. She's a drug, a forbidden fruit I'm not meant to taste but can't stop thinking about. The sound of her gentle voice, the feeling of her soft skin, the smell of her red hair is enough to drive me insane.

All of a sudden, the air gets knocked out of my lungs and I fall to the ground, the vision disappearing. I look around, gasping, before noticing the soldiers running ahead in haste.

"Issac, we need to go. We have to get to the safe spot." Alea is crouched beside me, her callous-covered hands gripping onto my arm, which I pull away from angrily.

"I can't. I have to go back." She stares at me in confusion before it hits her. I can't let Althea stay too far away. The command to capture her sets my brain on fire.

For the past few days, the thought of capturing her hasn't been pestering me as much. Sure, I've gotten annoyed and started uncalled-for arguments, but overall whatever Theo had insinuated worked. I'd been keeping a close eye on her. Until now, at least.

Everything inside me screams to go and find her, to make sure she hurts as I drag her back, but another side says something completely different. A side that has me questioning all the things coming out of my mouth ever since we had spoken. I recall hating her before, the way it came so easily, but not now. Now it feels like a punishment, like I'm stabbed each time she looks at me with betrayal, tears threatening to spill. This side is about to make me lose my fucking mind, that's for sure.

I rush to my feet, turning around to face the direction from which we came. The darkness had settled a while ago, the whole area covered in shadows. I hope to gods we haven't run too far. Otherwise, finding her might prove difficult. I know she had used magic. Our connection barely a whisper of what it usually is. I've got to hurry.

Ignoring the shouts from Alea, I move into the unknown. My eyes scan every tree, every movement in the distance, but nothing. I growl in annoyance. This wouldn't have happened if I weren't cuffed, if for some strange reason I hadn't lost my ability to walk and talk when saving her life.

It felt so wrong, so sinful to push her out of the way, but I knew if I hadn't, something inside of me would never forget this. I would forever be haunted by the sight of her getting hurt, and so I made a quick decision that ultimately fried my brain. It's a war, whatever's happening in my head, and I hate every part of it. I hate her, and yet when I think that, the word doesn't feel like it has meaning, like I believe it.

I come to a halt when the tree line thins out, unravelling the vast landscape. Ragged breaths escape my mouth as I slow my pace, trying to remain hidden. I have no idea what had happened between me blacking out and ending up far into the forest.

As I move ahead, no sound reaches my ears. Surprisingly, there are no cries or screams like I would expect during a fight. Instead, dead silence wraps the area. Have they moved somewhere else? Perhaps she did run away, and now I'm fucked. I stroll a bit further in, my eyes looking past the snow mountains, past the rocky hills, and suddenly… splash.

Water? I don't recall seeing any water. Especially in this temperature, it's impossible for it to just—

After a moment, my eyes adjust, and then I see it. The round circle of melted snow, the long-forgotten dead land hidden right underneath it now steaming from heat. Someone had burned this place. No, she had done it. Which begs the question: where is she?

As if hearing my thoughts, the sound of a whoosh reaches my ears, and I spin around to look for the culprit. Soon enough, I find the wisp flying in the direction of a tall snow bank. I waste no time chasing after it, discarding the fact I have no way to fight it, but that's not my biggest worry. What the entity is after, is.

I hop over the snow and slide down the hill, noticing the wisp charging at something down below. My eyes squint, and then I see her. Althea crouched down on her knees, her arms shaking as she tries to aim at the see-through woman.

It's like my common sense vanishes, like I don't care what will happen to me as long as she's unharmed, and before I know it, I launch myself between them. My hands are raised high, trying to subside the impact of the attack. Losing my limbs isn't important, nor is dying, but making sure nothing bad happens to her is. For whatever reason, the thought won't leave me alone. I've got to protect her. She can't die.

I land with a thud just in time for the wisp to raise her sharp nails, and suddenly the heaviness of the chain pulling me down is gone. My attention snaps to the cuffs. The metal still tightly wrapped around my hands, but the chain holding it together is gone. Perhaps I should celebrate that, after all, I've regained some type of freedom, but it can wait as the monster readies itself for another attack.

"Move!" Althea's voice is a ghost of a whisper, but I obey. Reluctantly, but still do. I can die by another's hand, not hers. I believe it would hurt my pride far too much.

Her hand raises high up past my face, and she yelps before speaking. *"Explodeo."* The red flames scorch everything in their path, and for once I'm happy I listened. This isn't the way to go.

The wisp melts away, her cries carried by the wind before the world goes quiet. I stare at the impact of Althea's spell, the amount of magic she put into it, and wonder when I missed it? Although my memory recalls seeing her train, I can't remember the part where she could take on monsters with such ease. Have I misjudged her strength, or just her in general?

A hiss pulls me back to reality. I turn around and look her over. The pale shade of her skin now red as if she stood above a lava pit for longer than she should, beads of sweat rolling off her scrunched forehead. Her whole body shakes so profoundly that when I put my cuffed hand on her arm to stop it, I begin shaking with her.

She blinks once, another groan trying to escape her mouth, but she suppresses it, bending down with her other hand squeezing onto her abdomen. I near myself carefully, our cheeks grazing, and when I touch her, I feel it. The unbearable heat. It doesn't take me a second to flinch away, my own skin hot to the touch like I've been burned by smelted iron.

"What did you do?" I ask, trying to flip her around so that I can take all these clothes off. She grimaces, letting me struggle for a minute before her hand unclasps the buttons on her jacket.

"I killed them all." Is the answer I get, and for some reason that makes me angry because only then do I understand what had happened.

"How many?" The words roll off my tongue with so much fury I think my vision starts to turn red.

She chuckles. "That was the thirteenth one." I huff, ripping the coat off her shoulders and gently putting her body on the snow blanket. Thank gods we're in Sebraycia because if she pulled this shit anywhere else, her magic would eat her up.

I'm sure someone warned her before about the consequences of overusing your powers. She knows damn well that going over the limit could permanently kill you, and yet she did it. At this point, I don't know if I should be glad that hasn't happened or perhaps furious that she was stupid enough to reach this point.

"You could have died." I snarl before brushing her wavy hair out of her face.

"Thought you might be happy to see that happen." She

attempts to smile, but it soon turns into a grimace as her magic feasts on her insides. I bite my lip, blood pouring down into my mouth before I can answer. Is she trying to piss me off?

I decided to keep my mouth shut for the time being and move to take off her vest. Dragon scales, although useful, can trap heat inside, and that's exactly what I don't need. She has to cool down as soon as possible. Otherwise, this whole trip will be wasted, and I'll sit here wondering if I should die or celebrate.

"Why did you come back?" She asks, her chest raising up and down rapidly. I want to know what kind of spell she had used, but bonding with someone you're supposed to hate isn't normal.

"Because I had to. Has your brain been fried too, or did you forget I'm supposed to keep you out of trouble?" I scan her shaking legs that minute by minute begin to calm down. Fuck, thank you, whoever watches over her.

She scoffs. "Supposed to, yet you hesitated."

"What?" I stare at her, puzzled.

"You hesitated. I saw it in your eyes. You saw the monster way ahead of me, and part of you wanted it to get me." I swallow hard, her words like a sword to my stomach, ripping me open. How can I argue against that when it's true? I did want to get rid of her, to have some peace and quiet for once in my life, but it doesn't work like that.

"Well, you should be glad I didn't listen to that part of me."

"Why?" Her dazed eyes catch mine, and I blink, thinking of the right answer. Giving her hope that the old me is trapped somewhere deep inside my mind isn't right. It'll only make her try harder, and I can't allow her presence to amplify. It's unbearable as it is right now.

"I don't know. Now be quiet and cool down. We've got to leave before more monsters gather." Her eyes fall shut, and with a single nod, silence slips between us.

It's neither comforting nor awkward. Just two people beside each other in the land covered by thick layers of frozen water and stars. Although my consciousness tells me to run far away, further than I can manage, my heart holds me still, keeping Althea before my legs. Her face now relaxed, any signs of her previous struggles gone if not for the couple droplets of sweat.

She looks so peaceful and trustful, like I'm not the person she should fear the most. Like I haven't admitted to the fact I was about to let her get killed. Right now, right here, she lets herself be vulnerable with a monster right at her side, and I'm not sure if I should call her brave or stupid.

The headache from earlier comes back for a short moment, another memory trying to test my limits, but before it manages to do any sort of damage, I push it away. I've had enough of going down memory lane for one day. Perhaps I can get tortured tomorrow.

A couple of minutes pass, and I notice Althea's face going back to normal, her breathing steady and her body still. We should be good to go, but before I'm confident her health is stable, I bring my cheek closer to hers one more time. Every muscle in my body tries to pull away, but I push through, finally feeling her skin.

Now that everything has settled, I smell it. The scent of vanilla and cinnamon seeping through my senses with such ease I almost choke. It's like she's the only thing here, the only person able to get a reaction out of me, be it good or bad. The softness of her skin brings strange comfort to my body, and so I relax, letting my eyes fall shut.

I'm playing a dangerous game here, walking on the edge, my feet ready to slip at any point and fall into the void she is. Yet I'm not scared. Confused, yes, but nowhere near fazed. Whatever it is I'm missing, she holds in her grasp, and I contemplate whether or not it's worth jumping for. What mysteries could she hold? What am I missing, and why does it make me feel so incomplete?

My eyes open, the moment gone, but then I catch a glimpse of dim yellow before it turns into a mesmerising gold orbit, like the brightest star in the sky staring right at me, into me. In the soft, sunset-like colour, I spot dots of brown scattered around, as if someone had made the greatest mistake in their life by flicking paint from their brush. The most entrapping and breathtaking artwork I've ever seen, belonging to a person I can't stand. How ridiculous.

She stays quiet, her mouth sealed shut, afraid if words come out I might pull away. Perhaps I would, but part of me doesn't want to. So I remain quiet with her, my breath controlled to not scare her away. She blinks, the colour intensifying and her pupils growing three sizes bigger, the golden shade getting swallowed by darkness I find comfort in. I don't know what kind of spell Althea Starbane had put me under, but in that moment, right here, I'm somehow all hers.

Suddenly, a shiver runs through her body, snapping me back to reality, and I jerk away. This time I'm not burnt by the temperature of her body, but by the questionable actions I've made. She shakes a bit more, her bottom lip quivering, and I focus on my cheek, noting how cold it's been ever since

I touched her.

"Let's go. You have to warm up." I rush her, struggling to pass her jacket in the process. She stares at me with a strange look in her eyes and slowly pulls herself up but fails as soon as her elbow tries to support her body. I catch her just in time, the wetness of her shirt rubbing on my wrists. "Shit, you're soaked."

"I'm cold." She whispers with chattering teeth, and I help her up. As quickly as possible, she puts on her vest and the jacket, but apparently that does nothing. Her legs are shaking along with her body. Who would have guessed that once you cool down after overusing your magic, your body will shut down on you and attempt self-destruction?

I kiss my teeth, looking around to see if we're safe to go. There's no way I can get her to our camp before she freezes over, not with the speed she'll be walking at least. "Fuck, come here."

My arm wraps around her waist whilst the other slips under her legs, picking her up off the floor. She weighs almost nothing. At least not something that could be a bother or stop me from speed walking. Her head falls onto my chest as she inches closer, probably seeking warmth.

I look ahead past the snow bank when another memory rips through just in time to stop me from taking the first step.

"Oh, come on, admit I saved our arses there." The words roll off her tongue in a playful manner. Her head nestled on my bicep. I reply to her, my lips moving but no sound filling the space between us. *"Don't act like you care what happens to me now."* Do I care? I'm not sure, my mind too absorbed by the vision of her blinking eyes, her lips curling into a genuine

smile.

I reply, she smirks, some words are being said, and suddenly my heart beats three times faster. It's such an intense feeling all my senses are thrown into overload, nothing and everything making sense. Like I'm supposed to be here, like she's meant to be in my arms, and I'm supposed to make sure she's safe. Nothing I do to try and stop this works, and nothing she attempts to do to break our contact helps.

Her fingers curl around my collar, and I'm snapped back into the present. Althea shivers, staring right at me through tired eyelids, her lips slowly losing the deep shade of pink that somehow makes this dull white land a bit more bearable. "Ar-e you o-okay?"

It annoys me. The fact that despite all my attempts at making her life miserable, that no matter how hard I try to make her hate me, I can still see the glimpse of care in her eyes whenever she looks at me. It's so foolish, infuriating, illogical, yet freeing because for once it feels like no matter who I've become, the person before me isn't scared. They don't want to back away because I'm too much work or because there's no redeemable part left in my tethered soul. They see me for who I am, and they're okay with that.

That's exactly why I need to keep her away. She's going to doom me in ways I can't comprehend.

"Just stay quiet."

***

We reach the camp in about half an hour. Thankfully, they'd gone to our planned stopping point as expected. My body relaxes, my brain finally quiets down after the long walk with a girl in my arms I'm supposed to avoid like plague. I was close to abandoning her and running away. My skin burned each time she nestled closer, indifferent to the fact she's being carried by someone who should be considered her enemy. I had to hold whatever it was building up inside my chest at bay until Desily's concerned face revealed beside a campfire.

"They're here!" She runs up to us, nearly ripping Althea from my grasp like I'm not supposed to be holding her this close, like it's wrong that I've enjoyed the weight of her body in my arms and the silence between us. Perhaps she's right. I'm toying with something dangerous here, a game I'm not sure I know how to play. "What happened? Why is she so cold?"

I crack my neck, staring ahead, trying my best not to spare them another glance. "She overused her magic. I had to cool her down, but now she's gone into shock."

"Is she all right?!" Ryo sprints out from his tent at such speed I'm tempted to trip him and see his teeth fall to the ground. He's only met her today, and she already has him wrapped around her fingers. But that's what Althea Starbane does. Slips into your life unnoticed and strips you away from all the things you hold dear, only to leave you with nothing but emptiness.

Desily replies to him, but I pay them no attention, moving away. I know she won't try to run away. She can't. So I decide to catch some rest. Any other night I would be watching her like a hawk, just as I did the night prior when she hadn't slept even for a second. The reason behind it a mystery I don't care enough to ask about. Instead, I make my way to where

Alea stands, guarding the entrance to Theo's tent. She spares me a single glance, something unknown swirling inside her grey eyes before it's gone.

I walk inside. The size of the tent enough to fit two grown men comfortably. Alea has probably decided to keep Desily company for the night, which I imagine she's been doing for a while but have no recollection of it whatsoever. Theo is leaning against a makeshift pillow, his eyes boring into mine. I rid myself of the jacket and fall onto the furry covers, exhaustion making itself known as a loud yawn rips past my lips.

The man scribbles something on a sheet of paper, his eyebrows furrowed, before he shoves the note into my palms.

'Did you do anything to her?'

"What? No. I saved her fucking arse if anything." I show him the broken chains, and he eyes me warily. How I wish he could just rid me of these, but if Theo doesn't trust me, then neither can I. He's the only person who knows me better than myself.

The paper is snatched from my hands, and he writes something down before passing it over.

'What happened to you earlier? You were not responding to any of us.'

I swallow the lie mustering in my throat. What am I meant to say? That I have visions I barely understand? That whenever I'm near this gods-forsaken girl, my world crumbles away and the empty cracks inside my head begin to fill with memories I can't process? He'll think I'm mad if he doesn't already. I do. I think I've lost all common sense for all the things I've thought through whilst being in her presence today.

"I'm just tired, Theo." He rolls his eyes, the paper taken away yet again. "Perhaps keeping me sedated for weeks is playing tricks on my mind." I breathe out, somehow telling him half the truth isn't so bad, almost as if I'm used to telling lies. Perhaps the person I can't remember was. The me right now, I'm not too sure.

I lay on the hard ground, the rocks underneath my makeshift bed digging into my back. Whatever. It's better than nothing. I need energy for tomorrow. Who knows what kind of torture Althea will throw my way this time.

Before my eyes close shut, the rustling of paper pulls my attention to Theo. A single sentence written down.

'I think it's not the sedatives that have you so perplexed but the memories of Thea you're trying to suppress so badly.'

I ignore him, turning away. What's with everyone and telling me about the past? Is it too much to ask for a clean slate? To try and live my life just as I desire? Yes, yes it is, because it's not my life I'm living but the life Lord Graham wanted me to. The life Aagon forced me to lead. Life with missing memories of a girl with reddish hair, golden eyes, and the smile of an angel.

Chapter 6

ALTHEA

Two days passed. Two long days since I quickly recovered from the wisp attack, thanks to Desily, and remembered the moment I shared with Issac. The worry and compassion in his voice, along with his frantic movements as he discovered me nearly lifeless behind the snow bank, still render me speechless. I find myself drifting to that moment from time to time, a part buried deep inside of him suddenly awakened. It brings me joy, courage to keep going, and hope that perhaps there's something worth saving, that I'm not striving in vain.

We set off shortly after everyone had their rest, trying not to waste any more precious time. This morning, as we reached the passage between the towering mountains, the spirit of celebration ignited within everyone. At last, we made it somewhere worth being happy about. In about two weeks, we'll arrive in Thehil, and from there, our trip to Yalan will be much faster. That's only if no more obstacles come our way.

I consider myself fortunate. The ability to walk and breathe after everything I've gone through seems like an incredible stroke of luck. When everyone left, when I knew I had no other choice but to take all those wisps down, I decided to raise the temperature as high as possible. The only other time I've done such a thing being during the battle against Wyrran. I had my doubts about whether this attempt would succeed. I felt as though I was on the brink of death, but when my body began to feel as if I'd traversed through flames, and the wisps emitted cries of anguish, I realised it had indeed worked. I succeeded.

The happiness was short-lived. The moment the final wisp descended, an overwhelming sensation coursed through me, as if every muscle and bone were fracturing inward. I was engulfed in darkness, gasping for air as my knees buckled beneath me, sending me crashing behind a snow bank. With every desperate inhale, it felt as if my lungs were on the verge of exploding, my skin burning. I knew it then. The urgency in the words written in the book about overusing your powers. I'd taken too much. Now it was time to give.

I glance forward at Issac's broad shoulders tensing as he talks to one of his soldiers. The mountain ahead of us, although joyous, brings many worries to some of the people. We can't stop walking, not even during the night, as the threat of being caught out in the open lurks around. It'll be a tiring journey. I know that much. He nods while attentively listening to whatever someone is telling him, and I keep staring, wondering what was going through his head the other day. Why did he look so deep in thought to the point he couldn't walk? Why did he decide to rescue me despite the previous remarks of hating my very existence?

"Thea?" I turn to face Ryo, his boyish smile spread wide across his lips. In the past few days, he became the only thing keeping me remotely sane, the only thing pure between all of us, a person I've yet to taint or lose. He's my beacon of hope that not everything I touch falls apart.

"Yeah, are they ready to go?" Once more, I glance over the high peaks and the resting snow along them. If we fail to remain silent, the deep, lingering snow will claim our lives more swiftly than we can escape.

"Seems so. General Edison is sending us all in small groups to keep the noise down." I furrow my brows in confusion. In those few days I've been unable to lead Issac took it upon himself to throw orders around. It's not that I mind because any help is better than none, but I know he will try to make my life harder than easier. The idea Ryo mentioned seems smart, still I'm not happy that I'll surely end up with Issac for the next couple of sleepless nights. Arguing and being able to put distance between us is one thing. Having to argue, keeping my voice in check, and not being able to run away is another. How can I maintain my sanity and awareness when every time I'll look, I'll be met with the sight of his contemptuous gaze?

"Do you know who I'm with?" I ask, glancing around. There are many soldiers I've yet to speak to, many who'd rather not say a word to me, but at the end of the day, I want to be near one person. The sun-kissed fairy smiling at me from ahead.

"No, but he will—"

"Everyone gather up! I'll tell you your teams." Issac interrupts Ryo, and the boy shrugs his shoulders. The feeling of dread gnaws at my stomach. "Theo, Alea, Aiena, Conall, and Desily will travel first."

Of course he didn't put me with her. Of course he had to

find some way to ruin my day. I swallow the hatred towards Issac and shove it deep inside my heart, hoping that if I leave it there, it won't grow into something bigger, something dangerous, one thing that could jeopardise our journey.

Des shoots me an apologetic look, but I smile, nodding towards Alea. I know she's happy to be with her, and I won't take that away. If I'm to be stripped away from people who don't see me as a monster, so be it.

Issac keeps on talking, giving out name after name that I'm not familiar with. I swear my legs start to shake when neither mine nor Ryo's names are being said, a flicker of hope flashing through the darkness. "At the end, it would be myself, Ryo, Venali and Jassin," my eyes drift to the set of twins. A boy and a girl, both in their elven thirties. The girl's black hair is twisted into a crown braid, whilst the boy's is cut short on the sides, leaving only a small piece left in the middle. They seem nice, is what I want to think, but their cold glare reminds me too much of someone I can't stand. "And finally, Althea."

Part of me rejoices as I realise there'll be one person amongst the monsters who will have my back. At the same time, I'm thrown into shattered glass, expected to manoeuvre around the danger. Balance.

***

The majestic mountains grip my heart tightly, their looming threats serving as a constant reminder of the challenges that await. This was the only way, I remind myself. The only route which would keep us hidden enough from Eclia's soldiers, from Aagon, from the monsters. I knew it was risky when I picked it. I knew people could get hurt, but as long as we stay quiet, nothing bad can happen. Or so I hope.

Ryo yawns beside me. We've been walking for eight hours straight, and the scenery of dull grey and white doesn't help to keep our minds entertained. Everyone's jacket is almost the same shade, covered in the never-stopping snowfall, their heads hidden underneath the fur hood. I pull the scarf over my nose feeling the cold air biting at it, and rub my gloves together for warmth. Layers on layers of clothing can't win against these conditions. Apparently they also can't win against Issac's gaze as it rips past the fabric and into my skull. I feel every emotion passing through his body as if we're connected by an invisible string, pulling back and forth on who's in charge.

I know we could communicate through Jinoro, but this seems different. Almost like our hearts have been slit open, all the feelings pouring into a big, stewing pot. I wonder if the woman knows anything about this. I wonder if she'd tell me if I asked.

"I wouldn't." She groans in the distance, and I roll my eyes. Ever since I used up my magic, it's been easier for her to slip inside my mind, to disturb my thoughts. The doors I try to keep shut are now cracked open enough for her to slither her way in. *"Don't flatter me, child."*

"Well, if you heard my thoughts, do you mind explaining?" I sigh deeply, stealing a curious look from Ryo. Sometimes it's hard to forget not everyone can hear her. That only Issac and I share this burden of being able to speak with the centuries-old demon. I shake my head and continue looking ahead.

"I do mind, but since you've behaved appropriately as of recent and finally went in search of my things, I guess I could reward

you in some way." She applauds, and I frown. Getting praise from someone you're trying to get rid of feels wrong, but I'll take anything at this point. *"The connection between you and the boy develops over time."*

"How do you mean?" I ask, my interest piqued.

She sighs, as if I asked her the most boring question anyone ever had. I probably did, given she's lived for years, seen many things, taken many lives, and almost destroyed our planet. Her mind hides stories far beyond my comprehension.

"First, it's the ability to telepathically communicate. Then, as your feelings grow, so does your magical connection, which allows you to hear their thoughts just as I do yours without asking." I blink, stunned. Have I missed a point at which I could hear Issac's thoughts? Has this ever happened between us? I want to ask him, to see if he's ever heard me the way Jino described, but she interrupts me by continuing her monologue. *"Over time, you'll be able to feel each other's emotions as if they've invaded your own system. Ultimately, you might be able to glimpse into their life as if you're seeing through their eyes, but that requires far more than just acceptance of one another."*

I gulp, her words swirling chaotically in my mind. I want to steal a moment where I could go inside her throne room, where two sets of doors are set opposite of each other. One leading to Issac's mind, the other a mystery she won't let me uncover.

My head turns to the side, hoping to catch Issac's eyes, and sure enough, he meets me halfway, his own gaze burned into mine. I wonder if he knew this before? If he had any idea that we were capable of all those things purely out of the connection to Jinoro? I want to know if he can hear my thoughts, so I push hard, but he just blinks in confusion, his lips twisting into a disgusted snarl before he pulls away, focusing his attention somewhere else.

"What's the requirement?" I ask her one last question, slowly turning to face the bleak road.

She chuckles, but there's no happiness attached to her voice, only despise. *"Love."*

For the next couple of days, I try to think to the point my head hurts from all the thoughts I let pass through it. I pick one at a time and ponder about it before letting it go.

There's no way he didn't know. He had to. She trusts him more than me. But then why would he never tell me? Is this not important to him? Information like this could save our lives. That's only if he cared, if he didn't wish I could disappear from the face of this planet. No, he must care. Otherwise, how could I feel so much rage inside me everyday? I know those feelings didn't belong to me, for what could I be enraged about? Sad? Yes. Worried? Absolutely, but not angry.

A flicker of hope grasps at my heart. I explore the possibility of Issac actually caring about me. He might hate me, of course, but there's part of him that actually cares enough to let me feel whatever it is he's trying so hard to suppress, and that's enough to keep me going. I won't give up on him, not because of the new discovery, but because I promised, and I never lie. Never.

"Gods, I'm so hungry, and my legs are about to give out." Ryo whispers beside me, and I smile, checking my pockets for slices of bread I stashed before we left.

"Here, perhaps this can help in some way because we're

not stopping any time soon." I smirk, passing him whatever food is left. He takes it with a thankful nod before stuffing his mouth.

"Are you not tired?" He asks, and I shoot him a confused look. "I mean, besides the walk. I haven't seen you sleep the other night."

"How—" I cut myself off and stare at him, shocked. The night Issac brought me back, I passed out from exhaustion, but the moment my eyes registered the brightness of the area around us, I couldn't fall asleep, too afraid someone might get woken up by my screams, by the nightmares still haunting my dreams. I can't possibly do that, especially here where monsters are waiting for the opportunity.

I let Desily live in the illusion I'm all right. That whatever happened on the ship won't be happening on land, at the cost of losing sleep and every ounce of my sanity. I let Alea and Theo and the rest of the crew escape the torture of my uncontrollable cries, knowing all too well how painfully awful it sounded.

"I woke up for a moment the other night and saw you staring into the fire. Is everything all right?" I know Ryo doesn't mean any harm in his questions. I know he wants to be my friend and worries just as Desily would, but I can't put that weight on his shoulders. This boulder is mine and only mine to carry, nobody else's.

"Yeah, I was quite well rested, so I decided to keep guard for the night."

"Just like General Edison." Ryo chirps in, and I tense. How many nights has Issac spent keeping an eye on me? How many times did I miss his glares? Usually, I'm careful not to disturb anyone, quietly sitting by the fire and staring into the dancing flames. From time to time, I'll glance around, making sure everyone's safe, but never have I seen him looking at me. Perhaps he's not. Perhaps he just watches from a distance every now and then to make sure I don't betray them, that I don't run to a place I wish existed. Some place I could call home.

My attention is shifted as two soldiers ahead of me whisper to each other. Their voices muffled by the heavy stomps in the thick layers of snow. The twins.

"Do you know anything about them?" I ask Ryo, nodding towards the set of elves. Ever since we began walking, our new companions have barely spared me a glance. They're the perfect example of dedicated soldiers, only doing what Issac asks of them. He could suggest severing each other's legs off or jumping off a cliff, and they'd do it. They wouldn't question his command, unlike me. They'd simply die for him.

For some odd reason, I get a feeling they don't like me. Although I've never met them before, there's a crack on the ground where we're standing, an abyss waiting for either of us to fall. On the other hand, if they came from Karul, I did give them plenty of reasons to hate my guts, and I wouldn't blame them if they did.

"Who? Venali and Jassin?" Ryo ponders. "Barely. I just know they've been here for a long time. Always the first pick when going on missions with General Edison." So they're from Karul, which means I've passed them countless times in the manor, oblivious to their existence, running amok trying to play pretend until it all backfired. They had to fight for their home, watch their friends die because some strange girl pushed into their perfect life and made them choose.

Their friends or their lives.

"I see."

We walk in silence until the sky turns black. Until the clouds clear the sky and the first stars appear. We travel for so long I can feel my stomach growl and my eyelids close from exhaustion. The only thing keeping me awake is small conversations with Ryo. To each of his questions, I answer truthfully. No need to hide who I used to be, who I still am. He always asks about the things I saw, about the lands I travelled and people I met. Question after question, I spill the knowledge gathered over the years, the books I've read, the food I've tried, the creatures I came across. As per usual, he listens. Never interrupts, never laughs or mocks as the most ridiculous things come out of my mouth. Instead, a spark of fascination dances in his brown eyes, light guiding me through the dark night.

"Why haven't you decided to become an adventurer instead? It sounds like it would suit you better." I ask at one point, a heavy yawn sticking to the back of my throat.

"These days we don't get to choose who we want to be. It's either die or live dying for something you might care about." My mouth opens, words ready to protest against his statement, but nothing follows. I know he's right. I know because my mindset is exactly the same. Our freedom had been taken years ago. We were given very few options from the start, like our dreams didn't matter, like our fate has been written down since birth into a centuries-old book and sealed shut. "Trust me, I wish I could travel the world, but people like us don't matter. We have no real place in here. Just another story waiting to be finished. It'd be great if everyone could see that the blood in our veins is the same, the heart in our chest beating to the same speed."

My throat squeezes so tight I have to fight for a small amount of oxygen. For a split second, I see myself and Issac at the lake during my birthday, the conversation we had about our future. My optimistic hopes and dreams and Issac's pessimistic view of everyone. It feels so surreal to hear someone say this, almost as if taken out of my memory and rewritten from a different point of view.

Ryo is us. The good and the bad, the foolish and the wise, the light and the dark. In the far future, a piece of hope carried over by generation, a candle that can never go out. He's everything I've ever wanted to be and everything I couldn't.

Finally, I allow myself to breathe, and the air tastes so cold, so different. All the worries dismissed by the young boy beside me. Fears that perhaps people born into this age would hate humans a little bit more, a little bit harder, but instead they see the world through the same crack in the wall I've been picking at my whole life. Hope is beautiful. Hope is the first flower in spring, the first laughter of a child, the first person to break the century-old chains holding them to who they were meant to be but chose to defy their fate, their destiny.

"Thank you," I say, my hand squeezing his shoulder, and he smiles, confused.

"For?"

I shake my head, the smile on my face growing wider. So innocent, just like I used to be once upon a time. "Don't worry."

The rest of the night we spend in silence. My eyes constantly move from the ground to the mountains, hoping to catch a glimpse of colour, something that would spring my imagination into action so that I don't fall asleep. The cold stopped bothering me ages ago. Now the air feels warmer than ever, lulling me to sleep as I fight against it. A few more hours, a couple more steps, countless amounts of snow.

A shriek so loud it rattles my bones rips past the three groups travelling ahead of us. Everyone stops moving, stops breathing, and I swear our hearts stop. I look ahead, my movements calculated to try and assess the danger. Nothing should have attacked us. No monsters reside in those mountains. Was I wrong? Are we trapped?

"Tinesi!" Someone shouts after the female soldier, and everyone's eyes fall on them in an instant. I see commotion, other elves trying to quiet the shouts of a man calling out for somebody who got hurt, or lost, or gods know what.

I turn around, my eyes finding Issac in an instant. He looks worried, disoriented as to what's happening, and before I manage to utter a single word, the ground beneath our feet begins to shake.

"Everyone run! Avalanche!" My head snaps up so quickly the muscles in my neck ache, and sure enough, I see it. The ocean of snow sliding down the side of a mountain right where we're standing.

"Ryo, quick!" I grab the boy's hand and dart ahead. Everyone's running for their life as the snow draws closer, consuming everything in its path. The tiredness I felt is gone, instead replaced by sudden adrenaline as I push myself to find a safe spot. We won't make it. We won't be able to get out of the way before everyone gets buried underneath the piles of snow. Even if we find a way, we'll be stuck under for gods know how long.

What do I do? What had gone wrong? Why did she scream?

Ryo's hand squeezes me tighter, and I turn for a second to look at his face. It almost breaks me. The distress caressing his features as he tries to keep up. The life flashing past his eyes, the future that might be stolen in a few minutes. I can't let him die. I can't let his dreams get destroyed like mine once did, because if there's nobody to have those dreams, then we'll all be doomed.

I stop suddenly, the magic in my body coming to life as I stare at the snow ahead. I can do this. I can hold it for a bit, letting everyone escape, and then perhaps hope to survive myself if the snow isn't too cruel.

"What are you doing?! We have to go, Thea!" Ryo tugs on my sleeve, but I pull away, thinking of a spell.

Think, think, think, think, think, think.

"Go! Go with them. I'll hold it back." As hopeful as I try to sound, my voice shakes, revealing the anxiety behind my back. This can go so wrong, but even if it does and I die, they'll live. Ryo will live.

"I'm not leaving you!" He protests, and I shoot him an urging glare.

"Ryo, please, go."

"No." He stands his ground, and I sigh. So stubborn. I guess if I were to compare him to someone, I wouldn't have to look far. It's like staring into a mirror.

"Fine, but it's about to get hot."

"What are you doing, Starbane?!" Issac slides on the snow, his brows furrowed with concern as he looks ahead and then turns to face me. I see the war inside of him. Should I go and save myself, or should I drag her away and die? Damn it, why can't they just leave?

"I'm going to hold it back. You have to go." It feels strange to give out commands, especially to him, yet I do it anyway, hoping he'd listen.

"Are you insane? Do you want to overheat your body once again?!" His hand extends to draw me back, but I leap to the side, my expression remaining as gravely serious as possible. If he doesn't trust me, that's fine, but he has to believe me, believe in me this one time, because I'd rather die than see everyone here get crushed under the snow due to my miscalculations. I can't bear another name added onto the pile of bodies I mourn for each waking hour.

"Either leave or stay. I'm not moving." Without sparing him another glance, I turn to face the nearing waves of white powder. My legs dig into the ground, my muscles ache, and I feel the strain from a few days ago, the magic yet to be replenished fully. Gods, kill me, kill me and take me away, but spare them, and if that's not enough, if I have to repay for my sins, then give me that ounce of energy I need to protect them.

When the first pile of snow tickles the front of my boot, I say the words Lisa taught me during one of our classes. A spell I've yet to master. Perhaps this one time my little knowledge and practice would come useful. "*Combustum.*"

Flames pour out of my palms, eating away all the snow coming our way. I created a shield, letting everyone pass safely to the spot where the snow won't reach them. Droplets of water fall onto my face, and soon enough the whole area turns wet. I grimace as the pain in my hands grows stronger, angrier, letting me know I'm gambling my life away, but that doesn't stop me.

The snow above my head roars, every particle turned into liquid, but it doesn't seem to cease. I'm not sure how much fight I have left, but it won't be enough to escape, not at this rate.

I turn to the side, noticing the last of the soldiers making it safely out of the danger zone, and a sigh of relief pushes past my lips. They're okay. They'll live, but now I've got to make sure I do as well, as do Ryo and Issac.

"Let's go," I tell them, and only then do I spot the twins standing right behind Issac. An expression of fascination mixed with fear is the first sight of anything human I saw them do.

The five of us move slowly as I try not to slip on the water below my feet, the parts of snow my magic wasn't able to eat away. The flames are strong, stronger than I've ever seen them, and if I'd done it on any other occasion, I might have set everything aflame, but not now. Perhaps one day I'll learn how to control the raw power. Right now, it controls me.

I sway to the side, my vision growing tired as my limbs become heavier. The magic's running out, and we're not even halfway through to where we need to be. Fuck, I've got to do this. I have to. I have no other option. Please, please, if anyone watches over me, now is the time to help. Please.

A sharp stab has me stopping, my knees buckling under my weight, as the flames turn the darkest shade of blue, borderline black, burning stronger, hungrier. I cough, the heat stripping me of any oxygen left to breathe, sweat rolling down my spine. The snow turns into water at such speed I'm soaked to my knees, still unable to move.

What's happening? Where is this magic coming from? Have I reached my limit and begun borrowing from nature, killing the innocent? Have I died and imagined it all?

My heart pinches, and I yelp, closing my eyes shut. Something's not right. I don't feel the same as I did whilst fighting the wisps. The never-ending pain doesn't come knocking at my door, stripping me of my sanity. No, I feel different. The magic isn't consuming me. It's restoring me.

A crack, then another, and another has me looking below my feet, and then the ground beneath me crumbles away. We're falling.

Chapter 7

Tap. Tap. Tap.

Cold. I'm surrounded by nothing. Frozen in the moment. My bones unable to move, my muscles unable to feel, my lungs refusing to draw a breath. Every inch of my body, every particle that makes me who I am refuses to cooperate.

Bang. Bang. Bang. Bang.

There's so much noise, so much chaos around me, inside of me. I'm burning with need to move, but part of me refuses to. I don't want to. The darkness calls out from the deepest parts of my heart. The laughter, cries, screams, and pleading latch onto my core with such force I find it hard to ignore. I've tried many times, but it's so much stronger. Their haunting whispers turn into words of a beautiful song, begging me to entertain them for just a moment, just a second.

I'm to perform, to dance until their vocal chords tear, until their mouths close shut and my feet begin to bleed. In this room full of no one, I'm the one skipping across the floor, trying to make them stay, to keep their eyes on me so that they don't notice the broken glass cutting through my flesh. I'm an entertainer.

Scratch, and then another, and another, and another, and

another.

I choke, trying to breathe. My body jerks up when I realise I can't. I can't breathe. I can't move.

"I found them!" A hand grabs onto my shoulder, shaking me into existence. I can finally see the first drift of air pushing into my nostrils. I gasp. "Shit! I can't get them apart!"

I blink once, my eyes readjusting to the sudden brightness. It doesn't take long before I spot Ryo standing right above me, his face a mix of relief and concern. The twins stand behind him, tiny scratches caressing their rough features.

My head falls to the side, a sudden realisation hitting me in the gut. I can't move, and it's not because I'm covered by inches of snow. No, it's the arms tightly wrapped around my waist that won't let go.

The scent of leather and blood is all I can smell. The weight of another body right below me, holding me in place, is all I can feel. Issac took the fall. He saved me from dying.

I start wriggling around in panic, my eyes catching every detail of where exactly we've landed, what happened. Ryo grabs onto my arm just as I feel the blood coursing through my veins, warming every inch of my body despite my knees being wet from standing in water. I struggle and struggle and struggle, surprised at the strength Issac's unconscious body holds.

"Help me pull her out!" Ryo shouts to the twins, and only then do they snap into reality, rushing to inch closer. I crawl out from beneath his arms, watching as they silently land on his abdomen. Not a single sound escapes Issac's mouth.

I stare up at the hole in the icy ceiling, a sudden epiphany. The route through the mountains was never safe. There was no ground beneath our feet. We were walking on millennium-old ice, thick enough to let a group of travellers pass, not strong enough to withstand fire hotter than dragon's breath. I caused this. I'm the reason why they're hurt.

"Issac? Issac!" I shake his shoulders, but he won't budge. His face is frozen still, a stoic expression engraved onto his features. My chest squeezes, tears pooling in my eyes as I reach for his neck with my shaky fingers.

No heartbeat. He's dead.

"No, no, no, no." I pound on his chest, crying harder than ever, fear of losing him to something so foolish, something perhaps not as obvious yet detectable, causing me to panic. What have I done?

"Thea." Someone calls my name, but I can't let go of his arms, my eyes unable to peel off his face, hoping that I'll catch a glimpse of a smile, a look of hatred, or a sudden outburst full of disgust. He has to wake up. He has to. "Thea!"

I'm yanked away, two sets of arms holding me on each side as I fight against them. "Let me go!"

"He's dead, but he'll come back. He's immortal. He can't die." Ryo's words are like a slap to my face, a wake-up call I needed so desperately. Right. Issac, unlike me, couldn't use his magic. He couldn't protect himself from the avalanche or the fall because I put him in that position, and now he lies at my feet, dead. Gods, I'm sorry, I'm so, so sorry.

I crawl away, trying to put as much distance between us as possible. The nightmares taunting me at night suddenly come to life as I stare at the person most important to me, gone. He'll hate me for it. He'll despise me more than before, and I can't do anything to make him forgive me. It was my fault.

Suddenly, my hand brushes against something, my back bumping into solid matter. With a thudding heart, I turn to the side, and only then do I see the young elven girl someone has been calling out for. Tinesi.

She must have fallen through a crack, or perhaps just stood on a flimsy piece of ice that had been waiting for a foolish person to free it. She was the one to do it, to discover that the person she'd put trust in had zero idea about what the ground we were walking on was made of, the danger right underneath our noses.

I stifle a sob, noticing the colour of her eyes has drained, blood everywhere. So, so, so, so much blood, and I can't stand it. My stomach convulses, and I'm ready to throw up before Ryo's hand pulls me away into a far corner where I can't see anything. Where neither Issac's nor Tinesi's body are in my field of view. Despite that, the image of their lifeless faces flashes before my eyes, and I crawl into myself, weeping.

I'm not sure how much time passes, but by the time I feel like no more tears can come out, fresh ones push through, spinning me into a never-ending cycle. My throat is dry from the cries, and my head full of thoughts I'd rather forget. I feel empty, yet every possible emotion passes by me at such speed I can't find the right moment to acknowledge it. There's a storm inside me, a tornado destroying everything in its way.

I glance ahead where the elven girl's body had been found, only to realise someone had moved it. Perhaps the twins decided it would be appropriate to give her some kind of burial before waiting for their general to come back from death. To my side, Ryo's arm is thrown over my shoulder, his hand drawing circles between my shoulders whenever I hiccup or jerk. He hasn't said a word since reassuring me that Issac will come back to life, as if knowing how much he means to me.

The next shaky breath I take clears my head just a little bit more, and for a moment I let myself gaze around. I'm glad everyone else had survived, but it'll be no good if we're stuck here, Issac's sacrifice going to waste. Gods, why did he do that? Why did he have to save me, making me feel like I'm in his debt now? Like I'm useless enough to be rescued by the last person wanting to do that on earth? I know he'll taunt me for this, come up with another way to torture me into insanity.

My eyes sweep along the long tunnel stretching to my left, the opening from which we fell metres away. We can't go back out the same way we entered. It seems we'll be forced to wander into the unknown.

The walls of the cave are the shade of deep blue. There's nothing around us except ice and snow, and never-ending darkness laying ahead. Perhaps years ago this was the route people took to travel, but at some point it sank under metres of water, freezing over. Should I be glad? Thankful? Or perhaps angry I was deceived?

"What happened?" The quality of my voice is foreign to me, as if I've clawed at my throat with jagged nails until it started to bleed.

"What?" Ryo's eyebrows are furrowed, sleep tugging on his eyelids. In this light, he looks like he's aged twenty years.

"What happened? How did he—we end up like this?" I nod towards where Issac and I were found.

The boy follows my eyes, the gears in his head shifting before he speaks. "I'm not sure. I just remember feeling the ground shake and your fire disappear. General Edison was by your side in a blink of an eye, before the ice split and we all fell. He held you close to his chest. He looked worried. We all did. It's a miracle we've survived the fall." I nod, my bottom lip quivering at his revelation.

He chose to save me, despite the war inside of him I saw moments before using my magic. Despite hating every fibre of my being, he decided to sacrifice his own life for the sake of keeping me safe and alive. He took the fall, probably broke his bones and passed away whilst I was oblivious to it all. Too consumed by the need for self-sacrifice, by the need to prove to myself and everyone else that I'm not a monster, another useless person in their ranks, I forgot that Issac was bound to keep me safe no matter what.

A hoarse inhale has the four of us turning to the pile of snow on which Issac rests. I'm the first on my feet, running to his side like it's the first time I've seen him in a long time. His feet shake, a grunt escaping his mouth before he lifts himself up and looks around.

I fall to my knees right beside him, my hand reaching out before I stop myself. He stares at me, an unreadable expression plastered on his face. He's in a daze, a moment where his brain is trying to recollect all the thoughts lost, all that happened before his death. It's not fun. It feels like a sudden rush of air forcing its way into every part of your head, latching onto the blank spots you've been left with to finally give you a clear picture.

The Issac in front of me doesn't remember he hates me. He can't feel a single emotion before he recollects himself, so I take my chance before it's too late. Before he starts screaming and cursing me out.

My hands wrap around his neck so tightly I'm scared I'll break it again, but I can't stop. Everything in me rejoices at the sight of him being alive and breathing. I feel the racing heartbeat underneath his armour, the deep, uneven breaths. He's warm, so fucking warm, and I can't get enough. The all-too-familiar scent of leather and smoke fixes every broken part of my heart in an instant. I'm full of words being unsaid, with emotions I can't explain and touch I've craved for so long.

"Thea… why are you crying?" The sound of his voice is sweet, sending ripples through my body that set me aflame. It's the first time he didn't call me by my full name, the first time I heard him be himself ever since the manor, and I know that moment's about to pass. We're at the end of a candle wick, slowly burning, stalling for time until it's gone.

His hands wrap around my shoulders, and I half expect him to push me away in disgust, but instead the cold metal of his cuffs swipes across my cheek, wiping the tears away. My throat squeezes, his brows furrow, and we're frozen. "You're safe."

A broken smile stretches across my mouth, and he blinks, wiping the care from his eyes and replacing it with uncertainty. I reach into my satchel and pull out a silver key on a brown string, something Theo had entrusted to me.

"Is that—" He nods towards the object, and I gently grab his wrist, twisting it around so I get access to the keyhole.

"Theo was never the one who could free you. I was." His body tenses, so much shock and wonder in his eyes as I scramble to free him. "He told me to get these off when I'm sure I can trust you," our eyes lock, so many unspoken words being said in the moment of silence, "and I do trust you, Issac. You might not feel the same way, but I do."

The cuffs fall free, and he pulls away, examining his hands like he's never seen them before. Long, slim fingers bending and folding. Issac is finally free, and now I have to trust my own intuition that I've made the right choice.

We're moving not long after, the twins informing Issac about everything that happened between us falling and waking up. He doesn't say a word, not even a change of expression when they mention the death of his soldier, too preoccupied with his freedom to care. I haven't said a word since pulling away from his body, since letting him roam without restraint. Part of me too afraid he might take this as an opportunity to be rid of me, whilst the other wants to live in the moment of peace.

I look ahead into the dimly lit tunnel. At some point during our time here, the night had passed and morning came forth, shining its light through the thick layers of ice above our heads. I have no idea where this might lead, but I'm hoping it'll get us back to the rest of the group. I'm sure Desily is worried sick, not to mention Alea and Theo.

Another step on more uneven ground shoots a wave of sudden pain from my ankle all the way to the tip of my hipbone, causing my teeth to sink deep into my lip. My nails dig into the flesh of my palm, crescent moons appearing on the rough surface. Shit, did I twist it during the fall?

"Everything all right?" Ryo is at my side in a heartbeat, and as glad as I am, I can't afford everyone present to worry. We need to get out of here, fast. This can wait until I'm reunited with Desily.

"Yeah, just stood on something." I force on a smile, a flash of Issac's suspicious eyes caught in the corner of my vision.

"Are you sure? I haven't really checked for any injuries, and I don't want you to be walking if you—"

"Ryo," I cut him off, my eyes hiding the agony I'm enduring with each step I take. "I'm fine. Let's just go."

We walk and walk and walk and walk and walk and walk and walk and walk. My mouth becomes dry, my eyes fight the tiredness tugging on the heavy lids. If not for the sudden surge of pain passing by every now and then, I'd pass out from exhaustion. The tunnel never ends. The darkness always lies ahead. I'm sure everyone thinks what I do. We're stuck here.

I catch the twins shaking their heads to wake themselves up every now and then. Issac beside them walks without a single care. In all fairness, he did sleep for quite some time. Not willingly, but he did. Ryo lets out the fiftieth yawn in the past hour, and I finally have had enough. "Right, we need to rest."

An echo of relieved moans ripples through the cave as everyone except me and Issac collapses onto the hard floor. "Right, I'll start on the fire."

"No, I'll do it." Issac cuts in, and before I can protest, he's gone, scavenging for any stick that might have gotten buried here in the past. That's one way to avoid an awkward conversation.

I find a bit of flat land by one of the walls, slowly sliding against it before I'm sat. The twins and Ryo are already laid on the ground with their eyes closed, drifting away to sleep. I'm glad they can rest. They deserve it. I, however, will try my best not to follow their lead. Perhaps once we reach the rest of the group, and I'm at a safe distance away from the camp, I might give myself the luxury of sleeping.

My hand unties the laces of my shoe before slipping it off. I don't have to take the sock off to notice the growing bulge on the right side. My ankle is a purple mess, pain intensifying with each second that passes in not-so-blissful rest. I groan and close my eyes. The exit to this cave better reveal itself sooner than later, or I might just tell them to leave me behind.

A few minutes pass before Issac returns with barely any wood. It'll last us an hour at best, but that's all we need. I observe him from a distance, the stillness of his movements as he gets the fire ready, trying not to wake anyone up. The gentle expression caressing his features makes him look approachable. Through the thick layer of ripped clothing, I see the outline of his lean body, and a smile creeps onto my face. I miss seeing him, being held in his arms during uncertain nights and lazy mornings. I crave the playful look in his eyes, his lips all over my body, his voice inside my head.

"Go to sleep like everyone else. You look like shit." He whispers as the flames come to life, and I blush, being caught in an embarrassing act.

"I'm fine." My voice is stern, but the grimace tugging on my lips gives me away.

He scoffs. "So you keep saying, but if anyone needs rest, it's you."

I roll my eyes, turning away to face the icy wall. I'd rather he wished me the worst than show a grain of care, because if he does, I might start believing it, and then, as per usual, I'll end up disappointed. "You should get some rest instead. That fall must have been horrible."

"Yeah, no shit. I died." I wince at his words. I guess the memories returned, but his old-new self is still finding his way through. "But I'm fine, so go sleep."

"Thank you, by the way." I turn to face him once again and find him already looking right at me. Confusion laced with curiosity. I guess he didn't expect the words to fall from my mouth. "For saving me," I clarify.

He chuckles to himself before taking a seat by the flames, his eyes not leaving me for a moment. "It's my job, isn't it? Not a single person here is foolish enough to try and save others at the expense of losing their life." I exhale the feelings caught up in my chest, hoping it'll loosen the grip they have around my neck. "Not anyone but us. I guess we're just that. Foolish." He shrugs and turns away. The conversation ends with the last breath he draws before gluing his eyes to the ceiling. I nod to myself and smile. Perhaps he doesn't hate me as much as I thought he would. Perhaps we'll be all right.

Chapter 8

I'm in a dungeon. A thick metal door shut tight in front of my face. There are scratches on the surface, stories engraved in a language I can't transcribe. The sound of shaky breathing draws my attention. Past the iron bars is a person, someone I know, someone I miss.

I take a step closer, every part of my body screaming to get away, but I can't move. The flames from the candles grow bigger, tenser. Their shadows dance along the stone walls, and I'm trapped in a trance.

Bang.

My head turns. A pair of blue eyes staring right at me. I stare back. Not a word is being spoken, but I see the horror in their gaze, the pleading, the anger. I'm stripped of every layer of my skin, my muscles melting away, my bones falling to the floor with a rattle until there's nothing left except for my soul. A bright light illuminating the dark space, and that's when I see him. Lathai.

He says something. I can't hear. I inch closer and closer until the ghost of my body passes through the space keeping us apart, and I'm in the cell with him. "Thea," he says, and I nod, my hands reaching to touch his cheeks. He's crying. "I'm sorry."

"For what?" My voice is a whisper, but in these four walls it becomes louder than ever, bouncing around. Lathai closes his eyes, his head shakes, and he steps back. I want to know what it is that he's hiding. What it is that he's apologising for, but he won't answer.

"I'm sorry," he says again, his eyes opening, the blue colour gone, instead replaced by deep amber. A nasty smile curls his lips upwards, and I step back. "For this."

A gasp pushes past my lips as his sword pierces through my stomach. I fall onto the floor, the light surrounding my person dimming little by little, second by second, and he laughs the kind of laugh that has your skin crawling with goosebumps and fear.

I reach out, words failing to be brought into reality. Lathai turns away, searching for something, and I try to stop him, try to avoid the inevitable from happening. Just a moment later, a swift movement of his hand, and Theo's body collapses onto the floor. Then Desily, Alea, Ryo, the twins, and Issac. "Stop! Please stop! I'll do whatever you want, just stop this!" I scream and scream, but he won't listen. Tears fall down my cheeks at such speed I'm afraid we'll drown. Everyone I've ever lost and everyone I'm afraid of losing is piling right in front of my eyes.

When the hill of corpses fills out the space around us, when I feel like my soul is ready to shatter into pieces from the pressure of all these bodies, Lathai turns. A thoughtful look spread across his face. "I'm afraid it's too late, darling."

Someone shakes me into reality. I'm shouting and throwing my hands in the air, kicking whoever is standing beside me in the chest. My body shakes and shakes and shakes, and I can't breathe. The air is too dense, the world is too fast, my head is too loud.

I choke on my tears, the pouring blood of my broken heart, and scream. I can't stop screaming. I blink and see figures all around me, somebody's eyes staring right at my face, and fear drags me across the floor far away. My chest raises and falls down, ribs threatening to break from my lungs expanding too much too quickly, yet I can't snatch a single ounce of oxygen.

My body goes limp, all the energy sucked out, leaving me helplessly lying on the cold ground. Someone reaches for my calf, and I wiggle away, crawling away as far as possible. "Don't touch me!"

A surge of pain flashes through my leg, a muffled sob pressing onto my tightly sealed lips. There's so much noise all around. Footsteps, whispers, shouting. Is it me? Is it someone else? I can't tell, everything is blurring into one disoriented image, and I'm in the centre of it, trying to push the smoke away, to save the broken parts and hold onto them with dear life.

The loud pounding of my racing heart makes me nauseous. My hands travel to my mouth before someone grabs them and tugs me away. I fight again, broken screams falling out of my mouth so loud they could shatter glass, they could snap my vocal chords in half, but I don't stop.

Suddenly, I'm pulled flush against a person. Their warmth seeps into my skin, their touch sending goosebumps over my flesh. My spine straightens, and I'm still. Words escape their mouth, but I can't hear them, too afraid if I do, the nightmares might turn into reality.

Thump. My eyes fall shut, the world goes quiet, I'm in the void. I fall and fall and fall until strange pain spreads from the top of my forehead. It's not the kind of pain I got woken up from, but one that slowly drags me away, sets my world straight.

I take a peek. Red. No, crimson in my vision. Is it anger? Is it pity, or just the blood of people I've lost? I can't tell. I blink, my reflection clearly visible. The messy, ginger hair. The golden, blank eyes staring right back at me. I'm a mess.

Another blink, one that doesn't come from me, has my head jerking away, but I'm firmly stuck against something, someone. "You're all right. I'm here. We're here." The voice of a man I thought I lost has my muscles relaxing, my heartbeat slowing down. His breath ghosts against my clammy skin, and I shake a little more. "Breathe, Thea, just breathe."

I watch as he takes a big, filling inhale. His lungs expanding, his shoulders raising, and I follow suit without a question. The air tastes so sweet on my tongue. I'm the anchor of a ship during the storm, finally finding my footing at the bottom of the ocean.

The world goes quiet, and I embrace it, live in it. Whatever nightmares had their grip on my reality are now gone, and I slowly adjust to the world around me, not the one my head loves to craft. As seconds pass, my vision fully clears, revealing Issac's troubled eyes assessing me for any injuries. But how can I tell him I'm all right on the outside when in reality my insides are slowly being eaten away? How can I begin to explain that day and night I run trying to uphold this façade, an act, but the beams on which I perform always slip away? How could he ever understand and believe me?

His nose brushes against mine, and I gulp down the feeling

of dread. The moment between us is about to come to its end. "Are you all right?" he asks, and I nod. He doesn't move, his eyes glued to mine as if worried the moment he shifts away I might fall apart anew. "Don't lie to me, Thea. If I have to bear the annoyance of keeping you safe, I need to know everything that's going on. Even inside that thick head of yours."

His voice is stern, laced with seriousness. His eyes are demanding, a glimpse of something I might mistake for pity passing through them. My mouth opens slightly, but no words come out. He keeps staring, and I grow uncomfortable. I want to tell him, I really do, but not this version of himself. This version will use my fears as a weapon to crush every ounce of hope left, every ounce of normality I cling to. "I know you're afraid of what might happen once the truth comes out, but fuck it. It's just me and you. So be straight with me for once." He sighs, his eyes shutting for a split moment. "I won't hurt you. You don't have to believe me. I wouldn't if the roles were reversed. But I do care, or at least some part of me does so be honest."

And in that moment, the walls separating the people around me and myself smash into tiny pieces. The silhouette of Issac waiting for me on the other side appears through the thick, intimidating fog, and I take that risk, leaping ahead past all the worries, all the taunting voices, the hatred, and for the first time in a long time, I feel at peace.

"*Nightmares*?" He repeats, uncertain, and I nod, my fingers laced over my legs. He's wrapping my ankle in a bandage to keep it steady until we make it out of the cave.

I've told him most of the things bothering me since leaving

the manor, leaving out parts I'm not ready to share. Like the fact I miss Lathai. Despite my previous worries of Issac mocking my current state, he took it rather well. Never interrupted, never made a face or gave me a bored look. He was just there, lending his ear to free me from some of the pressure.

At first, I hesitated, but his reassuring words made me realise that if I don't tell someone about what's going on, then we can't make any progress. If my head's not in the right place, it could doom us all. The team is only as good as their captain, even if the captain is a psychotic, deranged girl who has zero clue what she's doing. Either way, I confessed about being unable to sleep at night. About the worries occupying every waking hour of my day and the demons taunting me during the night.

I glance at him again. The outline of his jawline is sharp in the dim campfire light. His thick brows twitching as he ties another knot over my ankle. "When was the last time you had a proper rest?"

I swallow hard, embarrassment turning my cheeks bright red before I answer. "The day before we woke you up."

His eyes meet mine for a split second, and I turn away, biting my cheek. Him finding out about the things I did whilst he was unconscious is the last thing I want to talk about, but I want to be more honest, and that's what I'll do. For mine and others' sake. "What was different that time? Maybe we can try it again?"

"We can't." I cut him off before any more ideas roll off his tongue.

"Why?" he asks, letting go of my ankle, but his hand hovers above it, inches away, waking strange feelings inside my core.

I close my eyes, releasing a curt sigh. "Because we can't."

"But why?" He pushes, and I want to curl inside myself.

"Because the last time I had a decent sleep was next to your room whilst you were out of it, not threatening my life." I blabber out, meeting his cryptic stare with my fiery one.

A sudden laugh ricochets along the walls of the cave, and I'm ready to jump into the grave I dug myself. Yet I don't, because the sound of his laughter brings me a sudden rush of relief, happiness I'm not sure I deserve. "You fell asleep outside my door?" His head tilts back, exposing the sharp line of his throat, and I stare. "I mean, shit, I've heard we were close, but I didn't know I meant this much to you."

I scrape to my feet, shame of my past actions poking me in the chest. Revealing things like this is bargaining your life to a demon. You never know what kind of deal you might get. To this Issac, my behaviour might seem erratic, but the Issac I remember would find this proof of my devotion, of the unspoken word we were interrupted from saying.

"Whatever, laugh at me all you want. I knew you wouldn't understand." I huff and limp away, but his sudden grasp on my arm has me spinning around.

"Wait, all right, I understand." He hurries to explain, but I'm sceptical to believe him. There's still a part of him that hates me, a part that wishes me to be gone that heavily outweighs the side that cares. He can try to sympathise all he wants, to show me there are redeemable qualities in him, but I can't constantly throw myself into a haystack hoping to find the needle.

"But you don't, Issac!" I jerk my arm away. "You don't get it at all because you don't remember a single thing from that day! All you do know is that I've hurt the people closest to you, and yeah, that sucks, but I didn't mean to. I didn't want any of this to happen. I didn't want to lose you and bear this impossible weight of guilt on my shoulders."

Issac looks at me like he doesn't recognise me. Like I'm someone he's just met, his lips slightly apart, his eyes full of emotions I can't read. As he takes a step forward, the air around me seems to vanish, leaving me gasping for breath. "I do understand, because I remember." My brows shoot to the top of my forehead at his revelation, but no words dare to slip away. His eyes are burned into mine, looking for a sight of understanding. "Perhaps the memory of that day isn't matching yours, but I know what happened. I know what you might be going through because I've been there, and it's shitty. I know how it feels to be helpless and lost and lonely. I understand because for the past hundred years I had nothing but nightmares by my side until something changed. Until you showed up."

I'm speechless. The glass beneath my feet is swept away with a single blow, and the curtains close. My performance is over. I'm no longer expected to dance, and smile, and laugh like nothing ever happened. Like Lisa's death never affected me, like Theo losing his ability to speak doesn't make me want to cut my own tongue off, like losing my best friend in a split second didn't shatter my heart into a thousand pieces. Like the past hundred years I travelled through the world searching for the man I love, to find him and have him in ways I can't fathom, didn't rip my soul apart when I lost him all over again.

There's a strange sensation in the air, a mutual understanding between me and Issac, because for the first time ever since I lost him, we agree on something. We bond over the broken pieces in our life, and I'm all right with that.

He searches my face for an answer. I search his for the hidden agenda but find absolutely nothing. He's being honest, and I'm being freed from the cage I've kept myself in for a long time. "If all it takes for you to feel normal again, to get us to Yalan safely, is for me to be by your side, then so be it. I'll bear through every second of anguish it brings me to be in your presence if it makes you happy." His jaw ticks, and I swallow hard. The need to wrap my hands around his neck and bring our lips into an explosive kiss makes my head spin.

I want to thank him, to fall to my knees and tell him how much those words mean to me, but my body won't move. I'm paralysed, unable to give him any response at all, afraid if I do, he might not appreciate it. Instead, I watch as his hand reaches for the loose hair that got out of the braid and freeze when he tucks it behind my ear ever so gently. "It's fucked up," he whispers. "The way I can't stand you, but can't endure a moment without you by my side. Everything is so fucking messed up, but my job is to keep you safe, and that's exactly what I'll do." He confesses, but I know his words aren't fully true. I don't believe he still thinks of me as a mission. I don't think he believes that as well.

A half-smile creeps onto my lips, and I nod, letting his hand fall. We're in this together. The unexpected mess the universe threw at us we're trying so hard to conquer. Before, all we had was ourselves. Now, even if for a moment, we have each other once again.

"Are you done?!" Someone calls from the distance, and the moment Issac and I share is cut clean. We jump away from each other, our cheeks red, hiding within the shadows.

Ryo comes rushing from the darkness, and I smile, turning to fully face him. Issac's body looms over me. "Oh, I hope I didn't interrupt, but we found something you might find interesting."

"It better be a bloody way out of here," Issac growls low, the vibration of his chest sending shivers down my spine.

The young boy smirks, stopping metres away. He's out of breath, his chest puffed out, beads of sweat running down the sides of his forehead. "Something like that."

"This is our exit?" Issac announces, staring at a round hole. Shortly after we departed from our little rest stop, the twins and Ryo took us to the end of the tunnel which they discovered whilst Issac and I were busy bonding. It'd be great, cathartic even, if not for the thick layer of ice separating us from the outside world. "How are you planning to get past it, genius?"

He shoots Ryo a scolding look, and the boy begins swinging on his heels, his eyes searching mine. "No! Absolutely not! She probably hasn't recovered from what happened earlier," Issac cuts in, and I turn to face him. Ever since the conversation, he's been right behind me, and as grateful as I am, this isn't exactly what I meant when I said his presence calmed me. If anything, he makes me feel uneasy. My personal space being invaded by someone I barely recognise at any given moment.

"But General, there's no other way!" Ryo whines, and Issac rolls his eyes so far I can only see the white parts.

"There has to be another way. I said no."

"I'll do it." My voice draws their attention. The thankful look from Ryo fighting against the irritated one from Issac.

"Listen, even if there is another way, we don't have time. We barely have any food left, and everyone must be worried. I can handle this much ice."

"Thea—"

"No." I cut him off, a loud groan suppressing inside his throat, making it vibrate, making me lose my focus for just a moment. I pull him towards me so that nobody can hear the conversation. I've had enough of sharing and answering questions for one day. "I know you're trying to keep me safe, but you have to trust me, trust my judgement. I'll be fine, I promise."

His eye twitches, but he says nothing, stepping aside. Both twins and Ryo get behind me as the magic prickles the tips of my fingers, lightning setting my muscles into work. One breath, two heartbeats, and the ground begins to shake. "Explodeo."

The ice melts before splitting, little lines carving on all sides, forming into a spiderweb. I step away, dragging everyone to the ground just as a loud bang rings through the cave. Big chunks hurl past our heads, smoke mixed with snow, and finally light.

I never knew how much I'd miss the outside, the brightness. Even if all of it was so plain. Until now. It's blinding, painful even, but I stare ahead, a wide smile creeping onto my lips. We're out.

"Let's head to Thehil."

Chapter 9

The journey to Thehil was far worse than we anticipated. In the past four days, we've been hit with not one, not two, but three snowstorms, forcing us to take cover in any dented piece of land, caves so small my toes were touching someone's shoulders, and my arm was squeezed into my ribs trying to avoid touching Issac. He's made it his life mission to rest beside me whenever given the chance, and as sweet as it is, I can't bear another moment in his presence. He reminds me too much of what I lost, of what I need and crave, and that hurts in ways he can't fathom.

The day we left the cave, a trail of footsteps showed before us. I guess the rest of the group came across the cave but chose to make it to the town, hoping we'll catch up. I don't blame them. The weather is harsh, and we're running out of food. As long as they're safe, I don't care if they leave or stay.

I reach into my pocket, the rustling of paper a reminder our rations ran out two days ago. We've been living off any animal the twins could spot and hunt, which is almost nothing. Sharing a rabbit with four other people is like serving half a spoon of porridge to a toddler.

"When we get to that town, I'm buying all their food and

giving you none of it!" Ryo grunts under his breath, his hands lacing over his stomach.

Issac scoffs from behind me. "Who said you'll make it to the town?"

"What?" The boy turns to face his superior, brows shot high, furrowed in concern.

"I mean, perhaps another storm hits us and the twins won't catch anything tonight, and we'll be forced to sacrifice one of us. Who do you think it'll be, Erdove?" I elbow Issac in the ribs as soon as Ryo has that expression on his face that tells me he's ready to run for his life. The man moans, but a chuckle slips past his lips when Ryo eyes him warily.

"With all due respect, General, you won't do that." He raises his chin high and proud, and the sight almost makes me giggle.

"Oh yeah? Why's that?" Issac challenges, crossing his gloved hands over his chest.

"Because Thea won't let you." I nod in agreement, running to catch up to him. Our arms are linked, and I turn to face Issac with a fake, insulted frown on my face.

"He's right! What made you think I'd agree to this? Perhaps you'll be our next meal." I half forget that we're completely different people from the ones in the manor, letting myself joke around as if he hasn't threatened me weeks back. Often I find it strange, but the feeling of happiness is greater than the one of misery so I let it slide and enjoy those small moments whilst they last.

Issac rolls his eyes and shakes his head in disbelief. "Doubt the twins will be as easily bought by you as Soldier Erdove over here, but sure, you can try." He flashes his top row of sparkly, white teeth. Sharp canines blinking right at me, reminding me of what they're capable of. I have to look away before my thoughts wander somewhere dangerous. "But who knows? Maybe you'll wind up in front of me right on time?"

I'm sure my eyes are about to fall out of their sockets at his words. He knows too much about my feelings towards him. Perhaps he remembers some things too. And that became the new torture, to see how far he can tease me before I become flustered.

Of course, Issac's aware I'd never do anything he wouldn't agree to, but that's exactly why he's doing what he's doing. Playing with my feelings is the only way he can get to me since the war axe has been buried and our hands shaken unofficially. Unofficially, we're no longer at each other's throats, but tolerating each other's presence. Officially, he's allowed himself to toy with my heart for the sake of subsiding his inner voices because he knows deep down all of this affects me. The fact I can't have him kills me, and he's getting the most out of it. Smug bastard.

It's evening when the first sight of settlement comes into view. A carriage buried under piles and piles of snow stands right next to a pen that should host animals, none of them present. I wonder how they manage to provide food in these conditions. Given Sebraycia doesn't exchange with other countries, it must be hard, but somehow they manage.

I pull the hood of my jacket tighter as the evening winds begin to pick up, my eyes searching for something, anything in the distance. Just a single light speck, a person running towards their house in search of warmth, someone from our group posted at the tavern door keeping guard. Anything.

"We must be close. I see foot tracks." Venali announces,

and it must be one of the first times I heard her speak aloud, not only addressing Issac but also the rest of the group. What a couple of days in someone's presence can do to you, right?

Jassin scans the area, his long, pointy ears twitching as he tries to listen out for any noise. "There's commotion far ahead. Perhaps another thirty minutes."

"Guys—"

"Perhaps? I'm afraid my legs might stop working sooner than that." I cut through whatever it is Ryo wanted to complain about to add my own, very first complaint. I'm not the one to point out how tired I've grown, but lately I've been granted the luxury of having peaceful nights, so my body grows tired quicker than ever. Perhaps part of me just yearns to steal a couple of blissful moments beside Issac, and as shameful as it sounds, I can't wait to drift away knowing he's right beside me.

"I think you'll be fine for another half an hour, unless, of course, there's another reason you want us to stop so badly." Issac smirks, his eyes narrowed with sarcasm, and I stare at him with my skin ready to peel off, my bones ready to crack and assemble into a neat pile. A new source of energy springs into action, fuelled by something that feels like irritation. I appreciate how much easier it's become to be in his company, but I can't stand the way he uses my own feelings against me.

"No, I'll be fine, thanks. Perhaps it's you that needs something since you brought it up?" I inch closer without breaking eye contact. There's a spark between us, something that could go right or wrong depending on the words we pick next.

"Guys?!"

Issac scoffs. "Me? Trust me, love, I'm all good. I could

actually use one night without your snores."

"I don't snore!" My hands fly in the air, and Issac takes a step back, giggling to himself. Why am I getting so worked up over this idiot? I know he's doing it to piss me off, yet I fall for the trap each time, and when I do learn my lesson, he comes up with another way to throw me off the tracks. "If it bothers you so much, then sleep elsewhere. I'm sure Venali and Jassin would be thrilled to have their general drool over their shoulders."

"I don't drool!" He exclaims, a flash of embarrassment passing through his eyes. That's right. Taste your own fucking medicine, or in this case, poison. "You're unbelievable, making up lies to cover the fact you can't stay away from me."

"Me? It's you who always rushes to make sure nobody else rests beside me." I point an accusing finger at his chest. He can shame me for my feelings all he wants, find them ridiculous, but he can't hide the fact he cares. I see it in him, in his behaviour for the past couple of days. The hatred he had for me vanished, and now his head's messed up with things even he can't comprehend. This, whatever he's trying to do here, is just a cover-up, an excuse to get me to speak to him, to get a reaction out of me, a reason to be closer, to look each other in the eyes and try to solve the puzzle inside his head.

And I always give in. Why do I give in?

"Guys!" Ryo's third shout breaks the tension between us, and we both turn, shouting at the same time.

"What?!"

The boy is standing right behind Issac, his back fully facing us as his finger points at something in the distance. For me, it's too dark to see, but elves have the annoying ability to see better during night.

Issac grunts, stepping aside to face Ryo. "What is it, Erdove? If you're about to ask for more food, I've already told you. You ate it all—"

"No!" The boy turns slowly, and only then do I spot the outline of three creatures far ahead. "Do you think we can perhaps make it in ten minutes, per se?"

"Run!" I scream before darting in the direction of the village. My body, previously exhausted, is now pumped up with adrenaline and the remains of the argument still clinging to my skin.

I hear the heavy breaths dragging behind me, a sign that Issac and Ryo have listened and moved without question. So did the twins, the pair of them further ahead. I cough a little, my brain already coming up with an action plan.

"Don't even think about it!" Issac shouts from behind, his voice piercing through my chest.

"But—"

"There's no but! You've almost died. Just fucking listen to me for once and drop it. Your magic needs to recover!" He continues, and I bite onto my lip in frustration. Perhaps he's right, and continuing to use this power might bring us more trouble than salvation, but on the other hand, we can't keep on running, not from antlered polar bears.

A few minutes pass, and so far the vicious animals haven't caught up to us. I'm almost at my limit, my chest burning with fire I'd never felt before.

I try to speed up, but the next step I take has my knees buckling under the weight of my body as I tumble down to the floor. The unhealed ankle I've tended to in the past few days reminds me of its existence, waves of terrible pain taking a portion of my sanity.

Issac and Ryo come to a halt, both of them looking from me to the polar bears. They need to decide what to do, right here, right now. "Damn it, can you carry her?"

"Do you really think of me so little, General?" One look from Issac, and Ryo's back is straight, his hands glued to the sides like an actual soldier. Someone I've barely seen him be. "I'll take care of her."

"What? Wait, what about you?!" Issac ignores my shouts, his tensed back the only view I get of his person. I grunt as Ryo lifts me off the floor, slowly moving away from Issac and the dangers lying behind. Every nerve ending in my body hurts, every blood cell coursing through my veins turns into a needle, pinching me from the inside. "Ryo, stop! We can't leave him!"

The boy shifts me into a more comfortable position, my arms clasped behind his neck as my legs dangle. I look past his shoulder, past all the darkness to glimpse at Issac. "Thea, he's a general for a reason. Trust him to make the right decisions, just as we trust you."

I nod, but the feeling of dread and uncertainty doesn't leave my side for a split second.

ISSAC

One last stolen glance. One last shaky breath. One last pull on my chest as I watch them disappear off into the distance. Her betrayed, golden eyes the last thing I see, the last thing I might remember.

I turn around, realising the reason for my hold-up. I need

to make sure to stop the bears from reaching them before they make it to Thehil. With Thea unable to run, all we could do is stall for time. In this case, the duty fell on me. I'd never sacrifice any of my own people to save her. If it has to be anyone, let it be me. She's already carved a hole inside my chest, crawled into it, and sealed it shut. I'm a dead man either way.

I make a small incision on my palm, something I've grown used to. The pain doesn't bother me as much as it should. It feels oddly calming. The only constant amongst the chaos. Blood drips on the white snow, tainting it, making it impure, and I glance towards the bears. Getting my hands dirty isn't something new. I much prefer it to putting on an act of a good guy who's here to save everyone. I wasn't born a hero in this story. I've always been the villain.

The bears roar, their antlers crushing mounds of snow in their way. I haven't used magic in so long, but the feeling of the energy rushing into my bloodstream is so familiar. I build up a wall tall enough so they can't jump over and thick enough to stop them from just barging their way through.

When the last drop falls, I sprint away, just as the first scratch screeches along the crystallised blood. I could kill them, no problem, but the annoying tug on my legs has me following the rest of our group, specifically one vexing girl. I growl, looking ahead, wondering if they made it far enough, if I was right to trust that kid with her? Actually, scratch that. Why do I even care in the first place? Why has everything become so confusing lately?

There are times where I can't stand being near her. Where all I want is to slit my own throat and bleed out, but those are exactly the moments I choose to annoy her instead. It's a remedy, a shot of winter whisky poured down my throat, cooling my head, giving me a clearer image. Ever since I discovered how much she truly cares about me, the lengths to which she'd go to keep me safe, I decided to use it against her so she can see how it feels. How I feel being constantly told things I don't remember. Things I did or wouldn't do, expectations set too high. Even the mountain peak couldn't reach them. I want her to feel the same way I do. Helpless and lost, confused and hurt. Because that's what she does to me every time her hand brushes past mine when we fall asleep.

Those are the times I question my own judgement, the last grain of sanity and self-respect left inside, because, hell, I'm ready to throw it all away. To pull her closer, to be trapped by her addictive scent, to have her fingertips set me on fire, to taste her full, rosy lips and finally find out the truth for myself. Were those the same things that caught the past me, the one she's so madly smitten with?

Fuck, this wasn't meant to be this way. I was supposed to hate her, destroy her, just like I've been told to do all those years. She annihilated our entire village, put me in a place with a lunatic who found pleasure in pain, and then took away everything I've worked so hard on. My soldiers, my home, my family.

At least that's what I keep telling myself, but for a while now these things feel like words taken out of someone else's mouth. Like I've never stood there witnessing it all, but rather watched it from a stranger's perspective. I began questioning all things around me, even the girl I was made to hate.

She's never what I make her. Deceiving, horrible, devious,

or disloyal. I see it in the way she makes sure Ryo is never hungry or anxious during our journey. In the way she tries to get closer to the twins, knowing they trust me more than her, trying so hard to make sure we all feel happy, comfortable, and peaceful. Trying and trying and trying to build a bridge between us, even if it's just a flimsy plank. She'll cross it if it means I'll see her in a different light. She'll do anything. I admire that about her, the will to fight for what seems to be lost. Even in the darkest times, she chooses someone else over herself, and that really sums up the person she is.

Unlike me. I'd given up on fighting a long time ago, but she has this gift of making you feel things that feel forbidden, because how dare I care about a girl I wanted dead? How dare I try and make sure she gets some sleep, because in the time we've spent together, I watched her from a distance during the nights she didn't dare to close her eyes, too worried her screams might disturb others?

I truly, truly believed she was a horrible person until the wisp attack. The moment I nearly saw her die fighting for others woke something in me, a feeling long forgotten, drowned under all the shit I've invented. And then in the mountains, where she didn't think twice about herself but rather the lives of others, my life. At that moment, I knew I had to save her. Not because it was my duty, but because someone like her actually deserved a chance at life. I was willing to die if it meant she might prove my infuriating thoughts wrong.

That's why I've stopped accusing her of things she hasn't done, but rather focused on lesser evil. Part of me, one I can't hush away, still craves the pain in her eyes, the anger in her voice when we fight. Teasing her about things I can't remember but know are true is better than making her believe she's committed crimes I've imagined. I might be a monster, but not to that extent, not anymore.

A roar in the distance snaps my attention to reality, and I stop running, realising the bears had broken through the barrier faster than I anticipated. I guess Thea will have to wait a little bit longer for her beauty sleep. That is, if she still cares after being reunited with her friends.

A strange sensation pierces through my heart. The air heavy with a muddled cluster of emotions. I search for the right one. Is it irritation? Anger? Fear? No, it's jealousy. I'm fucking jealous of a girl I can barely abide. Add that to the things I wish to understand but can't, because what exactly am I jealous of? The fact she might find more comfort in being around Desily, Alea, Theo, or Ryo? The fact she might stop indulging my arguments and send me into a spiral of self-hatred, ultimately tipping my broken body over the edge and into the void? Or the fact I might not be able to be as close to her as I am, chasing her in the daytime and haunting her in dreams? Is it that I'm jealous or afraid of losing what isn't mine?

I release a chuckle, swiping the loose strands of hair off my face. At least one thing hasn't changed. I'm equally as fucked up as I was before dying for her, and even now, risking my own life to make sure she gets to safety and has a good night's rest. Gods, what the fuck is wrong with me?

Chapter 10

ALTHEA

"Thea!" A pair of hands wraps around my shoulders as Ryo sets me down, but I barely register anything. The sound of my twisting guts, the frantic beating of my heart ready to crack a hole in my chest. It's all there inside my head.

"What happened? Where is I—"

I stop listening. Eyes glued to the door without breaking away. Ever since we left, I've done nothing but stare behind, hoping to see him, praying he didn't get hurt or lost or kidnapped. The pain in my ankle doesn't matter, the long distance we crossed awfully fast now a sudden nuisance. Nothing around me matters.

I bite the skin off my chapped lips, drawing blood. I'm surprised there's anything left since all I've been doing is torturing my own body. The worry of making the wrong choice by leaving Issac behind, a sudden friend, sits beside me, laughing in my ear as I continue staring, oblivious to what's happening around me.

A tap on the shoulder. A raised voice. My view obstructed. My body twisted around.

"What are you doing?" I snap at Desily, who looks nothing but worried. She scans my face, her hands resting on my shoulders.

"What are you doing?" She repeats angrily, crouching down to remove my shoe.

I huff, shutting my eyes. "Des, get away. I'm serious."

"Why?" Her voice is calm, too calm for someone like me. I know I'm being unreasonable, uncooperative, and annoying. I know I deserve to be screamed at, to be slapped across the face and brought back into reality, but she does none of these things. Her eyes are solely focused on fixing my leg, unlike mine that try to catch a glimpse of a figure sneaking inside the building. "I've been worried sick about you, Thea." She whispers, and my heart aches. Why am I like this? "I wondered if you were safe, or even alive, so it's normal for me to ask questions, but your head seems to be elsewhere." She sighs and looks towards the door. "Few weeks ago, you wanted to be away from him. Today you seem ready to storm into the darkness just to find him. I can never figure you two out."

"Couple weeks is a long time for things to change."I snap, my voice harsher than intended. I can't tear my eyes away from the door, barely registering the warmth of her magic as she heals my shattered ankle. She could be pouring her energy into my head and I wouldn't even notice.

"Thea, look at me." Desily's hands tighten on my leg, forcing my attention. "Please, just look at me for one second."

I don't want to. I don't want to see the hurt in her eyes, the exhaustion, the desperation. But her voice cracks on the last word and something inside me breaks. When I finally meet her gaze, I wish I hadn't.

"I thought I lost you." Her words are barely audible, tears threatening to spill. "For four days, Thea. Four days of not knowing if you were bleeding out somewhere, if you were taken, if you were—" She stops, swallowing hard. "And the first thing you do when you get back is ignore me completely. You won't even let me help you without trying to run after him."

Guilt twists in my stomach, but it's not enough to drown out the gnawing need to know if Issac's safe. "Des, I—"

"No." She cuts me off, her calm façade finally cracking. "Do you have any idea what it's like? Watching you throw yourself into danger over and over for someone who wants you dead? Someone who made it very clear he wants nothing to do with you?" Her voice rises, the frustration she's been holding back finally spilling over. "I'm right here, Thea. I've always been right here and I'm trying to make you understand you can rely on me too, but you don't see me, do you? You only see him."

The words hit me. Gods, she's so right it hurts.

"I'm sorry," I whisper, but even as I say it, my eyes drift back towards the door. I can't help it. The pull is too strong, the fear too consuming.

Desily follows my gaze and lets out a bitter laugh. "You're doing it again. Even now, you can't stop." She releases my ankle, the healing complete, and sits back on her heels. "I know you love him. I understand you miss him but what happened, Thea? What happened that has you caring more about his safety than your own life? More than ours?"

I jerk at her words. I do care, I care about all of them but how can I begin explaining that Issac's the only person who can keep me steady. Who cures me whilst being the very thing that poisons me. "It's not like that—"

"Then what is it like?" She demands, her voice breaking. "Because from where I'm sitting, it looks like you've forgotten everyone who actually gives a damn about you. Ryo carried you here on his back. Theo secured this entire inn so we'd be safe. I've been healing every scrape and bruise, every broken bone, waiting and praying you'd come back." Her hands are shaking now. "But the moment you arrive, you barely acknowledge any of us. It's all him. Always him."

"I don't know Des! It all changes so quickly, time is slipping through my fingers and moments are passing by. I feel like I'm constantly at the edge of time when it comes to him." I rest my head in my palm fighting off a headache that threatens to knock me out.

"You're not though Thea. Not everyone's immortal like you two. Not everyone has the chance to live a different life every day, so talk to me. Tell me what's going on." For the first time since our arrival, I fully look at her, taken aback by her words.

Her brows are furrowed with concern, her eyes dark from the lack of sleep, and I finally understand it. She's not angry. She's tired. Tired because for the past four days she probably waited for us to arrive, worried we might not. I haven't thought about it this way, the fact I might vanish and she wouldn't know why or how, still convinced I'm immune to death, or the fact she might not share my luck and live to see another day herself. For some reason, Desily's death never crossed my mind because to me she can't do that, she can't just cease to exist.

Yet, in her eyes the story's different. She's lost someone close to her before, someone she wasn't able to reach in time before it was too late, and that's what has her so tired, so desperate for me to open up. She's afraid she might have to go through that pain again or perhaps the fact I'll go through it if I return one day and she's no longer here. I've been feeding her lies for the sake of keeping her feelings intact, and for what? Our last memories shared together will be of someone that doesn't actually exist, and she'll have to live with the fact that a person she considers her best friend didn't trust her enough to tell the truth. Desily knows how fragile her life is, and she wants me to acknowledge that one day she won't be here to say goodbye, that one day I won't be around to do that too, living in a fantasy where all of us are immortal like Issac and I. But that's far from it because I can die, I almost did many times and she has no clue.

The constant dream of saving everyone I'm living, instead of facing the facts, slowly falls apart, showing me a newer, more gruesome picture. I don't actually think of ever losing them, I don't allow myself to see the truth that they could just perish. Instead I focus on a person that can't die. At least in Desily's eyes it seems that way and it's all my fault because I chose to hide the truth from her, to pretend I'm indestructible when I'm not.

It seems at some point I slowly started to believe that lie myself, another version of my friends being untouchable inserting themselves in my mind, leaving Issac and me at death's doorstep. I tell myself I want to save my friends and keep them safe but it seems this whole time I've been pretending that can't happen, not when I'm around, not when Issac is. I've been so focused on saving a person who I know can die that I forgot about those who truly are in danger, whose lives are far more fragile than mine and unknowingly pushed them away for the sake of keeping them safe.

Shit, I'm a horrible person, a terrible friend.

"Des—"

"It's all right, Thea. I understand it's not easy, nothing lately is easy, and I'm sorry your life is shit and I can't fix it, but I want to be there with you, for you." She looks up at me, her eyes glossy with unspoken tears. It's a side of her I haven't seen, someone completely new. "Don't push me away, please. I've told you before I'm by your side no matter what, but I can't protect you if you won't tell me what's going on. You're like my sister, and I don't want to lose you in a worse way than I lost her, so please, please talk to me."

I struggle to breathe, my lower lip trembling, as her words turn my entire existence on its head. Perhaps I was never truly alone, and nothing was after me but the creations of my troubled mind. If only I trusted her a little more, if only I wasn't so afraid to lose her, perhaps the two of us wouldn't have missed so much sleep, perhaps we'd be happier sooner. The choices made in the past are forever engraved in this timeline, but that doesn't mean I can't make new, better ones. Decisions that'll keep us safe and closer than ever.

My eyes scan the room, realising we've been left alone. Whoever made it this far must be resting in their room or have just left, giving Des and me much-needed privacy. I wonder if Ryo heard anything? How long did he hang around for? Then a sudden memory of him promising to eat all the food available pops into my head. I guess some are sleeping and some are eating.

As Desily finishes with my ankle, I begin telling her everything that's happened since we left the ship. The nightmares, the conversations with Issac, the way he's stranger with each passing day. She listens without interrupting, her eyes focused on my leg even when I mention Lathai's name and the fact I might be missing him, or some parts of him.

"I miss him too, or who he used to be." She says with a sad smile, and I nod in agreement. Ever since that day, I believed I was crazy for having any good feelings left towards that man. I scolded and punished myself for even thinking he could still be saved, but it seems I wasn't the only one. Lathai was Desily's friend too, not just mine. She probably misses him just as much, worries about what might have become of him, and what she could have done to save him.

As I continue speaking, my mouth almost says too much when I want to tell her the truth behind my immortality and Jino. I quickly cover it by describing one of the nightmares, thankfully diverting her attention.

Gods, I wish it were easier to be fully honest with her, with everyone. No one except for a few people is aware I'm not fully immortal or that I can speak with the demon we're trying to rid ourselves of. That one day I might share Lathai's fate and lose control, but that day isn't here yet. I'm still fighting. I glance at her and purse my lips. It'd be better if she knew, less complicated, but I've promised Issac and Jino to keep it between us, at least for now. Though, if she knew, some guilt would lift off my chest and perhaps I could feel half as free as I do revealing my weaknesses to her right now. Gods, the nightmares and Issac are just the tip of the iceberg. I bet she'd flip if she knew I can die whilst using my magic. The only reason why Issac tries to stop me half the time.

"So what happened in the cave?" She lets go of my ankle

and gets up to plate me some food. Only then do I feel my stomach rumble and realise how hungry I've become.

"I'm not sure where to begin."

"Did he try hurting you?" She cuts in, and I wince at her words. Her eyes hold seriousness, a promise that if I confirm her worries she'll do something she might regret later.

"Gods, no, Des! Quite the opposite." I shake my head and lean forward to snatch the bowl full of stew off the table.

"Oh?" Her brows are furrowed in confusion, her eyes dancing with sparks of curiosity.

"He saved me from the fall and temporarily died. Not only that, he's promised to stay close by to help me with the nightmares after I told him I felt quite peaceful in his presence on the ship." Desily looks shocked at my words, her lips turned into a frown.

"When he was unconscious?" She asks doubtfully.

I nod. "Yeah, I did tell him that, but he was adamant about helping me, because it's his mission." I quote, rolling my eyes.

She chuckles. "I think it's more than a mission now." Her eyes drift off somewhere behind me, lips pressed together, before her tongue traces the bottom of her full lips. "That's why you wanted to go after him today."

My cheeks are red with embarrassment. But what exactly am I embarrassed about? The fact I fell in love with him all over again even if he hates me? The fact I should keep my guard up and stay as far away from Issac as possible, but instead I want to be closer? Or perhaps it's the shame of him being the only person who could pull me out of darkness. Not Desily, not Theo or Alea, but him. The man who despises my existence.

"I don't know what I'm doing any more, Des. All of this

is starting to feel like too much." I admit, before getting up to put the bowl away. The room we're in is quite spacious, usually serving as a dining space for travellers. I assume Theo paid quite a lot to rent this place for all of us, making sure we can rest in proper beds, with warmth, fresh water, and hot meals.

There's a fireplace on the right side with two fur chairs stood before it. I stretch my arms above my head and take a seat, basking in the bright light. Gods, I missed the comfort of being somewhere that reminds me of home.

Desily gets up from her chair and moves towards the hallway where the sleeping quarters must be. I decide to stay right here, in case Issac makes it back. In case I need to provide some help. In case I fall asleep and get woken up by nightmares.

"You know," she says before disappearing, "love is never easy, but that's what makes it so desirable. We'll always want what feels rare, what feels like it belongs to us."

After Desily leaves the room, I'm stuck staring into the fireplace with my head a bit calmer, with my thoughts more collected, but the fact Issac hasn't returned makes me worried just a little bit more. I reach into the bag hidden underneath my jacket and pull out one of the many letters neatly stored deep within it. The pages are becoming less full, filled with words that don't make sense, as if chaos resides inside the writer's head. I trace the page and begin reading, occupying my mind with something remotely similar to my own.

***

The sound of splitting wood has my eyes fluttering open. I don't know how many hours have passed, nor when I fell asleep, but the darkness behind the window tells me it's past midnight. I roll my neck and let it fall to the side, the sight of a person residing in the previously empty chair causing all the hair on my body to stand up.

"Seems like you'll sleep fine without my company." Red, piercing eyes. Freckles scattered across the pale face. Rosy lips twisted into a soft smile. His hand resting below his chin, his breaths steady. Issac is back.

The relief that washes over me takes away any worry, any doubt I ever had about his wellbeing. He's returned, and the first place he decided to go to wasn't Theo's room, but the scrawny chair stood at the foot of the fireplace. The chair right beside me. He kept his promise.

I want to get up from the seat and assess him for injuries, but the sudden, heavy material resting on my body stops me. I gaze down, realising someone has covered me with a blanket.

"Don't be so shocked, you looked cold."

"When did you— How— Are you all right?" The questions roll off my tongue. Issac eyes me cautiously, keeping himself reserved in case I mistake his act of kindness for something else, something more than it really is.

He slowly removes the armour from his body, a sigh of relief pushing past his lips because it's been a while since we've had the privilege to walk in normal clothes. These days, if you forget to dress appropriately, you might find yourself hurt, or worse, dead.

My lips press together at the sight of his lean body, the sculptured muscles hiding underneath the white shirt, a sight

I almost forgot about. It hasn't been that long, yet I feel like years have passed since I saw him so comfortable, so relaxed and careless. I guess in the land of nothing, time doesn't exist.

His hand brushes the longer strands of hair off his face, and I note they've grown since we left Karul.

"I should be offended you think I'd come back with nothing more than a scratch, but then, you're a paranoid one." He chuckles and exhales deeply, not a single body movement implying he might be in pain.

"Issac, I'm being serious. Are you all right? What happened? What took you so long?" I'm fully awake now, my head racing with questions I want answered. We arrived at the inn a while ago. He should have been back no more than an hour after us.

"Gods, you won't drop it, will you?" I shake my head, and he sighs, resigned. "When you lot left, I kept the bears away, until I couldn't any more because the weather got worse. I had to fight them for a while and make sure they don't come into town. Otherwise, what'd be the point of me staying if they made it here and lurked around?"

"So, you're not hurt?" I repeat the same question, and he groans, rolling his eyes.

"No, I'm not, and stop worrying about me so much. It's weird and I hate it." I ignore his words, knowing damn well even he doesn't mean them. If he did, he wouldn't have stayed. He wouldn't have put the blanket over me and taken the seat to make sure I don't wake up screaming. He would have walked away the moment I opened my mouth, yet he remains seated, with his eyes shut.

"When will you stop pretending?" The sentence comes out

of my mouth before I can stop myself. Something that was supposed to stay just a thought is now breathed into reality.

Issac's eyes are wide open, staring right at me in silence. I hold his gaze, my heart beating so damn loud it hurts.

"Pretending? Trust me, if I could, I'd just leave."

"We both know that's a lie. It's been for a while now." I'm not sure why I keep going, but a part of me wants to hear the truth. I know it might make him angry, livid even, but if I've learnt one thing about holding a conversation with this man, it's to always turn it into an argument and hope you win.

He laughs, but the laugh doesn't sound pleasant. It's more of a mocking type of chuckle, a warning, an act he plays so well he sometimes forgets it's just an act.

"Really? And you came to that conclusion how exactly?" I feel my skin crawl with fear, my fists opening and closing, trying to fight through the frustration and hatred heard in his tone. "Because I saved you from falling to your death? Because I promised to stay by your side? Because for the past couple of days I spoke with you out of boredom?" He huffs, and I wince. "Sorry to break it to you, love, but it's my mission, a task given by that fucker you brought into our home."

I scoff, my cheeks burning with fire, my vision clouded with resentment. "He never asked you to do any of these things. I know exactly what he said, word by word, because I lost you that day, Issac, and I've been trying so hard ever since to bring you back, but you make it so difficult." I bite onto my cheek, my eyes peeling off his face to look at a spot behind him, because if I have to stare him in the eyes any longer, I might just break. "Why are you fighting this? I see the change in you, the will to break free, but just as you get anywhere, you decide to ruin it all over again."

"Then stop." He shrugs, bringing my attention back to his face. There's no sight of reluctance, of second thoughts as he continues talking. "Stop fucking caring about me, Thea. It won't do any of us any good. Just leave me be and get it through your head I'm not who you want me to be."

I'm not sure what fuels my next move, but I can't help when my legs stretch out and touch the stable ground. I want to leave, to distance myself from this man before any good memory of our time spent together gets ruined by his stubbornness. All the noises around me are muffled by the inside screams of irritation at his words. I should have learnt my lesson by now. He's an arsehole, the worst one I've ever met.

The blanket rolls off my body, and from below it fall the letters I'd read before falling asleep. Embarrassment and anger sit on either side of my shoulders as I scramble to the ground to pick them all up, hoping Issac doesn't read their contents. Having him discover this secret, this one thing that keeps me remotely happy, would crush my world completely, and I'm not ready to fight another battle today. I've lost this one, I can admit it, and I'm not sure how I'm going to get up after it.

I hear him shift beside me, my movements faster as I collect all the scattered pages, but Issac has already taken one into his hands. His eyes read the paper covered in century-old ink, brows furrowed in what seems like confusion.

"Give it back, before you start hating on another person for having human feelings." I growl, trying to snatch it away, but he lifts it up, his eyes meeting mine, and I stop moving.

"Where did you get this?" He whispers, his voice slightly

shaking. I stare at him, perplexed. Two minutes ago he wanted nothing to do with me. Now he's asking questions. What the fuck is wrong with this man?

"None of your business. Give it back, I mean it." My voice is hard, laced with seriousness because I can't let him ruin this. I can't.

"Thea," he grabs onto my arm, pulling me closer. The space between us suddenly gone as I inhale his intoxicating scent, take in the rapid beating of his heart and the uneven breaths. "Where did you get this?" He seethes out the words through his gritted teeth like it pains him to even ask.

I purse my lips together, contemplating whether or not I should answer, but the pleading in his eyes makes me cave in. Fuck it, what can he possibly do with that information?

"I took it from Theo's office, back in the manor when I stole the books. Why do you care?"

His gaze sweeps across the page for a brief moment. Silence falls between us, and I wonder just what exactly has him so distressed. These letters belong to a prisoner kept by Lord Graham. Someone neither of us knew, so why would Issac care about such a trivial thing?

Another second passes, and his eyes are back, staring right at me, into me. It feels like whatever's about to come out of his mouth might change my entire world. It might just throw me into the void or pull me towards the shore. The whole universe might explode with his next words, and I'm unprepared for the impact.

"Because these letters belong to me."

Chapter 11

I always thought about what it would feel like to meet the man I grew so close to through the text he wrote. I wondered what colour his eyes were. I imagined green with a hint of brown, like the world he wanted to see so badly. I wondered what his voice sounded like. Kind perhaps, the sweetest melody in your ears, easing all those noises in your head. I wondered about his life before the manor, the girl he wrote about, the love he had for her.

Now, the truth stands before me, and it looks nothing like I'd imagined. The truth has crimson eyes. Its voice hard, clear of emotion, causing you to wonder what really goes on inside its head. Truth isn't a thing, a stranger. It's a man I spent my childhood with, who I searched for and fell in love with. Truth is cruel.

"What?" I blink, not sure if the question actually left my mouth or if I'd imagined it. The fantasy I've lived in for the past few months suddenly gone, burnt down and tossed away. All this time, I desired to meet the person I related to on a deeper level, to let them hear me out, hold my hand, and assure me it'll be all right. Yet now that I've met them, I'm not sure if I want to hear anything they're about to say.

Issac shifts away, his eyes avoiding mine. I'm not sure if

it's shame he's trying to hide, or surprise, but either way he's ready to bolt. All the things he wrote in those letters, all the stuff he said about me. How on earth is he going to deny it now? Play it off by saying it's just a mission, that he doesn't care about his old self writing he'd do anything to get me back, to see me one more time.

"Issac—"

"No." He cuts me off, shaking his head in denial. The letter in his hand gets crumpled by his tight grasp. I'm afraid it might get shredded to pieces, the last remaining proof of its existence residing in my head. "I can't— I've got to leave."

He rushes past me, but I'm quick to stop him by putting my frame in front of his body. I'm done with him running away when things get rough, when something that could bring him back shows up and he decides to leave it all behind. I want truth. I need it.

"You're not going anywhere." My palms land on his chest, the rapid beating of his heart pulsing against my skin. I gaze up, his eyes staring right at me with anguish. "I need to know, Issac. Is this true? Did you write these?"

"I— Fuck— Yes, yes I did!" He throws his hands up in frustration before bringing them back to cover his face. A deep, tired sigh slips past his shaking lips. "But that was years ago. I thought, shit, I thought he threw them away."

I assume he's talking about Theo, who'd often be mentioned in these letters. How did it not occur to me that it was Issac who wrote these? They just seemed so different, personal and open. Things I've never heard him talk about, words I wouldn't suspect him to say. The man trapped in the manor fought tooth and nail to hold onto a memory of us together. Tried his best to escape and find me, hoped I'd find him and forgive him for leaving without a word.

He loved me.

"Did you mean it?" I ask, my face stone cold, ready to take on any kind of response. Unlike my heart, which is two beats away from being shattered to pieces.

"Did I mean what?" He repeats, confused, his eyes finally meeting mine.

I exhale slowly, ready for whatever comes. "Did you mean what you said in those letters about me? Did you truly want to protect me, remember me? Did you really care about me this much? Miss me?" The last words come out more as a whisper, something I'd rather have neither confirmed nor denied. I just need to say it, to put it out there so that when he answers I might know some part of the truth.

His gaze lingers on me, as if I were a cherished memory from his past, a soul he once delighted in sharing laughter with, a person for whom he'd move mountains. I believe it, every second of it, and with that I grow more worried because the fantasy he lets me live in will inevitably come crashing down in mere seconds.

"What do you think?" He whispers, his heart beating faster, his breaths growing more rigid. My palms feel like they're on fire, like I should pull away and stuff them into cold water, yet I don't move. "Fuck, you weren't meant to find these."

"But I did."

"Yes, and now you let yourself foolishly believe that person's still here." He grunts, trying to take a step back, but instead coming closer. "It was many years ago. Don't give yourself hope."

"I beg to differ." I try to keep my voice steady, my head calm, but the way his body presses against me has the bones in my legs turn into mush. I can feel his breath brush against my face, his emotions waking inside my head. I'm him and he's me. "Perhaps you're not the same, but I know you meant all of it, Issac. I know that boy's still inside of you trying to win the fight, but you're too unyielding, too afraid." I slide my palm higher, letting it rest behind his neck as he remains silent, his eyes full of secrets. "What are you so afraid of?"

A beat passes. A storm forms inside my head, ready to destroy everything in its path. Another one. His eyes shift, his mask falls. He's present.

"You! I'm afraid of you!" His scream sends a shiver through me, his words slicing into my heart. I retreat slightly, my fingers trailing away from his skin, yet he seizes my wrist, drawing me close until our faces are mere breaths apart. "I'm afraid of what you're doing to me because none of it makes sense. You're fucking with my head constantly and I don't know why I let you, why it affects me." He exhales softly, his eyelids fluttering shut as he draws our foreheads together, creating a connection between us I've craved for so long.

I want to say something that would matter. Tell him it's all right to feel this way and that I'll always be there to support him, but my mouth is glued shut and I'm too scared of saying the wrong thing. Because what could I possibly say that would make him stay? That would make him hate me a little bit less and break away the seal keeping him bound to Theo's command? Nothing, or perhaps nothing that I can think of.

"Hating you is easier than admitting there's a part of me that feels something for you because you don't deserve this, Thea. You don't deserve a piece of shit like me." In an instant, he's pulled from my grasp, leaving me in a haunting silence. He dashes out of the room and into the shadowy corridor, carrying his words away, whilst my heart is left tethered to him by a fragile red thread he'd woven long ago.

***

When the first ray of sunlight slipped past the drawn curtains, the dining room filled with soldiers. It was only then I realised I'd spent the majority of the night staring at the empty chair Issac sat in, replaying his words in my head over and over again. The letters were safely tucked away into my bag, and I haven't dared touch them, too afraid to re-read the thoughts that had come out of his mind decades ago. Things he's been carefully hiding from me. I can't afford to give myself any more hope than I should. Whatever I've got left is enough.

Desily's laughter fills the space, followed by Alea's heavy sigh and Ryo's excited voice as he presumably tells them about our journey here. I shoot them a quick smile and move inside the building, hoping to find an empty room where I could bathe. It's been days since I'd had the privilege of cleaning myself from the dirt picked up on the road. Gods, I must stink.

As I take the corner, Issac's silhouette reveals itself from a set of doors at the end of the corridor. My heart burns in a way I can't understand, my cheeks turning red as the person I've grown to know suddenly becomes someone entirely different, someone more intimate, a forbidden lover. Right person, wrong time. I wondered about that last night, the fact nothing ever went our way. Were we always destined to fall for one another? Always meant to find each other only to be broken apart?

As I watch him close the door, my breath quickens. I can't face him, not after what he told me yesterday. Not when I know there's a part of him that wants me so badly it hurts. A part that, despite everything that's been thrown at him to pull us apart, fights against the very idea of fate day and night just to have me. I can't afford to look at him because if I do, I might just let myself believe I've never truly lost him, but I have, and we're far from being all right.

Without thinking, I tug on the first handle and catch his furrowed brows in the corner of my eyes before disappearing inside a room. Once there, I let out a sigh, holding onto my chest for dear life.

"Can we help you?" A woman's voice has me jumping like a scared cat. I look up, noticing Venali, one of the twins, dressing in her armour. It's the first time I get a proper look at her long face, the blue mixed with a hint of green dancing in her big eyes. She stares at me awkwardly, and only then do I realise I've barged into their room without knocking.

"Oh my, I'm sorry! I just— I needed to— I was looking for a room—"

"It's fine." She stops me, her eyes looking anywhere but at me. I bite onto my bottom lip, hoping she won't hate me any more than she already does. "Do or take whatever you need. I don't care. Me and Jassin were about to leave." She finishes tying her armour before swiping the black braid off her shoulder, letting it dangle on her back.

Right on cue, her brother appears from what I assume is a bathroom, and the way he stares at me matches the expression of his sister when I walked in. He turns to her, looking for an answer, but before she can give it to him I decide to cut in.

"I'm sorry." The two of them turn, disoriented by the whole situation. I exhale, taking a step forward, my palms sweaty as I hold my fingers in a tight clasp. "I know I've never said that to you and never really acknowledged your presence, but I'm sorry for taking your home away and destroying your life. Sorry for never getting to know you and dragging you along on this mission."

The two of them stare at me with such a muddled expression I begin to wonder if the words ever left my mouth, or if I'd just simply imagined them. Venali turns to her brother, her brows furrowed, her mouth opening and closing, before she decides not to speak, instead letting her twin handle the situation. Maybe this was a bad idea? Maybe I should have come some other time or picked a better moment to apologise?

"Miss Starbane—"

"Thea. Thea is just fine." I interrupt Jassin before letting him continue.

He scratches his forehead, eyes glued to the ceiling, and I wonder what it is he's thinking about. "Well, Thea, me and my sister appreciate your apology, but we don't need it per se."

"But—"

"Thea," Venali cuts in, her voice gentler than I've ever heard it. In this moment she's no longer a soldier, but a regular person. "We don't blame you for anything. We knew you were coming for a long time. Jassin and I picked this life. We knew what could go wrong, so we don't blame you for anything."

And suddenly, all that guilt and worry about people from the manor despising me gets blown away. Everything

I've hated myself for, everything I wish I could have done differently vanishes, letting my shoulders relax and my chest fill up with the biggest, most delicious breath.

The two of them look at each other before sharing half a smile and moving towards me. I step out of the way, my body so light I swear I could levitate. I could soar through the skies and watch everyone from above. Finally, the cage I've locked myself in for weeks has been opened and the key thrown away. I'm no longer a prisoner to my own thoughts.

Before the twins leave through the door, Jassin stops, his hand landing on my shoulder and squeezing it gently. "We're here to make sure you save the world. What happens to us doesn't really matter. We're but a grain of sand on a beach, two lost in the infinite. You're here to make sure that most of the sand remains, that the majority survives, not the minority. I know you try but you can't save everyone, account for all those grains. So please," his eyes search mine, and for a moment I find it hard to breathe under the urgency with which he stares at me, "save the world, not just us."

With that, they exit, leaving me feeling ever so free yet stuck. As if I began flying but the wind picked up, causing me to fight through the turbulent weather. I might have got rid of the guilt, but the pressure of everybody's life resting on my shoulders still remains. It's fine. For as long as I can stay afloat, everything will be all right. I'll save them all, every single one of them. I'll fight off the tidal waves and make sure everything remains intact. I have to.

***

After a long bath, I rush downstairs to meet up with Theo

and the rest of our squad. The dining room is filled with laughter and mixed-up conversations. I pass by a couple of tables, smiling at some of the soldiers before sitting beside Desily. She's become Ryo's next victim and is either forced to listen about his adventures or talk about her own. I chuckle and ask Alea to pass me a bowl full of steaming stew.

"How was it in the palace? Were the ceilings made out of gold? No, wait! Was the floor made out of diamonds?" Desily shakes her head in defeat and looks for help from either me or Alea, but the two of us shrug our shoulders and continue eating.

I take another peek around, noticing Theo is nowhere to be found. "Where's your brother?"

"Went to buy something with Issac. I think it's supposed to help him communicate." She explains, and I nod in understanding. I continue eating whilst eavesdropping on the conversation between Des and Ryo, laughing at their interactions from time to time. It's like a mother and son.

After the four of us are done, we decide to go shopping in the village. Although Thehil's not big in size, it still has many helpful shops for wandering travellers, lost souls, and its own residents. Des splits almost immediately, rushing to get her hands on any herbs possible, whilst Alea and Ryo take off to the blacksmith in search of an upgrade on their weapons. In the end, I'm left alone on my way to the market, hoping to get food that'll last us until we reach Yalan. Which isn't too long of a journey left.

I pass by running kids, their long, white hair a distinct feature of people from Sebraycia. It's said that anybody who's born here will be blessed with eyes blue as the cold ocean and hair white like the moon in the night sky. I always believed it.

Whether it's true or not, I like to think they have something that makes them special, something that makes them belong here. Even humans find happiness amongst magical beings who don't judge or use them. Perhaps my parents should have settled here, but life in the snow isn't as easy as it sounds. You need to work hard and stay cautious. Even in the most peaceful place, evil will lurk around.

I scan the first stand and pick a couple of loaves of bread as well as pastries and imported fruits. I'm ready to cry at the price I've got to pay when a familiar voice reaches my ears.

"I should have studied more when you told me to." Issac and Theo are leaving one of the shops, neither of them noticing my presence. The elf holds a small book in his palm, his eyes scanning the pages before he makes a small hand movement. "Theo, I have no clue what you're saying."

I mutter my thanks to the merchant before making my way towards the two of them. Theo keeps repeating the same hand gestures, growing more and more annoyed with the fact Issac has such a hard time understanding.

"He said you never listen to him." I cut in, holding my chin high and avoiding making eye contact with Issac. It's one thing being in his presence, but talking is another. The feelings from last night have been washed away in the long bath I took, along with my foggy head. Now that I've got a clearer picture, perhaps I might be able to work something out with the new information. Who knew spending an hour by yourself in a tub of water can change your life? Still, I can't bring myself to hold eye contact, the worry of being rejected by him still lingering.

"You know what he's saying?" Issac sounds more surprised

than ever, almost as if he forgot to hide away his emotions and put on a cold mask. Perhaps being in the presence of his best friend has that effect on you.

"Of course I do. I studied sign language decades ago, thought it might come in useful." I smile at Theo. "Though, I'm a bit rusty, so if you don't mind letting me study with you."

Issac scoffs, his head shaking in disbelief. "Course you did."

Theo stares at me, positively surprised, before signing another sentence.

"You're full of surprises." I smile at his words, ignoring the annoyed, six-foot-tall man on my right, instead focusing on the slightly smaller elf in front of me. "I'd be honoured if you could help."

"Your signing's not so bad either." I sign back, only to irritate Issac just a tad more. Keeping him out of the conversation is sure to get his blood boiling. Not only that, but being better at something he should have already mastered is such an ego boost I could jump high enough to touch the clouds.

Theo looks inside his book for a couple of seconds before signing back, some of the words not making sense, but I manage to put it all together. "I had to. Father made me learn, but not Alea. *We don't discriminate*." He rolls his eyes, and I know exactly what he means by that.

In the land of magic, everyone is respectful about your skin colour, the country you were born in, any disabilities. As long as you're not human or a woman, that is. That's where they draw the line. If you were born a human or a woman, Gods forbid, with any of those things, your life would be miserable. Not many would accommodate you, try to help out even a tiny bit. No, we're lesser than them. Always have been.

"Right, if the two of you are done chatting, let's get going. We need to pack up and leave." Issac mumbles under his breath before turning on his heels and speed-walking towards the tavern. I gaze at Theo, who's smiling from ear to ear.

"Somebody's moody." He signs, and I giggle, nodding towards our temporary home.

We walk in comfortable silence. For the most part, Theo's eyes are glued to the book before Alea and Ryo appear from the blacksmith shop, geared up as if we're about to march into a battlefield.

The two of them ask Theo about his book, and I explain for him before Desily runs up, her pockets filled to the brim with herbs.

"Well, I guess all of us got what we needed here." She smiles as her hand reaches for Alea's palm. She places a kiss on her cheek, which makes the younger elf blush, and turns to face me, sending a mischievous wink.

I guess we did get what we needed. Be it materialistic things or closure. Either way, we're ready to reach Yalan and finally find that damn ritual paper. Hopefully, our struggle will end there, and the rest of our adventure will go smoother. *Hopefully.*

Chapter 12

Five days of continuous walking towards our goal. Fifty conversations between twenty people. Four nights spent in the presence of one person. Six thousand, three hundred and forty-five words read in a small book filled with three hundred pictures. That's how our journey to Yalan was spent, my idea of productivity and staying sane becoming an obsession with counting numbers. Ever since the ship, I found peace when occupying my head with something other than the upcoming doom, the ever-lurking catastrophe. If I couldn't control the woman inside my head, or the man constantly slipping through my fingers, or the never-changing destiny, then I'd find control some other way.

Today was our final night before reaching Yalan. Lord Graham's notebook was now filled with changes and ideas about our route, and I worried that soon I might have to write on my hands as the pages grew thinner. This evening I found myself outside practising spells with Alea. For once, there was no storm or monsters, and we could enjoy the beautiful starry night sky accompanied by the silver shield.

"How are you feeling?" Alea asks as she deflects my fireballs. I exhale loudly and shake my hands, staring at the wet spots on the ground. Ever since the avalanche, I've been thinking about the strange colour of the flames. The deepest shade of blue swirling in black, a sight no one's ever seen before. It was different, so much stronger than the usual orangey-red I use, as if it didn't come from me but from somewhere else entirely. I tried asking Jino about it, but she barely gave me a shrug before disappearing.

"Alright, let's just keep going."

Alea assesses me cautiously, her eyes locked on something, or rather someone, standing behind me. "Are you sure? No signs of burning out?"

I roll my eyes and turn around to face Issac, who stands by the line of trees. He has his arms crossed over his chest, an irritated look playing on his face. I know I'm the cause of this, the reason why he seems so desperate to spark an interaction between us, even if it's just an acknowledgement.

"If it's Issac who's truly worried, he can ask me himself. You don't have to do his bidding, Alea." I turn back around to face the girl, her cheeks red from embarrassment before she nods and sheathes her sword.

The conversation in the tavern had given me a better picture of our situation, and I came to the conclusion I'm done entertaining his little games. There's a part of him that wants me, craves me, but each time he's ready to take the leap he decides against it and instead ends up hurting my feelings. I can't give in to his stupid games any more. It only assures him that the choices he makes are the right ones, but they aren't. I can't be getting a bit of happiness in exchange for a spoonful of misery. If he wants me to talk, to truly acknowledge him, he needs to try, and not in the way he's learnt is appropriate. No, I need it to be on my terms for once. I'm done being his punching bag and the very same thing he rushes to for comfort. It doesn't work that way.

So, in the past five days I managed to ignore his taunts, move away when he felt too close, too inviting. The only time I've allowed him to be by my side was during nighttime, but even then Issac never lingered when I woke up, most likely afraid I might call out his behaviour a proof of his hidden feelings, strip him of the last thing he's able to use as an excuse to be closer. Instead, he sneaked up on me once I drifted off, and vanished like a shadow once my eyes fluttered open.

"Well, I'm quite tired. Perhaps the two of you can train?" Alea proposes, at which I nearly laugh. I'm not asking him for anything any more. He knows what I want, and what he truly wants.

"It's fine, Alea. Go get some rest. I'll be alright by myself." She gives me a tight smile, her eyes going from me to Issac before settling on my face.

When she speaks, her voice is a whisper carried by wind and delivered right to my ears, keeping the man standing behind curious. "I know the things between you two are complicated, but arguing won't solve anything. There are times I wish I'd spent more time talking with my mother rather than staying silent, but I was young and foolish, and now it's too late. Don't ever take the time you have with somebody for granted."

I blink at her, surprised. Alea rarely speaks about her mother, unlike Theo, who is very open. I never expected her to say anything about her past. After all, she likes to keep her life as private as possible. Perhaps not even Desily knows about the young Alea, so when I hear those words leave her mouth I'm almost speechless. Almost, if not for the pair of eyes burning holes into my back.

"I wish he could hear those words. I know what I'm doing."

She half-smiles, her hand squeezing my arm. "Oh, he's heard it. Perhaps not from me, but still. I just wish the two of you could go back to being civil."

"Me too, Alea. Me too." I tell her, and she nods, walking away. I catch a glimpse of her stopping by Issac, saying words to him my hearing won't allow me to catch, so instead I focus on casting a few spells, looking for one that would draw out the blue flames.

A few minutes pass in blissful silence. I almost forget about the existence of a very stubborn man and lose myself in casting spell after spell. After my third attempt, which sets one of the trees on fire, I begin to grow impatient and annoyed. Am I doing something wrong? Have I missed some important step?

My palms rub together and I stare ahead with my fingers spread wide, facing forwards. The words of my next spell roll onto my tongue, but before I have a chance to say them, I hear the crunching of snow grow closer and closer to my body.

"What is it that you're trying to do?" He asks, and I grunt, throwing a fireball at the boulder ahead. The flames are the same orangey-red colour I've been seeing for the last half an hour.

"What does it look like?" I answer with a question and think of some other possibilities of accessing the magic I did before.

"Well, it looks like a waste of time." He scoffs, and I have to mentally stop myself from jumping into an argument.

"If you came here to bother me, don't. I don't have time to entertain you any more."

Issac's figure emerges from the side, cutting into my line of sight. His brows are furrowed in confusion and annoyance, a grimace twisting his lips downwards. "Entertain me? You're far from being the most interesting thing over here."

"Alright." I sigh and turn to face him.

He seems so puzzled. My reaction isn't what he expected. He's angry I'm not fighting him, throwing nasty remarks back and trying hard to win him over. It takes him a while to collect his thoughts and push for some kind of reaction from me, something that would make him feel the very feelings he's trying to suppress. "Alright? That's it? Why are you being so pissy with me lately?"

"Because I'm done entertaining your bullshit. I'm done trying to save you if you don't even know what you want yourself, Issac." I decide to look into his eyes, to truly gaze into his soul, but I don't have to search for long. The feelings of regret, irritation, hurt, and shock pass by me, lingering only for a moment to remind me they're not mine but his. "You said it yourself. I don't deserve an arsehole like you, so how about you just leave me alone instead of trying to do whatever it is you're doing right now?" I shrug and begin walking away. Anger is something I've opted to leave behind, letting it brush against my fingers. If one of us can't keep our emotions under control, then neither can win.

I take four breaths in, three steps away from him, two metres' distance between us, one heartbeat before the tension crumbles away. His hand wraps around my arm, my body spins around too quickly to register what's happening. I collide into his chest, feel the heat radiating off his skin, the shaky breaths ghosting against my frozen cheeks, the words ready to be said but kept locked away.

Our eyes meet once again. Issac looks at me in search of something that could pull him back up, entertain his dark desires and imitate a net that could pull him out of the depths he's fallen into. But his search is fruitless and my patience is running thin. He must've realised by now the fun is over. The games he got used to playing won't work any more.

I'm not the same girl who came to the manor searching for him and ready to sacrifice the world. Now, the gravity of the situation is much bigger, the weight much heavier, and I can't selfishly think of myself. Although my heart still aches for him, I'm constantly reminded that everyone besides Issac I've grown to love will perish if I continue on this path. This is bigger than me and him, us. I just wish I'd realised it a bit sooner. Perhaps then Lathai wouldn't have left the way he did. Either way, I have to save the world before I can save him, because if I don't do that, there'll be nothing to save.

"What? What do you want from me, Issac?" I break the silence, trying to ignore his scent trapping me from all sides, the desperation in his tightening grasp.

"I—" His mouth opens and then falls, his throat working up and down as he swallows words he's trying to fight off from coming out, things I hope to hear. "So what, that's it? You're just going to ignore me? Actually give up?"

I laugh. Laugh so hard it rattles my bones. "I'm sorry, are you upset over the fact I won't let you walk all over me? I might've been alright with that before, but that was before I knew what losing someone felt like, before I had nobody else but *you* to worry about."

He flinches, almost as if my words slapped him across

the face and kicked him in the chest. I see the pain and embarrassment flashing past his eyes, rejection dancing in the crimson, turning it almost black. I'm certain there's a moment in his mind where he questions whether or not to defy his orders, drop his guard down, and give in to his desires, but that moment's gone as soon as it appeared.

I rip away from his hold, the places where his hands rested now colder than ever. He stares at me without a word, waiting for all of it to turn into a joke, a façade I've orchestrated only to annoy him. Instead, he gets a pitying smile, because that's exactly what I feel for him. Pity. How terrible is it to desire someone but not be able to come to terms with it? To feel like it's wrong and forbidden, punishable even? I felt sorry for the dead, but it's the living I should really be pitying, for as long as they live, they'll never know peace.

"Figure your shit out. If you truly care about my company this much, then come to me when you're sure of what you want, not what someone else wants from you."

***

It's dusk when we arrive at the borders of the city. Everyone around cheers at the sight of the first buildings, lights, people. It's refreshing to be somewhere that's colourful, lively, and warm. The last time I was here, the town was much smaller. Now there are tall, blue or red buildings standing in every corner, green tents with merchants, orange huts with smoke coming out of their crooked chimneys. Yalan is no longer a town deserted from the rest of the world. It's truly the capital of Sebraycia.

I glance past the crowd and spot the castle on top of the hill. Wooden towers stretch towards the sky, their green roofs catching the fading light. The structure stands proud against the snowy landscape, a beacon of civilisation in the frozen north, noticeable even from this distance.

"I can't believe we actually made it in one piece." Desily chirps in at my side, and I shoot her an offended look.

"So you had no faith in me?"

She chuckles and slaps my back so hard I almost tumble to the ground. "Of course I did! I just thought we might die because of you and Mr Tight Pants over there." She nods towards Issac, who scans the area around, shooting murderous glares towards any passers-by. I roll my eyes at her words and step forwards. We need to reach the castle as soon as possible, and I can't be occupying my head with him right now.

Suddenly, the ground begins to shake just a little, vibrations travelling through my body and distributing evenly. I turn to face Theo, who shakes his head in confusion. Not a moment later, Issac appears right by me, following me like a dark shadow that I'm mindful of but choose to ignore. Alea runs up to Desily whilst the rest of the soldiers group together.

The locals move out of the way, and from the centre of the town come the first, real settlers of this land. Snow giants. I swallow hard, my lips pursing together as their long, white hair brushes against the tall buildings. Each step they take sends tremors through the ground, their massive shadows swallowing entire streets as they move. Their bodies are covered in thick, pale fur that seems to shimmer in the fading light, muscles rippling beneath with every movement. Now

I understand why the buildings have been built so tall. It's to make sure all the residents of Yalan can fit comfortably inside their homes.

I look down at the loincloth strapped to their waists with a club hanging on their hips. I'm sure it could crush us all into a bloody puddle in seconds were they to use it, but to my surprise they stop just before Ryo, who looks like he's shat his pants.

Without thinking twice, I push past everyone and move to shield the boy away. I don't need him to get into unnecessary trouble, especially here where those creatures stand at least five metres tall. One of the snow giants turns his piercing, blue eyes in my direction, scratching his fur-covered face with three sharp nails.

He growls low, a cloud of steam pushing past his flared nostrils and making its way to the worn out, blue horns sticking out of his head. "Althea Starbane?"

I stare at him in shock, my body frozen except for the drumming beat of my heart. "Yes?"

"The princess has asked for you. Come." He demands, and every ounce of heroism leaves my bones. How the fuck do they know who I am?

"What about my friends?" I gesture towards the small group of people stood behind me. I might feel like pissing my pants, but I won't let them get hurt. If anything, they can torture me for as long as they like if they promise not to hurt them.

The giant scans our group, his expression stoic before he speaks. "You all come. Follow us."

Well, this can either go really badly, or just terribly.

Chapter 13

The structure looms above us, all wooden beams and towering walls that stretch towards the dark sky. Square windows adorned with red drapes line the upper floors, their glass reflecting the dying light, whilst metal gates attached to the stone curtain wall stand open. The entrance to the palace is reached after we climb at least thirty steps and is placed under a triangular roof held up by carved pillars. Creatures native to Sebraycia's culture climb up the wooden beams in what looks like a chase. I resonate with them, my heart pounding inside my throat as the snow giants lead our group through the wooden doors.

I scan the carved-out moon on the left door. Right below it, a woman kneels by a lake, her hands cupped together as she looks up to it. On the other side is a star with five pointy ends, droplets of what looks like dust falling onto a child laid right below it. Perhaps it's something to do with their history, new information my brain didn't get a chance to absorb yet.

As we move inside, the strong scent of dried oranges, cinnamon sticks, and cloves invades me from all sides. I stare at the stone floor, the wooden walls, the paintings hung in any free space, the animal pelts scattered across the chairs.

This is nothing like the palace in Eclia, not as luxurious as the manor in Karul. This feels... homely.

We trace along the corridor, passing by many sets of doors leading to rooms we might get a chance to explore. That is, if the princess decides to keep us alive. I dare to turn around. One glance at Desily and Ryo tells me they think what I do. We're in trouble. As opposed to Alea, Theo, and Issac, who look rather composed, along with the rest of the soldiers. This shows the difference between those who were trained in politics and war, and those who were forced into that life.

The snow giant stops abruptly, his big hand knocking on the tall, oak door three times before we hear a click and they open. The next step teleports me into a completely different setting, another world. There are silver stars hanging from the black ceiling, candles lit in each of them, making it the only source of light. The floor below my feet is made out of moonstone, different colours swirling around in the clear void.

There are no chairs or tables in here, no decorations or people except for the guards posted at the very end by the stone throne.

"Althea Starbane, I presume?" My attention snaps to the melodic voice of a young girl that comes from behind the throne and with a help of her guards takes a seat. Clearly it wasn't fit for her but for a giant. She smiles, and her white eyes light up with golden sparks.

I clear my throat and speak with confidence, the only thing I managed not to lose on our way here. "Yes, Your Highness." I bow down, but her soft laughter erupts through the empty room.

"Thank you for seeing me Althea. Please do feel free to call me Coraenella, or Ella for short." She giggles, her hand three shades too white swiping through her long, silver hair. The young woman is dressed in a long, white fur jacket adorned with blue embroidered vines. I return her smile and examine her perfectly long lashes, her porcelain skin, and welcoming smile. Everything about the princess is so… white. Almost as if she fell off the night sky, as if she was the brightest star in the galaxy that longed for our planet and decided to stop by, gracing everyone with its beauty. "Oh my! Sorry, excuse me. I don't have guests often." She claps her hands together and rushes to get off the massive throne. For the ruler of Sebraycia, the land of snow giants, she's rather small. Perhaps a few inches taller than me, but nowhere near close to reaching the massive beasts standing right behind our group.

"I'm sorry to intrude. We were just simply passing by." I decide to speak up and hope to get out of this situation as soon as possible. She might've heard stories about me. Gods know from whom. But I cling to the hope she's oblivious to who I truly am and what it is I'm seeking.

The princess chuckles, her smile stretching so far two dimples appear on either side of her cheeks. "Oh, but of course you weren't." I wince, taken aback by her straightforwardness, and despite that she keeps on smiling. There's no malicious intent behind her kind gaze or the way she holds herself back from jumping in joy. "I know why you're here, and I'd love to speak with you over some tea if you don't mind."

"But my friends—"

She holds up her hand and I shut my lips instantly. "Your friends will be safe. I'm sure they don't mind if I steal you for an hour. Promise." I notice the wink she sends to someone standing right behind me, my mind already knowing the answer as to who it is but refusing to acknowledge it.

I nod in agreement, shooting a reassuring look towards Theo and Desily before I take a step towards the princess. "Fine, let's talk."

***

Everything in my body tells me I should be alert and careful, but somehow Ella's calming presence makes me more relaxed than I'd like to admit. Though I brush my hands along the daggers sheathed in my chest plate just in case this was all a clever plan to bring my guard down.

The tea room is located on the west side of the castle, past three sets of doors, two sets of guards, and one statue of a woman I remember seeing sculptured on the wooden door to the castle.

"That's my mother." Ella chirps in as if reading my thoughts, and I turn to face her. "She passed away during my birth."

"I'm sorry to hear that." I know losing your mother hurts. I was there when both of my parents died, but losing your parent before you get a chance to meet them hurts in a different way.

Ella smiles, but there's no sadness behind it, just genuine appreciation. "Don't be. She sacrificed herself so that I could be born, so that our land would know peace. See, my parents had a hard time getting pregnant, so imagine how relieved they were when after many failed attempts they found out they'd have a daughter."

"That's lovely—"

"It was." She cuts me off, a glimpse of sadness rushing past her eyes. "Until they found out their daughter wouldn't survive."

"I—What happened?"

"Magic." She pauses, letting the word settle between us. "The love for their unborn child led them to a folk legend, the only whisper of promise to save their daughter."

I stare at her curiously as she slowly takes the seat at the round table and I follow her right after. The flames of the fireplace dance behind her, illuminating a light that almost makes it look like a holy aura wrapped around her shoulders. "Long ago, a legend was told amongst our people where one could wish upon a full moon for anything, only if one were willing to sacrifice something in return." She looks away as if reminiscing, and I listen attentively in case she might share some important information. "As you might know, nature requires balance, so when my mother's prayers were thankfully heard by the Gods, I was born. She was a brave woman, kind and loving, or so my father told me. She wasn't afraid of death, not if it meant I was alive."

I look for words that could make her feel better, something that would justify the cruelty of the bargain her mother took, but my mouth remains closed, unlike Ella's, who continues her story with a smile. "She died shortly after giving birth to me, passing me to my father and making him promise that the people of Sebraycia would hear and rejoice over the power the Gods possess."

Ah, that explains why a smile doesn't leave her face. She's not sad, she's grateful and honours her mother's wish.

"That's beautiful. She was a wonderful person." I reach for

the teacup and pour some of the brew into Ella's cup as well as mine. She thanks me quietly and takes the first sip.

"She was. I know she was." Ella adds whilst nodding her head in agreement to her statement. "Hence why she's on the doors to the castle, and why her statues can be seen all over Yalan. A thing like this doesn't happen to just anyone. My mother was chosen and so was I. It was her destiny to bear me, and mine to become the princess of Sebraycia. The folk and snow giants couldn't defy the decision of the Gods, a prophecy come true."

"Prophecy?" I ask away, growing more intrigued by the girl sitting in front of me. Learning new information about someone's culture scratches my brain in a way I could never manage. It almost makes me forget about the real reason as to why I'm here, and Ella just doesn't feel like all those stuck-up Lords, Dukes, and Kings I've come across before. Perhaps I should keep my guard up, but it's hard to do so when I know my friends are safe and the person before me is being so open.

"Ah, yes! Centuries of years ago, an old witch foretold that one day the Gods would pick a mortal with a pure heart, ready to sacrifice their own life for another. She said the child of that mortal will be born with hair silver as the moon in the night sky, skin pale as the snow, and eyes stripped of colour just like the land it will be born into, and it will save Sebraycia from destruction—something that, as of recent, became a reality."

My heart aches because in this young princess who beams with kindness I see myself. A person who was chosen for a mission they never signed up for. Though Ella smiles and talks about her mother's sacrifice with pride, I know deep down just how burdened she must feel. I pity her just as much as I pity myself because I know deep down she's scared of making a mistake, of letting her people down and her mother's death go to waste. Though I'm sure she'd never admit it I know Ella wishes for a life she could've had, not the one the Gods gave her. As it seems, no matter what, human life will always be just that. A pawn to be played in a difficult and long game.

Ella's eyes avert my gaze, focusing on something behind me. It's such a subtle gesture, but I see it for what it is. The real reason behind our meeting.

"Do I have something to do with your mission?"

She half-smiles. "That depends on what you're willing to tell me, Althea."

"Thea is just fine." The princess nods and lets me continue. "So what is it that you need from me?"

Ella clears her throat, her fingers tracing over the fur collar of her jacket. I wait patiently, wondering just what does she mean by saving Sebraycia from destruction? I was under the impression this country was the only place in the whole world that wasn't involved in any sort of war, but I guess I was wrong. I'm wrong about a lot of things as of late.

"It's not what I need but what you need, Thea. The news of an immortal girl carrying a centuries-old demon inside of her that could destroy our world reached me, and ever since I'd known no peace." She begins, her brows furrowing in contemplation. "You must understand my surprise. Things like this don't just happen, and I knew I was born for the purpose of meeting you and convincing you to help us keep this place safe."

"Isn't your country already safe?" I question, and she sighs, her eyes darting towards the window where the night had long fallen.

"A message from Eclia reached me not long ago that the Eclian King began to punish humans in the capital, all to send a message to a girl that slipped through his commander's fingers." Her eyes drop to the half-empty cup of tea, her lips pursed as she thinks of her next words. "As you know the majority of Sebraycia consists of humans, I'm afraid for my people. Even the giants will struggle against an army of thirty thousand men."

"What?" The colour drains from my face, my fingers curling into a fist as I imagine all those suffering because I've escaped Wyrran, because I made a mockery out of him by nearly having him defeated. All those humans are in danger because he didn't get me.

"But that's not all." Ella continues and I have to push the grief away and make space for another wave of terrible news. "A couple of months ago before all of this began we were contacted by Eclia's king. He's demanded something I'm not sure I can provide, and then all of a sudden, two weeks ago a man appears at my doorsteps claiming he knows you and that you might be coming my way for the exact thing the elves have been pestering me about."

My face, although stone cold, might just be betrayed by my eyes as the flicker of surprise pushes past the barrier I've put up and into the surface. The ritual. They know about it. Not only that, some man knows about me and our plans. Was it Aagon? No, he'd reveal himself by now and cause havoc, but I'm in one piece and no lives were lost.

I clench my left fist under the table, my right hand curling around the fragile ceramic teacup. It doesn't matter who he is. Our squad might be in danger, or everyone on this continent. My leg bounces once, and I stop it immediately, the crippling feeling of anxiety I've managed to tame over the past few weeks suddenly reappearing. A pest you thought left, but in reality it never did. Instead, it watched you from the shadows, waiting for the perfect moment to take what it thinks belongs to them. In this case. My confidence.

"So how come you haven't killed me yet?" I ask her straight away. If things are going to go south, I'd rather it happen here and now where none of my friends will have to witness my death, where none of them are at risk of getting hurt.

Ella smiles, her eyelids hanging low from tiredness, yet the warm spark in her white eyes remains. She looks behind me, and the door creaks open, drawing my attention behind. A woman walks in, no older than me. Her face is washed of emotions, her blue eyes blank all except for the drawing smirk tugging on her lips.

She rolls her head, the short, curly black hair brushing against her shoulders with each step she takes. My brows draw in confusion, my eyes narrowing to get a better look at the stranger. She looks so familiar, almost as if I've met her before.

"She hasn't killed you because of me." The woman speaks, a smug expression now blending into the empty canvas she's left for me to paint. There's something about her I know, something I recognise, and it has nothing to do with the fact she looks like she hates me to the core.

"Thea, meet Myra Tratumal." The lights flicker as if the lightning broke through the ceiling, giving me all the brightness needed to see her face. The olive skin tone, the long dark lashes, the hatred in her eyes. I suck in the air, feeling like it's not enough, like it'll never be. My palm turns cold, sweat covering it from fingertips to wrist, and I shiver.

The woman before me is the sister to the woman who betrayed me, someone who died because of a stupid mistake, and ultimately it was my fault.

"Now, don't rush with your words of appreciation. I'm sure my sister never heard them." She hisses, and the cup I've been squeezing shatters. I jump away from the table, from the princess and the girl who's sure to kill me. The all-too-well-known feeling of betrayal spreads across me, taking over any rational thinking. I scramble to reach for my daggers, but Myra begins to chuckle, her hands raised high in the air to cover her face when she begins to uncontrollably laugh. It's then that I see it. The marks of a wielder.

"Fuck, I expected a show but this is incredible." She keeps on giggling to herself, and I stare at her in shock. At the black swirls that twist into waves.

"What the hell is going on?" I ask, ready to use my magic if needed, but Ella jumps between us just in time to stop her palace from being burnt down.

"Myra! Thea is our guest. No matter the history, please respect her." The girl wipes the corners of her eyes, a single chuckle escaping past her lips before she settles, and it's the exact moment my brain begins to process the whole situation.

"Right, I was just kidding. Gods, Ella, if I wanted to get to her I'd just have to mention Issac." Our gazes lock, and I feel it. The source of magic screaming to release it, just like the day I almost killed Lathai. "Whoops."

"What?" I ask through gritted teeth without taking my eyes off the girl. I don't care about her relationship with the princess or the things she's told her. If she's done anything to him, to any of them, I'll slaughter the entirety of Yalan without a care in the world. If her sister betrayed someone she knew for years, there's no way she might be any different.

"Thea, please let me explain, and you," Ella points at Myra, her previously calm and warm eyes now full of concern and irritation, "stop this at once. We're here to reach one goal, so let's work towards it instead of against it."

Myra, as if someone told her to eat a plate full of shit, grimaces and rolls her eyes before moving past me and towards the table where she takes my seat. I take a big inhale, the biggest I've ever taken, hoping it'll get rid of those dangerous feelings, of the magic threatening to pour out. There are a hundred things I want to ask and a thousand things I want to do to the woman I've met just moments ago, because why did she mention Issac?

"You have about one minute to explain before I find my friends, burn this place to the ground and leave you fending for yourself." I stare at Ella, my hands shaking, but my face keeping the unwavering mask of confidence behind my words.

Ella fixes her coat, waits for a moment as if searching for words that might ease my threat. "All right, well, let me begin by saying that I'm aware of what Lisa did to you and Graham's family, so is Myra. Neither me nor her are happy about that." Clearly, because from my point of view it looks like Myra holds a grudge against me for an unknown reason. "The man I mentioned earlier was John, Lisa's assistant. I'm not sure you were aware he's escaped and came to inform us immediately of what happened."

Dear Gods, John. The strange man who rarely spoke but

hung around Lisa. Well, I guess something did get her, and in the end he wasn't able to help. "I—no, I had no idea. More importantly, was he questioned? How do you know he can be trusted?"

Ella's lips purse into a thin line. "You can rest assured he was thoroughly questioned. We are aware how close he was to Lisa and didn't want to risk a threat like that staying in Yalan."

"He's here?" I ask, bulging my eyes out and instinctively having a look around to confirm he's not hiding in the shadows. They might trust him, but the same doesn't go for me. John was too close to Lisa, too close not to spot her plotting.

"Yes. You see, Myra has been staying with us for quite some time. The history between her and Lisa is complicated and I won't get into that. What matters is that John told her what happened and she vouched for him. Now, I need you to believe me Thea when I say I trust Myra with my life, and I know she wouldn't lie to me. She wouldn't vouch for just anyone."

I look at the girl, her eyes fixated on me like I'm a toy to be played with, a new weapon she can't wait to bash around, and I begin to wonder just how true Ella's words are. She might've vouched for John, she might be different than her sister, but there's still something about her that tells me she hates every fibre of my body. Perhaps for now, I'd be wise to hear out Ella and then make a choice.

"Well then, I assume John told you about the ritual?" Ella nods, her lips a shade of pale pink from pursing them for so long.

"He did, and so did the Elven King." She stares at me for

a split second as if checking if it's safe to approach before she does, her hands wrapping around my wrists and pulling them from behind my back. "We'll help you however we can, but under the conditions stated before. You'll help us keep Sebraycia safe, Althea. You have to promise." Her fingers squeeze around mine, and I notice how cold yet soft her skin feels, how desperate she is to receive my help.

I think about Lisa, about John and Myra. I wonder if they're going to betray me the same way their close one did, if they're plotting something behind my back. I consider our options, the many lives standing on the scales of life that I'm about to either even out or outweigh. Whatever choice I'll make, I'll have to make sure nothing happens to any of them.

"Fine, we have a deal."

***

After sealing the deal with Ella, she's revealed my friends are safe in their new accommodations. I tried to listen to whatever she was saying. Something about a banquet, a library, and a festival. But it was hard to focus on the princess when the other person in the room wouldn't stop staring. At moments it felt almost as if I'd found a female version of Issac, cursed to hate me for no reason whatsoever.

When Ella finished talking, she assured me her librarians would go through any papers indicating the whereabouts of the ritual and inform us as soon as possible. In the meanwhile, I was to be taken to my bedroom by no one other than Myra.

If being in the room with her was unbearable, the walk

through the castle proved to be far more difficult. She kept turning her head every now and then, sparing me a disgusted yet curious look before turning back around.

"What?" I snap after the fifth time, growing impatient. If she has a problem, I'd rather hear it now and deal with it than pretend everything's all right.

"So you're *her*." She scoffs, crossing her arms behind her head.

"Her? What does that even mean? If this is about your sister then—"

"Gods," she sighs deeply, interrupting me, before abruptly stopping and turning to face me. "I couldn't care less about my sister. She made her foolish choices and paid the price."

I wince at her harsh words, because I'd do anything to have a sister who's flesh and bone, connected to me on a deeper level. I know Desily would too, so what exactly happened between the two of them? "All right, then what do you mean?"

She exhales, her eyes narrowing into slits as she slowly takes me in, her lips twisting into a grimace. "I mean her, the girl Issac would never shut up about."

"You know Issac?" I ask, surprised. Perhaps her relationship with Lisa was still stable when she used to come to the manor to teach him how to use his powers. Perhaps Myra accompanied her many times and kept him company. After all, the three of us are a similar age. In looks, at least. She can't be older than thirty.

Myra smirks, something sinister behind it, and she slowly turns and begins walking away. "Know?" She grins. "You could say that." She giggles.

I mutter a couple of curses towards her inside my head

before following suit, a pile of new questions forming inside my already full mind. "Care to explain?"

"Oh baby, I don't think you wanna know what me and Issac got up to whilst you weren't around."

It's a slap to the face. A punch to the guts. A knife in the back, because what Myra's suggesting is that her and Issac were together whilst I wasn't around. I fight against the urge to throw myself at her, to shut her mouth and never let it fall open, to stop all the images of them being happily together running through my mind.

I know we've been apart for a hundred years. I know he had a life during that time, so did I, but he'll never have to worry about meeting my ex-lovers. Most of them being long dead. Unlike me. Myra is flesh and bone, a beautiful girl who could compete against her sister, with magic that's almost perfectly picked to fight mine off. It was as if we were meant to collide. A hammer and a nail, an asteroid and a planet, religion and science. A lot of things in my life seemed impossible, but this doesn't surprise me. What does, however, is the fact she appears to be convinced Issac missed her. If that's the case, it means they had a thing not long ago before I came back into his life.

Perhaps they did, given how young she looks. Perhaps I'm wrong, and that makes me want to scratch my skin off the bones, to dig past the ribcage and rip my heart out because I can't be competing against his twisted thoughts and her at the same time.

What if he decides to go for her? After all, his memory is all messed up, his view of me mixed up, and no matter how hard I try it might not be enough, not if his old flame is standing a few metres away from me.

"Issac's changed." I finally say, a bit of confidence still residing in my blood, pushing forwards to shut her up.

Myra giggles before taking a turn into a corridor. "So I've heard." She turns her head to face me, her smile laced with cockiness, arrogance, and ego shooting past the roof above our heads. "Apparently he hates you even more than he did when I was around."

The fire burning atop the torches blazes out in the length of the corridor, bringing so much light it's almost as if the walls have been ripped apart and the sun rested right before us. It quickly becomes hot, so hot I feel like we've entered a hot spring. A droplet of sweat rolls down my forehead and onto my brow as I stare at her, contemplating whether or not it's worth risking everything over the satisfaction of killing her.

Myra, previously confident, is now standing staring at me with fear in her eyes, unsure what to do. She looks around towards the torches, then back at me, and swallows. I see the cogs turning inside her head, the moment she realises she's poked the bear and woken it up. I force my feet to move, the fire growing bigger, angrier, almost making it unbearable to stand in its presence. "What did you say?"

Her mouth opens but closes as soon as the torch near her head roars with flames big enough to burn her to a crisp before she even has a chance to tap into her magic. I wonder if she's afraid of me, if she'll back away now that she knows my true power and the feelings I have towards the man she apparently thinks is hers. Tough luck. Only one of us lives a fantasy here, a delusion, and it's not me.

"Thea?" I blink and sway to the side to get a better look inside the corridor where Desily's head pokes from behind a door. "Is everything alright? Why is it so hot here?"

Suddenly, the other set of doors opposite Desily's swings open, and both Theo and Issac pop out to satisfy their curiosity. I look back at Myra and everything quietens down. The torches go back to being dim and calm, the high temperature dissipating, and I breathe.

"Myra?" I hear him say, and that's exactly where I feel like burying myself six feet under. My whole world falls apart, the hopes of him forgetting this girl's existence suddenly crushed under the hard-to-swallow reality. He remembers her. I see it in his eyes, the pleasant surprise something I wasn't given the day we left the ship.

Myra spares me a single glance, something telling me that she knows I won't use my magic against her if my friends are around, and then she turns to run in his direction. Her arms wrap around his neck, his wrap around her waist, and I fight the urge to fall down to the floor, to try and pick up the pieces of my heart that have been ripped out by the two of them. "What are you doing here?"

"Have been stationed here for a couple of years now. You'd know if you ever read any of my letters." I grit my teeth together, clenching my fists at my sides before deciding to disappear inside Desily's room. I hope that's where I'm going to stay, too afraid to be left on my own when my feelings are as untamed as a herd of wild horses.

Issac and Myra continue talking whilst I push past Des and drag her inside, letting the doors close with a loud bang. My skin is on fire, my mind a mess, and it takes me five whole exhales to realise Alea is sitting on the double bed in the middle, staring at me in confusion.

"I assume we should be concerned about her?" Des

questions, slowly moving away towards the bed. “Is it really that bad?”

I scoff. “You can’t imagine.”

Chapter 14

The mornings in Yalan are nothing like anywhere else in the world. It's not the chatter of people on the streets, the chirping of birds or barking of wild dogs that wake you up from sleep, but the giants as they walk past our windows, making our beds shake.

A knock on our door is all we have before a few women storm in and drag the three of us towards the bathing chambers. I rub my heavy lids, trying not to take a tumble from exhaustion. Three nights ago, on the day of our arrival, I spent the majority of my time telling Desily and Alea what had gone on between Ella and me in the tea room before Myra came in. Needless to say, Desily shares my hatred towards the woman.

Though a few positives appeared from meeting her. Like the lack of nightmares whilst I slept. Perhaps it was my sour feelings towards Myra that allowed me to temporarily forget about the past, or perhaps it was the exhaustion finally catching up. Or my brain simply realised we're somewhat safe and not in immediate danger and allowed me a moment of peace from the seemingly never-ending torture. Either way, I got some sleep without disturbing others, without Issac's presence, and hopefully it'll stay that way—that is, if

I can keep my mind occupied and exhausted. Shouldn't be hard with Myra around.

"She's been visiting us with Lisa for a few years. I never knew there was something between the two of them." Alea admitted when I finished my rant about the vexing, younger sister of the woman I had a part in killing. Of course, I figured this much out, but the fact Issac never mentioned her in the months we've spent together is what irks me. What's even worse is that I won't get the truth any time soon since the man I knew is long gone, and the one I have right now isn't sure about his own feelings.

The maids hand us three towels with neatly folded clothes as we enter a big room. You'd think you'd get used to it after a day or two, but that's hardly the case. On our first day, the exhaustion claimed us and we spent the majority of our time in bed. On the second, I managed to get to the dining hall before noticing Issac and Myra chatting and immediately turning back. And yesterday, Desily, Alea and I helped ourselves to the baths before being told the maids are supposed to show us here and that we shall expect them tomorrow morning. Well, tomorrow has come and claimed us.

I blink, trying to focus my vision, and for a second I think we've come into the herbal baths in Karul, but just as the heavy white curtains are being drawn away from the windows, the space around me shifts. Perhaps there are some similarities, like the greenish-looking water or the polished marble floor, but besides that it's a bit different.

Instead of a long rectangular pool, a circle was placed in the middle. There are no pillars, no torches, just the large body of water and the natural light falling through the windows.

"I hope none of the people from Yalan see my arse." Des murmurs before stripping away her clothes.

"Would you really care?" Alea questions, her hand tugging on the pins holding her hair in a braid. I take off each piece of clothing slowly, cautiously, as if an enemy's about to burst through the doors and murder us stark naked. Some parts of me just cannot be reminded of what it feels like to be in a place that feels safe, or I just don't want to let myself fall into the same dream I did whilst in Karul.

"No, but I'm not letting them see my beauty for free." Des scoffs and enters the water. Both Alea and I smile, shaking our heads at her comment. I'm happy she's still the same. At least some of us are.

I look at the walls around us. White stone with painted golden stars, almost as if we've entered a room that'll purify us of all the sins committed. Oh, if only it was that simple. I finally take off the last bit of my armour and join Des and Alea in the warm water.

"Truly royal treatment. Do we know why?" I ponder out loud as I rub the water into my skin, hoping it'd get rid of the ache in my shoulders and with it all the worries attached ever since we've arrived in Yalan.

"It's nothing special. That's just how they treat you in a palace." Desily answers casually, earning herself curious looks from me and Alea. "What? You lot do remember I used to live in one, right?"

"Yeah, just can't imagine you acting—" Alea stops, searching for the right word.

"Civil." I finish. Desily's mouth falls open before she splashes some water my way. Alea's giggle fills the empty space with happiness and warmth before getting replaced by the fairy's huffing and puffing.

"Screw you both."

We stay in the water for a while. Most of the time the conversation is about the ritual and its whereabouts before moving to Ella, her deal and the news about Eclia. I try to stay away from Myra. Any possible mention of that girl and my skin begins to boil. It almost drives me mad, the fact that she could be with Issac at this very moment, doing things with him I've craved since abandoning Karul. However, that's not important right now. My hatred towards the girl is outweighed by the suffering of humans.

"I can't believe he's punishing them." Alea murmurs staring into the water.

"I do, Wyrran's a sick fuck. Everyone knows it. Not long until he goes mad and kills his father." Desily spits the words like poison and I purse my lips.

"Those poor people. It's my fault this is happening. None of them did anything except for existing, and now they're getting punished for sins I've committed." I let my head fall into the palms of my hands, pressing them hard into my eye sockets as if to stop the awful images from entering my mind. I want to fight against the upcoming nightmares, but it's not as easy as I make it seem. The worries, the suffering of humans, the whispers of destruction didn't get much smaller in my head because of my anger—no, they're merely silenced whenever Myra exists in my thoughts. And though it pains me to think about her, I still force myself to, because I'd rather live angry at Myra and get some rest than wake up gasping for air with my friends worried.

"Thea, it isn't your fault. They've been treating humans like this for centuries, but now those people have a chance at having a normal life. You'll break their chains and set them free." Des rubs my shoulder and I exhale before facing the two of them.

"Set them free how? From where? From this palace? From this warm bath I'm taking or from the dinner table full of food I won't be able to finish whilst they starve?" I'm grateful for Theo and Alea, for Desily but my time with them made me forget just how the humans are treated without rich friends or special powers. I know they're upset over this, but none of them could ever begin to understand our suffering.

"Thea, your safety guarantees their freedom so don't take it for granted. Use it to your advantage to make sure they have a chance at living the same life." Alea half-smiles and I stare at her, taking her words in. She's right, this isn't forever. I won't be in this castle for the rest of my life. I'll be out there, with them fighting battles I never imagined myself in but can't stop thinking about as of late.

"You know, as much as I hated the palace, I do miss its perks." Desily changes the topic, her body relaxing into the water, her brown braids falling off her shoulders and into the water.

"What perks? Of course except the royal treatment." I mock, and she narrows her eyes at me. Alea scoffs from her side, and Desily sits up, water running down her toned body.

"You know what." She points a finger at me. "The chest plate you wear every day didn't come from thin air."

I scrunch my brows in thought. "Des, just how exactly did you get those scales?" She's never told me, and I've never asked, given we've never had a chance to talk like this, but the day started off well and I have a moment of peace, so why not use it?

Desily leans back against the stone edge, a smirk playing on her lips. "You didn't think I left the palace empty-handed."

Alea and I stare at the woman with our jaws hanging low. Each day she surprises us more and more.

"You stole them from the King?" Alea hisses, turning her attention to her girlfriend.

"No, they gave it to me." She rolls her eyes. "I mean, c'mon, you lot, do we really care who I took it from? The scales serve us all great." Hard to argue against that, given they've saved my life countless times and kept Alea's back protected whilst she uses her bow. I guess we can't say anything, even though it doesn't matter because the scales were in corrupted hands, but now they serve a better purpose.

My thoughts disappear as soon as a few maids walk in with vases full of scented oils and baskets full of white flowers. I send a questioning look towards Des and Alea, but neither of them has an answer as to what's about to happen. I roll my shoulders and watch as a few younger maids place a couple of the white flowers into the water, letting them float around. The scent I've never smelled fills up the space between us, something between fresh orchid and jasmine.

Three older maids begin pouring some of the oil on their hands and near themselves towards us. I jerk away as soon as their cold hand collides with my scarred body.

"Excuse me, it's nothing bad. We use this oil in Sebraycia to purify you of any evil attached to you." The maid explains, and I scoff. For the evil residing inside of me, they might need a lot more than just a drop.

"*Insolent child.*" Jino hisses deep within me, but I shut her out. Perhaps a detox from her and everything else is just what I need.

***

After the morning rituals I've never experienced in my life, I decide to skip breakfast. Some part of me warns that Myra and Issac might be seen there together, and that's not exactly what I need. We need to focus on the mission. I need to focus. Having that woman rubbing herself on the man I thought was mine would only serve as a distraction. Even if every fibre of my body inexplicably begs to walk towards his direction, even if my mind feels tormented and my guts are twisting from anger, I choose to spend my time in the library in hopes of speeding up the search.

Two tall knights guard the even bigger wooden doors to the room holding knowledge. I smile at them, and they nod their heads in return, reaching for the handle. The first step inside is breathtaking. The library in Karul, although holding forbidden knowledge, could never compare to what's before me.

Three, no, four levels of bookshelves filled to the brim with stories, knowledge, memories circle around me in a round room. There are a couple of people climbing up the ladders to the other floors, some reaching for books, some resting at the tables in the middle to read. I blink, unable to take it all in. This library might be one of the most wonderful places I've ever seen.

"May I help you?" A slender, older man comes from behind me. His skin ashen, his short hair white, and the tiniest circular glasses hang off the tip of his nose. I smile, clearing my throat, and he smiles back.

"Sorry, I'm Thea. I've come to perhaps lend a hand in search of what the princess had asked to look for." I explain quietly, trying not to disturb others, and the man nods slowly as if trying to collect his thoughts.

"Ah! Yes, yes, please feel free to look through whatever you might deem helpful. As you can see, there aren't many of us compared to the books we've acquired." He chuckles, his pebble eyes turning into thin lines decorated by wrinkles.

How I envy him. Oh, how I wish to experience turning old and living my last few years on this planet in peace and quiet, reminiscing about the past. Memories that'd be too precious not to replay in my mind over and over again until I die, instead of waking up each day knowing that what happened years ago might as well be almost forgotten. In my case, not many things are precious, but the things that are I hold onto dearly, knowing it's what still makes me human.

"Thank you. I'll make sure to help as much as I can." I smile at the man and begin walking towards the first shelf on the left side of the room. We've got to start somewhere.

***

Being inside the library feels timeless. I could sit here for hours looking through text and it'd seem like minutes have passed, when in reality it's been hours. I'm not sure how long I've spent reading book after book, but at one point I catch myself reading the same paragraph for the fifth time. Perhaps it's time for a break. After all, I'd managed to go through four bookshelves, only to come out with semi-useful information. Gods, this'll take ages.

"Miss Thea?" The old man whispers from behind me, and I turn around smiling, trying to hide the evidence the lack of human interaction had on me. "There's someone here to see you."

For a moment my heart skips faster, if only in hopes that Issac hadn't completely forgotten about me and held onto his promise to stay by my side. Even if it's only because his brainwashing tells him to, even if I made it clear I'm done with his games. Still, a part of me craves him. The same part that can't stand to think that Myra might be his new focus.

"Thea?" Desily steps from behind the pillars, and I try hard to hide my disappointment. Before reaching Yalan, the man wouldn't let me breathe, and now that we're here and he's been rekindled with his previous lover, I'm suddenly forgotten. Is that all we needed? To find him a good enough distraction? I clench my fists and grit my teeth. Nearly four days. Four days he didn't care to check up on me. "Thea!" Des snaps her fingers, and I blink, shaking my head.

"Sorry."

"Those books have drained you, Starbane." Desily scoffs before looking around the library. "We have to go through it all?" I nod, and she groans. "Whatever. We've decided to go out and explore the city for the night."

"I don't know, Des." I purse my lips together, scanning the stack of books placed before me. Some which I know won't hold any answers and some that might.

"Don't be like that. You need some fun. Come on! Just for tonight, please." Desily grabs onto my palms, flashing her puppy eyes and pouting her lips. It wouldn't hurt to go explore for one night. Besides, I don't think I can read another book, otherwise I might fall asleep.

"All right."

Chapter 15

It's night-time when the three of us exit the room. As it turned out, I've spent the majority of the day in the library, missing out on breakfast, lunch, and dinner. Luckily, Des brought some of it to the room, knowing I'd take her on the offer and would realise just how hungry I actually am.

I wrap the sage green scarf around my neck provided by the maids and rub leather gloves together. Now that I've got accustomed to the heat, going back outside might be a bit of a shock. After all, night-time in Sebraycia could go as low as minus twenty, which didn't bother us during the travels here as our lives depended on whether or not we'd make the journey.

Just as I hear the door behind me shut, the door opposite creaks open, revealing the silhouette of Theo.

"Oh! Haven't seen you all day, Thea. Are you all right?" He signs and I nod smiling. Glad to see his signing had improved. I'm sure years of not needing to use it had made him forget important bits, but a few nights together and he's talking like he's been doing it all his life.

"I'm fine. Are you going somewhere?"

"Actually—" Alea cuts in, scratching the back of her head.

I look at her with a raised eyebrow, demanding answers. "I invited them to join us."

"Them?" I hiss, twisting around, and surely enough, Issac stands right behind Theo, drilling the all-too-known holes into my face with his stare. I scoff and turn around, finding it comedic. How dare he look at me almost offended when he's the one who hasn't sought me out? No, he hasn't tried to talk to me ever since I told him to get his shit together. Of course, typical Issac, choosing to be as stubborn as possible and waiting for me to come running back like a fool. Not this time, not any more.

"Shall we go?" Des cuts in, feeling the tension, and I push forwards, trying to get away from him as far as possible. Perhaps I should've stayed in the library. At least there he wasn't forcing his way into my head.

We make it outside within a few minutes. I ignore the casual conversation between Alea, Theo, and Desily, and most importantly the heavy sound of footsteps following behind us. It's fine. As long as I don't look at him, I still have a chance at having some fun tonight.

The streets of Yalan are booming with people. There are stands with food almost everywhere, stretching from the gates of the palace all the way down the street. I look around at the colourful buildings, the lanterns hanging from structures, and the children running around with snowballs in their palms. A wide smile stretches across my lips, the memory of my childhood days during winter seasons spent with Issac flashing past my eyes.

Days where we'd wake up at the crack of dawn, eat breakfast, and race outside to build snowmen or an igloo. Days where we'd slide down the hill on a sack of hay and never get bored of it, no matter what. Days where it was the two of us against the world, not against each other.

We walk further, stopping by stalls every now and then to buy some food or look at the trinkets. It's a very fine reminder that there's still something worth saving in this world, that I shouldn't give up hope when it gets rough. These people haven't done anything bad. They're just existing within their communities, trying to make the best out of what they have. Even if the world is blank, they paint their own colours to make it livelier. Perhaps I should take a page out of their book and stop moping for once.

"Thea!" Alea's voice pulls my attention from looking at the stall with glass sculptures. "Come, we're going to this pub!" She points, and I nod, but not before I spot a stall with books.

"I'll come in a second!" I catch Des rolling her eyes before our groups rushes inside, and I giggle. Who knows, maybe I'll find something worth grabbing.

My eyes scan through the stacks of piled-up tomes, some of which I know, some which are newly released. It's strange to spot something fresh these days. Since the war began, the printing process had slowed down and books became much harder to produce.

Just as I'm about to grab one of the books about magic surrounding Yalan, a jolt of shivers runs from the tip of my spine until the very bottom. A hand is wrapped around my forearm. A strange sensation of anger, annoyance, need, and desire pours into my head from every direction all at once, as if I've holes inside my skull I wasn't aware of. My skin becomes hot, my breathing stops as I slowly turn, unable to make sense of what's happening to me.

Issac stares at me with his mouth slightly open. He shuts it only to open it a second later, as if making up his mind. I watch him do that for a while until the man tending to the stand calls out for me, asking if I'll buy anything.

"Yes, sorry, here." I mumble, passing the money and grabbing the book swiftly, wiggling out of Issac's grasp.

It's then that I feel my fast heartbeat and the warmth of my cheeks spreading all the way through my neck down to the spot where he held me. I lick my lips and realise just how dry they've become, just how messed up my head is. No emotion feels like mine. No matter what I try doing, I can't calm myself down. I push past the people, past the voices and the smells, the colours, the laughter, running from an invisible force trying to bring me closer to him.

"Thea!" I hear his voice call out for me, but I'm so busy running from something I can't understand that I can't control my legs when they take me down the alleyway. Every part of me screams to turn back around and throw myself into his arms, to steal the kiss from his lips I've been needing since we departed from Karul. Yet, at the same time, I can't make a fool out of myself, not when he's not sure of his own feelings and when his previous love is in the picture. I won't be fighting for a man who isn't strong enough to fight against all the odds to have me. I won't—

"Thea!" I'm slammed into the wall, panting. My body shakes as I slowly look up to meet his crimson eyes. "Where are you going?"

"I—" My eyes drift towards his hands on my hips, to his eyes fixated on my face, and my heart aches. Why is it so fucking hard to stay away? "Leave me alone, Issac. Just go away."

"What's up with you? Why are you acting so strange?" He questions, nearing himself, and it takes every ounce of self-control left within me to push him away just an inch further.

"Me? I'm perfectly fine! Why are you suddenly going after me? What is it that you want to say now?" I blabber out, hoping my words might save me from him discovering the hurt in my eyes and the need to pull him closer and get lost in his smell, taste, touch.

Issac's brows furrow. He swallows slowly and takes a moment to decide whether or not to give me the space I'm practically begging for. I see the concern in his eyes, the moment he decides whether or not it's worth bothering me, if it'd be all right to risk another disappointment just for a short-lived delusion. I feel the intensity of his stare when his lashes flutter and once again, Issac is too close.

My nails dig into my palms, fighting against the strange feeling of anguish and denial. I press my back against the hardwood of the building behind me and pray for a sign. For something or someone to tell me what to do, for them to tell me whatever it is I'm feeling is all right and I shouldn't feel crazy. That I'm not insane to have these bizarre emotions towards him.

"Thea, I just want to talk." He begs, and I shut my eyes. It's always the same story with Issac. He does something wrong, I get angry, and then we talk it out. I always end up forgiving him for whatever he's done. I always ignore my own feelings and push all the hurt aside if only for a moment of bliss spent in his presence. Even now, I can't decide whether or not I hate him, whether or not I should fight against these emotions or let him under my skin. Gods, I don't even sound like myself. If anything, I sound like—

My eyes snap open, and I stare at Issac in complete silence and shock. It's as if the wind blew through my head and cleared all the previous thoughts out. That's right. Everything I've contemplated up until this point didn't sound like me at all. No, it sounded like the man stood before me. I was experiencing what Issac was feeling and thinking. We were connected, just like Jino said.

Is it true then? Does he really care this much whether or not we talk? Does it really hurt to talk to me? Is he really in a constant war with himself about me? If so, I pity him. I truly do, because what I've felt wasn't just a person being unsure about their feelings. No, it was pure torture. Anguish beyond comprehension, and I can't imagine what it's like for him to have the memories of a person before him stripped away. All you're left with is half hatred, half desire for someone you shouldn't know, but your body tells you otherwise. Your heart screams to just make the right move and have them, but your head warns you against the unknown. As much as I'd like to help, I've done enough, and now it's up to him to decide.

A deep sigh pushes past my lips now that my head feels clearer. Is letting him talk alright? A few days have passed since we've spoken, days in which he had many occasions to ask about my conversation with the princess and show his concern. Time where he could've come and explained himself, the letters, the messed-up way of thinking, and worst of all, a girl I never heard about.

Although, to him it probably doesn't matter. This Issac doesn't know about our history the way I do. He wouldn't have considered the possibility that her mere presence near us might make me upset. To him, we're nothing more than acquaintances, ones that are far too close to be just friends but too far apart to be anything other than that.

"Can we?" He speaks again. This time I hear the urgency in his voice, the irritation at the fact I'm putting him in this position. If only he realised it's not me but himself.

"What is there to say? Unless you're willing to pick a side, I don't wanna hear it. I told you, I'm done." I hold my ground, levelling our looks.

Issac shifts away, his palms vanishing from my hips, and I bite onto my tongue at the way his warmth is being replaced by emptiness and cold. I've chosen this.

"Are you really angry with me because I can't remember stuff? Because I can't be who you want me to be?" He asks, and I scoff, rolling my eyes. Of course he still refuses to admit that the person at fault here is not me but him. I'm not his tormentor. He is.

"It's not who I want you to be, it's who you are, but for some bloody reason you choose to play around with your feelings even if your whole body tells you otherwise. Even if the Gods themselves came down from the sky and told you to stop, you wouldn't listen, and you know why?" I take a step closer, watching as his chest rises up and down in a quick motion. "Because you're scared, Issac. It's not because you hate me or because you can't remember. No, you're scared that what you're feeling is real, and if you let yourself be happy, that might come to bite you back."

"I'm not scared." He protests, and I groan, turning around. There's no point talking with him, at least not right now.

"Lie to yourself all you want. I felt the way you feel. You can't keep on living like this, so choose, or your own emotions might eat you up. Or it might just be too late." The last words come out more as a whisper, a promise that I won't wait for him forever. That I've done it before and I can't do it again. There are so many times I can put my heart back together for him and give it away before there's nothing to fix. "And if there's any part of you that truly cares about me, then choose wisely."

I begin walking away, the sound of the thick layers of snow crunching beneath my boots. I need to find Desily and Alea and hopefully get lost in a couple of drinks for tonight to forget about the mess unravelling before me.

"Is it about Myra?" I stop in my tracks. The sound of Issac shifting behind me tells me he said what he said on a whim. He isn't sure if this was the right course, and if my reaction is what he wanted, but after a moment passes I hear him huff. "So it is about her."

I turn around, only for a second to give him a confused look. "You remember her?"

Issac blinks and tries to take a step towards me, but I don't let him by moving away. He exhales deeply, resigned. "Of course I remember her. She was around the manor for months at a time when Lisa gave me training."

The way my guts twist and my chest squeezes nearly sends me to my knees, ready to puke. I'm not usually one to get this angry at someone. If anything, I need a good enough reason, but it seems the strange girl is just that. A person I've exchanged a couple of words with turns my blood into lava just at the thought of her. "Funny how you remember someone from long ago, yet you refuse to remember the person you've spent a whole past year with." I shake my head in disbelief. "What do you hope to accomplish here, Issac?

Truly, tell me. I'm intrigued."

"Gods, Thea, I don't fucking know. I just want us to go back to being civil." He groans, brushing his fingers through the messy strands of his raven hair.

I bite onto my cheeks and stare at him in silence. Always the same words, always the same excuse and the same favour. He'll never change, and it's all my fault because I've allowed this to happen too many times before. This time I won't make the same mistake. I can't and won't when I know there's a whole world depending on me.

"I'm sorry, Issac, but we can't go back to normal because normal in your dictionary means choosing to forget who we were and treating me well at times you deem acceptable." The man opens his mouth as if to protest, but I cut him off, with my body shaking ever so slightly under the pile of warm clothes. "I can't be a part of that any more, not when all of our friends' lives depend on me and with them yours. I can't keep on entertaining your games, so do me a favour this time." I reach for the scarf and wrap it tighter around my neck before turning. "The next time you wish to approach me, do it with an actual purpose, not just to get a reaction out of me. If you chose to remember Myra, I know you can remember me, so take your time picking what's more important. Hating me or being a part of my life."

I don't wait for his response when leaving the alley. My legs lead me towards the tavern at light speed, and the moment I set my foot inside the building, the sounds of music and laughter fill my ears. It's almost enough to cloud the pain growing inside my heart, almost enough to make me forget the way Issac had looked at me. Full of anguish and frustration because his foolproof plan didn't work.

I spot Desily shouting in the far-away table, joined by Theo, Alea, and surprisingly Ryo.

"Thea! You've made it." The boy grins, and I smile back. I've missed his company, even his constant talking.

"What are you doing here?" I nudge him and take the free seat next to Theo.

Ryo picks up a pitcher full of a strange concoction before taking a big swig and grimacing immediately after. "Decided to have some fun before shit goes down."

"Oi! Be more optimistic, youngster." Des cuts in, slamming an empty shot glass onto the table and calling the barmaid to bring her more. "I've had bigger worries at your age and made it through."

"Barely." Alea whispers, and Desily gives her a betrayed look. We break into laughter that's soon replaced by different conversations between us. I order a drink, and then another, trying my best to get rid of the feeling of uneasiness as I glance towards the door, waiting for Issac to enter. I've given him the ultimatum this time, hopefully made it as clear as possible I'm not here to play games. Even if it might cost me losing him, it's something the future me might have to deal with. The current me is too busy trying to get drunk.

A couple of minutes in, and two empty pitchers later, the door to the tavern swings open. I barely hear it through the shouts and the excitement in Desily's voice as she tells a story, but when I do, my eyes lazily drift away. I haven't drunk in so long that two pints begin doing tricks on my mind as my vision sways from side to side. I squint my eyes towards the door, blinking once, twice, and then I spot him.

Issac brushes the freshly fallen snow off his head and looks around the room from face to face until he spots mine and stops. I wonder then if he's angry or upset even that he didn't get what he wanted? Or if he's perhaps relieved I rejected his apology and let his hatred grow stronger?

I let my eyes linger on him for a moment longer, waiting for some sort of reaction, half-expecting it to be disgust, but to my surprise he seems miserable. Like the life's been sucked out of him, like he'd hoped to get a pile of gold but instead he received nothing. Like me walking away broke him in ways he can't begin to comprehend. He blinks, and I watch carefully for the change in his face indicating he's put on a mask, but yet again he surprises me by keeping on the same look. Could it be that Issac's grown tired of pretending? That he actually listened to my words?

"General Edison is here!" Ryo chirps happily, and I jump, startled. Suddenly the room becomes louder, and I realise it might be the best time to stop drinking.

Ryo waves his hand in the air to get Issac's attention, and the man sighs, slowly making his way towards us. I shut my eyes, praying he'll know better than to talk to me, but that doesn't happen as someone's voice addresses him out of the blue.

"Issac Edison? The Demon of Karul?" Our whole table becomes quiet to look at Issac, who's surrounded by two figures. Something inside me screams that I've seen them before, that I know who they are, but I'm far too drunk to even try to recall a memory from Gods know when.

"It is you! Fuck, we thought you'd died in that awful attack on the manor." The other stranger adds with notable happiness in his voice.

I tilt my head, trying to get a better look at Issac, and shockingly catch him standing there, pale as a sheet of paper, looking at the two figures in silence. This is unlike him. If anything, I expected them to be cussed out and beaten to a pulp, but Issac does neither. If I didn't know him any better, I'd say he looks scared, terrified even.

"Well, I'm glad we found you. Turns out your intel was helpful and we managed to sort our shit out." The man chuckles, patting Issac on the shoulder. "We've also managed to get some things for you, but by the time we were meant to meet you by the manor it was too late."

Wait a damn minute.

"Yeah, a shame really. At least the girl is safe, as promised." The other adds, rubbing the back of his neck. "It's been hard keeping the King and his army away from you lot, but hey, at least he's not here in Yalan searching for her, right?"

My mouth drops open at the realisation, my head spinning, and I'm not sure if it's from the shock at the sudden information or from the drinks consumed.

These people in front of Issac are the same two figures I saw him with in the forest. The same strangers I thought he was plotting with to have me kidnapped. Instead, as it turns out, Issac was doing the exact opposite. He was protecting me.

Chapter 16

ISSAC

The room is loud. Too loud. Suddenly the jacket I wore to fight against the cold feels too heavy, too warm and bothersome. I grab onto my collar and pull it away from my neck, but even then it's too hard to breathe, too difficult to think. I take a step back, but no matter the distance I'm suffocating with the incoming memories.

A glimpse of two elven soldiers working as spies in Eclia. I meet them by the manor, always late at night to exchange information. They ask for information about their family's whereabouts, and I ask… what do I ask?

Meeting after meeting I manage to find something worth coming back for. I know they'll take even the shittiest piece of intel because at the end of the day it's their family. They tell me one night the elven king took their close ones away as punishment for abandoning the battle with the goblins. I tell them I don't give a shit and walk away. They tell me the girl is safe, but on a track to finding the manor. Girl, what girl?

"Issac?" Someone calls out for me, but my vision is too

blurry and I can't keep up with anything that's going on inside my head.

I see those strangers again. They seem angry, furious even, because the King threatened to kill their families if the girl isn't found. I tell them I'll keep them safe, and they tell me they'll keep the King away from finding her. I throw some threats their way to make sure she isn't found, that she stays safe, and they promise to do everything in their power to keep that scum away.

Who the fuck am I protecting? Who is so important to me that I feel like slaughtering the entirety of the elven palace if shit goes bad? That I make sure we keep meeting each month for the sake of keeping her safe? Who the hell am I—

"Issac." A hand lands on my shoulder, shaking me awake. I jerk away and blink the memory away to the back of my head.

Everything around me comes crashing down at once. The sounds of the music, laughter from the nearby tables, and the smell of roasted meat. I blink once more and look ahead, into the eyes of a girl who's been driving me insane. "Are you alright?" She asks, and I swallow.

Not even an hour ago she told me to fuck off and sort myself out. Now she's staring at me with concern and care I know I don't deserve. I look past her, ignoring the way my body practically twitches to throw itself in her direction, and decide to focus on the two men staring right back at me.

Those men, the elven soldiers from Eclia Theo struck a deal with because I begged him to. I flinch when my head begins to pulse in a painful way, as if I got hit repeatedly by a brick. No matter how hard I try to push it away, it won't stop, and so my headache persists. Suddenly her voice fills my head, reminding me of the promises and threats she's made.

You choose to play around your feelings even if your whole body tells you otherwise. You're scared.

I grunt and stop fighting against the headache. Instead, I let my body relax. Only then do I realise the cause of my pain isn't just some random thing happening in my body, but myself. I'm the one preventing the door from opening. Without thinking twice, I yank the door open and a wave of memories rushes right at me.

It all starts to fall back into place. A part of my life I wasn't aware was missing is suddenly there, put back into place, making me just a little bit more whole. I remember those soldiers and the countless meetings I've had with them. I pleaded with Theo to make allies to keep her safe, because our soldiers had found out she's been getting herself known in Eclia. I remember staying up late to find some sort of information for those men, something that'll make sure they hold onto their side of the deal and keep Thea safe, away from the king and the dangers laying ahead. Away from me.

I remember how much I cared about her. How much I hated her at the same time, but couldn't stop worrying. Even if she wasn't present in my life, I made it my life mission to make sure nothing ever happens to her, that they don't find her before she finds me, before I am fixed.

I remember how she caught me one time and I brushed it off. How during that meeting they warned me against that idiot Wyrran getting closer to finding her whereabouts. How angry I was there was a possibility of her being in grave danger.

After all, it seems the past me and the present me shared

the same fate. To feel so perplexed by a girl we've been taught to hate because some strange part of us ended up wanting her closer rather than further.

"Issac, are you alright?" Alea calls, and I stare at her in silence. Everyone at their gods-damned table is looking at me as if I've lost it, and perhaps I have, because what the fuck were those memories? Is it what she's been telling me to let in? The reason as to why she's so upset with me? Why I see undeniable hurt in her eyes each time I refuse to cooperate?

"Let's go." I hear her whisper, and before I have a chance to reply she grasps onto my palm, dragging me outside. I ignore the way her hand fits perfectly into mine and the way our skin seems to burn through the leather gloves. We push past crowds of people, and soon enough we're on the outskirts of the city.

There are fewer houses here, with the orange light dancing through their windows. Most of the residents are in the town, because if there's anything enjoyable about living in this cold fucking country it's their nightlife. Fuck, even I'd spend more time outside if all I could see during the day was white, whilst at night colours I almost forgot existed popped from every corner.

Thea doesn't seem to pay attention to any of that, too focused on getting us away from the pub and the prying eyes. I wonder for a moment why she's decided to pull me out of that awkward situation when not long ago she seemed ready to break my neck. I deserved it, everything she said and more. After all, she was right. I was being an arsehole and ignoring her for the past few days, hoping she'd come herself and forgive me for my behaviour, but she hasn't. Instead, I sat in my room worrying out of my fucking mind if she's doing alright with the princess, and then Myra showed up and she looked like someone stabbed her through the heart. It'd be wise to admit to her she's right, I'm scared, but we both know I'm a stubborn and proud bastard. It'll take a lot to get me to break, like her threatening to leave, for example.

She stops suddenly, and I nearly crash into her before I manage to catch my balance. We're near the gates, our only companion the street light and the two outposted snow giants looking far into the distance. I wonder what's going on inside her head and if she's about to shout at me or ask me questions, but instead she remains silent.

Her hand wiggles out of my grasp, and I grimace at the cold feeling it leaves after it's gone. I purse my lips and watch her attentively as she shifts from foot to foot, the gears twisting in her head, trying to create a sentence without a loophole. Something I can't avoid.

"Just say it before your head explodes." I tell her jokingly, and her golden eyes snap on me. There are emotions behind them I can't decipher, all for one. Hope.

"These men, you know them." She states carefully, and I sigh.

"Seems like they know me more, but yes, I do know them." I decide to be honest with her. This one time I'm not going to bullshit my way through this because she was clear with me. I've got to show I care about her, not just about hating her, which by the way is pure bullshit.

I might've hated her. Gods, sometimes I still do, but it's not the same type of hate I felt when I woke up on the ship. No, it's more like the hate you feel towards someone who refuses to work with you, someone you wanted to be around but life keeps throwing obstacles your way, and to add to it your messed-up head keeps reminding you how horrible of a person they are, even if you don't believe it any more. That's exactly how I feel about her. Confused and torn apart about what's wrong and what's right.

"I've seen them before." Her voice shakes, and I note the nervousness behind her words. She's afraid of being lied to, of being made fun of or pushed away, and I curse myself for making her feel that way. If I could, I'd turn back time and beat the fuck out of the old me, the one who didn't know any better and who didn't manage to get some of his memories back. "Don't bullshit me, Issac. Be honest. Do they have something to do with me?"

I stare at her with half-formed regrets and half-hopeful thoughts that perhaps she might forgive me one day. That perhaps day by day I might let myself think about the future and remember the things she does. That perhaps the burning desire to hold her in my arms might be fulfilled, and the need to make her life miserable dissipates.

I'm just as fucking hopeful as she is that I can win her over, because for the past few days I've felt nothing but utter torment not being able to fall asleep by her side and not being able to bicker as if nothing matters.

"They do." The words come out of my mouth quicker than I can think. I see the worry being painted all over her flawless face. The freckles scattered across her pinkish cheeks, each one of them a different size, a different shape. Yeah, I've been staring at her more than should be allowed. Whatever, if that makes me a creep so be it, but if I'm not allowed to talk to her, the only better thing to do is to note every detail about her appearance. "Gods, don't look at me like I've plotted to have you murdered."

"You pretty much did." She mumbles, and I frown at her words.

"Yeah, but it turns out the past me actually cared a lot about you." Her eyes catch mine once again. This time a flame of joy dances through them. "I remembered asking Theo to get some intel in the elven palace, you know, in case they might be searching for you. These people were just that, our informants and the only reason why Wyrran hasn't found you sooner."

I wait for her to say something, anything that might change the course in which our relationship is going. I wonder if I've done the right thing revealing to her that I remembered a bit about our past together, a part of me that felt something towards her. Yet she remains quiet, her bottom lip trapped between her teeth as she thinks about her next question. A habit I've caught her doing often.

Finally, after a moment she exhales deeply and looks down onto her shoes. "So it was your idea to draft spies?"

"Yeah?" I answer, confused.

"So you remember why you've done that? You let yourself remember what I meant to you? Who I was in your eyes before you started to hate me?" She looks up, and her eyes are full of hurt and uncertainty. I want to tell her the truth, to for once be honest, but I know if I'd suddenly sprung onto her the fact I no longer see her as an enemy, she wouldn't believe me. Not when I've been acting like an arse, not when Myra purposely keeps messing with her head. She'd think I'm doing it to get her closer and start my torment all over again because she's too trustful, too kind. Things I'd told her before.

Well, if I'm to fix what's broken, it's best to do it slowly, cautiously. Althea is prey, a deer running through the forest whilst I'm the wolf chasing after her. A foolish wolf who appreciates her beauty but craves her blood. I'm a monster fighting against its own nature.

"I do, yes. Not fully, but some parts. I remember these people, and I remember talking to you about them in the manor." I tell her before turning around. We have to get back to the pub before everyone starts worrying, or so I say to myself to cover the fact that my body is aching to pull her closer.

"I see." She whispers, and my heart pains at the way her voice sounds resigned.

"You know," I start walking away, a part of me hoping she'll follow, and when the sound of the snow crunching beneath her boots reaches my ears, my shoulders relax. "I'm glad they've kept their promise of keeping you hidden. As strange as it sounds, I'm relieved that the past me kept you safe."

***

The next morning I find myself sitting at the end of the table in the big dining hall. Since we've arrived here, I've been nothing but surprised by the size of this building. All of it for one princess. The walls of the room are made out of wooden planks. Long, silky curtains hang off the arched windows overlooking the town.

I take a bite of the eggs before me and hear a slight shuffling to my right. Theo's eyes keep glancing in my direction, not in a subtle manner. Last night, after the two of us returned to the pub, I spoke to the men who'd spied for us, said my thanks, and bid them farewell. I ignored the curious eyes of our friends trying to figure out what Thea and I could've possibly been talking about for so long. It was none of their business, though I'm aware they know more about our relationship than I could hope for. Nosy bastards.

"What?" I ask Theo, who busies himself with pouring a glass of water.

He signs something, and I try hard to remember the things he's taught me in the past couple of weeks. "You and Thea all right?"

I scoff, shaking my head. "Peachy."

"Fancy seeing you here!" My eyes snap to the girl with short curly hair and eyes full of mischief.

"Where? In the fucking dining hall during breakfast hour?" I grimace at Myra and go back to eating, ignoring her as she takes the seat opposite mine. Gods have mercy.

The day we arrived in the palace, I didn't expect to see her. To be fair, I haven't expected to see her ever again after she had an argument with Lisa over their family loyalty and vanished without a word.

Sure, the younger me was a bit heartbroken at the fact someone I'd shared my bed with was gone, but the current me couldn't give two shits. So when she threw herself at me, hugging me like a day hasn't passed, I knew it wasn't because she missed me. It was to piss Thea off, which apparently worked.

Out of instinct, my eyes drift towards the other end of the table where she's sat, accompanied by Desily, Alea, and Ryo, and sure enough her eyes are throwing daggers at the brunette. Do I really need another thing in the way of winning her over? It's like I'm running up the hill and the

Gods themselves are throwing boulders in my path.

"Oh, don't be like that, Issac." She chuckles and follows the direction I'm looking at. I see her waving at Thea before turning back around. "Trouble in paradise?"

"Mind your fucking business, Myra." I snap at her and begin to gather my things. I can't stand to be in her presence. I don't even know what drew me towards her in the first place.

"Come on, Issac. Why waste your time with her when you already have me?" She pouts her lips, and I nearly gag. "It's fine if you're not in the mood. The banquet next week will surely relax you a bit. Perhaps a drink or two will make you forget about her and focus on me."

I stop and send a questioning look towards Theo, who just shrugs his shoulders. Great help there, as per usual. Fine, I'll bite and ask. "What banquet?"

Myra smiles, plating her food slowly. I know she's stalling for time to make sure Thea gets the wrong idea. I wish I could tell her there's nothing going on between us and that the brunette is just being delusional, but Thea in her current mental state isn't one to reason with. She'll believe what she sees.

"Just a little party the princess throws once in a while for the neighbouring lords from villages around Sebraycia." I roll my eyes. Surely it isn't a lot then. This country is covered in snow and ice, with monsters running everywhere. Yeah, it might be peaceful here, but at the same time it's easy to die in the dumbest way. Like I had. "Make sure you dress nicely, Issac. I've missed seeing you all formal. Always turned me on."

I don't spare her another look as I begin walking out of the room. Fuck the banquet, and the princess, and everyone else along with them. How am I meant to care when my head is nothing but a ship sailing through the biggest storm yet, and it isn't the safety of the land I sail to. No, it's a person a part of me loathes and craves the most.

The girl I wish couldn't speak to me but wouldn't stop at the same time. The girl I meet during nightmares at night and get greeted with a warm smile despite the obvious hatred during the day. The person who appears in the memories I'm so stubbornly trying to suppress, afraid of the truth they might hide. Of the truth the two of us created.

"I do sometimes miss the old you. The one who was focused on the mission more than the girl." Jino's voice rings through my head, and I visibly grimace at the reminder she can so easily read into my thoughts whenever I drop my guard.

"I miss the times when you stayed fucking quiet." I grunt at her in my head and cut off the connection before she can even think of a response.

Ever since yesterday I've been on edge. Torn between choosing what feels right and what could be right, I'm stuck walking a tightrope. How much time do I have before Thea decides she can't put up with my bullshit? How many times will she allow me to hurt her to satisfy this hunger inside of me? How many times will I reject the pleas of my own heart to let myself remember? Fuck knows, definitely not a lot.

Just as I turn the corner to make my way towards the bedroom, where I hope to spend the rest of the day staring at the walls and contemplating, the sound of rushed footsteps reaches me, and I halt, swinging around to check who's decided to bother me this time.

To my surprise, it's her. She has this pissed-off look on

her face, a clear sign of worry and jealousy passing by her eyes as she tries her best to hide it. I cross my arms and stare down at her, wondering if I should test my luck and annoy her further or hear what she's about to say.

"I've got a request." She mutters. Hearing her out it is.

"I'm intrigued. Do go on." I nod and lean against the wall.

She shifts from foot to foot, her eyes focused on the wooden panels, her bottom lip trapped between her teeth, her arms resting on her lean hips, her hair tied into a braid that rests atop her breast, and my heart begins to pound.

Something crawls from the back of my mind, a memory of sort, of the way she tastes, of the way her skin feels softer than silk, of the way her hair tickles my cheeks, and the way my hands fit perfectly in the dips of her hips. What the fu—

"Issac?" I blink and swallow the leftover taste of a memory off my tongue. It takes everything in me to compose myself and hold up the façade that I'm not fucked up in the head, that I haven't just imagined sleeping with Althea Starbane. She raises her brows, visibly irritated I haven't given her a response to whatever she said. But how could I when I just thought of having her below me? Or perhaps I remembered it.

"Sorry, what?"

She groans. "I asked if you'd be willing to spend an hour a day with me on training."

The smile that stretches across my lips might seem mocking in a way, but I'm nothing but surprised at her request. Had something happened during the night? Had someone changed her mind about me?

"I'm sorry, you're asking for my help?"

She kisses her teeth and rolls her eyes, the small amount of civility she mustered to speak to me slipping past her fingers. "Yes, yes I am, because according to Alea I need to stay in shape, and staying in the library won't do that."

"Right, but why me? Why not Theo or Desily or Alea for that matter?" I push, even though the two of us know the answer to that question. Still, I need to hear her say it.

Her eyes lock with mine. There's something brewing behind those golden discs, and I smirk. "Because we both know there's no one better at fighting in here other than you. The only other person who can use magic is you. As much as I hate to admit it, I do agree. I need your help."

I push off the wall and stalk towards her. She holds her ground, unsurprisingly, lifting her chin high to level with my look, but it's no use. I'm hovering above her, looming over her, and in any other case people would've run, but not her. Not Thea. She never runs when it comes to me.

"A week ago you'd rather cut your arms off than train with me. Today you want me by your side. I can't figure you out."

"Feeling's mutual." She huffs, turning her gaze to something behind me.

I can tell it physically pains her to ask me for help. It's the last thing she imagined herself doing after giving me the ultimatum, but her friends had convinced her that training with me might be worth a greater deal than our argument.

I wait a moment, wondering if being this close to her is the right option, if I should feed into this obsession over her I seemed to have developed instead of staying at a safe distance and watching from afar as she lives her life. But I know by now that I'm a horrible, selfish man who doesn't care if what I do might affect her. As long as it benefits me, I'll do it. I'll use every possible chance I get to be closer to her if it means my head calms down and my heart stops pounding.

"But I'll do it." I see the shock behind her eyes as she snaps her attention back to me. "If that's what you truly want, then let's do it. I'll meet you in the training room in two hours."

She looks ecstatic for a moment before a thought in her head ruins it and suspicion shadows her features. "How do you know they have a training room?"

I depart, a smile playing across my lips, despite my body's reluctance. An inexplicable joy fills my chest, simply from being near her once more. "I know a lot, Thea. It's good to know the assets and liabilities of your allies and enemies."

"Course you do, bastard."

"Heard that!"

***

It's well past afternoon hours as I bandage my wrists and prepare the space for the training. I might've arrived an hour or so earlier than agreed upon, but sitting inside my room and doing nothing was beginning to drive me crazy.

Almost as much as the thought of kissing Althea in the past. I glance up at the mirror-covered wall, my reflection betraying my inner turmoil. I'm utterly unravelling over this girl, my pupils dilated and my cheeks flushed crimson. Memories of our past seem to be resurfacing from the deepest recesses of my mind, and I despise every moment of it.

My obsession is a razor's edge between hatred and desire. She haunts me. Every stolen thought, every forbidden glimpse sending electric shivers through my body. I want to break her, possess her, understand her, and simultaneously flee from her completely. Distance torments me. Proximity drives me mad. She's a wound I can't stop reopening, a poison I can't stop consuming.

The door opens, and Thea enters. A vision that momentarily steals my breath. Her hair remains plaited, that familiar guardedness etched into her features, yet something has transformed. The borrowed castle attire becomes her: black leather trousers that trace every curve, a black vest that hints at the strength and vulnerability beneath.

Desire rises within me, a burning ache I can barely contain. My eyes are drawn to the mark on her arm. A dangerous promise, a potential salvation or destruction. I've watched her wrestle with this power, observed her desperate need to prove her independence, to demonstrate she requires no one's assistance. Each time she summons her abilities, she teeters on the razor's edge between mastery and self-destruction.

She's beautiful in her struggle, devastating in her determination.

"You're here early," she notes, taking a measured step forwards.

"So are you," I reply, crossing my arms over my chest. Her gaze sweeps over me, searching meticulously for hidden weapons, for any concealed agenda. Finding nothing, her features subtly soften.

Like her, I've chosen attire that allows for swift movement. Black trousers and a shirt cut asymmetrically from the neckline, revealing my own wielding mark. A symbol I never sought but have grown to appreciate. Were it not for this magic coursing through my veins, I'd have been nothing more than a memory, still stuck in that awful cell.

"So what is it that you're going to teach me today?" she asks, her tone a mixture of challenge and curiosity.

I smirk, tossing two pieces of bandage her way. "Hand-to-hand combat."

She scoffs, shaking her head. "Already learnt that, from Alea."

"Well, Alea isn't me," I reply, the words laden with unspoken meaning. The implication of my years defending the manor, fighting through countless raids, hangs in the air. A flicker of impression crosses Thea's eyes, quickly tempered by a hint of fear. She's too intelligent to provoke a confrontation that could prove fatal, and I'm not cruel enough to exploit such a moment of vulnerability. She's not foolish enough to make a move that might cost her life, and I'm not hateful enough to make it happen should she provoke an attack.

Once the bandages are in place, I rush her to stand before me, feet apart, hands guarding her face. "What would you do in this position?"

"Hit you in that smug face," she retorts, a smile laced with poison that neither of us truly believes.

"I'm sure you'd love that, but no," I counter. "Your enemy is quick and observant. Here, try it."

I ready myself for her attack. As her punch flies, I catch it effortlessly, pulling her against my chest. She stares at me, a storm of irritation and something deeper, something that resembles longing, before quickly donning her indifferent mask.

"Told you," I say.

"Fine," she grunts, wiggling away from my touch. The brief contact leaves an invisible mark, a connection that lingers beyond physical touch.

"What would you do then?"

"I'd use my whole body." I nod, gesturing for her to get into position. "You've got legs. Use them."

She pauses, analysing my instruction. When something clicks, her leg comes flying towards my side. I waste no time, catching her mid-strike and sweeping her to the ground. My arm slides behind her head as we land, her golden eyes burning into mine with a fierce intensity.

"You told me to use my legs!" she protests, slamming her hands against my chest.

I chuckle, enjoying how I can annoy her without crossing a line. "I did," I reply, my voice low and calculated, "but you shouldn't listen to someone you consider an enemy. Think of something better next time."

Something dangerous flashes in her eyes. A spark of defiance that gives me barely a moment's warning. Before I can react, her knee drives into my abdomen with precision, her palm forcing my chin upwards in a lightning-quick movement. In the midst of the chaos, she targets my elbow, causing my body to roll sideways. In an instant, she transforms our positions, straddling me with a predatory grace.

I stare at her. Half surprised, half impressed. As she gleams with a smile I haven't seen in what feels like an eternity. It's a revelation: she isn't the fragile creature others perceive her to be. Not the broken Thea who mends the world with delicate threads, but something far more complex, far more dangerous.

Sucks to be those who underestimate her. I've never seen her that way. Since the moment I awakened on that ship, something deeper had whispered a warning. Be careful. She harbours secrets beneath her skin, more than she ever shows.

"Well," she lowers herself, her braid trailing across my skin. I inhale sharply, fighting to maintain my composure, to prevent the mask from slipping. Her proximity sends electric shivers cascading across my body. "Seems I've got it figured."

I swallow hard, staring into her eyes as if they might unlock the mysteries that lie between us. A sharp pain travels across my head, and I blink as another memory forces its way into the light. Unbidden, unrelenting.

We rest atop a hill. The air cascades across my face. Cold and harsh. But the temperature isn't what captures my attention. It's the woman pressed against me, her heart beating alongside my own. Where are we? Did we fall after a fight, or did something entirely different transpire?

I delve deeper into the memory. A whisper echoes: *"You know my name too well, so drop it."* Have I called her something else? The word hovers at the edge of my consciousness, desperate to be remembered, yet my mind refuses to yield. What was it? What could I have called this infuriating, selfless, hot-headed wo—*Red.*

"What?" Thea's voice cuts through my thoughts, and I realise I've spoken aloud. Seizing her momentary surprise, I quickly reverse our positions, hoping to distract her from the word that slipped unbidden from my lips. Something clearly significant to her, yet frustratingly meaningless to me.

I pin her arms, my knee strategically placed to prevent another devastating strike to my abdomen. The room thrums with our ragged breaths. My racing thoughts competing with her rising and falling chest.

"What did you just say?" she demands, her eyes blazing with a mixture of confusion and challenge.

I scramble for an escape. "That you look red," I reply, my voice carefully measured. "Perhaps the colour might suit you well during the banquet next week."

I know my answer wasn't enough. The questions dance across her face, yet her mouth remains sealed. Her mind works meticulously, piecing together the puzzle, whilst I struggle to maintain my composure. If Thea discovers I've been following her unspoken instructions, I might just—

What? Be ashamed? Unsettled by the shifting landscape between us, where enemy lines blur into something more uncertain, more risky?

"What banquet?" she finally asks, deliberately changing the subject. We both understand the art of stubborn deflection.

"The princess will throw a celebration for her people. We've been invited," I reply, raising my eyebrows. She rolls her eyes, attempting to free her hands.

Instinctively, my grip tightens. My chest constricts. Her skin, impossibly soft, warmer than any hearth I've ever encountered, sends unexpected tremors through my resolve. She smells of cinnamon, a scent that echoes the constellation of freckles across her face, with an underlying whisper of vanilla hidden in places I've yet to discover.

From beneath her long lashes, she looks at me differently. Something has shifted. The sharp edges of our earlier confrontation softening into something more nuanced, more intimate. The woman who entered the room moments ago feels like a distant memory.

A cold reminder crawls across my skin. She's not to be

trusted. I release her hands abruptly, immediately mourning the loss of warmth. Cold rushes in, a stark reminder of boundaries.

"Let's return to training," I announce, my voice deliberately neutral. "We can discuss the banquet later."

I clear my throat, waiting for her to rise. Perhaps I should end this torment. Throw myself from the nearest cliff. Death might prove simpler than navigating the treacherous terrain of Althea Starbane, the woman who's become an inescapable red vision haunting my every thought.

Chapter 17

ALTHEA

I shouldn't have listened to Alea and Desily. I should've walked straight to the library, but how could I when Myra was making goo-goo eyes at Issac, constantly throwing me that *'he's mine'* look? It was exactly this that drew me to trail after Issac as he bolted from the dining hall. The same reason I see him far more often than I'd like.

Our group had found this weird sense of belonging. The castle was becoming our second home, and I was the only one on constant guard. I'd promised myself never to fall for the dream of settling down, not until we cleared out the evil lurking in our world. No matter how hard I tried to convince the others to stay alert, they simply didn't care.

Everyone was enjoying this illusion of peace whilst I was still living in the nightmare of having that peace torn away from me.

The past week had settled into a predictable routine. Each morning, maids would knock to provide baths and fresh clothes. After a quick breakfast in the dining hall, where Myra was always hanging around Issac's side of the table, I'd head to the library. There, I'd frantically research as many books as possible with help from the elder librarians.

Sometimes Desily would join me, sometimes Theo and Alea would tag along to polish their sign language, and on rare occasions Ryo would show up. He'd talk my ears off until I found him something to do, which was the only way to shut him up. It wasn't that I didn't want to spend time with my friends, but our total lack of progress since arriving in Yalan was driving me absolutely mad.

A few days after our arrival, the rest of Theo's soldiers reached us after their arrival in Keolin bearing news I wish I hadn't heard. Wyrran had ordered public executions of humans who seem to have any ties to magic, and imprisoned any human woman, man and child who appeared rebellious. Rumour has it he's been forcing them into labour camps, or just torturing them to get my attention. Lucky for him, it's worked as I grow more and more frustrated with being useless. I should be there, helping them, punishing Wyrran and his elven army for what they're doing to my people, but instead I'm stuck in a castle with my hands tied as I search for objects that apparently ceased to exist.

By now, I'd hoped to find the ritual paper or some extra information about Jino's blade. Instead, every book seems to strip away the hope I'd been desperately clinging to.

Late in the evenings, I'd meet Issac at our usual spot. Let's be clear. He isn't an easy instructor, never has been. Most times, I'd return to my room with bruises in hidden corners, aches that defied explanation. Yet, surprisingly, his lessons remain the sole beacon of progress in my otherwise bleak days.

No matter how many times I'd tumble to the ground, how unexpectedly he'd catch me off-guard, I'd rise. Each fall became another opportunity, another chance to prove my resilience. The proximity to him created a complex storm of emotions. My skin electric with a desire I'd desperately tried to suppress.

During our first encounter, I distinctly heard him call me Red. A nickname I thought had been lost to time forever. A ghost of a memory, whispered like a forgotten promise.

He swiftly redirected our conversation, and I hesitated to probe deeper. The fear of disrupting our fragile connection paralysed me, terrified that one wrong question might shatter whatever tenuous bond we'd rebuilt. A small flicker of hope crossed my heart. A delicate thought that perhaps Issac was fighting back, struggling to remember our shared history.

Today was the day of the banquet, and as much as I wanted to share the joy of my friends, I couldn't. This party was nothing but another distraction, another obstacle in our route to victory, but Desily had made me promise to join them all, and much to my dismay, I'd agreed.

Still, the banquet wasn't happening until later, and after going through four shelves of books at the library, my brain was begging for a break. I sighed, putting away the tomes of things I thought might be useful.

"Are you done for today?" Ryo asks from one of the tables, and I nod, rolling my shoulder to get rid of the tension.

"Yeah, do you have any plans before the party?" I ask, sliding one of the books into its original spot.

Ryo ponders for a minute, a finger tapping on his lips. "I was going to train, but Jassin and Venali told me my attire arrived, and I'd rather make myself more presentable to the ladies than swing my sword at some dummies."

"Are you sure Issac would approve of that talk?" I joke, remembering our lesson for today was cancelled. A strange sense of broken routine settling in my bones, then transforming into sadness at the fact I'd miss out on the only fun part of my day.

"General Edison gave us the day off, surprisingly. I guess he's not as boring as everyone thinks." I chuckle at Ryo's words and put away the last of the books. "Did you do any magical training lately?"

I shake my head and head towards the table where my research lies scattered, as if a hurricane had gone through it. A real reflection of how my mind looks. "No. It's safe to say I don't want to burn this place down, and since the entirety of Yalan is covered in snow, I find it hard to train somewhere I won't cause any damage."

"Yeah, I miss trees and grass and flowers and even the bloody mud," Ryo groans dramatically, slamming his head on the desk. A few passing librarians shoot disapproving glances in our direction.

I pat him on the shoulder, urging him to get up so we can leave and prepare for the wretched party.

As we walk through the corridors, Ryo regales me with stories about court ladies who've caught his eye. He's attempted to invite several to dance at the upcoming banquet, but without success. Apparently, he's too young for their tastes, and being an elf in Yalan doesn't help his chances.

We part ways at our doors, bidding farewell. The moment my foot crosses the threshold, Desily seizes my shoulders in a vice-like grip. My eyes widen in shock as she shakes me, her excitement palpable.

"You've got to see this!" Desily exclaims, her excitement

infectious.

"Wow, Des, hold your horses," I try to calm her, but she simply squeals in reply, dragging me towards the bed. Alea shoots me an apologetic look, yet I can't help but smile, unable to resist Desily's contagious enthusiasm.

I look at the clothes prepared for today's party, noticing how similar yet different they appear from one another. On the right lies a shimmering forest green dress with an asymmetrical hem—short on one side to expose the leg, cinched at the waist with a silver-buckled corset. Sheer sleeves gather at black bows, dramatic and flowing. People in Yalan take their parties more seriously than Theo ever had, that's for certain.

Moving to the next ensemble, I examine the two-piece set. Desily gasps, startling me.

"This one's Alea's! It's like it was made for her, isn't it?" she exclaims, eyes wide with delight.

"Let her look at it first, Des." Alea rolls her eyes, and I giggle. I suppose the green one belongs to the fairy. Rightfully so. Des will look absolutely breathtaking in it.

Alea's midnight blue ensemble features wide-legged trousers and a high mesh turtleneck with voluminous sleeves, silver chains draping elegantly at the hips. A short white fur jacket lies folded behind it—elegant yet formal, perfectly her.

"And?" Des quips like an impatient child, and I smile fondly. It must've been ages since she felt like royalty. Raised in a palace and then becoming a tavern owner must've been difficult for her. She rarely complains about missing the palace but I know how hard it is to revert from your old ways and try to fit in with the crowd. You can't extract a significant part of yourself from your life, no matter how desperately you try.

"They're stunning," I breathe, running my fingers over the luxurious fabric.

"Now yours. Look at yours, Thea!" She pushes through eagerly and reaches for the last piece of clothing.

The outfit before me is nothing short of breathtaking. And slightly daring. At its core lies a tight black corset that'd surely squeeze my waist to impossible dimensions, adorned with intricate silver decorative front closures that catch the light with every movement. The back features an elaborate lace-up design with satin ribbons criss-crossing. A crisp white linen shirt is cleverly sewn into the corset from the inside, providing an elegant contrast to the dark leather. The sleeves billow outward before tapering elegantly at the wrists, where shimmering pearl buttons offer the finishing touch.

I blink at the skirt attached to the corset. The front is short. Dangerously so. Barely covering mid-thigh, whilst the back falls in layers that remind me of dark feathers. Black fabric bleeds into crimson, silver threads catching the light as I turn it over in my hands. It shimmers like something far too expensive for someone like me to wear.

This design will have my legs fully exposed to the scrutiny of everyone present. If not for the modest triangle of black fabric at the front cut into a tasteful V-shape, I might as well attend the gathering in nothing at all. The thought makes heat rise to my cheeks.

Gods, how am I meant to conceal a weapon?

Desily shakes a pair of gloves in the air, much different from my usual ones. More elegant, cleaner, expensive.

Nothing like me. Still, the idea of joining my friends at a party dressed in something besides a white shirt and a pair of leather trousers has me feeling a touch more optimistic.

"Aren't they just amazing?" Desily beams, her eyes alight with excitement, and I nod, my apprehension about the party fading. Perhaps this event won't be so dreadful after all.

Chapter 18

The evening arrives quicker than anticipated. I almost groan at the sight of the moon peeking through the windows, nearly startling Desily, who's taken it upon herself to braid my hair into a crown, a few loose strands framing my face.

Her own hair has been twisted into curls and braids that cascade down her back. Alea stands behind us, struggling to pin her hair into an elegant updo for the third time, a silver needle with a crescent moon and sparkling diamonds holding it in place.

"Here, all done!" Desily clasps her hands together, finally letting go of my hair. For the first time since I sat down, I allowed myself a proper look in the mirror.

The person staring back isn't the same girl I remember fleeing the manor, the one who cried day and night, afraid of nightmares. Instead, I see a woman. An elegant façade masking the evil force within. Whilst I do look stunning, I can't shake the feeling this is all for show. This isn't who I truly am.

"Of course this isn't who you are, but you look presentable. Perhaps you might stand a chance against that infuriating girl," Jino's voice rings through my head, serving as a reminder

that Myra will also be attending the party. And so will Issac.

I wonder for a moment if Myra's looks will sway him, if he might give in to the temptation she presents. The mere thought twists my insides, my skin prickling with a layer of nervous sweat.

If she's who he chooses, then so be it. If fate is on our side, I'll get my Issac one day. But if we're not destined to be together, as time has shown countless times, then I'll have to accept the harsh reality and fully focus on the mission of saving the entire world.

"Let's show these folks what they're missing in their boring kingdom," Desily declares, wrapping her arms around mine and Alea's shoulders, drawing us closer. I offer her a half-genuirre smile. Let the show begin.

We walk down the endless corridors, the sound of our footsteps ringing through the empty halls. I follow behind Desily and Alea, who walk arm in arm, their hands entwined. My own hand slides to the back of my dress, where after a long time pondering about an accessible yet not noticeable place, I've hidden a dagger. This time for protection against everyone, not just Issac.

My cheeks burn at the memory of our last encounter, when days before, our relationship had taken a turn for the better. The feeling of his hand on my leg resurfaces, as if he'd never left. The memory of my fingers curling around the blade, bringing it close to his throat, is strong enough to knock the wind from my lungs, and I gasp, earning a questioning look from Desily.

I brush the memory aside and focus on the large doors at the end of the corridor. I don't know who the princess has invited, or if any of them can be trusted, but for my friends' sake, I'll behave. Perhaps some of these important lords might hold the answers to my questions. Though that doesn't mean I'll drop my guard.

As we reach the end, the guards posted on either side bow and reach for the handles, revealing the massive ballroom. What I've seen at Theo's manor can't compare in the slightest. The ceilings are tall enough to fit a snow giant, crystal chandeliers dangling above us and sparkling. Tables are set in each corner of the cavernous space, overflowing with fresh fruits, cooked meats, and pitchers of wine.

I swallow down the rising anxiety at the sight of so many unfamiliar faces. Every eye is upon us, their curious gazes shooting looks I wish to avoid.

Desily grabs onto my hand, pulling me towards Theo, who unsurprisingly is found standing in the far corner. I know he's afraid to reveal to these people that he can't speak, and to top it off, his name would surely cause a wave of gossip surging through the crowd. After all, his father was famous, more than I give him credit for.

"Where did you lose your plus one?" Alea asks, and Theo rolls his eyes, nodding to the opposite side of the room.

Our heads twist at the same time, searching for the man my heart is constantly bleeding for. Surely enough, I spot him standing in the company of Myra, his eyes focused solely on her and no one else, his hand grasping her shoulder, and that's all it takes for me to stalk towards the wine.

The image of Myra's dress has my hands shaking as I reach for the pitcher. Her corset is metallic, etched with vines that wrap around her torso. The neckline dips low into a sweetheart shape before sliding off her shoulders and everyone's looking at her. She appears ready for battle but somehow elegant at the same time. Sheer sleeves bell out from her arms, silver embroidery catching the light, whilst sparkles fall from her shoulders.

I look again even though I shouldn't. Her leggings look like they were made out of reptile skin, fitted tight, the colour shifting between deep blue and black when she moves. A belt with a red gem sits at her waist, connecting the corset to the trousers. I swallow hard and look up. She's already watching me. Her brow lifts, that mocking smile on her lips before she turns away.

With the first sip of the bitter wine, I can't help but wonder how Issac perceives her.

Is she pretty in his eyes? Has he missed her, waited impatiently for an opportunity to steal her away under the cover of this ridiculous event? The crimson liquid hits the bottom of my empty stomach, and I grimace, but waste no time refilling my glass.

I'd thought I could move past this, let Issac live his life. But gods, it's so damned difficult. Every inch of my body aches with a pain that's neither physical nor emotional. It just exists. Perhaps letting go of someone you love is harder than anyone admits, because it's when nightmares become reality that you truly understand what you're losing.

"Thea, you've made it!" Ella rushes to us with a bright smile, her navy blue gown shimmering with silver detailing at the heart-shaped neckline. Armoured shoulder pieces extend outward like pointed edges of a blade, connecting to billowing white sleeves that contrast with dark gauntlets at her wrists. A belt cinches her waist, the layered skirt parting at the front to reveal practical boots. She's dressed for battle as much as celebration—a reminder that she stands ready to protect her people, even in a land frozen in perpetual peace.

"Hello, Ella. Thank you for the invitation," I murmur, bowing with a smile I hope looks genuine. I try to ignore all the eyes on us, knowing full well this is exactly the attention I can't afford. Strangers wondering why the princess would approach me could spell disaster.

If whispers spread, news will reach Aagon fast, putting every soul in Yalan at risk. All because of me.

"But of course!" Ella reaches for my hands, leaning closer so her words remain our secret. "There's someone I'd like you to meet. An old witch from the Eastern reaches of Sebraycia. She rarely attends my gatherings, despite my persistent invitations. Yet today, she's here."

I stare at her, confused. The Eastern territories are brutal. Endless snow and merciless ice. Those who dared go there usually met one of two fates: death by cold or destruction by whatever monsters lurked in the shadows.

"Why?" I whisper, scanning the ballroom to ensure no wandering ears might catch our conversation.

"Apparently, because of you."

The colour drains from my face. This witch could be anyone. An enemy, an ally, a spy sent by Aagon, or maybe the key to answering my questions. If I meet her, I'll need to be careful. Using my magic in these wooden walls would reduce everyone to ash.

"She wishes to meet you after the opening ceremony," Ella continues, "in the third room east of the ballroom."

"Understood," I manage, swallowing hard to maintain my composure.

"Good luck, Thea." She offers a gentle squeeze of my hand before rushing off to greet her other guests, leaving me suspended in a state of tumultuous uncertainty.

Should I tell anyone? Does she expect me alone? If I go by myself, will my friends be furious that I've kept secrets again? Would Issac be angry?

The questions dissolve when Theo nudges my ribs, pointing towards the princess. I understand his frustration. In the manor, he was the strategist, the one who knew everything. Now he's left with nothing but unanswered questions.

I know that feeling. As much as I sympathise, he can't learn the truth. None of them can.

"Just catching up on our research," I lie, forcing a smile. I reach for my wine glass. "Let's have some fun."

The next hour drags. I watch, barely hiding my irritation, as Myra follows Issac everywhere. She greets guests with him, throwing me looks of victory as if our battle is over and I've lost.

Meanwhile, Alea and Desily seem to be enjoying themselves. They drift between tables, trying food and talking to people who could be dangerous. Part of me envies them, their ability to find joy despite everything. Ryo's the same. I watch him finally get a dance with a stunning, brunette girl after being rejected several times.

I retreat to a corner, losing count of the wine glasses I've emptied. Sixth or eighth, it hardly matters. My eyes track Ella's movements, desperate for the ceremony to begin and release me from the mounting uncertainty churning in my stomach.

Just as she's about to disappear behind a pillar, a figure materialises before me, blocking my view.

My brows furrow in confusion. I'm prepared to dismiss this intrusion, but before I can speak, the stranger bows.

Long strands of brown, curly hair fall softly with the movement.

"Forgive me, my lady," he says, rising. "I couldn't resist introducing myself. Duke Eric Reyfaren."

When he meets my gaze, his hazel eyes catch my attention. They remind me of wandering through a forest on a late summer afternoon. Warm, layered. His coat is black and shimmers like it's dusted with gold. A white shirt clings to his frame, an onyx cravat at his throat.

He smiles, waiting for a response, but I can't find words. Instead, I study his features. Sharp jaw, trimmed beard, high cheekbones. I wonder if he's mistaken me for someone else. Men like him don't usually approach people like me.

My gaze drifts to his ears, and I notice something off. Unlike Alea's or Theo's perfectly formed elven ears, his look unfinished, like their growth stopped too soon. An elf, but not quite, something in between.

"Ah, this?" He gestures towards his ears, and I feel the heat rising in my cheeks, caught in my unabashed scrutiny. "I'm half human, from my father's side."

My eyes widen. It's impolite, I know, but I can't help it. An elf choosing to love a human? It's unheard of, goes against every barrier that's separated our races. In all my years, I've never heard of an elf seeing humans as anything more than servants.

Yet here stands Eric. His existence proves the impossible, a love that broke through boundaries, two souls who challenged everything. He's proof that the most unexpected connections can happen, that love knows no limits.

What society calls impossible is often just a lack of imagination.

Eric purses his lips, glancing away clearly uncomfortable with my silence. I recover quickly, forcing a bright smile. "Apologies. Althea Starbane." I bow.

He chuckles. "No need to be sorry. I've heard I have that effect on people."

There's a playful cockiness in his tone, and I smirk. So he's decided to play that game? Fine. "What effect might that be?"

"Rendering them speechless, of course," he says with a smile that could've been carved from moonlight.

I pretend to look wounded. "I was merely surprised."

His eyebrow arches. "Hmm, was it my stunning looks or the strange shape of my ears?"

"Neither," I counter, wine glass light in my hand. "I was shocked someone dared approach me."

Eric touches his lips, eyes lifting. "And why would someone be afraid of approaching a beautiful lady like yourself?"

"That's a question you might get answered if you're ready to sacrifice your life," I joke. But the words hit my chest hard. Meeting new people is refreshing, nice even, but each one adds weight. Another name to the crushing pile I carry.

Eric laughs, drawing my attention back. "Well, that is quite intriguing. But first, I might need more information about who I'm throwing my life away for. You know, looks aren't everything."

What began as an irritating encounter transforms unexpectedly. I find myself drawn into Eric's stories. His Southern family lands, two younger sisters who adore him and drag him to tea parties.

He's unlike anyone I've met. Like an open book. No secrets,

no games. Just truth. Something I've desperately wanted from the men in my life.

"So tell me, Althea," he asks, "just who are you?"

Who am I?

A human girl who fled her home. Someone harbouring an immortality that could obliterate our world. A woman who fell for the wrong man, yet whose heart refuses to stop racing when their bodies collide. A mourner of those killed whilst protecting her, without understanding they died because of her. A nobody transformed into somebody in the briefest of moments.

Eric awaits my answer, but with each passing second, I find myself at a loss for words. My mouth opens and closes, devoid of a coherent response. Do I possess anything genuinely good to say about myself? Something that truly defines me beyond being a weapon or a monster unleashed?

"I—"

"I don't think that's any of your business."

The all-too-familiar voice slices through our conversation. Issac stands before us, his lips curled into a disgusted grimace, eyes boring into Eric with such intensity that I momentarily fear a confrontation might erupt.

Memories of Issac's previous violent encounters, particularly his heated exchanges with Lathai at the manor, flood my mind. I desperately search for a way to defuse this brewing tension, especially given Eric's unexpected kindness and Issac's persistent antagonism.

He doesn't get to do this. Not after repeatedly rejecting my attempts to help him reconcile with himself. Not when I know a part of him yearns to break free, yet he stubbornly refuses. Certainly not when that bitch continues to trail after him, and he does nothing to discourage her.

Eric's posture shifts, his chin lifting, nose slightly twitching as he assesses Issac with a calculated gaze. "And who might you be?" he asks, a hint of mockery in his voice. "Her father?"

Issac releases a chilling chuckle, something sinister flickering behind his furious eyes. "Might as well be," he retorts.

My eyes bulge, mouth hanging open in disbelief. Did I truly hear what I think I heard? Have I consumed too much wine, or is Issac genuinely displaying not just protectiveness, but something far more complicated? Jealousy?

Eric's jaw flexes, his biceps tensing. I can physically feel the energy around us shift. They're about to fight, and more bewilderingly, they're preparing to fight over me.

"I don't know who you think you are," Eric challenges, "but clearly she's enjoying my company. So how about you get lost?"

I recognise the moment Issac's cold mask begins to slip. His fake smile is a harbinger of impending chaos. Every muscle in my body freezes as he takes a step towards Eric, that calculated smile holding until he lowers himself, towering over the other man. Only then do I see the raw emotion drain from his face.

"We've already established who I am to her," he says, his voice a dangerous whisper. "Perhaps it is you who should get lost? After all, it is not your name she's calling, but mi—"

"Enough!" My hand flies to Issac's mouth, heat rushing to my cheeks. What the fuck is he saying?

I mutter a quick apology to Eric before seizing Issac's hand, dragging him away from the watchful eyes of the ballroom. How dare he create such a scene? How dare he interrupt a conversation with a man I had deemed worthy of my time?

Once we're far from the crowd, I shove him behind a wall separating the guests from a set of doors, likely leading to the kitchens. My anger blazes through my eyes. My chest heaves with barely contained fury as I pin him with a potent glare, a litany of curses dancing on the edge of my tongue.

"Have you lost your bloody mind?" I hiss, half-shouting, half-whispering. Unsurprisingly, Issac merely smiles, mischief dancing across his features. "Why would you say those things?" I demand.

"Me?" He points to himself, scoffing. "I'm only telling the truth, or so I assume, given how smitten you are with me. What about you?"

"Excuse me?" The words escape me, too stunned to formulate a proper response.

"You heard me," he spits, the words dripping with venom. "What exactly are you doing talking to that wannabe prince charming?" His tone suggests the mere thought of Eric is something toxic he wishes to expunge.

"It's none of your business!" I jab a finger into his chest. "I trust my judgement, and he's decent. Unlike you."

Issac rolls his eyes. "Trust your judgement, hmm? Where has that taken us before? Oh right, our fucking home burned to ashes." His hands clasp together, and I instinctively retreat a step. His words strike where they were meant to, straight into my heart.

My head shakes in disbelief. He never cared before, and now suddenly he's determined to ward everyone away from me, as if I'm some rare artefact only he can possess. As if I belong to him.

The realisation strikes. I laugh, the sound sharp and incredulous. "This isn't about my judgement. You're jealous, aren't you?"

Issac's smirk vanishes instantly, as though my words have completely dismantled his carefully constructed façade. For a moment, he looks exposed, caught in a truth he desperately wishes to deny. I wait, letting the words hang between us, watching as his lips remain sealed as though he doesn't trust himself to speak.

It seems that somewhere along our journey, Issac began to consider my offer, or perhaps the seeds were planted long ago, and I merely helped push him in the right direction.

Truth be told, I'm uncertain whether I should feel happy or surprised by this discovery. A part of him chose to fight against his own will for me.

"You wish," he finally manages to say, the words hanging between us.

I sigh, disappointment washing over me, a familiar sensation born from countless lies I've heard far too many times. Whether he likes it or not, he has let his carefully constructed mask slip in front of the wrong person, and for once, I hold the advantage.

"Whatever," I retort, my voice cutting through his defences. "Seems you're not trying to convince me, but yourself."

Just as he's about to reply, the sound of music and Ella's voice pulls me from our intimate moment. The opening ceremony has begun and I must leave. Whatever lies between Issac and me will have to wait.

I begin to shuffle away, feet carrying me towards the door. Before I can pass through, his fingers wrap around my wrist, twisting me back to face him.

"Where are you going?"

"None of your business," I snap. "You're not my father,

and you've certainly made it clear you won't be my lover. So go back to that venomous bitch and seek answers from her mouth."

I wrench myself away, my heart racing far too quickly. My skin burns with invisible flames where he touched me, a ghostly reminder of our connection. Perhaps my words were harsh, but I've been wounded too many times by the person I desire most. It's only fair I return the favour.

As I said, I'll deal with Issac later.

Chapter 19

Standing before the door, my heart threatens to rip from my chest. The dagger I've managed to hide burns against my back, its presence both a comfort and a curse. This woman could be anyone. A killer, an aid, a mystery wrapped in shadows. Whatever she wants from me must relate to Jino and Aagon, because who am I without them? Just a name carried on forgotten winds.

With a deep breath, I push the door open, hoping death won't be waiting on the other side.

The smell of herbs hits my nose. Sharp, pungent, overwhelming. Earthy sage mixing with something bitter and ancient. I blink away the sting in my eyes and look around, noticing a woman beside a dancing fire with a small cauldron suspended above the flames. Whatever she's brewing in that black pot is about to turn my stomach inside out.

"So the girl came after all," she says, her voice soft and melodic, spilling into the room.

"Was I not meant to?" I manage, my own voice steadier than I feel.

She chuckles whilst stirring her concoction. "There are always two outcomes out of things, Althea Starbane. How it happens depends on you."

I furrow my brows, scanning the room for any hidden threats. Gods know that I've learnt my lesson by now. Can't afford to trust anybody, especially not the people who sought you out with smiles that don't reach their eyes.

The interior is simple, with red wallpaper faded by time and dark timber furniture adorning the inside. Not many places to hide her—

"There's no need to worry. I came alone." The woman interrupts my thoughts as if reading them from an open book, and I stare, surprised. With each second, this encounter is becoming stranger.

"It's good to stay cautious."

"Cautiousness might drive people into madness, as it has with many before."

The woman lets the ladle fall with a thud, her silhouette rising from the chair. I take a silent step back, hoping my movement didn't offend her. For some strange reason, it feels like I'm being evaluated, as if she has her hands in my head going through my thoughts, only picking the ones she deems interesting enough to keep.

"Let me perhaps introduce myself to ease your mind. I'm Ligaya, pleased to meet you." She bows, her long, black hair cascading down her shoulders and onto the floor between us.

"That's it? No surname?"

"Is my surname what you need to feel safer in my presence?" She peeks from between her hair, and a shiver runs down my spine. I can't tell if she creeps me out or intrigues me.

I follow her movements as she settles on the nearby couch. Her long, black dress drapes behind her. There are no decorations adorning her attire, no expensive fabric or hand-sewn gems. Just a simple satin dress, save for the velvet cape hanging off her shoulders.

My eyes drift to her face. Big, doe eyes stare back at me, brimming with secrets and knowledge I'm so hungry to consume. Her lips curve into a smile, the red lipstick a stark contrast to her bronze skin. I notice how young she appears, yet upon longer inspection the signs of ageing can be spotted. She can't be more than thirty, but Gods, she could fool people into thinking she just entered her twenties.

She blinks once, the long lashes sweeping away the emotions I've seen earlier. She's a blank sheet of paper, and I'm the writer ready to tell my story, though I suspect she already knows the ending.

A few moments pass before I decide to take the seat opposite her, my bottom lip trapped between my teeth as I wonder just who exactly she is, and why would she seek me out of all people?

The woman smiles, her fingers carefully laid on her legs, a gesture meant to show me she means no harm. I've heard that story before, and will not fall for it again.

"So what is it that you want from me?"

"Perhaps to change the course of your life." She ponders, her words hanging in the air. I grimace. If only it was that simple. "Do you believe we're born with our fate or is fate unravelling before us with the choices we make?"

I purse my lips, taking a moment to think. "I believe our choices matter in how our life goes."

"But were these choices already made for you before anyone knew of your existence, or did you will them into life?" I open my mouth, but no words follow. Whatever riddles she's trying to have me solve are straining my brain. I'm afraid my answers matter just as much as the fate she speaks of.

Ligaya tilts her head to the side, watching me carefully as I search for the right answer, if there even is one. Her eyes reflect the firelight.

"I think we're born with purpose, but how we execute it is entirely up to us. Perhaps even the smallest choice will matter at the end of our journey."

The woman smiles, her face revealing nothing beside sheer curiosity. She's trying to work me out, or make me work myself out, as if I'm unaware of the things around me. Perhaps I'm not seeing clearly, not to the extent I wish to be. The world suddenly seems larger.

"Very well. As you might've heard, I don't often attend gatherings as such, but once in a while a vision is bestowed upon me. That's how, after all, I told the princess's mother of the prophecy."

I stare at her, shock spreading through me. This woman before me is not just a nobody from far away corners of Sebraycia. She's the very witch that warned the people of this country of the upcoming danger. What's even more shocking, she's still alive despite her prophecy being centuries old. How is this even possible?

My eyes instinctively peer at her ears, searching for signs but notice nothing out of shape. "Wondering how I look so young but am old? You'd be surprised what the herbs on our planet can do to you." She chuckles, and I swallow, unsure of what to do next. This person before me indeed holds answers to many questions in my life, and if I play her game right, I might glimpse into my future.

"I don't believe it. Just who or what are you?" I shift in my seat uncomfortably. Ligaya appears to be a mere human, yet older than me and Issac combined. She's lived on this land way before any of us existed, before the war broke out, and probably before humans became not just slaves but the rock bottom of our world.

"If I told you I work with the Gods, would you believe me?" She asks, and I scoff. There's no bloody way, but recent events twist my mind, making me want to entertain her. "Doesn't matter, that's not what you're here for."

"Am I here to hear my own prophecy?" I ask and try not to lean backwards, remembering the dagger is still there if things go south. Ligaya smiles, her eyes glinting with mischief.

A feeling of dread re-emerges from deep within me. I'm tired of learning things about my life, things out of my control, but if what she's going to tell me might change my future, might help my miserable life, then I'll sit here for as long as it's needed.

"You're a smart girl, aren't you?" She giggles and claps her hands together. Only then do I catch a glimpse of something. A faint mark of black circling around her wrist, or perhaps a chain worn so long it became part of her. It awakens something in me, a feeling of worry or perhaps curiosity, but as they say, curiosity killed the cat, so I sit still, trying hard not to let my tongue loose and ask the wrong questions.

The woman suddenly gets up from her seat and stalks towards the cauldron where her mysterious brew is now coming to a boil. She pours two cups and sets one before me and one before her.

"Couple decades back I woke up from a terrible dream.

Dream where our world stood in flames, where bodies piled on top of each other, where magic ceased to exist." She begins, and I listen attentively, eyeing the cup with cautiousness.

"I'm aware of the prophecy about Jinoro and Aagon."

"The dream wasn't about them." She stops me, her voice sharp, before taking a sip of her brew.

I sigh and grab the cup, hoping it won't kill me anytime soon. If she wants me to trust her so badly I'll do it, as long as she pays with information. I sip the liquid, the faint taste of chamomile, lemon balm, valerian and something I can't quite name drowning my taste buds. "Then about who?"

"You, of course." She answers without emotion. "You who stood in the middle of it all with blood tainting your hands, with no one by your side."

The colour must've drained out of my face, my body frozen from her words. I'm not sure how but I feel like I'm falling despite sitting. Like the paths I've recently chosen were for nothing upon hearing her words.

I meet her gaze slowly, my heart thudding inside my chest. "What?"

"Does the vision of our world ending scare you, Althea?" I stare at her with my mouth agape, unsure if she's having a laugh or being deadly serious.

"Does it not scare you?" I manage to counter.

"I've lived through many things. I might even live through a time where a girl possessing both an evil sorceress and fire magic comes to end our world." She shrugs her shoulders, and I furrow my brows.

"I can control my magic," I snap back, heat rising to my cheeks.

"I never said you couldn't, but I think it's rather your magic controlling you, won't you agree?" She takes another sip of her brew, eyes watching me over the rim of her cup. I bite my cheek until I taste copper, thinking of the times where my fire moved on its own as if it were an extension of my emotions. "Doesn't matter, after all you're still afraid of it, still won't come to terms that it's a part of who you are."

"I'm not afraid of it," I insist.

"Yet you see yourself as a monster each time you wield the flames. The villain of the story, the creator of destruction, and that might be why your fate is moving towards that course. Perhaps the choices you've been making aren't entirely good, perhaps they are. Who knows?"

"Enough, tell me what you know." My voice comes out shaky despite the demanding tone. Her words strike true, and every part of my body hates it, even the bloody magic she assumes I loathe. I can feel it now, simmering beneath my skin, responding to my anger.

Ligaya sighs, her eyes tracing the corners of the room as if she's painting a picture of her vision in the air between us.

"Although at first I thought of it as nothing more than a dream, that changed once the visions came with relentless clarity," she says, her voice dropping to a hollow whisper. "Each night I'd witness the same terrible scene: two people lying on the floor, blood pooling around them. And then there was you, standing between them in tears, shouting until your throat was raw, praying to gods who wouldn't answer, begging for mercy that wouldn't come."

She pauses.

"No matter what you did, it had no effect. Their lives slipped away, and ultimately the vision always ends the same way. With darkness consuming you from within, with your fate straying towards evil, rather than good. I watched as something inside you shattered, and what emerged from those broken pieces was something unrecognisable."

My hands shake as I set the cup down, the porcelain rattling against the wood. Words rise in my throat but die on my tongue. Just who is she talking about? Who could be in danger and why do I become the very thing I'm trying to avoid being?

"W-Who was it?" I finally manage to ask.

Ligaya shrugs, her eyes drifting to the ceiling. "I can't see their faces, but I do know they mean a lot to you. It seems someday in the future something awful might happen to the ones you hold dear, and that might be all it takes for you to stop caring about this world."

"That's impossible. My friends could never—I would never—"

"I'm not accusing you of the things you're yet to commit, Althea," she says, her voice softening. "I'm merely informing you of the future that might come, that is if you're not going to change it."

My mind races with the possibilities. Could it be Issac? Desily? Alea or Theo? Maybe Ryo who grew on me in the past weeks, or perhaps our other comrades? Who should I protect, and how do I begin to do that when danger is nothing but a shadow without form?

"Tell me how, just tell me what to do and I'll do it." I lean forwards, my hands grabbing onto the table for support. The fire crackles louder to my right, flames roaring with uncertainty.

The woman smiles, her hand reaching for mine across the

table. Only then do I notice the mark of a wielder. Black ink swirling to create something oddly close to an eye, dotting her skin with multiple of those all the way up to her shoulder where it disappears beneath the cape. She isn't lying. The vision she saw was true.

"You're a wielder."

"I'm many things, an aid to humankind among them, hence why I sit here telling you things that might very well threaten my existence were they not to be executed correctly." She smiles and squeezes my hand. "I can't tell you how to avoid what's coming, as I implied you're the writer of your own story, so grasp it and change it, Thea." Her voice carries weight. "All I can tell you is that whatever path unfolds before you, the key seems to be the survival of the ones you love."

She pauses, her eyes searching mine.

"After all, the people around you bring you hope, and once that's gone, well then darkness will swallow you whole."

I stare into her eyes, searching their depths, hoping for something more. For a way to see what she saw and protect the ones who need it. How am I meant to keep my friends from dying? Keep myself away from turning into the very monster I've spent the past year fighting against?

My teeth trap my bottom lip, and I wonder how have I not chewed it off yet? Just what is going to happen in the next few days, months or years? Just who am I going to have to mourn all over again? No, I won't let it come true. I'll do everything in my power to make sure none of them get hurt. That none of them have to shed tears once more all because of me.

The cost doesn't matter any more, not my blood, not my

soul, not my life. I'll fight against my fate even if it means I'll have to rip through the paths already built. If I have to, I'll burn it all down, and from the remains, I'll write my own damn story. The future isn't carved in stone, but in choices, and this choice is mine to make.

"Our future rests on your shoulders, Althea, and I believe you can rewrite it. One way or another, I know there's good and purity in your heart no matter what you believe." Ligaya smiles. She rises from her seat, the dark fabric of her dress flowing around her. "Do feel welcome to finish your tea; it'll help to ease your feelings."

"You're leaving?" I ask, worry etched into my face.

"I did what I was asked of. There's nothing more left to say."

"But I have so many questions. How are you a wielder? How are you alive? Just what is the right thing to do?" I blurt out the questions all at once, hoping at least one might hold her here a moment longer.

Ligaya chuckles before reaching for the handle. "I don't know what's right to do per se, I do know however that the hardest choices in your life are often the ones that turn out to be the best." Her eyes meet mine one last time. "Remember that, Althea. When the time comes, don't let the darkness consume you, light it up."

With that, she exits, the door closing behind her with a soft click. She leaves me alone with my spiralling thoughts and dozens of unanswered questions hanging in the air around me.

I need to make sure everyone lives to see another day, however possible. Their faces flash through my mind. Each smile, each shared moment suddenly precious. I'll change the course of my future, even if the only way to do it is by sacrificing myself to the darkness. My life for theirs. A price I'd pay without hesitation.

I won't become a monster, the very thing I've avoided becoming. I won't lose anybody else. I'll make sure of it. This promise to myself etched in blood and bone. Death won't be the winner of this battle this time.

Chapter 20

I'm not sure how much time passes before I peel my eyes from the door where Ligaya stood. I've been sitting here contemplating ways I might alter my future, pondering the darkness the woman warned me against and wondering what on Eatera am I meant to do?

Who precisely am I meant to safeguard? A person I already know? Someone yet to cross my path? The questions accumulate, stacked impossibly high, until I can reach no higher.

I sigh and lean back, my mind a labyrinth of uncertainty, my future a looming shadow. What was meant to be a meeting that could help me defeat Aagon has transformed into a desperate search for the right path. A way of preventing myself from becoming the very monster I fear.

"What did the woman say?" Jino's voice startles me, and I jump, clutching my chest. She's been unnervingly quiet throughout the entire meeting, though I didn't expect her to participate. She simply doesn't care.

"Didn't you hear?"

"If I had heard, I wouldn't be asking." She snaps back and I furrow my brows. I'm certain I didn't block the connection; there was no reason to. So how is it she didn't hear a word

exchanged between us?

My gaze falls upon the vacant teacup, and comprehension washes over me. The tea was meant to hide the revelation from her. She purposely blocked her out, but why? Somehow Ligaya knew Jino could hear everything going on around me and that must've meant she knew I communicated with her. How? Just who exactly is this woman and what other secrets does she hide?

Before more thoughts cascade through my mind, I restrict my connection with Jino, preserving it solely for dialogue rather than permitting her to sift through my innermost contemplations.

"She's warned me against my future," I say, choosing my words carefully. If Jino discovers I'm going to become exactly who she wants me to be, or worse, succumb to her influence, I'm certain she'll throw a celebratory revelry inside my mind.

"Your future? Who is she to know anything about it?" Jino scoffs, her spectral robes swirling around as if a gust of wind had passed through my consciousness. Though her voice sounds steady, an ounce of uncertainty can be noted in her question almost as if she knows something.

I bite the inside of my cheek, staring at the door where the woman stood. Is telling Jino a poor choice, or did Ligaya give me the option of revealing it myself and having the upper hand? Gods, why must everything be communicated through games and riddles?

For a moment, I wonder if perhaps Jino might offer a solution. If she knows of a way to prevent my future from becoming a horrific disaster. But that thought alone nearly makes me laugh.

"Do tell me, girl, what is so amusing?" The edge in her voice

cuts through my thoughts.

"Have you ever tried changing the course of your life?" I blurt out and await her mocking laughter, but surprisingly, nothing follows. Jino remains silent, as if my question interests her more than she's willing to admit.

"Perhaps," she finally murmurs. *"Is that what she told you? That your life might not be proceeding the way you desire?"*

I rub my tired eyes, the irony of the situation making me want to weep. What am I doing discussing the future with the very entity who might bring about my downfall?

"More or less," I chuckle bitterly. Perhaps I'll descend into madness before any of those calamities materialise. Crushed beneath the weight of problems I'm already struggling to resolve. "Anyway, if you know a method by which I might prevent a disaster from unfolding, do enlighten me."

Yet again, I'm met with silence which both intrigues and worries me. The heavy pause stretches between us. Clearly, the woman knows something, perhaps a bit of information that might help, but she's keeping it to herself. Her presence lingers in my mind, inscrutable and unyielding. As per usual, I'm not surpris—

"I'll offer my aid, Althea, but at a cost. I'm sure whatever she said has your mind racing with possibilities since you've blocked me out, but mark my words. When the time comes, I'm sure you'll seek me out." I flinch at her words, their meaning painfully clear.

It's what must've happened to Lathai, a deal made with Aagon in exchange for his family's safety. His haunted eyes make sense now. He was cornered and left without a choice, but that won't happen to me. I have time and resources, advantages he never possessed. What's more important. My mind hasn't gone mad yet.

I've thought about this since Ligaya departed. Issac is immortal; that's one person I don't need to worry about, but the rest of our group might be in danger. What if I'm also wrong about him? What if me thinking he's untouchable is the very reason I let my guard down and let the vision come true? Gods, if I can find a way to somehow keep them away from harm, then everything will be okay. I'll be okay.

But what if my plan doesn't work? The thought circles back, and I get up from the worn leather sofa, pacing around the room with Jino now gone, my mind in shambles.

Am I really willing to sacrifice everyone for the lives of my friends? A deal with Jino that'd somehow keep them all alive and protected? Am I truly ready to sacrifice my soul for the sake of people who deserve happiness?

No, I won't let these thoughts consume me, over my dead body. Gods know what'd have to happen before I decide to make any deal with her. If anything, she's my last resort, and before that, I have time to do research, to find a way to keep everyone safe. I'll work harder, longer, with better focus. I won't disappoint them, I won't lose it—

The creaking of the door stops me in my tracks. My head turns quickly. I half expect Ligaya to walk in with a smile on her face and tell me it was all just a big joke, that she didn't mean to rip away whatever hope and peace had settled in my heart, but it's not her I see standing in the doorway.

"Why are you here?" The door shuts with a click, and I cross my arms over my chest. I stare at the man who has me thinking of things that shouldn't happen. A man that has me contemplating the unthinkable. Giving myself away to Jinoro just to ensure his safety.

"You've been gone a while, and in case you've forgotten I'm meant to keep an eye on you." He rolls his eyes before taking a step forward.

I study his face in the dim light, the irritated expression etched deeply across his features. I wonder with a sudden, sharp ache if I might lose him today, tomorrow or in a month. I wonder if I'll regret ever turning away from who he became, if I'll be angry at myself for breaking the solemn promise of never leaving his side.

My heart squeezes painfully in my chest, and I turn away, walking towards the fireplace where my eyes settle on the dancing flames. The fire crackles and hisses, casting flickering shadows that dance across the walls.

"If you've confirmed I'm not a danger to anybody, leave." I take a shaky breath in, my hands unsteady as I fight the panic wrapping around my throat.

Will Issac ever hate me for who I become? Will he be mad I didn't fight hard enough to bring him back, instead I let him make his own choices? Will I be mad at myself for wasting the precious time we have left?

I hear him shuffle behind me, the sound of his footsteps nearing, and the fear in my throat tightens until each breath becomes a struggle. I can't bear to face him right now. In truth, I can't face anybody and especially Issac.

"I'd gladly do that." Yet he doesn't; instead I feel the proximity between us close with the way my skin grows hotter.

"Then do it, I've had enough of you for tonight." The words taste like poison on my tongue, because there'll never be a time I've had enough of him. Every second of the day spent in his presence is a blessing, and I scorn myself for trying to put distance between us.

“Really? Are you expecting someone else?” He spits the words out like they burn, and I turn ever so slightly to look at him.

“And if I am, then what? Do you care?” Slowly, I let my body twist so that I can fully face him. Issac is stood behind me, his tall frame casting a long shadow across the floor. One step and I’ll be able to get lost in his scent, feel the heat of his body despite the coldness growing at the tips of my fingers.

“I don’t,” he counters, the words clipped and sharp, and I scoff, moving away.

How am I meant to cherish these moments when he makes everything so damn hard? How am I meant to save him when he doesn’t want to save himself?

I run my hand over my face and try to swallow all the worries down but my throat constricts and I fight to grasp a bit of oxygen. “Is it that joke of a duke you’re waiting for?” He scoffs, disgust dripping from every syllable. “Disappointed he’s not the one standing in my place?”

“You’re impossible!” I run at him, shoving him with all my strength which only makes him sway a bit to the side. “You want to stay away from me, but always find a way to come back. You don’t care about me, but are always first to jump in whenever I talk with someone other than you. Tell me Issac, which is it? You don’t care or you do, because I’m getting confused over here.”

I take a shaky breath in, the air not filling my lungs to the brim. Everything in my life is a disaster, even my own body failing to cooperate when I need it to. My hands grasp onto Issac’s coat, my vision blurry with unshed tears, and before I can stop myself I decide to look at his face.

He stares at me with a puzzled expression, one I've rarely seen grace his usually guarded features. Something caught between regret and denial. His eyes bounce around my face, searching for answers, as I stay silent, my lip quivering despite my desperate attempts at keeping it still.

"What's wrong? Did someone do something to you?" I jump when his hand travels to my shoulders, squeezing them gently.

"What?" I ask, voice barely audible, just as his finger swipes over my cheek, his expression growing serious.

"Thea," he asks with a demanding tone. "Why are you crying?"

Just then my senses kick in, and I blink away the tears gathered in my eyes, letting them fall down my cheeks unchecked, but not before Issac captures them with his finger. My body shakes and I try to say something but no words come out, no thoughts follow. I'm hollow and lost.

I blink at him, looking for an answer, but it's almost as if the connections in my head have been crossed and are unable to work properly. My fingers squeeze his jacket tighter, tears falling harder now. The next thing I know, Issac's arms wrap around my shoulders, drawing me into his chest, embracing me in a hug I never expected from him.

It takes exactly twenty seconds for my brain to process the fact that another human is holding me in their arms, ultimately telling me I'm not alone. It takes another five before I break into sobs, letting my head fall into the crook of his neck just as he wraps his arms around me tighter, in a more protective manner which has my heart beating ten times faster from joy despite the state I'm in.

His hand swipes over my head with unexpected tenderness. Somewhere along the way my carefully put hairstyle had fallen out of its construction, strands of my hair now cascading freely against my back. Issac's fingers tangle between the silken waves, his chin resting on top of my head. I breathe in his scent, listen to the steady rhythm of his heartbeat against my ear, and for a second let myself believe this is the Issac I've lost, the one I'm searching for. Perhaps this is the hope I need at this very moment. The reassurance that the man I love is here, right where I need him, not entirely gone but hidden beneath layers I have yet to peel away.

This is a reminder I needed that the sacrifices I'm willing to make aren't for nothing.

Chapter 21

ISSAC

I ask myself for the tenth time how exactly did I end up in this situation? What made me leave the banquet and search room after room, my heart hammering against my ribs as I silently prayed nothing happened to her? Was it because of our fight, bitter words still lingering on my tongue, or because of that idiot guy she kept smiling at?

Perhaps it was Myra who wouldn't leave my side despite telling her repeatedly I don't want to speak or look at her. Yet she still lingered, following me around. No matter who I had to greet to keep up the façade, she'd show up right beside me and insert herself into our conversations. I was ready to leave this bothersome party if not for the sight of Thea speaking to that man.

The way she looked at him with curiosity in her eyes; the way her shoulders relaxed beneath her far too tempting gown; and her lips stretched into a smile I've never seen her make at me. It struck something I thought was long severed, and before I could think, my feet took me in their direction. Though my body had its reasons to tell him politely to piss off, my mouth had known no restraints, and once again I fucked everything up. Each selfish attempt at winning her over shoves us further apart instead of closer, all because out of instinct I have to prove to myself I don't care about her. That she doesn't make my days feel half as shit as they should.

After her sudden departure, I wasted no time questioning Theo who only shrugged and returned to a conversation with some higher-up people. My next stop was Desily and Alea, but the two of them disappeared shortly after the princess announced the party had started. That left Ryo, but Gods help me the boy was in no state to talk. Surrounded by women, on his third glass of wine, I think a mule would've told me more than him.

I waited a good while before my feet dragged me out of the room and somewhere deep within the manor. Usually, there's a sense of her lingering around, but when that connection disappeared, my rational thinking scarpered out of the window. The cold corridors stretched endlessly before me. Surely enough, after opening my fifth set of doors, I found her sitting there, in an empty room with a look on her face that expressed... nothing. It was almost as if she wasn't there, as if her body was a mere vessel.

Her body trembles underneath my touch, and I squeeze her closer. I'm not sure what drove me to this reaction, but the way she looked at me, helpless and resigned almost as if hoping a part of me wouldn't leave her. There was absolutely no way I'd just leave. I wouldn't let my messed-up head tell me at this very moment that what she needed was punishment rather than aid. Over my dead body.

I let her cry for as long as she needs, time slipping away as for the first time ever we're far too close, far too intimate, something I've only wished for in the quiet corners of sleepless nights. Her tears seep through to my skin, each sob a confession without words. I wonder for a moment if something happened to her, if she'll ever tell me, but suddenly she breaks away, taking her warmth with her and leaving a gap between us that my hands, still warm from holding her, can't bridge.

"Will you tell me what's wrong?" I ask as she moves further away, wiping the last stray tears finding their way down her flushed cheeks. She doesn't meet my eyes when she answers.

"It doesn't matter. It won't change anything, you can just go."

I clench my fists, her rejection stinging more than it should. "Don't do this."

"Don't do what?" She raises her head, anger flashing in her eyes where sadness pooled only a moment ago.

I take a step forward, praying she won't move away, and she doesn't, her feet firmly rooted to the floor. "Don't push me away."

"Me? Pushing you away? You must be joking, Issac." She throws her hands in the air and I purse my lips. "It's fine when you do it but when I do it you don't like it?"

"It's different."

"How?! Enlighten me please because as I said this is all tiring, fighting with and against you is one battle I can't win no matter how hard I try."

I sigh deeply and look past her. "You know well I can't be what you want me to be. I can't be the man you're searching for in me. I'm not him."

"I know and it bloody hurts!" Her scream shatters the stillness between us, sending a shiver down my spine. I hate how she hopes to awaken the person in me I only glimpse in fragments of our memories. I hate how she doesn't want to fight for this version of me, how easily she just gave up, and how the bitter truth that I'm not good enough lingers between us.

I hate how I drove her to this state. My countless taunting words, snappy comments and questions left hanging in the air. Perhaps if only I'd known sooner how much I'd grown to yearn for her presence, perhaps if only she knew how I wage war against myself daily to be better for her, to shape myself into the person she desperately searches for in my eyes.

"Well then tell me, tell me exactly what it is that you want me to do. Who do you want me to bloody be, Thea, because I'm trying and you don't care." My voice breaks on the last word, revealing the raw longing I try so hard to conceal.

"Trying?" She scoffs. "If you were trying, the two of us wouldn't feel like strangers rather than partners."

My heart aches at her words, a hollow pain spreading through my chest. I cut the distance between us in two determined strides, my body drawn to hers. She attempts to move away, her back colliding with the wall behind her, and I stop just before I can make her feel threatened. Like I'd ever do anything to her besides offer protection, besides wanting to hold her in my arms until they fall away from my body altogether.

"You're insufferable. Gods, sometimes I truly hate how stubborn and unwilling to listen you truly are. How you've built a wall between yourself and the whole world, too afraid of what's to come as if you can see the future, as if you know the outcome of all things."

"I do." She bites back, her chest rising with each heated breath. "I do because I've seen it happen before and Gods help me if I let myself feel that pain again. The pain of losing all these people, our home and you."

"You've never lost me!" I raise my voice, running my hand through the loose strands of my hair. She blinks at me, too stunned to answer, too stubborn to acknowledge my revelation. "For God's sake, Thea, why won't you ever cooperate? You're driving me mad!"

She lifts her chin up, her brows furrowed in anger though her eyes betray what her words never would. Emotions swirling beneath that carefully maintained façade. The restraint of what she truly wants to say, the denial that I'm right about her, that she despises the truth.

"You have yourself to thank for Issac, for making me like this." She snaps back at me and my heart cracks just a bit at her words knowing damn well how true they are. "You can't stand me, I get that." She shrugs her shoulders, her mind visibly searching for escape routes from this conversation before it transforms into something she can't retreat from. "I've heard it before, Issac, so why don't we just move on?"

I place my palm against the wall beside her head, my wrist brushing against her hair. "Hate?" The word tastes bitter on my lips, a sentiment I once embraced but have come to reject in the past few weeks we've spent in each other's presence. In those moments where fragments of memories returned, shared times together that sparked a longing in me so profound it bordered on physical pain. "Ask me to name all the things I can't stand about you, I'll name you a hundred."

She scoffs, her head shaking in disbelief. "I know, you've

told me bef—"

I bring myself closer to her face, the words dying on her lips. Her breath ghosts against mine, warm and sweet, her eyes growing wider at the vanishing distance between us, pupils dilating with something beyond fear. "And then ask me to name all the things that drive me mad and the living won't know peace. I'll tell them how your eyes put me in a trance, making it impossible to look away. How your touch ignites the coldest corners of my heart. How you're underneath my skin, your soul latching onto mine, and I can't escape no matter what I do, no matter how desperately I once tried. No matter how much hatred is embedded into my heart, you've got me under your spell, a captivity I no longer wish to break free from. You're the only person that grounds me, shines light into the darkness and guides me through it. You're my curse and my destiny, Thea."

Silence settles between us as I await her answer. Will she reject me? Will she understand that I'm no longer the same person she saw on the ship? Will she finally believe me when I say I want her? Her heart might be guarded by walls far too tall and far too strong, but there are no lengths I won't go for her, no barriers I'm not willing to break just to have her back. I know that now with unwavering certainty.

She blinks at me, her mouth opening then closing, as if searching for the right response, but is there even one? Perhaps I'm too late, perhaps the damage is far too great, but I'd be a fool to surrender now of all times.

"If it's too much to handle, I'll go—"

Her hands wrap around my neck, and without warning she brings me towards her, colliding our lips in a kiss that shatters my world. Everything around me erupts into colour as the feeling of her soft skin burns against mine, as her scent fills my lungs. I get lost in Althea as if she's the earth beneath my feet, as if there is nothing else and never was.

Chapter 22

My hand encircles her waist, drawing us closer, yet never close enough. I need her to be a part of me, as if we're one being, as if we came into this world tethered together. She lets out a soft moan when my fingers trace along her spine, and I lose what little restraint I have left.

I grasp her thighs and lift her up, letting her back rest against the wall, her weight in my hands precious. A quick glance reminds me of the dress she decided to wear tonight, and the fire inside me ignites anew. Her bare legs make me wish I could trail kisses up their length, mark her in places everyone can see and let them know she belongs to me, as it seems she always has.

I lower myself down and begin leaving a chain of kisses down her neck, before I reach the crook where I bite down, sucking on her skin in the most torturous way, making her squirm beneath my touch.

"W-Wait a minute!" She breathes out, and I look up at her, her expression awash with desire as she reaches behind her, pulling out a small dagger that she tosses behind us onto the floor with a metallic clatter.

"Bringing a weapon to the banquet?" I raise a brow, and

she smirks. "Was it for me?"

"Maybe." She chuckles, her laugh vibrating beneath my fingertips in a way that makes me forget what exactly I intended to do.

"Don't worry, perhaps you'll still have some use for it." I go back to kissing her chest, lowering my head to the valley between her breasts.

She arches her back towards me and I smirk against her skin. "For you?"

"For whoever you want, darling. If you wish for me to be dead, I'll let it happen. Your enemies are my enemies, and I'll make sure they end up exactly how you want them."

"Even if I want them naked?" She whispers, and I stop moving, slowly raising my head to meet her eyes.

"Fuck sake, Thea, what are you doing to me?" She squeals as I move us onto the couch, where I gently lay her down, without breaking our kiss. Gods help me if I did. I've denied myself the pleasure of having Althea for far too long, and I don't know how I could ever stop now that I've started.

Her small hands wander across my chest, driving me to the point where I'm ready to tear her clothes off and forget about the history between us, but that very reminder is why I decide today isn't about me. It's about her. I want her to know I'm not here for a quick, desperate fuck, but to show her that I'm fully devoted to her and she can fully rely on this newer version of myself.

Thea's leg brushes against my inner thigh as I push my tongue inside her mouth, her lips yielding without protest. She tastes sweet, comforting, far too divine for someone as broken as me, but I can't afford any regrets when the woman I've forced away has finally cracked a part of her fortress and let me inside. With a swift move, I take her wrists, pinning them above her head, my mouth leaving hers to trace a path of kisses along her jaw, across her cheekbones adorned with freckles, and the delicate curve of her button nose.

She blinks at me, so much love and longing shimmering in her eyes that I waste no time bringing my lips to her neck to leave yet another mark.

"Issac—"

"Don't," I warn in a low growl. "Don't say anything or my composure around you might just crumble to dust."

She sighs, and I gaze up at her. Pleasure twists into her expression as she battles the urge to take this step further.

"Why?" She asks in protest, and I move away from her neck towards her chest, my fingers working to undo the tricky lacing and far too many buttons. How the bloody hell does she breathe in this contraption?

"Because if you so much as beg for me, I'll lose all control, Thea, and I don't want to. I can't. For you, I can't." I catch her eyes, thoughts racing behind them as she weighs her options. I silently pray this once she'll heed my instructions, and when she does, I let out a ragged breath.

"You're such a tease," she murmurs, before sucking in her breath as I finally allow myself to kiss her exposed stomach, her skin silk beneath my lips.

"You've got no idea." In a swift move, I wiggle her out of the dress and toss it somewhere to the side. My eyes devour the black lingerie she's decided to wear today, and every rational thought is consumed by desire too powerful to tame. It's as if I've got a wild beast caged within me, something impossible to restrain no matter how desperately I try.

I get up for a moment, making her groan in displeasure

which brings a smirk to my lips. Without wasting any more of this precious time, I take off my coat, leaving only the crumpled white shirt that still makes me feel far too feverish. My hands wrap around her calves, her eyes tracking me, and I wonder how I could have ever harboured hatred for her.

She's a masterpiece. Despite the scars gracing her body which many might find confronting, I find them beautiful. A story of who she is, of how hard and fiercely she fought to be where she is today. With or without them, she's utterly mesmerising.

Slowly, I raise her leg and begin to kiss her exposed skin, her body trembling under my touch as if my lips brand her.

Something in the recesses of my mind whispers that we've been here before. A memory struggling to surface, but I push against it. Not now. I need my full focus on her; I can't afford to stop, to remember what I once had and lost.

My other hand finds her waist, squeezing it gently, which draws a delicate moan from her lips as I bring myself to her centre.

"You've got no idea how long I've waited to taste you," I tell her as my fingers brush against the fabric, her body arching towards my touch, which has me withdrawing slightly. I can wait, build her desire until she craves me so thoroughly that when next time comes, she won't think of any other man but me.

"I've heard that before." She groans, her eyes fluttering closed as I play with the hem of her underwear.

"And I'm sure I haven't complained." I chuckle but move closer, my breath caressing her most intimate place, which has her eyes opening in an instant. "Did you?"

I throw her legs over my shoulders, raising her slightly, my hand moving her panties aside so that I have access to her, to witness how desperately she needs me.

"Issac, I swear to Gods if you don't—" Her words dissolve into a gasp as my mouth claims her centre, my tongue quick to savour her sweetness, nearly undoing me with how divine she tastes.

Thea's hands search for something to latch on as I stare at her from underneath my fringe. Her eyes are closed, lips twisted in a slight grimace as she fights against pleasure.

I play with her for a moment, letting myself memorise every aspect of her body, every droplet of sweat trailing down her temples, every moan escaping her lips and every pleading look she flashes my way. I wonder for a moment if my former self felt this desperate, this close to the edge. If I was ever this bloody grateful for being chosen to be the one between her legs, drawing expressions I've never before witnessed.

Thea's fingers reach for my hand, her nails digging into my arms, and I release a growl before plunging two fingers inside her. I watch as her eyes widen in surprise, as her breath catches and her body tenses.

"Want me to keep going?" I smirk, and she looks nearly offended I asked.

"Do you really need to ask—" I cut her off by moving my fingers in and out, making sure to hit the spot that has her eyes rolling to the back of her head.

I bring myself closer to her face, her hands immediately finding purchase at the nape of my neck, and I lean in for a kiss. It's rushed, desperate and filled with unspoken promises. My heart beating wildly against hers, our ragged breaths mingling together. Every now and then I feel her pause, just as my movements quicken and I silently congratulate myself for eliciting such reactions. A few hours ago she wanted to throttle me; now she doesn't want me to move away even a fraction.

Once again, I find myself grazing the delicate skin of her neck with my teeth, her hands in my hair tugging whenever I move with slightly more force.

"Answering your question," I whisper against the freshly made mark on her neck, "I do, because if there's still a part of you that hates me, I need to know."

"Why?" She huffs out, her eyes squeezing tighter, her centre throbbing which tells me she's about to come.

"Because I'm about to make sure you're mine, and that comes with a whole host of darkness, Thea. If you think you might still hate me for how broken I am, then say it now or never."

She forces her eyes open, the gold in them sparkling, and I'm entranced. Her lips curve into a smile, her expression softening for just a moment before she speaks.

"I've told you before, though you don't remember, but I could never truly hate you, Issac. I'm always yours."

I stare at her in wonder because that's not what I expected. Not after everything I've done and said. I thought she might come to her senses, push me away and tell me to get lost. I thought I wasn't good enough, that I'd lost my way, but it seems in Thea's heart there's still a place for another version of myself.

"Fuck, Thea, I'll give you the whole of me even if you give me only a fraction of yourself." With that I kiss her, this time with more intensity, pouring forth words I can't say, emotions I can't express, hoping she understands the depth of what I can't articulate.

I feel her body quiver underneath me, her walls tightening around my fingers, and I hasten my movements. It doesn't take long before she's leaving marks across my back, whispering words I can barely comprehend.

My head falls into the crook of her neck, my breaths uneven not from this encounter but from the memories practically cleaving my head in two from the force with which they're trying to resurface. Damn this. Just for a moment, just a glimpse to find some peace.

The floodgates open and I'm left breathless from the torrent of images pouring forth. So many moments happening at once, so many words spoken in the darkness of my room but long forgotten, now returning.

I grasp onto the first vision my mind can latch onto. It's a memory of Thea and me in what seems to be my bedchamber. She looks battered, her body covered in dirt, blood and bruises. I argue with her, or perhaps against her as she tries to convince me to give us a chance. The feeling of fear fills me from crown to sole, fear of having and losing her in the same heartbeat.

She pleads for an answer, I give it to her and then it happens. We kiss. *'I've always been here,'* she whispers, and my heart pounds a beat faster. She has, and I was a fool for ever turning her away, for ever waging war against myself.

Suddenly, I'm transported to a different memory. She's right underneath me, bare, listening to something I'm saying. The words barely register, but I strain to hear what the old me had promised, what the two of us once dreamt of together.

'You're everywhere I go, even if you're not there you still haunt me and it's not fair because I want nothing more but to have you,'

I hear myself confessing.

She smiles in return, her eyes full of love that perhaps the old me deserved, something the current me must earn anew. 'You have me,' she answers, and I smile. I had her once and lost her due to a wretched mistake neither of us saw coming.

I linger here a moment longer, observing the two of us, wondering if I could ever make her look at me like that again, but when the memories vanish, I'm met with Thea's present face, her eyes gazing into mine, telling an unspoken story.

"I've got you back." I hear the thankful whisper of her voice inside my head and before I can stop myself, my arms encircle her shoulders, pulling her closer to my chest. Relief washes over me, and I exhale breath I didn't know I'd been holding. She does have me, not how she wants it, but nevertheless she's got some part of me back and it seems that's enough.

Chapter 23

ALTHEA

The sun never felt so good on my skin. I stretch in the bed and smile. For once it's a smile full of hope and relief at all that unfolded last night in Issac's presence. His confession, the fact he's battled against himself to have me, the clear truth that the two of us will triumph against even the most formidable obstacles. It nearly feels as if he could be brainwashed a hundred times over, yet would always find his way back to me. As if our souls are tethered in a way neither of us comprehends, as if my fate was to end with him from the very beginning.

A cloud rolls over the sun, hiding its warmth and bringing a sudden chill to my body. Just like that, I'm reminded of my conversation with Ligaya, the vision waiting to happen, my fate lurking for me to misstep and wander in the wrong direction. Even after partially winning Issac to my side, I know no peace as another challenge emerges. This time it's not merely about him.

It's about my friends, the people of this world, and myself. It's greater than anything I've ever thought about, and I can't waste precious hours lying in bed, replaying our moments from last night as if there were no cares in the world. I must research, I must prepare, and above all, be vigilant. I need to protect them all from myself.

"Awake already?" Alea's voice startles me for a moment, and I rise on my elbow to spot her in the door frame. She's fresh from her herbal bath, something I ought to consider. My eyes drift to the bed before me and discover Desily sound asleep. Worry tugs at my heart that she might be the one I lose. The girl who never misunderstood me, never left my side, and stayed steadfast as if nothing else mattered. "Thea?"

"Yes, sorry," I whisper and scramble out of bed. I've got to search another row of books today, and I doubt Ryo will accompany me, considering how much revelry he enjoyed at the banquet.

"Library?" Alea asks, and I nod. "Let me come with."

I halt midway through pulling on my trousers and gawk at her as if she'd grown a second head. It's rare she wants to spend time in my presence. Ever since she and Desily became involved, it's been nearly impossible to separate them, not to mention that since Issac took over my training, her duties of teaching me swordsmanship have vanished.

"Sure, let me just take a quick bath and I'll meet you in the library shortly."

"Perfect." She smiles and climbs onto the bed to wrap her arms around Des, who remains blissfully unaware that her girlfriend wishes to accompany me. I observe the two of them for a fleeting moment whilst lacing my boots. The tender smile playing on Alea's lips, the sparkle in her eyes as she watches Desily breathe, her fingers tracing gently along her skin. Gods, they deserve what they have because it's rare to find love these days. Especially one as pure as theirs.

***

Alea and I have gone through at least ten different bookshelves and thousands of various titles. Nearly all of them concerned matters that don't interest us, at least not now. I let out a frustrated growl as I take the seat opposite Alea, clutching a book about magical weapons crafted by goblins centuries ago.

"This is way more difficult than we thought." She sighs from behind her tome. "I mean, it should be here, shouldn't it?"

"Right, that's at least what the letter to your father stated." The girl freezes for a moment, and I scold myself for bringing the man up. I know he's been gone for a long time, but a wound like that is difficult to heal, if ever possible.

"He was a bastard whilst living, and still remains a bastard whilst dead," I hear her mutter. "I mean, why couldn't his letters be more specific? Why remain so bloody cautious?"

"Cautiousness drives people into madness," I hear myself echoing Ligaya's words from last night. Perhaps it wasn't me to whom she referred but Lord Graham. Perhaps it was merely a warning of what I might become if I don't lean on my friends for help.

Alea sets the book aside, her eyes wandering across the ceiling. "That it did to him," she admits quietly. "At times I miss my mother. She had a way of calming us, of dispelling our worries."

"I know the feeling." I allow myself to smile at memories of my own mother. Her face nearly unreadable now, faded with time, all except for her kind eyes and gentle touch. That's something even the relentless march of time can't pry from my grasp.

"Anyway, how are things with Issac?" Once again I'm surprised by her sudden interest in my personal affairs, but don't hesitate to answer.

"It's safe to say he won't be contemplating my murder anytime soon." I chuckle and flip the page, scanning a drawing of a battle axe designed to cleave cleanly through an enemy's neck.

Alea doesn't immediately follow up, her lips pursed as if restraining herself from prying, but one look at her and she caves. "Was it because of that man speaking to you?"

"Alea! Were you spying on me?" I giggle and playfully swat her hand.

Her cheeks flush pink, a reaction I never expected to witness from someone normally so composed. "It wasn't me! Desily saw the two of you, and well," she sighs, her shoulders slumping in defeat. "Desily must be rubbing off on me."

I break into laughter, and surprisingly, Alea joins in, her face partially hidden behind her slender fingers. The small scratches on her fingertips reveal she's been practising her archery during what little free time she has when not with Desily. I wonder for a moment how I never found the opportunity to enquire about her life, how we spent months together and all I knew about Alea was that she was the daughter of a cruel man, sister to a powerful lord, and the beloved of my dearest friend.

Just as our laughter subsides, I realise that perhaps this time we're spending together today is a chance for me to draw closer to her, to discover who she truly is beneath the carefully maintained exterior. And that I most certainly do.

We talk for what feels like hours, ignoring the disapproving glances from the librarians at our animated chatter. She tells me that she enjoys horseback riding and waking at the crack of dawn because that's when her mother could usually be found in the greenhouse, watching the sunrise. I listen, captivated, to tales of how as a child she'd constantly get scrapes and bruises, and Theo would always be the first to tend to her wounds. Something I relate to deeply, as Issac and I shared a similar bond, though not connected by blood.

I observe as her face twists into a grimace at the mention of her father and how he insisted she become a proper lady when her heart yearned to be a soldier. How he rarely let her play with Theo and forbade her from going beyond the manor walls.

I witness the transformation when I ask about her mother. Her face lights up in a way that warms my own heart. Stories flow about a woman who'd move mountains for her children, who'd sneak Alea into the greenhouse to teach her swordsmanship, and guide her on woodland trips to teach her archery. A mother who'd sacrifice her very existence to keep her children safe, a woman who died by the hand of someone she believed loved her, but who in reality wanted power more than family.

That's the Alea I never knew. A young woman with such passion, kindness and love, concealing those traits from the world because it was her mother who died for possessing those very qualities.

"Theo was unbearable as a child!" I flip another page of the book I've barely glanced at whilst Alea regales me with stories of her brother. "I kept warning him about sneaking to Issac's cell, but he'd never listen, and then I'd catch a glimpse of mother scolding him. Gods, truly he just likes to do things his own way." She rolls her eyes and I giggle. I can see why she and Desily are drawn together, why they cherish each other so deeply. One is composed and thinks rationally, whilst the other is forthright and untamed. Both lost someone dear to them, both concealed their pain from the world, but not from each other. And I find that beautiful.

"Duke Reyfaren, what brings you here?" One of the librarians speaks in a startled tone, the surname rolling off his tongue catching my attention.

Whether I wish it or not, my head turns to see the man from the banquet standing at the entrance. He wears that polite smile stretching across his lips, a smile that nearly won me over along with his honesty and warmth.

"Forgive me, I've come to return books my sisters had borrowed since our last visit." His eyes sweep across the library, landing on me, and I turn away just as his smile broadens, my cheeks flushing with heat. Alea shoots me a curious look, but I nod my head slightly to avoid drawing more attention to myself.

I should be apologising to Eric for the dreadful things Issac said. He hasn't just embarrassed himself, but me as well with what he implied. And yet even after that, I allowed him to do those very things—

"Miss Thea." Eric bows, and I curse inwardly but nod. Alea rises and extends her hand. "Miss Alea Graham, if I'm not mistaken?"

"You're correct, Duke Eric. Lovely to finally meet you in person." Alea skilfully slips on her formal mask, whilst I sit still and quiet, attempting to devise a suitable escape plan.

"Likewise."

"Wait." I interrupt them. "You two know each other?" I look between Alea and Eric, both regarding me with practised smiles.

"Of each other, yes. Our families conducted some business together back when you resided at the manor. My condolences for what happened." A sombre expression passes across his eyes, one I'm certain he didn't need to feign. What happened to them is truly dreadful. Their entire existence vanished in the blink of an eye, family heirlooms and memories now nothing more than cinders. And as much as I strive to accept their forgiveness, not a day passes when I don't burden myself with blame for what occurred.

"If you'll excuse me, I believe it's time for lunch." Alea gathers her belongings and I follow suit, hoping not to remain alone with Eric for too long. I dread the explanation he might demand, the expectation to indulge his fantasy of us together. It's something I haven't properly considered, haven't strategised.

"Miss Thea, if I might steal a moment of your time." I squeeze my eyes shut, my teeth sinking into my bottom lip. Well, damn my plans, I suppose.

I turn to face him, plastering on a smile that might just reach my ears. "But of course."

We wander through bustling corridors. People hurry past us with either stacks of papers clutched in their hands or trays of food balanced carefully. I dig my nails into the spines of the books I've borrowed from the library as the silence between Eric and me stretches longer than I'd hoped. Alea left so quickly, I barely had the chance to ask her to come with me to the dining hall. I suppose our bonding time has come to an end, and she has other matters needing attention, like Desily.

Eric clears his throat, and I steal a glance at him. "Did you enjoy last night's banquet?"

"Very much. It's not typically something I find myself drawn to," I explain as we round a corner. There are countless activities I prefer, and formal gatherings rank amongst the last. Unless they involve my friends, I won't be found attending such tedious affairs.

"What is it that you do enjoy?" Eric asks, genuine interest sparking behind his eyes, and once again warmth creeps into my cheeks. My heart may belong to Issac, but heavens, this man has a way of making me feel self-conscious. It's as if he's the most courteous, good-hearted person I've encountered in ages, with nothing but sincere intentions.

I pause to consider my response. "Perhaps spending time with my friends, or practising my swordsmanship, or—"

"Exploring your magic?" I halt abruptly at his words. The mark on my arm burning as if suddenly aflame. Eric meets my gaze with an apologetic expression, as if he's uttered something meant to remain private. "Forgive me, word travels swiftly."

"And with it curiosity, it seems," I add, feeling much more uneasy around him. Just as I lowered my guard, somehow I needed to be reminded that strangers can't be trusted.

Eric scratches his neck, his lips twisting into a grimace. "I apologise, truly. I didn't mean to cause offence. It's just these days it's hard to find one of us you see."

"One of us?" I blink at him in surprise. Is he saying what I think he's saying?

"Well, beside me and Myra, there aren't many other wielders in Sebraycia. My sisters are too young—" I stop listening momentarily. Although I was fully aware Myra was a wielder, Eric was definitely the last person I'd assume could use our magic. With his parents being both human and elf, I'd presume he'd have to rely on crystals, but it seems I was far off. As it appears, he received a choice, just as I did, just as every other human before us.

My eyes instinctively travel to his arm, but his shirt covers it in a way that prevents even a glimpse of the mark. Questions about him flood my mind, possibilities of who he might be, of whom I've begun lowering my walls for—

"I wield the power of psychometry." His words pull me back to reality, and I stare at him, mouth agape, because no one has ever been this forthright with me, not without expecting something in exchange, not without an ulterior motive. "That's what you wanted to know, isn't it?"

"I—How did you—What?" I stammer, not even sure myself what I'm trying to say. Eric steps back, giving me space to breathe, and I take a moment to collect myself before asking, "What does that mean?"

"The power isn't exceptional, but I'm able to gain knowledge about an object's history by making physical contact with it." He offers a half-smile as I process his words. A gift like this is surely more than exceptional. It's extraordinary. To touch something and know everything about it.

My eyes narrow as suspicion begins to grow. "And people?"

"Just objects, don't worry. I haven't been spying on you in secret as most assume." I exhale and mutter a quick apology. Gods, everything that transpired between Lathai and me has made me excessively paranoid. It matters not if the person seems amiable; I simply can't trust anyone. "Sorry to spring all this information on you out of the blue. I sometimes forget how to conduct myself around ones like myself, so I'll leave you to it, but if you have more questions, don't hesitate to seek me out."

With that, Eric walks away, and I'm forced to make my way towards the dining hall where I'll have to pretend as if I haven't just discovered something equally amazing and terrifying. A power like his. So many possibilities. From what I understand, he might know when the table I'm about to reach was made, and who exactly crafted it. He'll know who made the silverware and the burning candles. He'll see everything those objects consist of, every detail that might be useful or merely interesting. How amazing.

"Thea!" Desily's voice catches my attention as I snap out of my train of thought. I take the seat opposite Alea and shoot her an annoyed look for abandoning me with Eric, to which she replies with a noncommittal shrug.

The entirety of lunch consists of us discussing the banquet and any new rumours circulating around the castle. I barely listen, too fascinated with my discovery about Eric, when suddenly I hear a noise.

"Have your parents not taught you to never steal others' toys? Or were you just too dim to understand?" I shut my eyes and smile, but the smile isn't kind. It's the sort of smile that conveys precisely how much you despise someone.

Desily clears her throat and crosses her arms over her chest, whilst Alea's vigilant eyes won't leave Myra's spiteful face for even a moment.

"Hello to you as well," I turn to face her, my lip twitching. I still don't understand how one person can evoke so many hostile emotions from me. I've barely spoken to her, know almost nothing about her, but there isn't a flicker of doubt in my mind that every particle of my being loathes her.

"You know," she begins, bringing her finger to her pouting lips, "I was prepared to overlook the fact Issac had been training you, since you're such a pitiful case, but having him abandon me during a conversation. That I can't overlook."

"Perhaps he's not interested in having a dog," Des remarks, and I scoff, which makes Myra shoot her a venomous glare.

"Listen—" I swing my leg over the long bench and attempt to face her properly, even though looking at her countenance fills me with revulsion.

"No, you listen," she interrupts, all playfulness and artificial kindness vanishing from her features. "You might think you have him wrapped around your finger, but once upon a time he was wrapped around mine when you were nothing but a blight on his existence."

"Yet even during his worst moment he still chose to pick me over you. That must sting, Myra." The girl's fingers curl into fists at her sides and I smirk. I won't let her bully me anymore, not when my future with Issac is a bit more certain.

"You were merely forced into his mind. That's the only way he could make himself think of you." She spits back, her eyes glaring at me with hatred I match without breaking a sweat.

"Seems I occupy a great deal of both your minds, but in his case, I suppose he'd rather choose something that makes him feel genuine rather than delusional." The way her face grows increasingly flushed with each passing second has me wanting to perform pirouettes from sheer satisfaction. I'm finished being beneath her boot; she is not the master of me or anyone else, and Issac certainly doesn't belong to her.

Myra scoffs, the annoyance wiped from her face in seconds,

replaced by that composure I typically see her wear. As if she owns the bloody world, as if she knows Issac could be hers.

"Funny, that's coming from you, since you've spent a hundred years searching for him, whilst he wanted nothing to do with you."

"That has—"

"Not to mention, during those years you were barely on his mind," she lowers herself, her voice dropping to a whisper. "I made certain of that, especially when he dragged me into his bed. As it seems, you're receiving what I taught him."

The flames of the candle spark, and I inhale sharply, wondering if they'd throw me into a cell for murdering this woman. Perhaps they would, but it might be worth it, even if only for the momentary satisfaction of striking that smug face.

"Fuck you," I spit out, my knuckles becoming white from how hard I'm squeezing my fists, and though Desily's hand wraps around mine, I tear it away to point a finger in Myra's face. "What sort of fantasy are you living in? Do you truly believe he gives a damn about you?"

"Oh, he does." She nods in a way that appears way too confident as if she's sure of her words and ready to die were they not true.

"Funny, your name was never mentioned during our conversations," I bite back.

Myra's hands cover her lips as she giggles. "Yours was. Not in a nice way though. But he soon forgot about that too. I suppose he was too preoccupied getting distracted in writing me letters." Letters? What bloody letters? I hear the fire to my right crackling louder, the heat building, but I can't restrain myself, can't prevent these furious emotions from consuming me.

"Sorry to disappoint you, Myra, but that's all you were to him. A distraction. A thing to replace for momentary satisfaction whilst I wasn't present." Myra's eyes grow increasingly hostile, her carefully maintained composure crumbling with each word escaping my lips. I'll bloody strike where it'll hurt the most. "Not even your own sister liked to speak about you. Says quite a lot, doesn't it?"

"You bitch." Myra's hand moves so swiftly I barely have time to register as she manipulates the water from the vase, suspending it above my head. "Don't you dare speak about my sister."

"Or what? It's not like she cared, even in her final moments it wasn't you who she thought about but her lover."

Before I have a chance to react, the water cascades down, and I'm drenched. I'm not sure what happens next or how exactly, but the flames from the candle leap towards Myra's leather attire, burning through the linen cuffs of her shirt.

My body shakes and I wait for a moment to pounce at her and pound my fists into her face until they bleed, a wicked smile stretching across my lips until Desily's urgent grip shakes me back to reality.

"Thea! Stop this!" I blink and Myra's panicked screams reach my ears. All the emotions pour down on me and I clutch my chest trying to dissipate all the anger, all the hatred and craze. This feels so odd, almost like these weren't mine, almost as if I lost control over my magic once again just like back then with Lathai. Without thinking twice, I extinguish the flames and my eyes involuntarily scan Myra's arms for any burns. Bloody hell, do I want to hurt her or not? Was it even me or the magic acting of its own accord?

"You're insane! No wonder he wanted to stay away from you, you absolute looney bitch!" Myra is poised to launch herself at me, but Alea rushes past the table and intercepts her, tackling her to the floor with swift precision.

I look around the room and unsurprisingly every pair of eyes is on us. Their whispers barely reaching my ears, but I don't need to hear what they're saying to know what they're thinking. It's written all over their faces, I'm dangerous, a monster compared to Myra. Whilst I'm left a bit cold from being wet, Myra could be seriously burnt. Her power barely able to hurt me whilst mine ready to consume it all, and what's worse I enjoyed it.

I enjoyed seeing her hurt. I drank her screams and got full on her worries. I truthfully was ready to see her burn over a man.

I get up from my seat and race past everyone, past all the judgement and guilt trying to make it through my head to flood me with new worries. Before those feelings manage to consume me, my feet take me to one person that might just be able to get rid of this burning desire to kill.

Chapter 24

The door to the training room swings open with a bang, and I curse under my breath as I catch the handle and shut it behind me. The space before me stands nearly empty, save for the confused man on the right side in nothing but linen trousers and a vest that clings to his muscles entirely too well.

"Thea?" He drops whatever he was holding, his eyes scanning my body for injuries, and my heart momentarily melts.

We haven't seen each other since last night, and a part of me half expected him not to appear. To laugh in my face for believing his words, as if planning some elaborate plan to destroy me further. But no. Issac is right here, walking the fine line between the person I once knew and this version I've had to grow used to.

It's as if I'm juggling fragments of him. Pieces of his childhood, his awkward teenage years, those precious moments at the manor. Now this current version stands before me, someone familiar yet not entirely so. The scent of his skin, that mixture of leather and smoke and something uniquely him, drifts through the cool air between us. I don't mind these contradictions; as long as everything between us remains stable, I don't care.

My feet drag across the wooden floor, the scrape of leather against polished oak echoing in the room. My mind whirls in chaos as I try to reason with myself. Issac blinks twice, his brow furrowing with concern, before his arms open. I fall into his embrace, my head hidden beneath the thick curtain of my wet hair that clings to my neck and shoulders.

The warmth from his body is nearly as soothing as yesterday. The steady rhythm of his heartbeat thrums against my cheek, calming my racing thoughts, and I realise that hugs from him are far better than anything intimate we've ever shared. It's as if in this simple gesture we tell each other all there is to know. I've got you.

"What happened? Why are you drenched?" He whispers before resting his chin atop my head, his breath stirring my damp strands.

"Did something have to happen for me to get a hug?" I mutter, trying to change the topic and lighten the mood to get rid of the persistent feeling of guilt that coils inside my stomach.

"No, but the Thea I know wouldn't just approach me for a hug out of nowhere. If anything, it feels like the last thing you'd do." He says, and I chuckle, the sound hollow even to my own ears.

"Then you don't know me that well." Issac reaches for my chin, his calloused fingertips gentle yet insistent as he tilts my face upward, forcing our gazes to lock. I sigh in defeat under his soft look, my resolve crumbling. "Myra happened."

"Oh?" His voice carries a note of understanding that makes my stomach clench.

I pull away, the warmth and security within his embrace

torn from me by a force I can't understand. Almost as if we were bonded together, held by some invisible power, now severed. I brush my fingers through my hair, droplets of water falling onto the floor. My mind races as I search for words to best describe what happened, to make myself appear less like a villain, but in truth, I fell for her bait and nearly burnt her alive. The smell of smoke still clings to my nose, a reminder of how close I came to crossing a line. Whether it was her plan or not, I'm at fault. I should've known better, and now everyone in the castle will be wary of me, if they weren't already.

"I can almost hear your thoughts. Tell me," he urges and leans against the wall whilst I continue pacing around the room, my wet footprints marking a chaotic pattern across the floor.

"She's just bloody insufferable! She provoked me once again but this time it nearly ended up with her becoming an ash pile." I bite on my nails, the metallic taste of blood touching my tongue as I avoid his gaze at all costs. What if the part of him that hates me takes it as a threat, a chance to strike? I've nearly hurt one of his friends, or whatever she is to him. The thought sends a chill down my spine despite the warmth of the training room.

"Is that why you're soaking wet? Did she do it?" He asks, his voice carefully neutral, and I grunt, the sound echoing off the high ceiling.

"Doesn't matter! I'm tired of her, tired of her acting like you two are together and I'm the bloody issue here." I stop to finally face him, the floorboards creaking beneath my sudden movement, half expecting disappointment flashing past his eyes, but all I see is sympathy, warm and genuine in his crimson gaze.

"But you know that's not true," he points out, and I shoot him a look.

"Of course I do; doesn't mean it makes it any better. She's making my existence absolute hell, putting these ridiculous ideas inside my head." My voice rises and falls, echoing against the stone walls.

"Like what?" He presses, pushing off from the wall, his muscles flexing with the movement.

"Like the two of you being together before us." I throw my hands out in frustration, my wet sleeves sending droplets flying through the air. My head searches for answers as to how I can convince everyone I'm not bad, how I can get rid of Myra without a fight breaking out, but nothing comes. It's almost as if I'm dry out of answers which doesn't surprise me. I put far too much pressure on myself, but who wouldn't when the whole world is depending on you? The weight of it presses down on my chest, making each breath hard.

Issac kisses his teeth and stalks towards me, his movements fluid. "C'mere."

I sigh and slowly move towards him in defeat. With each step, his scent gets stronger in a way that despite everything, still feels like coming home. Inches away from being far too close to him, his arms land on my shoulders, their weight both comforting and confining. He shakes me a little, which brings my full attention to his face, to the tiny scar above his left eyebrow, to the flecks of black in his crimson irises that I'd forgotten about.

"Does it bother you? The fact me and her shared some history?" His voice is soft but serious, his warm breath fanning across my face.

"No, it's just that—I don't know. I just want to know the truth, Issac. There are things you haven't told me about, like the letters, or why she's never been mentioned before." My voice catches on the last word, betraying the emotion I'm trying desperately to hide.

"What the past me told you can't be tied to the present. I'm sorry for not being honest with you about her, but if telling you what was between us will make you calmer, then I'll do it." His thumbs trace small circles on my shoulders, the gesture soothing despite the tension crackling between us.

I want to say it won't help. I want to tell him that listening about him and Myra living their best life whilst I spent my days searching for him and dying each night is the last thing I want to hear. The very thought makes my stomach twist into knots and my chest tighten. But at the same time, it's the truth I've been craving.

Ever since my arrival in the castle, it's been nagging me why Issac has never told me about her, why hasn't anyone else? Not to mention, the letters I read back to back and can practically recite from memory, are full of answers yet none straightforward. The only person able to tell me the full story is Issac himself. I have to hear it. I have to know. The truth, no matter how painful, is better than this gnawing uncertainty that eats away at me from the inside out.

"Let's start with the letters then." I see the uncertainty in his eyes, the fear of something far too complex for me to understand. He moves away and takes a seat on the wooden floor, urging me to follow, and so I do. The boards creak beneath our weight, the sound echoing in the emptiness of the training room.

His mouth remains closed, but I can see the cogs twisting

and turning behind his crimson eyes. Issac isn't trying to hide the truth, or sugar coat anything; he's trying to remember. It must be hard, to recall things you wrote decades ago, and I wouldn't blame him if he just simply didn't tell—

"The first letter I wrote was shortly after Theo sneaked in and brought me something to kill time and take my mind off torture. I wrote them as a way to talk with you I think at least, that memory is still a bit foggy but I know I was writing them so that I have something to offer once that important person in my mind showed up and demanded explanation as to why I'd disappeared for so many years." I purse my lips, recalling the words of the mysterious writer, his hopes of seeing the only person that brought a smile to his face during the darkest of his days. "See it as a journal of sorts. I believe I just needed to have something to remind me of you, a way to latch onto the memories of us."

I nod as understanding settles between us. His memories aren't fully back, but getting them this way, talking about lost time is the best possible way for the two of us to strengthen the connection. I've received that piece of Issac I needed. Although he told me the story before, reading those letters, imagining his days changes things a bit. I'm no longer on the sidelines watching; I am there with him living through the pain and the longing he felt. If I ever needed proof he missed me, it's right there in those letters, in the tremble of his handwriting when he wrote of home.

"Well, I guess it worked how you wanted. I've been able to imagine your days there." My fingers fidget with the hem of my damp shirt, the fabric cold against my skin.

"Nothing spectacular, I know. Just a bit of torture here and there." He chuckles and I swat him on the shoulder, my palm connecting with his warm skin. A part of me still feels horrible for not finding him sooner, but that's a story long resolved and buried, and the only person still reliving those moments is not Issac but me. The guilt coils in my stomach.

I bite my bottom lip before speaking the next words, the metallic taste of blood touching my tongue. The feeling of dread chains me in place. "What about Myra? I barely know anything about her, but it seems you do."

Issac rolls his head back, a deep laugh escaping his throat that shakes me to the core. The sound bounces off the walls, filling the training room with momentary life. Strange how things between us can change so quickly. How we can go from despising each other to holding civil conversations just because our bond was at threat of snapping. The fragility of what we've rebuilt haunts me constantly.

"I met Myra during Lisa's second visit. She was young, perhaps couple years younger than me, and I could see travelling with her sister was the last thing a teenager wanted to do." I listen closely, my mind hungry for new information to fill out the blanks left by time. "Lisa stayed with us for a while to teach me magic, a week each month, and inevitably whether I wanted to or not, I ended up speaking to her sister."

My heart skips a beat faster, the image of cold-hearted Issac being kind to a girl who was losing her childhood to go with her sister with no peers around making me oddly sad. Not because I wish I was in her place but because Myra had nothing. No friends around, no people to go through forests and fields with and make up stories, or stay up late at night to talk about her hopes and dreams. Lisa was a formal woman, and I doubt she'd spend her time doing those things; if anything, she probably made Myra train alongside Issac.

The room suddenly feels colder as I imagine their isolated existence.

"Since she had nobody, I was the closest thing to calling a friend. We were forced to be in each other's presence as Lisa wanted to help Myra hone her skills in wielding her power. Of course I wasn't happy, but a few years fast forward, she became someone I could talk to when Theo wasn't around." Issac's eyes find mine, and search in them for a glimpse of anger but find nothing except curiosity. Perhaps their history is much different from what I imagined, not purely sexual as Myra implies but rather two people looking for some sort of connection to break away from a constant. "Seven or so years in, we'd spend every free moment with each other. Whether it was getting dinner or studying, she'd be there, and I hate to admit it, but it helped me forget about the mission Lord Graham forced into my head."

"The mission to capture and kill me," I add quietly, ignoring the shiver running down my spine.

"Myra would try to reassure me you weren't coming back, that we were safe in the manor, and I listened because I had no other option but to believe her words. The rest of the story goes as you think. We got closer, ended up doing things, but not because either of us had feelings for each other but because we needed a distraction." I blink at his words. That's what I said to her, and perhaps I was closer to the truth than I thought. The revelation sits heavy in my chest.

"I don't think she feels the same way, Issac." My voice is barely above a whisper, yet it seems to fill the space between us.

"Maybe, I- I guess I always knew, and fuck, I feel so bad for ever letting her believe we could be something more. I thought it was nothing more than sex, no strings attached, but in her eyes, I must've been the one and only. The person who pulled her out of misery and gave her purpose amongst chaos." He sighs, the sound full of regret, and I squeeze his hand for comfort.

My judgement of her was wrong; she is not as evil as I made myself believe. She is simply a girl in love with a man who she thinks saved her, and if that's not tragic, then I don't know what is, because I know deep down it pains her to see him pick me over her. A girl he once despised. A girl he vented about to her day and night now being the only thing his eyes can see. The irony is almost too much to bear.

"What was her relationship with Lisa? It seems she hates her." I decide to change the subject and find out a bit about the history between the sisters. The wooden boards beneath us creak as I shift my position, my wet clothes beginning to chafe uncomfortably against my skin.

Lisa never spoke about Myra except for that one time she had compared me to her, and now as much as I hate to admit it, I can see the similarity. We're both stubborn, both ready to fight for what we think is right, but that's not what I care about right now. Some part of me, the part that wants knowledge, needs to find out why exactly the sisters fell out, and why Issac had stopped seeing Myra. The question burns in my mind.

"Their father was the main reason from what I gathered. She'd often tell me how he'd force Lisa to become the perfect lady, the heiress to the throne of their clan." Issac's voice drops lower, as if sharing secrets not meant for these walls. "Growing up they barely had any interactions if not for the moments Lisa had to train her, and let me tell you, I could feel the awkwardness from miles away. Myra wanted a sister, but Lisa needed a soldier, a right hand, and then two worlds collided and exploded."

I look away for a moment, a strange feeling of sadness swirling around my chest. I shouldn't have spoken those words to her; I shouldn't have reminded her that to her sister she was nothing. Yet perhaps we're both wrong because the day I spoke to Lisa, it seemed like she missed her for reasons beyond their family feuds. She missed her sister, not her perfect soldier.

"Few years before you came back, Myra and Lisa arrived at the manor, and from the way they avoided each other, I knew something was wrong." His fingers tap a gentle rhythm against the floor, the sound barely audible. "Surely enough, Myra clued me in, and as it seems, they had a big fight over her future. Lisa wanted her to go into Sebraycia as per requested by their father. Something about the princess needing help from a wielder, but that's not what Myra wanted. She wanted to stay in the manor with me, with Lisa maybe, because over the years they grew closer. Those stupid moments with us training were the only moments Myra could really speak to her sister, build some sort of connection and bond."

"I gather with her being here she didn't get her way." My voice sounds hollow even to my own ears, the words echoing faintly in the room.

Issac shakes his head, a flash of pity passing by his eyes before it's gone. "The last time I saw her, she and Lisa got into an argument. She shouted at her for being a terrible sister, cussed her out, and wished her all the worse for taking away the reason as to why she was happy. She said she wanted nothing to do with the family, and though Lisa kept her composure, she finally snapped and told her it wasn't just about her, and that she should be grateful for what she had, but Myra didn't care. So Lisa did the only thing she thought was right."

"Which is what?" I swallow hard, the need to hear the truth holding me still, my breath caught in my throat.

"She had John put Myra to sleep and taken away from the manor to their home. What happened there is a mystery." He speaks the words softly, almost regretfully.

I blink shocked that John would go to such lengths for Lisa, but that's not what has my heart squeezing painfully in my chest. It's the fact that Myra's freedom was stolen away and probably replaced by her family's needs, a mission given to her out of nowhere.

The bitter taste of injustice floods my mouth. Even now, she still can't let go of the grudge, still can't see past the hatred she felt towards her family for tearing her apart from whatever happiness she managed to gather. Perhaps her anger comes from the fact she knows she'll never get to ask her sister questions as to why was she the way she was, why she chose their entire clan over their non-existent bond and why ultimately she betrayed that very family for no one else but her lover, but could never bring herself to do the same for her sister.

Yeah, we're more alike than I thought.

"Is that all?" Issac's hand cups my cheek and I melt into his touch. A surge of warmth spreads through me, starting where his skin meets mine and going outward. Honestly, it's like nothing bad happened between us, like last night blew away all the worries and anger far, far away to a place it won't return from. Still, a question nags at me.

"Yeah." I nod and pull away, the sudden absence of his touch leaving my skin tingling. "What is happening between us?"

Issac smirks in the way that has my legs grow weak. He wastes no time to spring up and trap me between his arms, his body leaning towards me whilst I lean slightly backward. The scent of leather and smoke wraps around me. I stare into his eyes, into the crimson depths of the soul I've fallen in love with for the second time. Every version of Issac is a version I'll accept without a second thought. We might have our highs and our lows are low, but we make it through every storm. Even at the edge of time it's us.

"Whatever you want, pet. I am yours, and I've been an idiot for ever refusing to acknowledge that." His voice is low, husky. The next thing, Issac leans into a kiss, capturing my lips in a soft and slow exchange.

I let my body fall onto the floor with Issac's hand now holding onto my back for support. The cool wood presses against my still-damp clothes. He follows through without breaking contact, my skin burning in a pleasurable way I forgot it could. My thoughts twisted, and my insides melting with each time our lips brush against each other. The training room fades away. Its wooden floors, its high ceilings, its emptiness. All that exists is this moment. I drown into him and he drowns into me.

My fingers thread through his long raven strands, my chest aching not from pain but relief because as much as I believed I could get him back, the bigger part of me believed I couldn't, and that feeling was eating at me from the inside. But here we are now, doing things we used to do like no time passed, like we've never left the manor and never had to face a terrible choice.

His hands remove the damp shirt over my head, and I sigh as the cold meets my skin, goosebumps rising along my arms and torso. But soon enough Issac's lips are all over my stomach, kissing and biting, the heat of his mouth chasing away the chill.

"You know," I breathe out as he sucks on my chest to leave a mark, the sensation sending sparks down my spine, "the old you used to call me that as well."

"What? Pet?" He breathes out through ragged breaths and I nod, feeling the vibration of his words against my skin. "Seems we're more alike than I thought."

He comes back again to capture my lips in another kiss, this time hungrier and more rushed, and I almost forget that we're in a public space where anyone can come in. The thought flickers briefly before dissolving. Screw it, let me have some happiness since all I've been given lately was nothing but misery.

Issac's tongue demands entrance and I let him in, the faint taste of something like herbal tea still lingering on his tongue. I dig my nails into his back and momentarily we're back at the manor, back in his room, in his bed where nothing mattered. The scent of him, the weight of him, the heat of him. It all comes together into a familiar comfort I've missed desperately.

Though I miss parts of the old him, this Issac is much more open, less aware and carefree as if the worries his previous self carried are now vanished. He doesn't hide anything because he has nothing to hide, because he isn't afraid of losing someone he hasn't lost yet. He doesn't remember.

"Sounds like the old me was quite an arsehole." His voice echoes around my head and I jump, the sudden intrusion startling me back to the present.

"Get out of my head!" I try swatting him on the shoulder but he skilfully catches my wrist and pins my hand above my head, the wood cool against my skin.

"Hard to when all you do is think, and not once do you just let yourself simply enjoy the moment." I roll my eyes though he can't see it, momentarily forgetting about our conversation as he bites my bottom lip, the sharp sensation sending a jolt through me.

"With you around? Impossible." Issac chuckles, the sound too sweet not to remember for the next couple of centuries, deep and resonant.

"From what it sounds like I won you over three times now; you can rest assured I will always find my way back to you." His words drift between us, settling like a promise.

"Three?" I pull him away, our gazes locked, our breaths mixed before he sweeps the loose strands of my hair off my face, his fingertips tracing my cheekbone.

"Three, because I lost you as a young boy. I lost you as an adult, and I lost you now during the attack." I blink at him, surprised because I never thought of it that way, but what he says is true. We got back to each other three times, so if the next time ever comes I won't be worried; fear won't win this time. The realisation settles within me, a comforting weight.

I gently push him away, remembering the purpose this room serves us, but before I have a chance to look away, I catch the glimpse of his disappointed look, his crimson eyes darkening slightly. There will be plenty of times for us to carry on, hopefully in a place that everybody doesn't have access to.

"Let's begin the training," I say, my voice steadier than I expected.

The next hour passes in a blink of an eye, and surely enough I'm covered in sweat from avoiding Issac's ruthless attacks. The wooden floor now bears the marks of our movements, scuffs and scrapes telling the story of our dance. By now I'm sure I could take someone far stronger than me. He made sure of it by throwing me to the floor every time I hesitated and demanded immediate solutions. My muscles sing with exertion, my lungs burning with each breath.

I know what to do when trapped and what to do when it seems like I'm running out of options. Issac's always coming with a plan for our lessons, a new weakness of mine to be targeted and honed to perfection. He believes I'm capable of great things and so do I, but that's not the reason why I torture myself each day, no. I'm preparing in case another attack comes because I'll be damned if I let him or anyone else get hurt this time. The memory of the last attack still burns fresh in my mind.

By the end of our lesson, I'm laid on the floor, my chest rising and falling rapidly, the coolness of the wood a blessing against my overheated skin. After this, I'm meant to go back to the library to research more books, but I doubt I'll be there anytime soon with the way my muscles ache.

"Any progress with the ritual paper?" Issac asks whilst putting away the training equipment. I peek at him and admire the outline of his back muscles, the strength usually hidden behind heavy armour now glistening with a fine sheen of sweat.

"Not really," I grunt in response and let my head fall back

onto the floor with a soft thud. "I just wish there was a way to see where exactly it was hidden. What the smudged part of the letter hid." The frustration that's been building for days colours my voice.

Issac chuckles as he approaches, reaching his hand towards me, his palm calloused but inviting. "I bet you do. I think anyone would love to see what mysteries could be hidden within an object."

I get up to my feet as my eyes grow three sizes wider whilst I stare at him, my thoughts racing. That's it, that's what I need, someone to be able to touch the letter and see past the things neither of us can. Someone with a power to read objects and their information. The solution suddenly seems so obvious I want to laugh.

"That look on your face tells me you've just found something." His voice cuts through my revelation, amused and curious.

"I have an idea," I say, the excitement building in my chest. Perhaps all is not lost after all.

Chapter 25

I don't remember the last time five of us were gathered in the same room without a reason. It must have been one of those lazy days at the manor when the sun settled slowly beyond the horizon, and none of us had anything pressing to do. Back when Lathai was still around and normal. Whatever defines normal these days.

His absence hangs in the air, felt most in those little moments where his laughter would've filled the room. When Desily would bicker with him over their royal treatment. When Issac would shoot him those evil glares that sent shivers down everyone's spine. When I felt like I truly had a friend, someone I could trust without constantly judging them. The empty space beside us speaks volumes.

My attention snaps back to the present as Ryo enters the room hastily. His chest heaves with uneven breaths, cheeks flushed crimson from exertion, showing he's run here rather than taking his time. We've come to the conclusion that three other people should be included in this conversation. People I've gradually grown to trust and who could prove valuable to our cause. Jassin and Venali shoot him disapproving looks from their positions by the door. Issac, well, he just looks thoroughly resigned.

"Sorry, sorry I was a bit preoccupied," Ryo mumbles, nervously fixing the collar of his rumpled shirt. I giggle despite the tension in the room, noticing the telltale purple marks dotting his neck. Evidence of a passionate encounter with someone he clearly spent the night with.

"Was it one of those court ladies I saw hanging onto you last night?" Desily throws her arm over Ryo's shoulder and rubs his head with her fist, mussing his already messy hair. "Bloody hell, our little boy is growing up before our very eyes!"

"I—well—" The boy stutters, his face turning an even deeper shade of scarlet. I break into a genuine laugh, the sound bubbling up from somewhere deep and nearly forgotten, joined immediately by Des's hearty chuckle. Issac and Alea roll their eyes in perfect sync, whilst Theo remains seated with a soft, knowing smile playing on his lips. Jassin and Venali stand rigidly on guard by the heavy oak doors, being the essence of true soldiers. So unlike the flustered young man who arrived noticeably late. I suppose when you're younger, not much matters beyond love and living your life to its fullest.

"Leave him be, Desily," Issac interjects, his voice carrying that edge of authority that immediately shifts the atmosphere in the room. "After the meeting, I'll make bloody sure he makes up for the training he's missed today." A calculating smirk crosses his face, and all the colour drains from Ryo's face.

"Tonight?" He gulps audibly.

"Tonight," Issac repeats, a mischievous grin dancing along his features. Gods, he loves to punish that boy, but in all fairness, he's the general, and that's precisely what he needs to be doing. Maintaining discipline even as our world threatens to crumble around us.

I clear my throat, the sound echoing slightly against the stone walls, and pull out the weathered leather satchel full of books, letters, and research done carefully over the past few months. Lord Graham's journal lies on the table, its pages yellowed with age and filled with my rushed handwriting. Ideas and plans sprawl across the parchment in chaotic order, now no longer needed. Not with our secret weapon around.

The scent of old paper and ink fills my nose as I arrange the materials before me. My fingertips tingle with a mixture of anticipation and dread.

"Right," I begin, my voice steadier than I feel inside, where my heart pounds against my ribcage. "I've asked you all to gather here tonight because I believe I've found a way to discover where the ritual paper is."

Everyone's eyes focus on me, eight pairs of gazes burning into my skin. The room suddenly feels smaller, the air thicker and harder to breathe. I'm in the spotlight now. The reluctant leader, the one person they will listen to should things go south because I'm the one with the plan. Not Theo with his royal blood, not Issac with his military experience, but me. Me, whom they'll blame if things don't work out as intended.

My hands shake slightly as I reach for the letter hidden within my bag. "I've discovered today that Duke Eric Reyfaren has a wielding power of psychometry."

"Psycho-what?" Ryo interrupts before receiving a hushing glare from Issac that could wither flowers. Our eyes lock momentarily across the polished surface of the table, and in Issac's intense gaze, I see the unspoken promise of a private conversation after this meeting ends. After all, this is the first time he's heard about it. In truth, any of them have.

"It's an ability to gain knowledge about an object from just a simple touch," I explain, my finger tracing over the fragile sheet. The texture of the parchment is rough beneath my fingertips. "I think looking through the library is too time-consuming. This could be our shot. Perhaps our only shot before it's too late."

My eyes search the room, taking in each face as they process my words. Everyone appears deep in thought, the only sounds the occasional creak of leather armour and the distant call of night birds outside the windows. I linger a bit longer on Theo, who stares at the table, his brows drawn closer together as he thinks about something. Desily catches my attention from her position by the hearth, where the dancing flames paint her in shades of gold and amber, and nods ever so slightly to reassure me she's with me. But Alea remains quiet, her face unreadable in the flickering light. So does Issac, his jaw working silently as he weighs options and consequences. Venali and Jassin stand like twin statues, their hands never straying far from their weapons.

The silence stretches between us.

"I understand your concerns—" I begin, trying to bridge the gap of uncertainty.

"How are you sure he can be trusted?" Alea cuts in, her voice sharp with suspicion. I turn towards her, noting the way her fingers nervously twist the silver ring she always wears.

"I'm not," I admit. "But it's the best lead we have right now." Everyone except Desily, who stands firm in her support, and Ryo, who looks like he has absolutely no idea what's going on, seems doubtful. "Let's face it, we're slowly running out of time, and Gods know where Aagon is right now."

The mention of his name sends a collective shiver through the room. I can almost taste the fear it brings, metallic and sharp.

"It's a good idea in theory," Theo finally signs, his graceful hand movements carrying the weight of his royal upbringing, measured and thoughtful. "But what if he betrays us just like Lathai did and puts everyone in Yalan at risk?" He sighs deeply, the sound filled with the burden of potential consequences.

My throat tightens, anxiety coiling in my chest. My hands shake more visibly now, betraying the doubt that gnaws at my insides. That's precisely what I'm worried about too. The terrifying fact that Eric could be one of Aagon's spies, cleverly positioned to beat us to the ritual. And if I let him get his hands on the letter, then a tragedy far greater than the one that hit Karul will be brought upon the innocent residents of Yalan. A disaster perhaps even Ella herself is desperately trying to prevent.

The weight of this decision presses down on me, making it difficult to breathe. One wrong choice, and thousands of lives hang in the balance. But doing nothing is no longer an option.

Suddenly, I feel the atmosphere in the room shift as a warm hand rests on my shoulder, squeezing it gently. I turn and find Issac's gaze meeting mine, his red eyes no longer hard but full of something rare. Trust and unwavering honesty. Not the disapproval or disappointment I've braced myself against.

"I've made the grave mistake of not listening to her before," he says, his voice resonating through the chamber. "I know we all suffered devastating losses during the attack, but that wasn't Thea's fault." The candle flames seem to still as he speaks. "None of us could've seen that betrayal coming. If you want someone to blame, then blame me too, because I was right there and let it slide. We all were."

Issac's words wash over me, lifting a weight from my chest. A boulder of guilt I hadn't realised I'd been carrying until its absence makes me feel lighter. I look around the room from face to face, the firelight dancing across their features, showing the shame that flickers in their eyes for ever doubting that my word could be trusted. I don't blame them though; I too often punish myself for those same failures. But it seems I'm no longer alone in carrying this overwhelming burden. I've got these people, my friends. My chosen family. To help me navigate the treacherous path.

Desily eyes me suspiciously and I know she's itching to ask just why Issac and I are suddenly on better speaking terms, and why he's become so nice. I'm sure I'll be questioned later in our bedroom, but right now that's not the priority and we both know it as she turns to Alea, thoughts running through their heads.

The tension in the room dissolves.

"So what's the plan, then?" Jassin asks, his deep voice breaking the silence. Beside him, his sister's posture softens visibly.

I draw a steadying breath. "Well, convincing Eric to help us, of course."

"That should be easy enough," Alea adds, a knowing glint in her dark brown eyes, "since he seems to be utterly intrigued by you."

I shoot her a warning look just as Issac's grip on my shoulder grows firmer. My hand finds his, our fingers intertwining in a silent promise, and I give him a reassuring squeeze. There isn't a man on this continent or beyond its shores that could tempt me to leave Issac's side. No matter how honest they are, what titles they hold, or how striking their appearance. My heart made its choice long ago.

"So when are we doing it?" Ryo asks quietly. His eyes dart everywhere but towards Issac, clinging to the vain hope that his mentor might forget about the promised punishment, but I know the man better than I know myself. He won't let it go.

"Sometime this week. We need to prepare for any outcome." The decision forms in my mind with clarity, and everyone nods in understanding.

A movement catches my eye as Theo's elegant hands dance through the air. "We're with you, Thea," he signs, and my smile grows.

***

I go through the map of the world, the possibilities of the artefacts hidden within it for the thousandth time and sigh. Two days have passed since our meeting about approaching Eric and ever since I've not only been avoiding meeting him, but also Issac who seems to need answers. Whether from curiosity or jealousy, I don't know.

I've worked with Theo to approach the topic carefully. Eric barely knows anything about our plan, about the woman residing inside of me, and if I were to reveal that information I might risk our entire cause. People won't be happy to hear that the very monster threatening to destroy their world is just sat there right in front of their eyes. Gods, who knows what he might do. Perhaps he'll shred the letter into pieces, and throw it into the fireplace alongside me.

"Fuck's sake," I grunt and lean back, my head tilting until my gaze becomes lost in the high circular ceiling and the books spiralling upwards into the library's towering heights. I wish my mind were so organised, that it was this easy to reach for information and find the right answer.

"What's got you looking so defeated?"

My attention snaps back to reality as Ryo approaches the table, his slender arms laden with heavy books I'm sure he's dreading to read.

"Life, as per usual," I grunt and try to read the titles he's brought with him. "Issac making you practise crystal magic?"

Ryo sighs dramatically and takes the seat opposite mine. "Yeah, he said I should learn how to use them properly, but honestly, what's the point? We don't even have any resources."

"Knowledge is power," I reply, a smile softening my features despite the weight of my own concerns. "You never know when you might need it." My fingers idly trace the outline of a continent on the map before me.

Though what I said is true, knowledge is also dangerous, especially in the wrong hands.

My mind circles back to Eric, and I exhale slowly, my eyes tracing over the map once more. The ritual is somewhere here, somewhere close I know it, but the rest of the things, Gods know. Perhaps that's what I need, divine help. Nivlan, if you can hear me, please drop a crumb of information, anything that might help me figure this out before it's too late.

"When will you be talking with the Duke?" Ryo asks, his eyes fixed on the text before him but his mind clearly elsewhere. I know he's stalling his studies, but a conversation with someone in our inner circle might be exactly what I need right now.

I tap my quill against the edge of the inkwell, watching tiny droplets splatter across the corner of my parchment. "I don't know. Soon, I think. Theo said I can go for it, so I just need to find the right moment to approach him."

Theo and I spent the last few days talking over the best plan. We've even informed Ella of it, and what could follow were things to go south. The princess, of course, assured me she'll inform her guards as well as giants that in case of a sudden fight breaking out they're instructed to evacuate their town to Keolin. I guess that eased my mind a little, but not as much as I'd hoped it would.

"Will it be before or after you speak with General Edison?"

My mouth hangs open, words dying on my lips as my eyes widen in surprise. Ryo peeks up from his book, a mischievous smirk pulling at the corner of his lips.

"I'm sorry, what does that have to do with anything?" I cross my arms over my chest, taking a defensive stance that's both playful and genuinely curious.

"I mean, he's been absolutely killing us lately during training sessions," Ryo continues, leaning forward. "And I saw the way you two looked at each other during the meeting. I'm no idiot. He doesn't like that Duke fellow, just like he didn't like me at first. He doesn't trust men around you." He shrugs.

My eyes bulge in surprise, a warmth creeping up my neck.

I know Issac is overly protective, perhaps because of his twisted past or the unique bond we share, but going so far as to say he doesn't trust men to be around me seems a far stretch. Doesn't it?

"That's not true. He likes you," I try to fight my case, but Ryo meets my protest with a soft, knowing chuckle.

"Yeah, now that he finally understood I'm not interested in you the way he thought I was." His grin widens. "I mean, come on, you're like a grandma to me. Gross."

I reach over the table and swat Ryo over the head with a pile of papers. "I'm not that old!" I giggle, as he shields himself with upraised arms, our laughter filling the empty space.

"You so are," he nods with mock seriousness, and I fall back into my chair as I shake my head in disbelief. Kids these days.

We both study in quiet for a while, the only sounds the occasional turning of pages and the distant shuffling of books being shelved somewhere in the vast library. The silence stretches between us, comfortable yet heavy with my unspoken worries, until I finally gather enough courage to make a decision about Issac.

He should be finished with his training by now, and will surely be waiting for me to join him for our class. Which I've managed to avoid swiftly by begging Desily to tell him I'm overwhelmed with research. Still, something tells me he came to the training hall regardless, in case I showed up, in case I needed his company. When did we switch roles? When did he become the one needing answers and willing to wait, whilst I became the one hiding truths, running away at any given opportunity?

I mutter a quick goodbye to Ryo before gathering my

papers and leaving, the map rolled carefully and tucked into my leather satchel. The corridors of the great hall stretch before me, torch-lit and eerily quiet as I head for the training room. My mind races, coming up with every possible question that might be thrown my way and any good enough answer that might satisfy him without revealing too much. Will he be angry that I've avoided him these past days? Will his trust in me waver, sending us back to those early days of suspicion and distance? Gods, why is this so complicated when once it was as natural as breathing?

My steps halt before the heavy oak door to the training room, my heart hammering against my ribs. I brace myself for whatever might await inside, my hand hovering over the iron handle. *Inhale,* my hand grabs the iron handle. *Exhale,* the door opens with a creak.

Chapter 26

The room is awfully quiet, empty if not for the man sat in the middle, staring at a spot on the floor. Sunlight streams through the high windows, lighting up the weapons mounted along the walls. I doubt he notices me until the heavy door falls closed behind me with a thud.

Issac turns to face me, his expression unreadable as he blinks, remaining perfectly still. I take a tentative step forward, my fingers fiddling with the frayed hem of my shirt. I've dreaded this conversation, but I know it must be done. It pains me to hide things from him, especially now that we've found some peace between us.

I scratch absently at my hand as I stop before him. His eyes are softer than I expected, calm, something I didn't expect after days of avoidance. He reaches for my leg and pulls me closer to him, his head coming to rest against my stomach. The warmth of his touch seeps through my shirt.

"Have the past me made you so scared of telling me things that you've refused to see me for a few days?" he murmurs. I feel myself relaxing as his arms wrap around my waist. "Or has it been me, now, who made you afraid?"

His words make me jerk. Though a part of me wants to deny it, a larger part recognises the truth in what he's asked, and that realisation hurts. I don't want him thinking I'm afraid of him. I've never been. I'm just afraid of failing him and everyone else, of watching the trust in his eyes fade to disappointment.

"It's not like that," I try to explain as my fingers tangle in his soft hair, brushing through the silken strands. The scent of him, freshly fallen snow and timber, fills my senses.

He looks up at me, and I catch a flash of sadness passing through those crimson depths. I purse my lips, uncertain of my next move. Should I lie and spare him the pain, or stick to honesty?

"Then how is it, Thea? Why didn't you come to me to talk about Eric? Why have you been avoiding our training sessions?" he asks. I swallow hard and slowly lower myself so our gazes are level, knees pressing against the cool wooden floor. He's been honest with me; I should do the same.

"In the past, you weren't very keen on the men in my life," I begin. "Honestly, right now it seems like you aren't either." My voice comes out as a whisper.

Issac licks his lip and looks away for a moment, and I give him that brief break. My eyes scan his features, tracing the line of his jaw, the curve of his mouth, the furrow between his brows.

"It's not that I don't trust you," he finally says. "I don't trust them. I don't want you getting hurt." His eyes meet mine again, and I sigh.

"I'll be fine, Issac," I assure him, reaching out to trace the line of his cheekbone. "Not everyone is a threat."

"In your life? Yes, everyone is. Including me." His words catch me off-guard. There's never a time when he doesn't view himself as the villain, though I see him as so much better.

Yet somehow, he always ends up voicing his darkest fears whilst I remain silent with mine. Will there ever be a time when we don't have to be this way?

"Issac," I begin, my voice steadier now, "do you think we have a chance to work?" His head shoots up, his eyes wild with emotions I can't read. Fear, hope, desperation perhaps. He's on his feet in seconds, strong fingers wrapping around my wrists, as if he's terrified I'm about to slip away from him.

"Why? Did I do something wrong?" The urgency in his voice makes me fight off a smile, because this Issac is so different from the one I first knew. This one behaves like his younger self, like the man he was before all the dreadful things happened. Around me, he's a boy in his twenties, and it's as if the world hasn't yet hurt him in countless ways.

"No, no, I just—" I pause. "Well, it seems like I'm always diving into this with no worries. I don't care about who you were, and what might happen. I just see us. But you seem to see things differently." I squeeze his hand, feeling my heart thundering inside my chest. "I feel like you live in constant fear that you might be the one to hurt me."

"Fuck," he growls, pulling away, his fingers raking through his hair as he paces across the polished floor. The sound of his boots echoes. "Of course I'm scared. You can't deny there's a risk, Thea. My mere existence is a risk to yours, and I always find a way to fuck things up."

"Issac," I say firmly, rising to my feet, "there are always risks. Our whole lives we've been at risk, with or without you, but this. Us. Is different." I take a step forward. "I will always risk being with you because that's the only thing in my life that has proved to be worth living for."

He stops suddenly. The turmoil behind his eyes is evident but begins to fade as my words sink in. I need him to understand that he's not in this alone. I'm here; I've always been and will continue to be. Without him, I don't know who I would've become.

I watch as he crosses the distance between us in a few quick strides, and suddenly I'm pulled against his chest, my body melting under his touch. The familiar shape of his body fits against mine perfectly.

"I wonder how many of those risks you're willing to take before your heart can't bear it anymore," he murmurs against my hair.

I smile and reach up to cup his cheek, feeling the slight stubble beneath my palm. "As many as you do," I promise.

Issac lowers his head and captures my lips in a kiss. The silent training room fills with sound. The beating of my heart, our quickened breaths, the rustle of fabric as we hold each other close. Through the high windows, the late afternoon sun bathes us in golden light.

I arch my back into him, pressing the length of my body against his. His warmth wraps around me as I become drunk on his scent. Pine, iron, and something uniquely him. Issac's hand slides to the small of my back, fingers pressing with a possessive intensity that ignites something inside me.

His tongue traces my bottom lip with deliberate slowness, raising goosebumps across my skin despite the layers of clothing between us. The wet heat of his mouth sends shivers down my spine. I pull away for just a moment, my lips trailing kisses from his jaw to the hollow of his neck, before stopping at the collar of his shirt where I can feel his pulse hammering.

I hear him release a deep growl that goes right through me, making my knees weaken. Even so, I don't stop when my hands cup his cheeks and pull him closer again.

Issac, as if plucking the thought directly from my mind, suddenly grasps my arse with both hands, lifting me effortlessly. The unexpected movement pulls a surprised yelp from my lips before my back meets the cold stone wall, knocking the breath from my lungs. The contrast between the chill of the stone and the burning heat of his body sends a shudder through me.

The kiss deepens into something wild, all pretence abandoned. His tongue plunges into my mouth as I try and fail to ignore the unmistakable hardness in his trousers pressing against me. Each movement of his hips sends sparks of pleasure through my veins.

"It's not my fault your thoughts almost drown me when you're like this," his voice echoes through my head.

"Stop spying on me and get out of my head," I respond, though the command lacks conviction.

"Would love to, because if we don't stop soon I will fuck you right here, on this floor." My body shakes at his crude promise, pleasure spreading through me faster than I can process, pooling hot between my legs. His hands squeeze and knead my arse, lifting me higher against the wall. His breath ghosts over my flushed cheeks. His teeth capture my bottom lip. Not quite painful but thrillingly close. And I shiver from pure need. My arms circle his shoulders, fingers diving into his hair, tugging just hard enough to make him groan against my mouth.

"As much as I'd like to continue," he huffs out between heated kisses, "I want to take you somewhere."

"Must be important since you're willing to stop this," I chuckle breathlessly, but quickly fall silent as his grasp becomes rougher, his fingers pressing into my flesh.

"Trust me, Thea," he murmurs, his crimson eyes darkened, "there's nothing else I'd rather do, but I want to create memories with you beyond sex."

I stop suddenly, my body stilling against his as our gazes level. Issac's eyes tell me everything. The raw honesty there steals my breath more effectively than any kiss. He isn't lying. He wants me. That much is evident. But this isn't the type of need that'll be satisfied merely in bed. He wants what lies beyond my body; he craves the approval of my very soul.

Something shifts between us, something deep and wordless.

"Let's go then," I whisper.

***

Dressed in a heavy coat, the dragon chest plate beneath with daggers safely tucked in its hidden pockets, we forge our way through the snow as the silver moon hangs above us. My gloved hand finds Issac's warm grasp as he leads us higher up the mountain.

I must admit, even after countless training sessions with him, conquering this path in such conditions tests my endurance. My breath comes in heavy clouds before me. Perhaps it's the biting cold or the restrictive weight of protective clothing, but sweat forms beneath my garments as I struggle for the tenth time to wrench my boot from the clutching snow.

"Where exactly are we going?" I finally ask.

Issac's low chuckle echoes in the stillness, but he doesn't slow his pace. If anything, I sense him quickening his stride. "You'll see soon enough," he promises.

"Hopefully I won't die before then," I mutter under my breath, but nothing escapes his senses. He yanks me forward with a playful tug that sends me off-balance, my body colliding briefly with his before I right myself.

My gaze drifts upward to the vault of night above us, the deep indigo expanse studded with countless stars. Their scattered pattern reminds me of Issac's freckles. Constellations I've mapped with my fingertips in intimate moments. Glancing back at our path, I realise we've climbed far beyond the reach of any watchful eyes. Strangely, this isolation brings comfort rather than fear. Out here, my magic can flow more freely. Though I temper that freedom with caution. An errant spell could trigger an avalanche.

We continue in silence, the rhythmic crunch of snow beneath our boots and the whistle of wind creating a wild symphony around us. After what feels like both a moment and forever, I catch sight of our destination. The summit emerging from the darkness ahead. We've reached one of Yalan's highest points. Yet I wonder what purpose drove Issac to guide me through this gruelling climb.

"Close your eyes," he commands softly. I regard him with unveiled doubt, but something in his expression. A rare vulnerability. Melts my resistance away. His hands guide me forward with unexpected tenderness, supporting my weight whenever I falter. Finally, we halt.

"Is the torture finally over?" I huff out, flexing fingers that have grown numb.

His chuckle warms the space between us, defying the biting

cold. "Yes," he affirms. "You can open your eyes now."

I roll my eyes beneath closed lids before slowly lifting them, blinking against an unexpected brightness. And then I see it. The reason Issac has brought us here. My hand slips from his grasp as I turn in a slow circle, first gazing down at Yalan spread below us. The city's lights. Warm glows from hearths and homes, torches, lanterns and bonfires. Create their own constellation against the darkness. From this height, the imposing structures appear tiny, reduced to mere specks.

My gaze travels further, beyond the city walls to where Keolin's more distant lights glimmer faintly, and beyond that to where darkness stretches unbroken. The snow-covered landscape glitters, each crystal catching and breaking the moonlight.

I turn towards the ocean, where the vast expanse of water stretches to the edge of the world. Far below, mighty waves crash against the mountain's base, their distant roar reaching us as little more than a whisper. The sea appears as black as spilled ink under the night sky.

Suddenly, something in the water captures my attention. An unusual flicker of colour reflecting off the dark surface. My eyes lift skyward, and the gasp that escapes me hangs suspended in the frozen air.

The heavens have transformed entirely. Where moments before stretched deep blue infinity studded with stars, now unfolds a sight of such beauty it steals the breath from my lungs. Vast curtains of light cascade across the sky. Shimmering emerald green pulses with vibrant life, rippling and folding upon itself. Violet so deep it borders on midnight blue weaves through the display, occasionally erupting into brilliant flashes of cobalt that light up the entire sky. Ribbons of ruby red and salmon pink dance amongst the other hues.

The auroras move with purpose and grace, expanding and contracting in rhythmic waves. Their edges shimmer and dissolve. Each shifting pattern tells a story older than human memory.

The glow bathes the snow-covered landscape around us, transforming our world into a kaleidoscope of colour. The pristine white reflects back the celestial display, making the entire mountain seem alive with magic.

I hear the soft crunch of snow behind me. Issac approaches slowly, perhaps allowing me this moment before his arms circle my waist. The solid strength of him presses against my back. The heat of him goes through our layers of clothing.

His chin comes to rest atop my head, his breath creating a gentle rhythm that somehow syncs with the pulsing lights above. Though his touch grounds me to earth, my gaze remains captured by the heavens.

The connection between us deepens in this shared silence. No words could express what passes between us. The towering mountains around us stand as ancient witnesses.

I've lived for centuries. Yet somehow, I've spent those long years with my vision narrowed, my gaze fixed downward on immediate threats, on politics and survival. I forgot to look up, to pause and witness beauty purely for its own sake.

As the auroras continue their dance overhead, something long-knotted within my chest begins to unravel. Our problems remain: Eric, the ritual, the threats that circle us. Yet viewed beneath this cosmic spectacle, they appear smaller, more manageable.

Issac's arms tighten almost imperceptibly around me. I allow myself to lean fully into his embrace, perhaps truly resting against his strength for the first time without reservation or fear. Together we stand, bearing witness as the heavens paint stories only the stars will remember.

In this moment, I can't think of anything else but the two of us as children, witnessing the wonders of the world together for the first time. Memories cascade through me. When I'd chase crimson fireflies through the twilight forest; when Issac and I would walk barefoot along fields dotted with glowing mushrooms; when magic didn't seem like a curse but simply what it was. Magical, wondrous, a gift rather than a burden.

"Was the torture worth it?" Issac whispers from behind, and I chuckle softly.

"I guess it was," I admit, watching as a ribbon of emerald light unfurls across the sky. "How did you know I'd like the view?" I often retreat into the past, thinking about the forgotten beauties of our world, but I rarely voice these thoughts unless directly asked.

"I listen to you sometimes," he jokes, and I elbow him gently.

"Thank you for showing me this," I say, turning to face him, finding a soft smile stretching across his lips. It truly melts my heart knowing he planned this for me. A sight he knew would dissolve my worries and bring joy to my burdened spirit. The fact that he remembers the things I love speaks volumes.

"Don't thank me yet. This doesn't even equal what you deserve." His fingers brush my hair behind my ear, his eyes searching my face. The crimson of his irises catches the aurora's light. "If what it takes to bring a smile to your face is to present you the wonders of our world, I'll search for them anywhere."

He places a kiss atop my forehead, his lips lingering there a moment longer. "Still, I'll argue the most breathtaking thing here is you, but that's just my opinion."

"Are you trying to steal my heart, Issac Edison?" I giggle and playfully swat his arm.

"Already done, darling," he responds, the simple phrase carrying the weight of our shared history, our present, and all the uncertain future that stretches before us. A future that, for this perfect moment under the dancing sky, seems a little less frightening to face. "C'mon, let's get going before you freeze to death," he says finally, his reluctance to break the spell evident in his tone.

"I could warm us up," I offer, longing to stay here longer beneath the shimmering curtains of light, but I know Issac is right and we need to begin our descent. Cold might not be the only danger lurking in the darkness; the monsters of Sebraycia are surely waiting for their next easy meal.

Issac entwines our fingers, a gesture that sends shivers down my spine no matter how many times we've done it. Something about us now though feels much different to what we were in Ķarul. We're no longer two friends separated after a long time, forced into each other's presence and rashly admitting their feelings, but two people who, despite the odds and struggles, have fought for each other. We're something completely different, something new. Another story entirely.

"I know you could, trust me," he chuckles, and I push his shoulder playfully.

We make our way down the mountainside over the next hour or two, finding the descent less hard than our climb. I'm surprised when the subject of our mission isn't something Issac asks about, but instead he asks about the person he was before. The old Issac had refused to be connected to his past, whilst this version of him is full of questions. I suppose Theo's words and Lord Graham's brainwashing took much more than a mere memory of me; he was stripped of who he was entirely.

So I tell him everything. I tell him about how we met, the mischief we caused together, the nights we spent sneaking out from our rooms to stargaze, and the afternoons we'd spend going through forest paths known only to us. I tell him about his mother and the books she read to us, the stories she told by firelight. I tell him how he'd always dreamt of becoming a soldier, and how I was uncertain about my future, naively thinking the world wasn't cruel.

I talk for so long that by the time we reach the castle, most of the lights are out. But Issac doesn't interrupt me. He doesn't grow weary of my stories or silence me with his own questions. He just listens closely, as if making mental notes of each detail, each fragment of his lost past, and that alone is something that makes me fall in love with him even more deeply.

Just as we step through the front doors, our breath still clouding in the cold night air, a guard rushes towards us, his face covered in sweat despite the chill, his eyes wild with worry. Out of instinct, I prepare to let go of Issac's hand, but he holds me firmly at his side.

"Miss Starbane, we've been looking for you everywhere!" he rushes out in ragged breaths, and my heart sinks to my stomach. Something isn't right.

"What happened?" I demand.

"It's Miss Stardove, she's been hurt."

Hurt? The single thought eclipses everything else. The world narrows as fear wraps its cold fingers around my throat.

Chapter 27

I've never run so fast in my life. Not even when rushing home to tell my parents we needed to flee the country. Not when escaping Karul and certain death. My feet scream in protest as I tear across the castle corridors, fingernails digging crescents into my palms. Cold sweat beads at my temples despite the chill. I pass faceless figures in a blur, my heartbeat thundering. Questions spin in my head, each breath hard, the taste of copper coating my tongue. Desily is hurt.

Despite everything we've endured, I still forget our lives hang by a thread. Acid guilt churns in my stomach as I realise my carelessness. Keeping my friends at arm's length is the only way to protect them. Dare I find a moment's happiness, and the world hurls another obstacle in my path, a cruel reminder of my destiny. Not joy, but a sentence to misery and worry. My jaw clenches tight.

"Thea, wait!" Issac's voice echoes behind me, but I can't tear my gaze from the heavy oak doors at the corridor's end. The medical wing awaits. Where the guard directed us before I bolted ahead, driven by raw fear.

My limbs quiver. Dread coils in my stomach, each terrible possibility sending waves of nausea through me. Vision blurs at the edges as panic rises. Did someone get into the palace? Is Aagon hunting me? Did they target Desily knowing what she means to me? The metallic taste of fear floods my mouth.

Ligaya's warning echoes. My friends in mortal peril, their safety my responsibility. Sweat trickles down my spine as I struggle to steady my hands. Even Jino's unspeakable offer seems possible now as terror tightens my throat. I can bear losing everything, but what remains if my "everything" is the people I cherish? My heart pounds against my ribs with such force I fear they might crack.

I shove the doors with such force they nearly tear from their hinges, slamming against stone with a thunderous crack. I halt, drawing a deep breath before looking around the room. Ten beds line each wall, and at the far end stands a solemn gathering. Theo, Alea, Ryo and Ella, each as pale as midwinter frost.

Their heads turn in unison, eyes widening. First, Theo's gaze meets mine. His face drains of colour as he shakes his head. A silent warning. My attention shifts to Alea, eyes crimson and swollen, tear tracks staining her ashen cheeks. Her usually perfect hair now hangs in disarray, strands caught in trembling lips. Arms wrapped around her middle as though holding herself together, she quakes violently, knuckles white from gripping her elbows.

I step forward, legs nearly buckling. Ryo's normally bright eyes now appear bloodshot and hollow, his face ashen. The boyish innocence I've always admired has vanished, replaced by a haunted stare that chills me. His hands shake uncontrollably, breathing shallow. Dread tightens my chest. One question burns in my mind. The one question I desperately don't want answered.

"Thea." Ella's voice carries unexpected steadiness, contradicting her twisted lips and furrowed brow. Her hands clench rhythmically, knuckles cracking. Angry red veins spider through her eyes, dark shadows beneath them. A muscle jumps in her jaw as she swallows hard. I push forward, breath caught in my lungs, frozen in place as each second stretches endlessly.

Alea's sobs pierce my awareness. I'd been deaf to them until now, somehow. Each broken cry twists deeper into my heart, a cold wave of horror washing over me. Could I be too late? Have I lost my best friend? The thought nearly makes me collapse, knees weakening beneath me. I inch closer. My hands tremble against my chest, pulse racing until lightheadedness threatens to overwhelm me. What horrors await?

Mere inches away, both Theo and Ryo step aside, and finally, I see her.

"Des," I whisper, my voice breaking as I rush to her side. My heart pounds painfully, hands gripping the bed's edge until my knuckles blanch. Her dark skin, normally radiant with warmth, appears ashen and dull, lacking that sparkle that usually dances across it. Tears burn down my frozen cheeks. Her clothes hang tattered, body lined with vicious wounds. Blood. So much blood everywhere. The metallic scent fills my nose, making my head spin as I fight back nausea. My hands hover above her, trembling, afraid that even the gentlest touch might cause more harm.

"I'm sorry," Alea chokes between sobs, clutching Desily's hand. "W-We just went for a walk. I didn't realise we'd wandered so far from the gates." Fresh tears cascade down her cheeks. I turn back to Desily, motionless on the bed, desperately searching for signs of life. The cruel gash running from her left brow to cheek has been cleaned and bandaged.

I study her parted lips, then her chest, which rises and falls with shallow breaths. She's alive. Thank Ovian the God of life for letting her stay another day in this wretched world.

"Will she be alright?" I ask, turning my attention to Ella, who has been nervously fiddling with the frayed ends of a woollen scarf hastily thrown over her trembling shoulders.

"Myra did everything within her power," Ella responds, her voice barely above a whisper. "We can't say in what state she'll wake, but she'll live."

"I'm sorry, I'm so bloody sorry," Alea gasps between shallow breaths, breathing so hard that I worry she might collapse at any moment. Her entire body shakes with each sob, fingers clutching at her throat as though fighting for air. Tears and mucus streak her face, shoulders hunched forward. Her eyes dart frantically around the room, pupils dilated with pure terror. So I do something I wish someone had done for me right after the attack. I embrace her, pulling her shaking body against mine in a fierce hug. I feel her heart hammering against her ribcage, her skin clammy and cold to the touch, as her fingers desperately cling to my clothes.

"I didn't mean to." Her voice catches, barely audible.

"It's not your fault," I whisper so that only she can hear it. "It's not your fault, Alea."

I repeat because I know firsthand how hard it is to believe those words. Because I still haven't believed them myself but I wish I could. Her body slumps in my arms, her cries muffled in the thick layers of my clothing, and all I can do is hold her with all my strength. My fingers brush her hair in a calming manner, and despite everything, I let myself pray that Desily will be okay, that this isn't the awful ending I've been promised. Albris, please, if you can hear me, I need some miracle, an ounce of luck.

"You know there's a way to protect her from dangers." Jino's voice slithers in. My whole body tenses as rage fills my bloodstream.

"Get lost Jino, now is not the time," I grunt out, trying to be mindful of the crowd around me, even spotting Issac trying to sign something to Theo only he will know. When did he get here?

"Are you sure about that? Your friend seems to be in a bad state and you're telling me you won't consider my offer?" I close my eyes shut, rage boiling beneath my skin. I let myself appear before her. Not as the restrained version of myself, but as fury itself. My hands itch to do more than gesture; they crave to connect with her smug face. The thought of silencing her with violence instead of words floods my mind with dark satisfaction.

"Offer? There is no offer and there won't be. Falling for your tricks is the last thing I'll do." I poke a finger at her, but she dances away, her laughter echoing off the stone walls. Hollow and unhinged. Each cackle scrapes against my nerves.

She circles me, her footsteps making no sound against the cold floor. Though her gaze flickers toward the weathered stonework, I feel the weight of her attention pressing down on me. Her presence fills the room with something unsettling and terrifying. Like the air before a devastating storm. A cold shiver runs down my spine, each bone turning to ice one by one. The hairs on my arms stand rigid beneath my sleeves, my skin prickling with warning. This isn't just fear; it's something primal, something my body knows is dangerous long before my mind can process it.

"Oh Althea, and will you take responsibility if something happens to her? Will you blame me for not offering help?"

"She's fine," I grunt out through closed teeth, and suddenly she stops. Her purple eyes bore into mine with such intensity that I feel my legs grow weak despite the previous confidence. Those eyes seem to peer straight through my defences, exposing every fear I've tried to bury.

"This time, what about the next one? What if you're not around again? What then? Do you think you can protect them all the time, everyone here?" Each question lands like a physical blow, each word precisely aimed to find the cracks in my resolve.

I swallow hard, the sound deafening in my own ears. Her words sink in, burrowing deep beneath my skin because I know-Gods help me-she's right. My heart pounds a reluctant admission against my ribs. I might be able to protect two, perhaps three people if I manage to stalk their every move. But our entire group? The very thought stretches before me, too wide even for someone as stubborn as me to bridge.

Truth is, since that hushed conversation with Ligaya, her warnings still ringing in my ears, I've come to a haunting conclusion. Desily needs my protection most. Though her fingers dance skilfully with a sword, though her powers can stitch wounds closed, if thrust into true battle, her light would falter. She wasn't raised for violence and bloodshed. She was meant to heal, to mend what others break, working alongside her kind with gentle hands. Her sister at her side, continuing a legacy of mercy. Everything changed, the world turning upside down, yet to her core, she remains unchanged.

A healer forced to bear witness to destruction.

I think back to her still form on the bed, chest barely rising with each shallow breath. The vision haunts me. Two people closest to me, their fates sealed in blood. Who else could it be but Desily and Issac? He moves through danger like it's merely an inconvenience, a river to be crossed. I'm certain he'd survive nearly anything this cruel world hurls at him. But Desily… she isn't made from the same unbreakable material as us. Her spirit shines too brightly, too purely. She's nearly as vulnerable as any human, her mortality a constant shadow at her heels.

"Tell me, girl, have you come to your conclusion?" Jino's voice slithers into my ear, her breath carrying the chill of ancient tombs. I feel her words more than hear them, vibrations against my skin raising goose flesh along my neck. I swallow hard, my throat dry. The deal dangles before me. Tempting, poisonous, perhaps necessary. But who says the time will come when I must taste it? I'll find another way. I always do.

"We will talk later." My voice comes out steadier than I feel, each word weighted with resignation and determination in equal measure.

"I'm sure we will." I hear her say before diving back into reality. Before facing the fact that I might've just agreed to do the worst thing in my life.

***

Eating in the main hall without Desily's presence feels exactly as it should. Horribly lifeless. Three days have passed and she still hasn't woken up. Both Alea and I have been visiting her at every opportunity, but with Issac trying to pull my thoughts elsewhere, I find myself trapped between constant worry and necessary training.

Yesterday, we managed to leave the castle for just an hour, as I refused to stray too far in case Des woke up. During that brief break, Issac had me practise every magical spell possible. It felt exciting to wield fire again, to create a shield with a mere thought, to hurl a fireball across the frozen air and change temperature with the flick of my wrist. Surprisingly, even weapon creation wasn't the challenge I'd expected. I switched between a gleaming sword and a crackling whip without faltering.

A part of me yearned to stay longer, to absorb something new and useful that might protect us all, but the larger part. The paranoid, anxious part. Had my feet moving before the sun could sink behind the jagged mountains.

"Ugh, I hate veggies." Ryo's voice yanks my attention back to the present moment, interrupting Alea's listless prodding of her untouched food. "Don't you guys? I mean, look at this." He gestures dramatically at the vibrant greens wilting on his plate.

"What are you doing here?" I ask, gently shoving away my own plate, the food barely disturbed. My appetite vanished that night and likely won't return until I know my best friend is safe.

"Ouch, sorry for joining you guys. I didn't know it was a closed party." Ryo clutches his chest in mock offence, wiping imaginary tears from his cheeks with theatrical flair.

"No, no, I meant—"

"I know, we came to cheer the two of you up." He interrupts, before contradicting his earlier disgust by shovelling a heaping spoonful of greens into his mouth.

I stare at him, confusion furrowing my brow. "We?"

Right on cue, the weathered wood beneath me creaks as the weight around our table shifts. I turn to find Issac settling beside me, whilst across the table, Theo takes a seat, his eyes drifting left to his sister with unmistakable concern. I can't blame him. She's barely spoken to anyone, hardly appearing for meals unless I physically drag her from our room.

Issac's warm hand slides beneath the table, landing on my thigh with a gentle, reassuring squeeze that instantly melts some of the tension from my rigid posture. His gaze falls to my barely touched plate, and without a word, he firmly pushes it back under my nose. I open my mouth to protest, but one meaningful look from those penetrating eyes has my spine straightening in reluctant compliance. Under different circumstances, I'd fight until the bitter end, but surrounded by friends, I can't bring myself to cause a scene over something as trivial as food. Especially when his actions stem from genuine concern. Though lately, any reason to rebel feels like a good one.

I've been balancing on a knife's edge, so tightly wound that even Myra's snarky remarks and venomous glares are enough to set me ablaze. My thoughts scatter. I'm not thinking clearly. All I want is release from this emotional prison: the guilt gnawing at my insides, the fear coiling around my throat, the worry burning behind my eyes, the constant anxiety prickling beneath my skin, and the shame that weighs on my shoulders. Even with Issac somehow returned to me, I feel myself drowning beneath an avalanche of thoughts, and what's worse. I can speak of this to no one. Not my best friend lying unconscious, not Theo or Alea with their own burdens, and not even Issac, whose presence should bring comfort. Gods know how desperately I wish to unburden myself, but if they discovered what's been happening behind the scenes, I fear they'd never look at me the same way again.

"Any plans for today?" Ryo asks cheerfully, and I glance toward Alea, who merely shrugs one shoulder before Theo taps her arm and begins signing.

"Want to help me research a few things?" Theo's suggestion hangs in the air. We all know there isn't much to be done, and Alea surely realises her brother mostly spends his days filling out endless paperwork and studying musty tomes, but neither of us contradicts him. This isn't about Alea's help. He wants private time with his sister to make sure she's coping.

Just as Alea's lips part to decline, I interject, "That's a brilliant idea. Alea could look through our preparations." The lie rolls smoothly off my tongue.

She shoots me a bewildered look before I subtly nod toward her brother, making it painfully obvious that he's worried and won't be deterred. They need this time together. "Fine," she relents with a sigh. "I'll come to your room."

"Then I can leave for tonight. You two deserve some quality family time." Issac interjects, setting down his fork with a soft clink.

"And where will you go?" Alea asks, one eyebrow arching sceptically in my direction.

"Plenty of rooms in the castle," he answers casually, and I can't help but smile. It's another side of him I've discovered. How he quietly shows kindness without drawing attention to it. Like coming with me to Desily's bedside each night, secretly monitoring her healing progress, or coaxing me on late-night walks through echoing corridors where I can speak freely about our shared past. Or how he slips away after our training sessions to the library, teaching himself sign language so he can better understand Theo. He might think these gestures go unnoticed, but I see them all, and they only deepen my feelings for him.

"Not every room will have Thea in it," Ryo whispers beside me, and I gawk at him before delivering a swift elbow to his ribs. The boy grins triumphantly, but his smile falters as he notices Issac's withering glare boring into him. "I'll shut up," he mutters, suddenly fascinated by the vegetables he claimed to despise.

"It's fine, I might stay up longer with Theo. Issac and you can do whatever the two of you usually get up to." For a second, Alea's lip curves up in a knowing smirk, and I stop myself from hushing her in front of everyone because her smile is worth more than the secrecy of my private time with the man. If that's what makes her happy, so be it.

For the rest of lunch, the five of us dive into discussing our next destination. Everyone seems eager to prepare in any way possible. Whether it's extra hours dedicated to honing combat skills, researching potential threats, or stacking up on provisions we might need. Eric's name is called more times than I'd wish, which only serves to remind me of that dreaded conversation the two of us desperately need to have. I promise myself that the next time we cross paths, I'll speak to him properly. It's better to get this uncomfortable matter out of the way.

"Good afternoon to everyone. I hope you're enjoying your meal." My eyes snap open, and I look up to find Eric standing right behind Alea, his shadow falling across our table. Right.

Who planned this little coincidence?

Issac's grip on my leg tightens instantly, his fingers pressing into my flesh with barely controlled tension. I slide my hand beneath the table to give him a reassuring squeeze. This might be the perfect opportunity I've been looking for, and since I made that promise to myself less than a minute ago, well, it's time to stick to my words.

"We are," Alea replies, her usual formal smile faltering slightly at the edges, the constant worry over Desily's condition still weighing heavily on her. "What brings you here, Duke Eric?"

"Just stopped by to grab food before returning to some paperwork and heading home." He smiles warmly at Alea, though his eyes linger on me for a heartbeat too long, sending a prickle of unease down my spine. "No need to be formal. Eric is fine."

Theo coughs, catching my attention, and I look past a vase with water to see that his fingers are already twitching with unspoken words, eager to engage with Eric. I'm certain it's just more aristocratic nonsense that I could never comprehend, but I clear my throat nonetheless. "Pardon me, Lord Graham would like to speak with you."

"But of course." Eric flashes his pearly whites, and I struggle to maintain my composure, knowing full well that on my right, Issac sits brewing, his glare so intense I can feel it burning in my peripheral vision.

As the two men begin signing rapidly back and forth, I make sure the rest of our group is sufficiently engrossed in conversation before opening the connection leading to Issac. I've promised myself to be more honest with him, and if telling him I'm about to speak to the man he loathes is what needs to be done, then so be it.

The mental door between us cracks open, and almost immediately I'm hit with the full force of Issac's turbulent emotions. Anger, fear, uncertainty, jealousy. It's all there, swirling, though I hope to clear it by letting some clarity in.

"I'll speak to him after lunch," I project, watching Issac's expression carefully, noting the way his eyes meet mine with silent pleading, as if he wants to come with me, as if he's afraid something beyond his control might happen in his absence.

"Are you sure?" he asks, dark brows drawn together in concern. My fingers intertwine with his beneath the table, hidden from prying eyes, and I nod my head ever so slightly so that only he can see, so that only he understands my resolve.

"I'll be fine. If you're still not convinced, then just make sure to keep our connection in proximity." In the manor, the effective distance was probably only a quarter of this sprawling castle. I'm certain if Eric and I end up in one of the rooms not far from the dining hall, Issac will still be able to talk with me, to hear my thoughts clearly.

"I always do. I always listen out for you." His mental voice wraps around me, both comforting and possessive in equal measure.

The connection between us shuts with a decisive click, and I look away, suddenly conscious of the others at our table. Is it wrong to admit this Issac is way easier to convince, more willing to compromise than I remember? The one in the manor would've fought tooth and nail to keep me away from Eric, consumed by fears he could never quite put into words.

I think back to what he just said. That he's always listening for me. And wonder if his words ring true. Has he truly been standing silent guard over my thoughts all this time? The question lingers, but evaporates just as quickly when I see Eric rise from the table, offering polite goodbyes with practised charm. Right, it's now or never.

Going over the carefully rehearsed phrases I've been mentally practising for days, I push myself up from my seat. Issac's warm hand slides reluctantly from my thigh, and in its place settles a peculiar chill. Eric's eyes find mine across the table, curiosity flickering behind his diplomatic smile as I stand still.

"I'd like to speak with you." The words emerge with a steadiness that surprises me, a confidence I hadn't known I possessed until this moment. Despite the trembling uncertainty beneath my ribs, my voice doesn't betray me.

His smile widens, revealing perfect teeth. "Then let's go."

Chapter 28

The room is spacious, easily twice the size of the one I share with Desily and Alea. Through the tall, frost-kissed arched windows, I spot the mountain Issac and I conquered a few days ago, with several houses and tents nestled at its base. I flex my fingers as I take in the crimson interior of the office Eric has brought us to. This is where he spends his time, buried beneath piles of paperwork resting atop a mahogany desk.

A couple of bookshelves stand near the entrance, and a luxurious couch stretches before a long table, but taking in the details of this room isn't what I've come here to do. Almost instantly, my eyes land on the man examining the documents yet to be read and signed. I take a shaky breath before approaching the desk.

"That's a lot to do," I observe, my voice quieter than intended.

He chuckles, the sound warm and genuine. "Yes, indeed, and almost no time when I have to leave by tomorrow."

His hand slides through the long strands of his hair, and I purse my lips. Even now, he's dressed in expensive clothes adorned with silver. The fabric of his shirt made of silk and something I could never afford. Sometimes the difference between royalty and a mere commoner strikes me with painful clarity. They have everything whilst we have to fight to keep from starving. Lately, I've forgotten about that privilege, but my past self would fight with dogs for a piece of stale bread. Some of us are born lucky, even as humans, into a life others could only dream of.

"I didn't realise you had to do so much," I say, deciding to take the seat before him, my legs slightly wobbly, betraying my nervousness.

"Well, this is just a few matters between the Royal family and the people from my village, though Thea." He stops and looks up at me, mischief dancing behind his deep eyes. "But I don't think paperwork is the reason you wanted to speak."

"Right, sorry." I clear my throat and straighten my posture. I've got this, I tell myself. If things go badly, then Ella will have to forgive me for burning this part of the castle down. Hopefully Theo has already informed her that the meeting has began."I'm sorry to ask so suddenly, but we need your help."

Eric stops reading whatever had drawn his attention, his focus now fully on me. He quirks a brow, his lips curving into a curious smile before he settles back in his chair. I know he looks harmless, and I know he's been nothing but kind, yet I can't help but remain cautious. Perhaps Issac was right and I'm bad at reading people. Perhaps I search for kindness in anyone, to have a reason not to feel disappointed, not to kill them.

Back in the manor I was warned countless times about Lathai, and I've always looked past it. Back then it felt almost as if Issac knew something I didn't, as if him and Theo hid some truth about the man I'd yet to discover, but that changes nothing. Practised smiles, and kind words are just a part of someone's life, for others they're a weapon and I don't know Eric well enough to tell which one is which. I can't afford to sit here and guess, I have to play these games right and stay alert.

"My interest is piqued. Do tell," he encourages with a gentle wave of his hand.

"Let me start from the beginning."

I tell him in detail about my powers, about who I am and the reason as to why I'm staying in Sebraycia. I tell him about Jino and Aagon, and the prophecy, and why it's important for us to find the ritual paper. I make sure to note his expressions, the changes in his eyes for any signs of sudden betrayal, but Eric remains composed, only nodding when needed, leaving nothing for me to read besides curiosity.

A part of me secretly hopes he might turn out to be evil, that he will betray me and show me kindness doesn't exist. That he will somehow prove that what Lathai has done can be done again, because then hating him would be easier. I wouldn't need to feel half as guilty as I do about missing him when I shouldn't, when my friends are suffering and want him gone. If only any of them knew my true feelings about the man that made our lives a living hell, they'd scream at me until their throats bled, and I wouldn't blame them.

"This brings me to my main point. We need your power to find out what was written in those smudged lines," I blurt out quickly, trying to finish this awfully long story so that I don't have to relive it again. Talking about the past, especially this period of my life, isn't something I enjoy, but rather something I torture myself with on a daily basis.

Eric leans back into his chair, an unreadable expression

clouding his face. The urge to bite my fingernails from anxiety is so strong I shove them under my thighs and pray for the best outcome. Albris, let this go well, let him be on our side.

"So just so we're clear. You want me to use my powers to find a ritual that will stop an evil sorceress from thousands of years ago from destroying our world once she meets your ex-friend?"

"Her ex-lover actually, who possessed him," I correct Eric, and he smiles.

"Right, an ex-lover that used to be your friend but became evil. Okay." The man nods, a smile I can't place in any category playing on his lips. A moment passes where a droplet of sweat traces down my spine, where the ticking of the clock becomes the only sound filling the room, where my heart shakes my body. "That's fine, I'll help."

"Really?" I sound more surprised than I should, nearly jumping out of my seat at his words, the leather creaking beneath me, but quickly compose myself when Eric chuckles, his eyes scanning my frame in a way I know would make Issac's blood boil. "I mean, thank you. How could I repay you?"

He shakes his head before leaning forward, the smell of parchment and perfume surrounding me, musky and expensive. "You don't have to. I'm happy to help, and also from the sound of it I'll be saving the world alongside you."

Without thinking twice, I launch myself across the table and wrap my arms around Eric to pull him into a hug, papers crinkling beneath my elbows. No words can describe how grateful I am, how much his help means, the weight lifting from my shoulders. We are finally going somewhere, finally might be able to tick one thing off the never-ending list.

My body tenses when I realise what I've just done, muscles going rigid. Hugging a duke I've barely known is probably punishable, but suddenly Eric's hands come from underneath me and return the gesture, warm and reassuring. I blink at his behaviour, at how a person can so easily trust someone, at how a half-elf half-human wielder decided to help a girl who he barely knows, believing the crazy story that once upon a time I found hard to believe myself.

Perhaps I was wrong, and so was Issac. Perhaps I am good at reading people, and some of them can be kind and trustworthy, not everyone hiding bad motives. I pull away slightly, going back to my seat and trying to hide the blush warming my cheeks, the heat spreading to the tips of my ears. What I've done was embarrassing, but how else could I express my gratitude without words failing me?

"When do I have to do it? Since you know, I'll be leaving tomorrow."

"Tomorrow morning is fine, whatever suits you." I can't wait to tell the rest of our group about the news, they'll be thrilled. "I still wish I could repay you somehow."

Eric looks away for a moment, his eyes betraying him as I spot signs of a challenge in them, a glint of something hopeful. "You could join me for dinner," he states boldly, and I freeze in my seat, body going still. I'm sure since the party he's under the impression Issac and I are not together, but things have changed and he deserves the truth, no matter how uncomfortable. I can't make the same mistake twice like I did with Lathai and be blind to his true intentions.

"Eric, I'd love to but it wouldn't be fair to—"

"General Edison?" He finishes for me with a tight smile

that doesn't quite reach his eyes. I bite my lips and nod, hoping I haven't just killed our chances at uncovering the truth. "It's fine, Thea. I gathered you two might be together but just wanted confirmation. You truly don't owe me anything, but if I could ask for one thing, it would be to be considered your friend."

"Of course, that's something you don't need to ask for, Eric." With that said, I get up from the seat, making sure to tell the man where to meet me tomorrow morning. Eric shoots me one last smile before turning to his paperwork whilst I make my way to where that persistent, invisible connection prickling my skin feels strongest.

The door to the training room is cracked open, and I wonder if Issac left it like that in case he urgently needed to leave, always prepared for danger. As per usual, I find him in his vest punching a dummy that wobbles with each hit, droplets of sweat glistening on his pale skin.

I lean against the wall and watch his footwork, the way his body moves with controlled strength, each step precise and deadly. His broad shoulders flex with each movement, muscles rippling beneath the surface, the fabric of his vest clinging to his back, darkened with sweat. My thoughts begin to wander as my eyes trace the defined shape of his arms, following the lines of strength from shoulder to wrist.

Issac's biceps tense when he throws a punch, veins visible along his forearms, and the dummy nearly splits in half from the impact, stuffing threatening to spill out. The power in his body is impressive. I'm sure if he wanted, he could pick me up with one hand, throw me over his shoulder and—

"You just gonna stand there and stare?" he chuckles, bouncing side to side before delivering a hard kick to the dummy's side, making it fall with a dull thud. The movement causes his vest to ride up slightly, revealing a glimpse of toned stomach, a sight that sends heat rushing through me.

I clear my throat and push off the wall, heat creeping up my neck as I try hard to suppress indecent thoughts about this man who has somehow become the best part of my days. Issac wipes the sweat from his forehead with the back of his hand, and I get rid of the unnecessary clothing knowing he will put me into training as soon as I tell him the news.

The shirt rolls off my shoulders revealing simple, white cloth tightly binding my breasts in place. Issac's eyes darken noticeably as they trail over my exposed skin, lingering a moment too long before meeting my gaze again. I reach to plait my hair, but he rushes to my side and stops me, his fingers grazing mine. "Let me, whilst you tell me how it went."

I stare at him with a smirk, but allow him to braid my hair, his fingers surprisingly nimble yet purposefully slow. "I didn't know you could do that."

His fingers brush against my exposed skin, each touch deliberate and lingering, sending electricity racing through my veins. My eyes flutter closed to suppress a sigh as his breath warms the nape of my neck, making it nearly impossible to ignore the growing ache inside me. The heat from his body radiates against my back, an invisible pull that has me fighting the urge to lean into him. "You still don't know a lot about me, now go on," he murmurs, his voice lower than usual, rough around the edges.

"Well, I told him the most important bits and the reason as to why we need him to use his power," I begin, but my focus scatters with each deliberate brush of Issac's fingers along my exposed skin. My words falter when his knuckles graze the sensitive spot where my neck meets my shoulder. Each warm breath ghosting over my skin creates vivid images of what we could be doing instead of training. "He agreed to help," I manage to finish, my voice betraying me with its breathlessness.

"That's great, I knew you could do it." His voice attempts composure, but the slight huskiness gives him away. The way his body gradually presses closer to mine tells me his thoughts have wandered to the same forbidden places as mine. His chest occasionally brushes against my back as he works, each brief contact sending a fresh wave of yearning through me, the tension between us thick enough to cut.

I jump as his finger lands on my shoulder blade, tracing along a scar from long ago, way before I'd ever heard of the manor. The touch is gentle but deliberate, following the slightly raised line that runs diagonally across my skin. The sensation sends a conflicting mixture of vulnerability and comfort through me.

I tilt my head to the side, catching his expression and to my surprise his brows are drawn together, a grimace twisting his lips. His red eyes darken with something that looks like pain, perhaps imagining how I received such a mark. His finger hovers over the scar for a moment longer, as if he could somehow erase it with his touch, before he withdraws slightly, the cool air replacing the warmth of his skin.

"Did I have something to do with it?" I pull away, the braid he's made for me whipping around and landing over my chest.

"What? No, this is from a couple years ago when I was exploring Nahrius and ran into some monsters," I tell him, my hands reaching for his as he listens, his red eyes intent on mine.

"You went back to Eclia?" The question catches me off guard, his voice carrying a hint of disbelief mixed with something that sounds almost like guilt. I thought he knew exactly of my whereabouts but as it seems the brainwashing took away whatever memories had to do with me, even the ones where we weren't together.

"I did, to the parts that felt safe. I've been to many places whilst looking for you." My voice softens with the admission, the words carrying years of searching, of hope repeatedly kindled and put out.

Issac purses his lips before clicking his tongue and taking a step forward, his arm circling my waist to pull me closer, his touch firm but gentle. "Seems fate wanted to keep us apart."

I swallow the ball of guilt forming in my throat, because the truth I'm about to say tastes far more bitter than it should. Yet, honesty with Issac is what matters and bringing his memories back is my priority, even if they're hurtful.

"It wasn't fate, it was you," I whisper, bringing my hand to palm his face, feeling the slight roughness of stubble beneath my fingers. Issac stares at me for a moment, confusion and a bit of anger swirling in his eyes before he leans down, placing a kiss on my lips. Short enough to be missed, but long enough not to be forgotten.

"And I was an idiot. Never again. I am never letting you go again," he whispers, his lips brushing against my ear, sending a delicious shiver down my spine. He pulls me into an embrace, and I feel my body melt against his, curves fitting perfectly against hard planes. The solid warmth of him surrounds me, his heartbeat quickening against my chest.

One of his hands splays possessively across my stomach, fingers just grazing the underside of my ribs in a way that makes my breath catch.

Whatever happened back then is nothing but the past, and though I like to dwell on what's been, I prefer to look forward to the future that seems to get brighter with each passing day. With my friends by my side, nothing seems impossible, even stopping Aagon and Jino and having a happily ever after with Issac.

"Now, let's get to training," I grunt, reluctantly pulling myself from his arms and slowly moving towards the centre of the room. My skin still burns where he touched me, my body already aching with the loss of his warmth.

"None of that, young lady. Let's see if you can take me down," he challenges with a dangerous glint in his eye. His gaze rakes over me with barely restrained hunger that makes my pulse quicken and my mouth go dry. Gods, let this finish fast enough.

***

An hour into the training and I'm feeling my legs shake with each step I attempt to take, muscles burning beneath my skin. For whatever reason Issac decided to be ruthless, throwing me to the floor at any given chance, and I'd be mad as hell if not for the fact every time he did so his fingers managed to brush against my exposed skin. At first, I thought of it nothing but a mere coincidence but when I ended up on my arse for the tenth time, his hand sliding deliberately behind my shoulder to ease the fall, his thumb grazing the sensitive spot near my collarbone, I knew something was up.

I take a deep breath in, fixing my stance as Issac bounces from side to side still full of energy, his vest now clinging to his torso, outlining every defined muscle beneath. Sweat glistens on his pale chest where the fabric dips open at the neck. He raises his arms to guard his face, the movement causing the muscles in his forearms to flex enticingly. I feel the sweat tracing down my spine, a single droplet sliding between my shoulder blades and disappearing beneath the white fabric that binds my chest. I curse in my head for having such a formidable opponent as him against myself. I'd have to train a hundred years to manage tipping him over.

My lunch threatens to come out as I run at Issac sliding down and avoiding his punch, the movement bringing me close enough to catch his scent. I quickly throw a kick to the back of his knee, but he rolls away with unexpected grace for a man his size, and I stand up without wasting time. In a few quick strides I throw a punch to his side, swiftly avoiding another punch and then leap backward when I see his feet shuffle. Our eyes lock for a moment, his crimson gaze alight with something that has nothing to do with combat. We will be stuck doing this all evening if I don't come up with something.

An idea pops into my head, and I try hard to hide the mischievous grin threatening to stretch my lips. Issac might be strong but I am far more agile. I can move faster, and I take it as an opportunity when running at him to then duck to the side and come behind him, my breasts brushing against his back as my hands move to restrain his arm whilst the other reaches for his throat. My fingers press against the warm skin of his neck, feeling his pulse jump beneath my touch as I squeeze gently and pull him towards me, my lips mere inches from his ear.

"If you don't stop playing games with me I'll choke the life out of you, Issac," I threaten, though my threat comes out in a breathless whisper that sounds more like an invitation.

The man laughs, his throat vibrating underneath my touch, the sound sending tremors through my fingers and up my arm. My skin grows hotter, a flush spreading from my chest upward. "What games?" His voice drops lower, rougher at the edges.

Suddenly, he grabs onto my arms and without any struggle yanks me over himself. My body slides against his as I'm pulled forward, the friction sending a jolt of electricity through me. I just about manage to land on my feet before turning around and kicking him in the abs. His hand comes into my vision ready to throw me off him, but I am faster, grabbing onto his wrist and letting him do his thing. As expected, Issac resists, his body tensing as he tries to pull me towards him, muscles coiling beneath my grip, and when that tension builds up, I let go, watching as his eyes widen when he stumbles backwards and falls. Quickly, I send another kick to his stomach and then launch myself at him when he loses balance, my arm pinning his throat making it slightly harder to breathe. The position brings my face close to his, our ragged breaths mixing in the small space between us. If I had a dagger the enemy would be dead, but in this scenario, this will do.

"You know what you're doing," I hiss out, narrowing my gaze, my lips close enough to his that I can almost taste him.

Issac smirks, eyes darkening to a deeper crimson, and uses the moment I let myself breathe as an opportunity to twist my arm around, switching our positions where I am now facing the floor whilst he's behind me, his body pressing against my frame. The heat of him wraps around me, every hard plane of his chest and abdomen moulded against my back, his breath hot against my neck.

"I have no idea Thea, tell me." He whispers as his lips land on my shoulder making me shiver.

I consider the idea to stop this sparring lesson and turn it into something far more intimate but my pride will always win against need. I have to prove to him and myself I am better, that I can take him.

Using his own tactics at distraction I push my hips up, letting his erection press against my arse which makes Issac's breath hitch, his attention momentarily somewhere else. Without wasting a moment my elbow flies towards his cheek and makes the man jerk to the side.

I roll away and jump behind him, wrapping my legs around his torso, my arms circling his to immobilise them. The hard lines of his back press against my chest as I let my lungs fill to the brim. It might not be a win, but I'll take a moment of rest over anything right now, even as my body registers every point of contact between us.

"I know what you're doing. Don't try to distract me, it's not fair," I squeeze harder, my body gradually losing its energy, muscles trembling from exertion and something else entirely.

Issac shifts underneath me, the movement creating a delicious friction. His hand finds my leg, fingers grazing along my calf with a strange gentleness that doesn't match the intensity in his eyes when he turns his head slightly. "You know what, Thea," he begins, his voice no longer playful but deep and possessive. Each word feels weighted, deliberate.

I try to maintain my focus, but it's nearly impossible when his fingers trace patterns on my skin through the leather trousers, each touch precise and knowing in the most pleasurable way. "I don't play fair."

All of a sudden, he grabs onto my arms and my vision blurs as I fly over him once more, air rushing past until I land between his legs with a thud, the training mat firm beneath my back.

I look up and spot him grinning down at me, his red eyes alight with triumph and hunger. Every inch of my body feels ready to explode with tension, every bit of my pride hanging by a thread I desperately cling to. But in the end, it's my heart that wins over mind. I raise myself on my arms and throw my legs over him in one fluid motion, my thighs now straddling his hips as my arms come to rest on his shoulders, bringing our faces mere inches apart.

He looks at me half surprised, half expecting this exact outcome, his pupils dilating as his gaze drops momentarily to my lips. I do what I think is the best reward possible after this torturous training, the only thing that might quench the fire building beneath my skin. I kiss him.

Issac's hands land on my hips instantly, fingers pressing into the flesh with enough pressure to leave marks, pulling me closer until not even air could pass between our bodies. His mouth parts without hesitation, allowing me entrance as I feast on his taste. My hips rock back and forth deliberately, a punishment for his earlier behaviour, yet another reward for myself. The friction creates sparks of pleasure that race up my spine. He can't spend an entire training session edging me and expect to get away with it.

I feel myself momentarily fall forward as Issac lets his

body lay back on the floor, our kiss maintaining without a break, deepening as his tongue slides against mine. It feels so incredible I'm nearly ready to cry from relief. Though I kiss him more often than ever these days, this is different. Almost like the room around us has ceased to exist, almost like my whole body has dissolved into pure sensation, every touch, every taste, every sound amplified.

The way his fingers brush over the hem of my binding, calloused tips tracing the edge where fabric meets skin. The way he growls into my lips whenever I move my hips, the sound raw and possessive, rumbling from deep in his chest. The way he arches upward, seeking some sort of sweet relief that I deliberately withhold. No, I'll make this a torment for him just as he has done to me, drawing out each moment until he's as desperate as I am.

Just as suddenly as the kiss began, it ends when Issac pulls away, his chest heaving against mine. He stares at me with a look that promises much more than kisses, his eyes now the colour of spilled wine, dark and intoxicating.

"What—" I yelp as he grabs me by the waist and throws me over his shoulder in one swift movement, my body folding easily over the hard plane of his shoulder. He strides hastily towards the doors, each purposeful step jostling me against him. "Where are you going?!" I scream, though a breathless giggle slips past my swollen lips, betraying my eager anticipation.

"You better fucking pray Alea has left the room already," he growls, his free hand coming to rest possessively on the back of my thigh as he carries me toward what promises to be a much more satisfying conclusion to our training session.

Chapter 29

The time to get from the training room to my own is cut in half as Issac rushes his steps, his breathing heavy against my lower back as he ignores the passing maids and confused guards. I'd try to hide my embarrassment if not for the heat pooling in the pit of my stomach, making my skin hypersensitive to every jostle, every brush of his hand against my thigh. I know Alea must be long gone from the room, still I cross my fingers as Issac kicks the door open to then shut it with one hand, the sound echoing through the otherwise silent chamber.

"Bath or shower?" He growls out, voice rough, looking around until he spots the door leading to our bathroom. His fingers dig deeper into my flesh. I draw my brows together in confusion trying to process his words when suddenly his grip on my legs grows tighter and I squeal, the sound embarrassingly needy even to my own ears.

"What?" I ask, confused, raising myself on my arms to look past his broad shoulders, my body sliding against his with the movement.

"I won't repeat myself, Thea. I don't have enough restraint left so pick now." He grunts out, his head falling down in defeat, muscles tense beneath my hands. I hold back on the shiver threatening to race through my body, but can't suppress the way my breath catches at the raw need in his voice.

"Shower." My answer makes Issac nearly sprint for the door, his footfalls heavy with urgency. He finally sets me down onto the floor, the cool room a stark contrast to the heat of his body. I watch as the door closes slowly, wrapping us in darkness save for the single, tiny stained glass window high in the ceiling. Not that it does much since it's probably late at night, only the moonlight transformed into vivid colours left to guide me through the shadows.

I look around trying to hear or see Issac, but the room remains silent, almost as if he's disappeared. I wonder if he has some sort of super power that allows him to see past the dark, to track me by the sound of my racing heart. I move backward, my back colliding with the cold tiles, a gasp escaping my lips, and suddenly the sound of the handle twisting has me jumping as the cold water collides with my skin, shocking a yelp from my throat.

"What the fu—" My words are caught between Issac's lips as he pushes into me, his body a wall of solid heat against mine, letting the water fall between us, creating streams that trace paths down our bodies. I wrap my arms around his neck, bringing him closer until there is no room left, not even for breath. He grunts out, the vibration travelling from his chest to mine, and I feel him remove the shirt over his head before he's back to my lips, kissing and biting whilst I try to remain sane despite the onslaught of sensation.

By the time his lips end up on my neck, the water is warm enough to be considered enjoyable, steam beginning to rise around us. I moan as his tongue circles around my collarbones before he bites down and begins sucking on my skin, marking me. Droplets of water cascade down my forehead and into my eyes keeping them closed shut as I drown in pleasure, my head falling back against the tiles. My hands trace over the defined muscles on his back, feeling them flex and shift beneath my fingertips, my nails digging in as he continues torturing the same sensitive spot where neck meets shoulder.

"Fuck, I can't get enough of you," he murmurs against my wet skin, his breath hot in contrast to the water, and suddenly steps away. My eyes have adjusted to the darkness well enough that I catch him fiddle with the ring over his finger before a single drop of blood falls onto the floor, dark against the white tiles.

Whatever he has planned takes me back to the time where he had used his magic to keep my hands bound behind my back. The memory alone sends a thrill of anticipation racing down my spine. Surely, he wouldn't…

Right on cue, I feel the cool liquid wrap around my wrists, waiting to strike. Just as I'm about to pull away, the liquid hardens and my arms are pulled upward. I watch in fascinated arousal as Issac's blood wraps around the metal shower head and turns solid, leaving me on my tiptoes with my hands once again bound, this time above me, stretching my body into a taut line before him.

His hand lands on my arse and squeezes it possessively, water making the contact slick and smooth. His nose brushes along my jawline, inhaling deeply as if memorising my scent beneath the water. "Forgive me for my selfishness, but I have a feeling we both enjoy you begging." His lips curl up into a wicked smile that I feel rather than see, and I moan as his hand slides to my waistband and with a single swift move removes my trousers and underwear.

"*You* enjoy me begging," I try to correct him, at the same time fighting hard to stay up as his solidified blood digs into my wrists in a pleasurable way that borders on pain, heightening every sensation.

Issac chuckles, the sound dark and knowing. His hands cup my arse cheeks before he lifts me up, my legs circling around his waist out of instinct and to make myself more comfortable, the new position bringing our bodies flush together. He quickly unwraps the binding around my chest letting the material fall to the wet floor. "Really?" He whispers against my ear, his lips grazing the sensitive shell, sending shivers cascading through me despite the warm water. One of his hands slides between my legs, the touch almost reverent. I suck in a sharp breath when his fingers brush along my folds, teasing and deliberate, sending tingling sensations down my legs that make my toes curl. "I think you enjoy it just as much."

I nearly lose it when his finger slips in, his thumb circling around my clit with deliberate precision, but Issac is quick to hush any noise with his mouth, swallowing my sounds of pleasure. I moan into the kiss, trying to focus on anything but how can I when his skilled mouth is making me lose my mind, when the heat of the water feels like ice in comparison to his bare skin pressed against mine, and when his fingers are plunging inside of me, curling to find that perfect spot, tipping me over the edge with each movement.

I squeeze my eyes shut when he adds another finger, stretching me beyond what my body remembers, the sensation overwhelming. But with his mouth working against mine, and his other hand gripping my arse to hold me steady, the initial discomfort is quickly forgotten and replaced by waves of pleasure that radiate outward from my core.

Gods, if only I could see his face right now, read through his expression to know exactly just how much he wants me, how much satisfaction it brings him to see me in this state, bound and wanting, completely at his mercy yet willingly so.

"Use your magic," he whispers before his lips land on my neck, teeth grazing the sensitive skin there.

"What?" I moan out as his movements speed up, each thrust of his fingers more insistent than the last. My eyes roll to the back of my head and I begin to think about just getting our own room if it would mean we'd end up like this after every training session, his body against mine, water streaming between us.

"Use your magic to light up the candles, *Red*." The nickname has my senses return just for a moment, allowing me to process his words through the haze of pleasure. I look around the room to spot a few candles scattered around on the shelves, near the bathtub and high on the windowsill. My lips curve into a smile as I understand his desire to see me.

"You once told me not to play with fire," I chuckle, but quickly snap my mouth shut as he hits that sweet spot that has my back arching towards him for more, desperate for the pressure to increase.

"I think we are way past that, darling," his words, hiding the double meaning, bring me closer to release as he relentlessly makes sure I feel nothing but the building pleasure coursing through every nerve. "I'm telling you now to do the opposite, so please listen, I need to see your face."

As difficult as it is to concentrate, I split my attention away towards my magic, searching for that familiar warm glow in the darkness. When my mind grasps it, I focus carefully to light just the candles and not accidentally set the two of us ablaze. That would be awful. With a simple flicker of my fingers, the few flames spring to life and with them, I finally get a glimpse of Issac's face in the golden light.

Unsurprisingly, he looks borderline feral. His pupils are blown wide, nearly eclipsing the red of his irises, his lips parted as he takes me in, an expression of raw desire etched across his features before he leans down into the crook of my neck and works his movements to bring me to my release, his rhythm becoming more urgent.

"Issac," I curl my fingers into fists above me, the restraints keeping me suspended and heightening every sensation.

"Come on darling, just let go," he encourages, his voice rough against my ear, and I feel everything fall away. The orgasm comes crashing against me and making my back arch forward, my eyes and mouth wide open as I struggle to make a single sound, the pleasure too intense for voice. My body trembles around his fingers, muscles clenching as the sensation washes through me, leaving me boneless and gasping in its wake.

When the moment passes, my head falls onto Issac's shoulder, my breaths ragged as I try to slow the frantic pounding of my heart. This man somehow knows exactly what he's doing and which desires to awaken. Perhaps I don't make it challenging enough for him.

"Don't fall asleep on me, Thea. I am not done with you yet," he murmurs, and before I fully register his meaning, the blunt tip of his arousal presses against my entrance. I raise my head and lock eyes with him, a slight smirk lifting the corner of his mouth, and suddenly—

"Shit!" I grasp onto the makeshift shackles he's created, an electric shock shooting up my spine as pleasure explodes through my core. I haven't even descended from the previous climax and I can already feel the next one gradually building, coiling tight within me.

Issac studies my face, pride painted across his features, but also concern for my wellbeing. I inch towards him, my breath ghosting over his parted lips, inviting him for more, and he seizes the bait. His mouth crashes against mine just as his hips begin moving, twisting my expression into a delightful grimace as I surrender to every aspect of our connection. The sensation of my breasts brushing against his chest, the way his hands grip my flesh, lifting me for deeper contact, everything about this goes beyond perfection, a realm of intimacy I've never before experienced.

I break away from the kiss, allowing my lips to trail down Issac's jaw, down the column of his throat to where I feel his pulse thrumming beneath my mouth. Then I do what he's been doing to me in our past encounters. I bite him. He emits a guttural sound, his fingers digging into my flesh, and I smile against his skin, sucking harder, my tongue tasting the salt of sweat on him.

"Fuck, Thea," he whispers just as his rhythm intensifies, striking that perfect spot within me. My head jerks backward, my hands clutching the solidified blood as I search for some form of anchor. Every sensation around me feels magnified beyond reason, as though each touch is amplified tenfold, defying description. "I want to be the only one able to witness your face make those expressions."

"You are," I confess, my head falling back to connect with the tiled wall.

"Good," Issac growls, his body colliding with mine, and I cry out, the candle flames surrounding us roaring, growing in intensity. "I'd kill any man who dares to touch you in the way I do. You are mine, and I am yours."

"Ah!" I clench my jaw shut, the room becoming increasingly heated, and I can't determine if it's my magic or the water cascading over my flushed skin.

"If I have to battle with myself another hundred times to have you this close, I'll do it. Even if you loathe me, even if you doubt us, I know nothing could truly keep us apart. Not when we've been this close. Not when I know exactly what expressions I can draw out of you and not when my heart threatens to stop if you're not around because I can't live a second without your presence." My lips part, my mind unable to produce any coherent response beyond a series of breathless exclamations.

Issac's movements abruptly slow, and I shoot him a look of frustration before his hand releases my hip and moves to my throat, applying gentle pressure, just enough to restrict my breathing slightly.

"Gods help me if I ever lose you forever, not even the heavens will be able to keep me away." His lips brush my jaw, then my nose and cheeks, as though he can't decide which part of me demands his attention most.

"Who says I'm not going to hell?" I mutter, my vision growing blurrier. Issac chuckles, his fingers brushing against my artery.

"Who says I won't follow you there?" My mouth falls open,

words I wish to say forming on my tongue but none come out. I'm too concerned with Issac stopping me from reaching climax to fully acknowledge what he said.

"Tell me what you want, Red." His voice sounds sweet, but poison drips off it. He's doing it on purpose, he wants me to beg.

"I-" my voice diminishes as his hand tightens around my throat a fraction more, a playful curve dancing across his mouth, desire reflecting in his crimson gaze. "Make me come again. Please, I can't stand this Issac."

"As you wish," he chuckles, and suddenly delivers a powerful thrust that has my body shuddering uncontrollably, my legs trembling from another approaching release. "For you I'll do anything."

I'm ready to plead for sweet surrender when he speeds up once more, and the flames around us grow so intense that the entire room bathes in their glow. I glance around, amazed that my magic responds so strongly to my emotions, but my attention swiftly returns to Issac as he claims my mouth in another searing kiss. The sound of our passionate exchange draws a moan from deep within me, as I wonder how many different ways he could bring me to ecstasy.

"You enjoy this, don't you?" he murmurs, his breathing becoming laboured as the room grows unbearably hot. "Perhaps I should allow you release for the sake of our survival, though the notion of being consumed by your fire sounds strangely appealing."

"Issac!" I warn him, my knuckles blanching from my grip on his blood-formed restraints, and he offers me a knowing look.

Suddenly, his body presses fully against mine, my back

flush against the cool tiles. I gaze at him as he rests his forehead against mine, his strong arms lifting me in a precise rhythm that has him striking that exquisite spot repeatedly, until my limbs begin to quiver, until my abdomen tightens with impending release, until my magic saturates me with sensations beyond comprehension.

"Come for me Thea," he commands, and I obey, nearly weeping from the overwhelming intensity. The flames expand, their colour shifting to azure as Issac guides me through the climax without faltering for a moment.

"Fuck! I can't—this is too much," I plead with my eyes, but he persists, instead capturing my lips again, finding his own release with several deep, final movements.

We remain breathless, the flames gradually subsiding to their natural size, the water now feeling noticeably cooler than moments before. As reality slowly returns, I find myself wondering if this connection between us is as rare and precious as it feels in this moment of shared vulnerability.

Issac chuckles to himself before releasing my throat, and with a casual flick of his finger, his blood dissolves and spirals down the drain in thin crimson streams. His arm wraps around my waist gently to help keep me steady as I shiver beneath the shower spray, gazing at him with a raised brow, my legs still unsteady from our encounter.

"Did the lava beetles die in there?" I glance up at the shower head, and he laughs softly, shaking his head, water droplets flying from his damp hair.

"No, I turned it down as soon as I asked you to use your magic. I knew you'd spice things up." I swat him playfully on his shoulder, feeling the firm muscle beneath my palm, and watch as he adjusts the temperature. "Here, let's actually take this shower properly."

Strangely enough, we slip back into a moment of tender familiarity. Issac works the shampoo into my hair with careful fingers, massaging my scalp as I remain motionless, thinking about the day he ran a bath for me, mere hours before the attack. Though contentment fills me now, a creeping fear sneaks into my heart, casting a shadow over my thoughts.

What if the past repeats itself? What if this is our final night before everything crumbles? Before I lose him again to forces beyond my control? I swallow hard, watching the droplets of water dance off the tiles around my feet. Lathai isn't here; he can't steal my happiness away, but others I've yet to truly know remain threats, and the Gods only know what intentions they might have. After revealing our plans to Eric, he might well be plotting his next move. Perhaps I've made a terrible mistake, cut our precious time in half with my trust.

My heart threatens to sink, the weight of Issac's hands on my shoulders suddenly feeling like a weight I can't bear. I can't endure losing him again, not when he's so eager to rediscover himself, not when he's unafraid to be honest and vulnerable in my presence, not when I haven't properly expressed what I feel for him in words that could anchor him to me.

Out of impulse, I spin around to face him, halting his movements mid-stroke. His brows draw together in concern as he studies my expression, water streaming down his face, catching on his eyelashes. My hands rise to cup his cheeks, feeling the slight roughness of stubble beneath my fingertips. My heart hammers against my ribs, swaying my body from side to side. If what follows is wrong, that's okay. At least I'll have unburdened myself of this weight and discovered if we truly can weather any storm together.

"What's wron—"

"I love you." The words escape my lips, my eyes searching Issac's for any reaction that might confirm my darkest fears. For a breathless moment, time suspends itself. He blinks at me, droplets clinging to his lashes, his expression shifting from surprise to something deeper, more profound. Then unexpectedly, he pulls me closer, one hand cradling the back of my head, and places his lips against mine in a kiss so achingly tender that I feel myself unravelling. It's different from our passionate exchanges. This is a kiss of reverence, of promise. Every worry instantly dissolves, every dark thought banished as he holds me steady, his lips moving against mine with delicate precision, saying without words what his heart feels.

When he finally draws back, his eyes shine with an emotion I've rarely witnessed in him. Vulnerability, raw and unguarded.

"Do you mean it?" he asks, his voice barely audible above the shower's patter, as if I had just offered him the most precious gift he dares not believe is truly his. That simple question breaks something in me, because beneath the exterior of this powerful, confident man is a soul who considers himself unworthy of love, damaged beyond repair.

I nod in response, unable to find more words, the lump in my throat making speech impossible. I watch as his bottom lip quivers almost imperceptibly, a flash of naked emotion crossing his features before he pulls me into an embrace that feels like coming home. His arms wrap around me completely, his heartbeat strong against mine, his face buried in the crook of my neck.

"I love you too," he whispers against my skin, the words sinking into me, taking root where once there was only uncertainty. And in that moment, with water cascading around us, I know that whatever comes next, this truth between us will remain unshaken.

Chapter 30

I wake up to Alea standing in the doorway, a knowing smirk playing across her lips upon spotting Issac peacefully snoring by my side, his chest rising and falling. The soft golden light filtering through the curtains tells me the day has barely started, yet she is already up on her feet, dressed and alert. I shift my position carefully, letting Issac's warm arm fall from my waist, and pull the sheets closer to my chin to shoot her a questioning look.

One word falls from her mouth that gets me scrambling out of bed. "Desily."

The two of us race to the medical wing, our hurried footsteps echoing against the cold stone floor, nearly stumbling around corners in our haste. I barely had a moment to dress before bolting out, my attire consisting of a hastily buttoned, crumpled white shirt and beige linen trousers that hang loosely on my hips. I'm certain my hair is in an even bigger mess, but none of that matters since Desily has woken up.

We push the doors open, Alea first to spot someone next to Desily's bed. A woman with short hair, dressed more appropriately than me. Myra.

She turns around upon hearing our ragged breaths, her relaxed face quickly transforming into a grimace once our eyes meet. I'm ready to match her energy when suddenly I'm reminded of Issac's story about her and Lisa, and the fact I said something awful. Perhaps apologies are in order since she's been the one tending to Desily, making sure her healing process goes well.

My eyes catch a movement right behind Myra, and a familiar face comes into the light. Though half of her face is bandaged, it doesn't stop me and Alea from running straight at her.

"Des!" I wrap my arms around her, tears streaming down my flushed cheeks as the scent of medicinal herbs clings to her skin. A half-sob, half-laugh escapes my lips when she hugs me back with all the strength she can muster, her fingers digging lightly into my shirt.

"Missed my presence that much?" She giggles, and I move away for Alea to take my place.

Alea's already crying as she approaches the bed, silver tears catching the light. Her bottom lip quivers as she reaches towards Desily, who extends her arms out, the white bandages stark against her bronze skin. Alea grasps her hand and takes a free spot on the edge of the bed. There's a moment of silence between them, silent words that will never need to be spoken, apologies that neither of them needs to voice.

"I am never going on walks with you, Alea," Des chuckles, her palm cupping Alea's face. The girl leans into her touch and smiles.

"Yeah, maybe not in Sebraycia," she breathes out, before Desily pulls her closer, their lips colliding.

I stand there smiling like an idiot because I'm happy for them, happy because she's safe and alive, and because I haven't lost her this time. None of us have.

As I give the girls some space, my attention returns to Myra who is focused on putting away the medical equipment. I grit my teeth and swallow my pride before deciding to approach her.

She doesn't turn around instantly, but the way her shoulders tense when I'm inches away tells me she doesn't want to face me. I don't blame her. I nearly set her on fire and cruelly reminded her of the pain her family caused. I'd be mad too, still, the way she behaves towards me isn't right or excusable, but a part of me wants to bury the fighting axe and move forward. We might not become friends sharing secrets over tea, but acquaintances nodding respectfully in hallways seems like a peace we can reach.

"What do you want, Starbane? Your friend is over there," she barks out, with her back still facing me.

"I know," I try to keep my positive thoughts, though her attitude makes it hard. "I came to talk to you."

"Oh? What is it now?" She spins around suddenly, throwing her medical gloves onto the table. "Are you going to cuss me out and set me on fire or bring up my dead sister to get a reaction out of me?"

"That's hardly true. Last time you've—" I stop myself, taking a deep breath in. She's mad and hurt, and so am I, but I need to be the bigger person. If neither of us takes the first step, then we will be stuck standing on opposite sides instead of by each other. "I came to say I'm sorry, for what I said about Lisa. I didn't mean to."

"Oh?" Her brow quirks before she leans onto the table, tilting her head slightly as if to urge me to continue.

"I also wanted to thank you for healing Desily," I say,

fidgeting with my fingers. I'm trying my best not to let the vulnerability show in my voice or the way I look at her with pleading eyes.

Myra looks at me in silence, her dark blue eyes cold, thin arched brows drawn together. Her slender fingers tap against her crossed arms as she considers my words. I'm ready to apologise again, but a loud sigh escaping her lips stops me.

"Didn't expect to hear that this morning, but I guess I'll take it," she scoffs before pushing off the table and moving towards Desily's bed. "Don't think I've forgotten about Issac. I might let go of a lot of things but not this one."

I roll my eyes at her words but despite everything smile because apologising seems to have actually worked. She might not know it, but Issac and I are closer than when we arrived at the castle, our relationship growing in the direction only she could hope for, but I won't say that. I won't be the one breaking her delusions, because I don't have to. I am no longer anxious about what future will bring; I am now certain it will be in my favour.

"Thea, you need to tell me everything," Des calls for me, and I step closer to her bed. Despite her injuries, she sits with her back straight, her remaining visible eye alert and bright. "Gods, I can't wait to get rid of this bandage, what a bother." She scratches at the fabric, huffing in frustration, and I chuckle, looking at Myra who shoots me an odd look, her head tilted slightly.

"What?"

"Well, though my magic can heal a lot of things, I'm afraid this is the limit. The damage might be permanent." I blink at her words, my eyes darting between her face and Desily's bandage, a cold dread settling in my stomach. Is what I'm hearing true? Is Desily going to be partially blind?

"Your water can heal?" Desily speaks first, her curiosity about healing magic a bigger priority than losing her sight. Myra nods in reply, her eyes once again landing on me as if I might have something to add. Yet I'm too stunned to say anything, because in my mind there might've been a chance I could've prevented it.

"Maybe it doesn't work like your magic, but water can do a lot of things and this is one of them, but unfortunately I can't mend what's been broken."

I see the way Alea's face grows paler, the colour draining from her cheeks as guilt gnaws at her. She chews nervously on her lower lip until it reddens, her shoulders hunching forward as if trying to make herself smaller. She thinks it's all her fault, not the fact that whatever attacked them that night just happened to be there, not the fact that they were unlucky to end up in that exact spot at the exact time, not the fact she wasn't the one who did this, but I know she thinks she did. I know she feels like her hands are bloodied by sins she didn't know she could commit. I know she wishes she could've done more, thrown herself in Desily's place and sacrificed her own body, but what's been done can't be undone, and none of it is her fault.

But she won't believe our words, just like I refuse to believe theirs. When something you think could've been prevented by you happens to the people you love, it's a burden you'll be carrying for the rest of your life no matter what.

"Well," Desily sighs, and I stare at her with my lips pursed. "I guess I could become a pirate."

"Des, it's not funny! I did this." Alea throws her hands out in frustration, her slender fingers trembling, her bottom lip shaking as she looks over Desily's bandage. Her voice cracks, growing higher as she speaks. "Because of me you won't be able to see properly."

"Alea, you've had nothing to do with it. As long as I have one eye that lets me see your face I don't give a shit about anything else." Desily moves away from the headboard, wincing slightly as she shifts her weight, her bronze skin glistening with a thin sheen of sweat from the effort. Her working eye, a warm brown that catches the morning light, fixes on the girl as she reaches forward, grasping her hands to pull her closer, their fingers intertwining. "Even if I go blind I don't care, I will hear you, and when I go deaf I can feel you, and when nothing else is left of me I'd live off memories of us, because I don't care about anything else."

I smile at her words, and the way her finger gently swipes Alea's tears off her flushed cheeks. I'm sure some of the guilt has been lifted off her chest, not enough to let her forget but enough to make her believe that Desily isn't mad, and that this isn't the end of them. I guess some people would do just about anything for love.

In the next few minutes while Myra is gone, I try to fill Desily in about what's been happening. From my research to the sudden development in the relationship between Issac and I.

"I told you forcing them to be around each other will work!" Desily turns to Alea who just shakes her head while trying to suppress a smile.

"Ah! Should've guessed the miseries in my life come from you." I tilt my head and cross my arms over my chest in an accusatory way though I'm only joking.

"What can I say? I'm full of surprises, besides, who else other than your best friend would ruin your life?" I stick a middle finger at her before the three of us break into a laugh that sounds too sweet to my ears, almost reminding me of the time when Lathai was around. When I thought life couldn't get better, but it can, it does.

I continue telling Des about the tense conversations with Issac and then Eric. I tell her about him agreeing to help us, and try to hide the bitter taste of distrust that spreads across my tongue.

"Here, she needs to drink this." Myra passes me a glass of some strange mixture and I eye it warily. The glass feels heavy in my palm, the liquid a murky amber that smells of tangy fruits though I doubt the girl will taste them. My finger brushes across the rim before I pass it to Desily, droplets of the mixture sticking to my skin.

"So when will you meet him?" Des asks before gulping her drink down and grimacing at the taste.

I gaze at the fancy clock on the wall that shows it's well past nine, and suddenly realise I was meant to meet Eric in the morning.

"Now."

***

I sit on the couch with my hands gripping onto my thighs as Eric's slender fingers graze over the letter. The same letter I've read over a hundred times trying to match the right words, trying to find a way to figure out where exactly they could have hidden the ritual paper. My leg bounces up from impatience, I gnaw at my fingers until I taste copper as Eric's face remains stone cold though his eyes seem to be moving all over the place. Almost as if he's seeing things I can't.

Suddenly, he places the paper onto the table, his hand reaching for the pen and my breath hitches. He scribbles something down, the scratching of quill against parchment filling the otherwise silent room, filling out the blank spots that have been smudged, and I lean forward.

Silence settles in the room as the pen falls from his hand with a soft thud. "Right, I think I have your answer." He looks at me with half a smile, and I nearly lose it when reaching for the paper. He hands it over slowly, a strange look passing through his eyes, something dark, before he masks it with happiness.

Did I just imagine it or did he really just look pitying and almost like it was towards me, not the content of the letter? It doesn't matter, he seems to be happier now and so the letter must hold the answer. Perhaps he saw something about Lord Graham he didn't wish to; that man was terrible.

The paper crinkles under my fingers as I bring it closer to my face, reading the first paragraph with my heart thudding inside my chest.

'To Lord Tarron Graham,' I swallow the ball of thorns growing inside my throat. Just like the last time, I ignore all the unimportant news about this person's daily tasks and get straight to the point.

'As for the woman, she has now relocated to Eclia. Our spies tried to pin her down but she's been hiding in an unknown place. We will do our best to track her down since she holds the books about the magic from the burnt library and we know how important they are to you. Thousand years will come in ten years, and since we've acquired the spell it shouldn't be a problem

to retrieve the blade. It is rumoured the elves hid it somewhere, I will make sure to look into that. The ritual paper remains hidden in Yalan within Giant's castle grounds like you've asked. It will take someone years to figure out the castle once stood below and not above.'

I rise from my seat, the wooden frame creaking beneath me, Eric's gaze not leaving me for a moment as I rush towards the door with the letter clutched in my trembling hands. This tells me more than enough; it tells me where the other artefact might be hidden, it tells me that all this time we should have searched underneath the palace rather than above it, a place not even Ella might know about. It tells me about a person I've never met. A woman who knew about this magic, knew about the ritual and the magic and Jino and Aagon. I wish I could meet her and ask her the questions building up inside my head, but so much time has passed since then I doubt she's still with us.

"Got what you needed?" Eric asks as I reach for the handle. I stop abruptly to face him, nearly on the verge of tears from the information provided, my vision blurring slightly at the edges.

"More than that. Thank you, thank you so much Eric." I nod, my voice thick with emotion, and the man stands up, dusting off his dark trousers before moving towards his desk. It feels strange to say I will miss him now that he has to return back home, but something tells me our paths will cross again.

"Don't mention it Thea, I'm just glad I could help. Now go tell your friends," he chuckles, and I smile, nodding in agreement before pulling the door open.

"But Thea."

"Yes?" I pause once more to acknowledge him before completely vanishing.

Eric looks torn apart between doing what he's always done, telling the truth, and lying. I can see it in his eyes, the way they dart nervously to the side, the way his jaw clenches then relaxes as he thinks about whether or not he should say whatever it is that has him looking so sour. "Be careful out there. Not everyone who you think is honest lives up to those expectations."

His words, almost reminding me of Issac's back in the day, have me halting my movements. I want to ask more, to dig the truth out of him, but on the other hand, this is more important than chasing after words with potential meaning. I'm sure there isn't a lie in this world that could destroy me. After what happened with Lathai, there couldn't exist a betrayal far worse than his, so whatever Eric saw in this letter will remain a mystery until the day we meet next.

"Safe travels, and I hope to see you too." I bow down before letting the door shut behind me with a soft click.

In less than an hour a meeting is called. Everyone who knows about our mission is in the room I first met Ella in. Well, everyone except for Desily who is still recovering. The last time I was here I shared tea across a small circular table; now before me stands a long rectangular table of polished mahogany that has seats for the nine of us.

The room has grown quiet ever since I've told them about what Eric had discovered. Both Myra and Ella seem to be giving each other meaningful looks none of us can understand. On my right, Issac's mind seems to be somewhere completely different. It has been ever since I've relayed the whole message about Lord Graham, the woman and the whereabouts of the ritual. His pale fingers drum silently against the table's edge, his crimson eyes focused on some distant point beyond the room's walls. A part of me believes it's because of the mentions of his captor, but something deep inside me tells me otherwise.

Alea and Theo are both deep in hushed conversation between each other, their heads bent close together, voices barely above a whisper, glancing around the room as if to make sure nobody can hear them, and opposite them Ryo, Venali and Jassin just sit still awaiting the next orders from one of us.

"Very well then, I think this calls for an even bigger meeting." Ella's voice breaks the silence and all eyes are on her.

"Bigger?" Ryo repeats, arching his brow.

Ella smiles in reply, and rises from her seat before striding off to a set of doors located at the back of the room. I don't remember seeing them the first time there, but perhaps I was too distracted by the princess, her own prophecy and a woman that clearly hated me.

All of us follow suit, stopping inches behind Ella as she pulls the handles open and the harsh wind blows into our faces. A cold shiver runs down my spine, before something lands on my shoulders. I look back to spot Issac in his black shirt, his two sizes too big jacket now resting on me, the fabric still warm from his body heat. I mouth a quick thank you before wrapping up tightly and secretly getting a whiff of his scent.

Ella walks into what looks like an open balcony. The sky has turned pitch black, reminding me of the night a few days ago when Issac had shown me the aurora. The memory brings a smile to my face despite the nervousness in my bones, because deep down I know there will be plenty more moments like those shared between us.

I watch as Ella grabs onto something, and upon further inspection I recognise that something to be a horn, an enormous curved instrument carved from what appears to be ancient bone, its surface etched with symbols I can't read. The woman takes a big breath in, her chest expanding, and blows the air into the thing. All of us cover our ears as something similar to a battle cry rings through the city of Yalan, shaking every house, every human, every pebble, but luckily not the mountains around us.

When she stops, we all shoot her a confused look that quickly changes when the ground begins to shake in a way that's much different from the one before. I grab onto Issac as my feet struggle to find balance, the rest of our group lunging towards furniture or someone stronger. Whatever Ella summoned, it's big enough to lift the castle with its bare hands.

A moment passes, the shaking subsides and then a cloud of mist rolls in faster than I've ever seen it move. I cover my face, the cold air biting my cheeks, and then I hear a low growl.

"Holy shit. When you said bigger I did not think of that!" Ryo screams and I hear his feet shuffle behind as he scrambles to hide behind Venali and Jassin.

"Good evening, Zodhor." Ella bows low, and I have to shake myself into reality to realise that the white mist before her isn't just a randomly occurring thing, but the hot air coming from a giant's mouth. He's far taller than the others we've met, older, and paler. His white hair reaches past his shoulders in thick strands, his beard probably touching his waist, and his blue eyes are focused solely on Ella.

"Princess, you called," he answers, his voice making every bone in my body shake. I swallow the uneasy feeling that settles in my stomach as I imagine this giant crushing us with his fist.

"My friend, Miss Thea has discovered something I'm sure you'd know about." The giant's eyes move in my direction and I swear everything in me screams to run. It must be my fight or flight response because never in my life have I felt this scared. I fought terrible creatures, enormous monsters, and things that shouldn't be real but this is different. This is a creature who's nearly fifteen metres tall, who can think and see through my lies and movements.

Issac nudges me gently, his warm shoulder brushing against mine, and I blink, bracing myself for the meeting. "Zodhor is one of the eldest giants in Sebraycia. If anyone knows about the place you're talking about, it's him," Myra explains, and I nod, moving forward, slowly, my knees threatening to buckle with each step.

I fight against my own body as I get closer and closer, my legs trembling with each step, my muscles tensed ready for a speedy escape. The giant looks at me quietly, his ancient eyes scanning me from top to bottom, his expression unchanging, and I reach for an ounce of courage so that I don't make a fool out of myself when speaking.

"Mmm, Althea Starbane," the giant speaks, and I wobble as his breath sways my body, warm and carrying the scent of frost and stone.

"You know me?" I ask sheepishly, trying not to sound

terrified.

"Our kind has heard of you, as have many others. Your magic speaks to us." I blink, surprised at his words. I've been aware for a while now that magical creatures can feel this magic, but not to this extent. Not to the point they know who I am beyond this magic. "So tell me what is it that you wish to know."

I fill my lungs with the cold air, hoping it would cool me down, the chill burning my throat as I inhale deeply. Everybody's eyes burn into my back as they await my words to come out. For some time now I've stopped being on the sidelines, I become their leader. "I've learned about a castle that stood here centuries ago belonging to your kind. I was told that's where I will find what I'm seeking, but I don't know how to get there."

Zodhor chuckles, the sound like boulders rolling down a hillside, his lip curving into a smile almost as if he's thinking about a memory from long ago, something he has nearly forgotten. "The palace, yes, how could I forget it. It stood here before the humans came to our land, before we made peace with them and before the avalanche swallowed it below the ground."

"An avalanche? Is it buried?" I ask, taking a step closer, all the previous worries vanishing as I get drawn to the information.

"Mmm, it has been for years." The giant nods, and I bite my lips trying to figure out a way to somehow get below without destroying the current castle in the process. "But there is a way. Humans always find the way to get to what they need."

"Could you please tell me how?" I grasp onto the railing,

my knuckles turning white, my hands absorbing the coldness of the metal, but I discard the painful feeling hoping to hear more.

Zodhor blinks at me, his eyes the size of my head and as blue as the deepest glaciers, and I stare into them as if they're the clearest oasis I've ever seen. He then turns his head towards the highest peak, his massive hand raising to point to the foot of the mountain, the movement causing a brief gust of wind that ruffles my hair. "The entrance is between the mountains, but it's been frozen with ice. The smallest disturbance might cause another avalanche, so tread carefully, Althea Starbane." I nod, letting him continue, hanging on his every word. "The humans said there is a tunnel that leads down. It should take you to the castle, but be careful. Gods know what could've crawled down there over the years."

"Thank you, thank you so much." I smile and the giant nods before slightly bowing towards Ella and dismissing himself.

My heart beats like a galloping horse when I spin around, everyone staring at me awaiting the next command, and I decide on our next big move. "We will go there in a week. Let's find that bloody ritual."

Chapter 31

"Is that all you've got?" I blink fast, trying to steady my racing heartbeat as clouds of mist flow from my heavy breaths into the freezing air. The cold bites at my face, though I can't really feel it, my sweaty skin sticking to my clothes.

In the past week all I've done is training. Morning, afternoon and night I'm either found inside the training room or outside the palace, past the gates where I can use my magic freely. Only when the hard work is done, and my body feels like it can't take another step do I drag myself to the library to check our plans.

"Thea! Focus." I duck as Issac's blood spike flies past my ear, missing by inches before it stabs into the old oak tree. Pieces of bark crack off, the tree seeming to shake.

I turn to him, my vision going spotty for a moment. "That could've killed me."

He shifts his stance for hand-to-hand fighting, his black hair stuck to his pale forehead, sweat drops catching the bright midday sun. Issac looks focused, yet that annoying playful smirk stays on his lips, his crimson eyes shining. I envy how calm he is whilst my nerves feel like they're falling apart, tomorrow's mission weighing on me. "Then you better focus instead of thinking of other things. I need you prepared." His lean body tenses, muscles tight under his training clothes as he waits for me to move.

I shake my hands, the dragon scale gloves warm from using magic. Taking a deep breath that fills my nose with the smell of pine and frost, I charge at him, throwing a punch which he easily blocks. I swing my leg up to hit his side. As his arms come down to grab my leg, I slam my palm against his chest and call up my power, feeling it rush through my veins before bursting out, sending Issac flying backward through the air.

Gone is the need to say the spells I already know out loud, and that's only because Issac showed me it's possible. Training with him has many perks.

He lands gracefully despite the force, not wasting a second before his blood begins to dance through the air, red ribbons weaving patterns as they snake towards me. I back away quickly, jumping to avoid them, but just as I leap, a stream of blood wraps around my ankle. My balance breaks, and I crash hard onto the frozen ground. I'm dragged across the rough surface, my fingers clawing at the frozen ground, desperate for purchase as I try to think of a way out. In this moment, I remember a gift Myra handed me a few days ago.

Shortly after Zodhor left, Myra appeared at my room doorway holding a book I'd never seen before. She looked hesitant when I greeted her, messy and flushed. Silently, I hoped she couldn't tell Issac was hiding right behind the door, trying not to laugh as I had to answer her knocking in such a state.

"I asked my father to send me this when you arrived at the castle, though I had no intention of giving it to you, but I think now it could become useful." She handed me the time-worn volume, its pages bound in faded crimson. I looked it over twice before realising it was a book about fire magic and spells that my ancestors used.

"Thank you," I whispered, looking through a few pages with detailed descriptions and drawings. Myra nodded with a soft smile, though her eyes drifted towards the centre of the doors and I prayed she didn't spot Issac, not when we just started to become civil. Her jaw clenches then relaxes.

"Don't burn yourself, Starbane."

Okay, time to try something new.

I twist my body mid-drag, focusing my magic into my shaking palms until it forms a blazing sword, the heat burning the edges of my sleeves, the sharp smell of burnt cloth stinging my nose. As soon as the weapon is hot enough, I slice through Issac's hardening blood, knowing his clever mind is planning some deadly counter-attack. I refuse to give him the chance. I watch with growing fear as his blood gathers, ready to swallow me whole. Desperate, I decide to try a spell I've only read about, taking a deep breath whilst praying the fire doesn't burn me from the inside. My heart pounds so hard against my ribs I'm afraid they might crack.

I curl my fingers into a fist and bring the small opening between my palm and fingertips to my mouth, blowing with every bit of strength I have left, hoping it's enough. A moment passes before flames, born from somewhere deep inside me, spiral through the small hole and crash into Issac's approaching blood wall. The fire stops its progress, holding the red tide at bay. I watch, amazed, as the flames grow bigger, hotter, changing from soft yellow to deep red to bright blue at the edges. But never black, that never shows up no matter what I do.

Through our magic connection, I feel Issac's power weakening, his surprise clear across our shared mental link. He never expected this move. Honestly, neither did I. Part of my scattered mind still thinks my insides will be charred when I stop the spell, yet strangely, there's no pain. Instead, a wonderful feeling spreads throughout my chest before flowing outward through every vein, a glowing warmth wrapping around me.

The moment his blood gives up, falling lifelessly to the snow-covered ground, I stop the flames and get back on my feet. We could end the fight here, but they all taught me one thing: a battle only ends when your enemy can't get up anymore. My limbs shake, a mix of adrenaline, tiredness, and raw magic energy rushing through my body.

Issac prepares to retreat, muscles bunching under his clothes, but before he can run, I stretch out my arm, pointing my finger at his core, calling up one last spell. Something that won't hurt him badly but will definitely knock him down. The world around me fades away, reality shrinking until only he exists in my vision.

"Boom." The tiny fireball, no bigger than a pebble, is flicked off from my finger as if it's nothing more than dust and hits his stomach with perfect aim. I watch as his face changes from shocked to stunned, his pale fingers spreading out to block it. His quick mind searches for a defence, but the fireball's speed makes it almost impossible to dodge. He has no choice but to take the hit, his body thrown backward before crashing into the pristine snowdrift, white powder billowing around him. "I am prepared," I say, my voice sounding strange to my ears.

"I should ask you where did you learn all those things, but I'm in pain and strangely turned on by the fact you kicked my arse." He chuckles, the sound half-choked.

"Did I hurt you?" I worry a bit knowing how powerful the spells can be when in my palms they feel like nothing but warmth and comfort.

Issac smirks, his hand lifting his armour a bit higher to reveal crumbling blood. "It'll take a lot more than a tiny spark to take me out love."

I squint at him, annoyed. Of course he used his blood to harden around his torso, I assume that's why he doesn't care about dragon scale armour and why he rarely loses battles. "Next time I'll aim at your head."

I stand over him, arms folded across my chest, as the cold wind cuts through my sweat-soaked clothes, sending shivers through my body.

"Next time knock me out."

I yelp as his hand shoots out, grabbing my ankle and yanking me down beside him. I fall into the snow, the cold blanket cooling my overheated skin, the sudden temperature change making me gasp. "You just can't let me win."

"If you kill me, I'll count it as a win." He peeks at me through his thick eyelashes, and I roll my eyes, though my stomach's flipping.

"I'd never do that," I whisper, the words heavy with hidden fear.

He scoffs, reaching his arm out to pull me closer before holding my face between his pale fingers. "Then I guess I should count myself lucky because I'd hate to be scorched alive." His lips brush my forehead in a light kiss. "At least I can say you're ready."

I sigh and rest my head against his chest, where the steady beat of his heart plays against my chaotic thoughts. My gaze drifts up to a sky that, for once, isn't an endless sheet of white but rather a blue dome so bright it hurts my eyes. My mind breaks apart, splitting into countless pieces of worry about tomorrow, Issac's fate tied to mine, and all the things that could go wrong despite our careful planning.

"What's wrong?" He asks, threading his pale fingers through my hair.

"Nothing, just—" I pause to look up at him, our gazes locked. "Worried, that's all."

Issac shifts beneath me, leaning on his elbow as his palm rests on my shoulder, squeezing it. "You're ready, more than that, I'm certain you're better than before. We've got a plan and a strong team. What else is there to worry about?"

I hold my breath, looking for words that could describe the storm of feelings inside me, but nothing I'd say would make sense. Issac can't possibly know that someone's life's at stake, that I'm afraid of becoming the monster everyone fears I might become, that even after our preparations I still worry that my magic might not be enough, that the horrors in the manor will repeat themselves all over again. My hands tremble slightly at the thought.

"I guess I just don't want you guys to get hurt because of me. Not again. I worry I made a mistake." The words feel inadequate compared to the crushing weight pressing down on my chest. What ifs run around my mind endlessly asking questions I can't begin to answer. The biggest one of them is was telling Eric the truth a good choice?

"Eric is not Lathai, Thea." Issac states, his presence in my mind barely a whisper, door slightly cracked open.

I roll my eyes, resigned, exhausted of worrying about trusting people in my life. "But you didn't trust him, at first until I convinced you." There is a knot in my stomach, pulling and twisting as the words settle between us. I look away, into the distance trying to form the question in my mind the best way before it reaches his ears.

"It already did, so say it." His voice wraps around me like vines with odd gentleness, and I push him away shutting the door closed. I need to remember to keep them locked around Issac before he decides to rummage through my thoughts and discover things I can't afford for anyone to find out.

"Fine, I've been wondering...why didn't you trust Lathai in the manor?" I look him in the eyes, search for that subtle change in his expression before he lies, but Issac scrunches his brows in confusion as if unsure what exactly I'm asking. Right, with his memories scattered like leaves in the wind I have to be a bit more specific. "Well, on multiple occasions you warned me against him, you and Theo. It always seemed like the two of you knew something I didn't."

The question is out, and my mind feels a little less heavy. Issac seems opposite, his head now full of thoughts as he searches through his lost memories. Perhaps he forgot, though it has nothing to do with me but I need to know. I need to know if he just disliked Lathai and me because of the brainwashing or did he know something and decided not to tell me too scared of how I'll take it because if that's the case then perhaps I was wrong again, perhaps he knows something about Eric he won't say just not to hurt me, per—

"I didn't trust him because this whole thing seemed strange to me." I stare at Issac, mind going quieter as I listen. He gets up to sit, his shoulders relaxed, his eyes putting words together, words I'm desperate to hear. *It was your fault Thea, your trustworthiness, your bad judgement* or *we knew but didn't tell you, we were afraid you won't believe, you will leave, he might do something.* "I guess it was weird to Theo and I. I mean our enemy shows up claiming he's here to help you after raiding the manor few years back in search of you. He claimed he left the army to find and help you even though he's been searching for years and suddenly he's decided you're not a threat to his people, suddenly he's not a bad guy, he doesn't want to blindly serve his king and just walks away? He just left his family who still lived in Eclia while he was openly committing treason? Yeah it didn't add up, and then all that talk about saving the world, pressuring you. It was all very suspicious to us."

I thought relief might wash over my heart. I thought I could finally understand what others saw and I didn't but what Issac said is things I knew. Things I simply paid no attention to because Lathai was kind, and understanding and wanted my help. Because he was the first person in hundred years able to stick by my side, promising companionship I craved, ear willing to listen. He was exactly who a person like me needed.

My fingers go cold as I press them into the snow. It was that obvious, huh? His life story a proof he's willing to help because of the stakes, and a lie that makes zero sense in Issac's and Theo's eyes. So it was me. Not the two of them, not destiny or divine intervention, or Lathai.

"So I was really the fool. I let the monster into the manor." The words leave my mouth before I can catch them, drifting away with the wind into the sky where they will forever remain.

"That's not true Thea, you couldn't have predicted—"

"You did, Theo did and yet I didn't. Someone who spent hours with him." I mumble, my head falling into my palms heavy with guilt and regret. "Gods how can you trust me now, how could you trust me with Eric, trust me with keeping you safe?"

"You're not responsible for our lives Thea. It was our choice to join you, to trust the people in your life, not yours so don't beat yourself over something you've got no control over." Issac's voice is stern, his words something I'm meant to understand and accept but how can I? I was a fool and even now I doubt myself because I trusted someone I barely knew with a secret that could get us killed.

"But I could've had control, I could've only if I had listened to you, if I chose to look through your eyes—" My words stop abruptly as Issac's hands grab onto my wrists and pull me towards him. I stare into his eyes, part of me hoping to see anger, to see something that would feel like a punishment, but instead I am met with understanding.

"You couldn't have seen through my or Theo's eyes because you didn't live our lives, because we didn't live yours. You spent hundred years alone, aching for someone to stay by your side when nobody would whilst I stayed surrounded by friends, by soldiers and four walls I could call home. I had shit to lose that's why I was suspicious while you had nothing, nothing beside a man who stuck around and gave you hope and purpose so you'd never question him like I did because for the first time in a long time he was something you couldn't afford to lose."

A tear runs down my cheek, falls onto the snow in silence while I stay still wondering just who exactly is the man before me? A man who understands? Who doesn't judge and overly protects? It feels like years ago I had the nightmares, had arguments with him all over again about how much he hates me, and now we are sat here and it's not me who comforts Issac but the opposite. It's the person I took the most from telling me to forgive myself, to trust myself a bit more, to let it all go.

He pulls me closer, the warmth of his body a stark contrast to the biting cold around us, and I let my chin rest on his shoulder, letting his words sink in so that I might stop obsessing over what could've been and hopefully one day forgive my foolish nature and trust my own judgement. "Come on, we've got to train some more so that I'm sure you can beat Eric's arse if he turns out bad."

Chapter 32

We finish the training once our stomachs begin to growl from hunger and our muscles ache with exhaustion. I want to push myself to train a bit more, but my magic is weak. I doubt Issac would continue training when I can barely keep my eyes open and so we leave.

Back in the castle Issac and I stop by the dining hall, the rich aroma of roasted meats and freshly baked bread wrapping around us as we enter. Desily is sat at the long wooden table with Alea, chatting and eating their food to gain some strength. Myra let her leave the hospital wing a few days ago, after making Des promise to visit regularly for a bandage change and healing sessions. The girl, of course, agreed after making a joke about getting an eye patch and soon changing from a healer to a pirate.

As it turned out Myra was right, the damage done to Desily's eye was too severe to fix, and though she accepted it in front of everyone with a brave smile, I see her sneaking out late at night to the bathroom to try to heal her eye with her own magic. Each attempt fruitless, her soft sobs barely audible through the thick wooden door as she silently comes back to bed with shoulders slouched down in defeat.

Alea and I pretend not to notice, it's something we all got good at. Pretending. If she's happy, we'd be happy with her. If she wakes up a bit under the weather, we'd be there for her to lift her spirit up, acting like it doesn't hurt us to see her this way.

"Oh! Look who finally showed up." Des blinks at me with a bright smile. She's been trying to convince me to bring her along on the journey but I refuse to put her at risk since she's still adjusting to the new changes. Safe to say she's not happy about that, her frustration showing in the slight tightening of her fingers around her spoon.

"Yeah, I have to look over the plans." I pour four glasses of ruby-red juice, handing one to Issac, one to Alea, one for me and one for Des. She takes it slowly, her eye narrowed into a slit. "No, you are not allowed to come," I add before she can speak.

"Thea! I can help." She protests whilst gulping down her drink with a grimace like a six-year-old child that wasn't allowed to go out to meet their friends.

I roll my eyes and plate myself some varieties of food. "I saw you stub your toe on the bed today, no way you're coming."

"You're cruel," she huffs and stuffs her cheeks with food.

"I'm protective," I rephrase her words with a smile that doesn't quite reach my eyes.

Desily scoffs but doesn't say anything else. She knows there is no way to win me over, and I hope to Gods she will use her time in the castle to regain strength and learn to live with the damage. I wish I could be there for her like she was for me on the ship, but I'm not as good at comforting, not good at getting used to something so severe because guilt is my friend and I'd sooner feel the way Desily feels rather than make her realise it's all okay. In my head I want the people in my life to be well and safe, but most of them live with invisible scars, some on the surface, and it pains me there is absolutely nothing I can do. Even with all those new powers I remain useless.

Theo, Venali, Jassin and Ryo show up not long after Issac and me, chatting quietly about our trip tomorrow. I even spot Myra at the end of the oak table with someone who I recognise, nodding her head in a greeting manner.

"Is that—" Des whispers, but I shush her hoping not to get attention. John, Lisa's ex-bodyguard sits with Myra. A person I thought was dead but turned out to be alive, a wielder who escaped using his powers and informed the princess of our existence. I haven't seen him once since we arrived here, I just assumed he must've returned to Eswos, to his boss and moved on but as it seems he came back. For what? That's a mystery that makes my skin prickle with unease.

The man turns as if feeling the eyes of eight people, and the whole table looks away, plates suddenly becoming the most interesting things in the world, all except for me. We look at each other for a moment, his bored brown eyes scanning my face, before he turns around and I hold back from getting up to ask him few questions.

Did he know Lisa was going to betray us? Did he realise she was disappearing to meet with Wyrran? Did he feel sorry for her?

"Thea." I snap my attention back to Ryo who with a grin begins to get up from his seat. "Ready for some reading?"

"He can read?" Issac murmurs and I elbow him, feeling his

ribs through his thin shirt. Though Ryo hated being in the library at first, my company seemed to change his mind, or the fact to each of his questions I seem to have an answer. After all, he's still a kid with a curious mind that I seem to feed with vivid descriptions.

"Yeah, let's go. I want to finish the fire wielding book today." I kiss Issac on the cheek, his skin warm against my lips, before throwing a quick goodbye to my friends and catching up to Ryo. Oddly enough I find most comfort in the boy's company out of everyone. Even with Desily and Lathai I never felt that way when sitting in the stillness of the library. Around Ryo everything seems to come alive, becomes interesting once again, no longer a task I might get tired of after few hours. With his young spirit I find a spark in myself that I thought was long gone.

We walk in silence, though the boy smiles every now and then, deep in thought. As we turn the corner, he turns to look at me with bright eyes, and I can't help but return his smile.

"What?" I ask.

"Nothing! I just can't wait for tomorrow." He jumps up, his boots momentarily leaving the ground. I chuckle, shaking my head at his energy.

"That excited, huh?"

"Don't get me wrong, I enjoy General Edison's training sessions, but Gods is it boring here. I need some action." Ryo throws fake punches at an invisible opponent. I burst out laughing. Only if I shared half his enthusiasm instead of growing more and more worried about the mission, hoping every detail is checked three times over and perfectly planned. Anxiety coils in my chest. Nothing can be missed.

"I'm sure you'll have plenty of fun," I respond, unable to keep the edge of worry from my voice as we approach the library doors.

***

I rub my tired eyes as I pass the quiet corridors, my footsteps muffled by the thick stone walls. I've nearly finished the book about fire wielding, though some spells are harder to remember than the others. I'm sure I won't be able to cast them without proper practice. If I had more time perhaps I'd feel stronger, I'd feel more secure and confident about the mission tomorrow.

The torch by one of the doors near my room flickers with sudden movement, and I nearly faint as a hand reaches for me and drags me inside. Everything in me screams to use my powers, but my body tingles in a way I know all too well, so I drop my guard down.

"Did I startle you?" Issac smirks at me, his crimson eyes gleaming with mischief, and I look up to meet his gaze before swatting his shoulder.

"Are you trying to give me a heart attack?" He smirks and plants a soft kiss on my forehead, his lips warm against my skin.

"Not in this way at least." I take a quick peek behind him to notice an empty room, similar to the one I share with Desily and Alea, lit by a crackling fireplace. "I've asked the princess if we could use this for tonight. I want to spend as much time with you before tomorrow."

I smile before cupping his cheeks, my fingers brushing against the day-old stubble that scratches pleasantly against my palms. Something awful must be coming my way because having Issac with this personality is so strange yet rewarding. He cares about things I'd never imagine his old self think of. Back then I've had a general who tried his best to keep the manor and the people inside of it safe. Now I've a man who doesn't care about anything else beside me.

"Can we just lay down?" I ask, and the smile I get in return makes my knees weak. Issac doesn't just look at me with care but with love, undeniable, unshakeable and unexplainable love like I'm all he's always wanted. Like I'm his oxygen, his life purpose, the most precious person in his whole entire existence.

"Of course we can." He lifts me up unexpectedly, and I lock my hands behind his head, feeling the soft strands of his dark hair between my fingers. We land on the bed with a soft bounce, my head resting on his chest where I can hear the steady rhythm of his heartbeat. I trace my finger over the outline of his muscle through the thin black shirt he's wearing, picking at the white buttons and wondering if they might come off.

Issac's fingers thread into my hair, and my eyes fall shut at the pleasant feeling of having him touch me in a way far more intimate than I could ever explain. We are not naked nor are we ready to swallow each other whole, yet my body shivers in a relaxing way, melting into his touch as if we're doing something forbidden. The weight of his body underneath me serves as a reminder this is real, and so is the faint sound of the fire burning up the wood in the fireplace.

"What's on your mind, love?" His voice sends ripples through my body, low and husky, and I slightly gaze up at him.

"Love? Is that a new nickname?" I quirk a brow at him, feeling heat rise to my cheeks, and he smiles before kissing the top of my head, his lips lingering against my hair.

"You could say that. You are the only being in this vast world and far beyond it that I could ever possibly give my heart to." I lift myself up to get a better view of his face, my eyes watering just from his words. "And if I ever get torn away from the path we take I will find my way back to you no matter where it is."

I blink rapidly as a strange feeling settles over my chest making it heavy but light at the same time. My lips quiver and I try to stop them from shaking but without success. Issac's brows draw together in confusion, worry creeping into his crimson eyes, and in a second I am straddling him as he frantically tries to get rid of the tears falling down my cheeks with his thumbs.

"Wha—"

"You know," I interrupt him with a smile, my fingers wrapping around his wrists, feeling his pulse beneath my touch. "There used to be a time where I thought having you as my best friend was the best possible thing that could ever happen to me." I take a shaky breath in, my heart pounding inside my chest louder than the words coming out of my mouth. "Then I lost you and I prayed to have you back in any shape or form, but I'd never expect it'd be like this. If I knew I'd thank the Gods every day for letting me have this life, for letting me meet you the way I did and every part of you whole or broken."

Without a warning Issac pulls me closer, his arms wrapping around me and hugging me tighter to his chest. I rest my chin on top of his head, breathing in the familiar scent of him, tears still rolling down my cheeks but by now I hope he knows they're from happiness. If I could freeze time and let us stay like this forever I would, and I'd never return back to normal.

I look down as his body tenses a little, and ignore the faint sound of his shaky breath against my neck. I'm sure I'm not the only one crying, but mentioning it might ruin this perfect moment I'm imagining in my head, so let's stay like this for longer until one of us gets tired of holding another.

"Are you ready for tomorrow?" Issac whispers as his hand brushes against my back in soothing circles. I swallow hard and try to forget about the dangerous mission ahead.

"Will I ever be?" I chuckle and exhale as the part of me that worries tries to come back. "If you guys are there that's all the reassurance I need."

"No, as long as we have you that's all the reassurance we need, Miss leader." His voice carries a hint of teasing.

"Oh shut it!" I playfully push him away but Issac doesn't let go. We laugh for a bit, and then talk about everything and nothing until the fire dies down to glowing embers, until my eyes are too heavy to keep open, and until our bodies feel like they're about to melt into each other. The room grows dim and peaceful around us. Tomorrow feels brighter than ever now, wrapped in his warmth and the promise of his unwavering love.

Chapter 33

The morning wind cuts through us, as though warning us to turn back. My boots sink into the deep snow, the small pack weighing against my shoulder. I glance towards Alea, watching her struggle to communicate with Theo. Each time she raises her hands to sign, the fierce wind threatens her balance.

Behind us, Ella and Myra stand flanked by one of the towering snow giants and John, whose presence feels both familiar and distant. I've decided to let them join, it's quite hard to say no to royalty and her personal guard. Although, I don't mind their presence, it's John who makes me a bit worried.

We haven't spoken since his arrival, only acknowledged each other's existence with curt nods and mumbled greetings, yet his sudden investment in this mission burns with an intensity I think comes from grief, perhaps guilt over Lisa's fate. I could turn him away, after all I still don't fully trust him but it was Myra who begged me to let him tag along, her father sending him as extra protection, as a way to check on us. Whatever that means, Myra wouldn't explain and I didn't push. I don't have time to learn new information about her family right before our mission so I agreed for him to come knowing we need extra wielders and that he'll be under Issac's watchful eye, as well as Theo's, Alea's and mine.

Near the entrance, Ryo, Venali, and Jassin gather around Issac as he goes over their roles for the tenth time. His attention to details brings me relief; one burden less for my mind. Everyone must remain alert, prepared for whatever horrors the ice has kept sealed. The gods alone know what lies dormant beneath those frozen layers.

My gaze drifts towards the castle's silhouette, and my heart tightens. One crucial member is absent from our group, and her missing presence echoes through our ranks. Desily, despite the darkness clouding her remaining eye, had demanded to join. Yet as group leader, the weight of refusal fell to me. I know what dangers await her. The hurt that flickered across her features before she stormed away cuts deeper than any blade, but sometimes you have to be cruel.

"Is everyone ready?" Issac shouts from the entrance, and we gather closer. I clench my fists, the dragon scale gloves rough against my palms, then brush my hand against my armour to make sure all weapons remain secure. Issac's crimson eyes flicker to me before a proud smirk spreads across his pale lips. "Let's start, captain."

I swallow hard as all eyes fall upon me. Nine. Nine lives depend on me now, and I can't afford a single misstep. These people trust me enough to guide them through the unknown, perhaps they trust me more than I would ever trust myself.

"Right, the mission officially begins now. As established, do not under any circumstances split from the group. Make no loud noises inside the cave and grip your weapons tight. May the Gods guide us." Everyone nods, and I turn towards the entrance where Issac prepares to forge a hammer from his blood to shatter the thick wall. One strike and it will all crumble…

"No!" Jino's voice rings inside my skull, and I glance at Issac poised to swing. He halts his movements suddenly which tells me Jino's talking to us both. *"Do not strike it! It will cause an avalanche, you fools!"*

Issac lowers his weapon and turns to meet my confused stare. He sighs but recalls his blood. I purse my lips, wondering how I failed to consider this earlier. How are we meant to enter if we can't break through from outside?

"What should we do then?" His fingers wrap around my wrist, trying to pull me from my thoughts, but it's useless. I'm trapped, searching for a solution that won't expose my first mistake so early.

"Dear mortals, use your magic. Fire won't cause damage if you maintain control." The look Issac sends me confirms he heard Jino's message too. I nod and move towards the ice wall, my fingers sliding against the freezing surface as cold seeps through the leather.

Control. Easier said than done, but what choice do I have except to master what lives within me?

Magic floods through me, and I trace its path along every vein until it reaches my fingertips. Steam begins to surround Issac and me as ice melts away, and I focus on containing the heat to one spot, nowhere else but my fingers.

The air grows increasingly hot, but I hold my position, bringing my other hand to the wall and channelling all my power into raising the temperature. A spark ignites, red, then gold, then brilliant blue. I blink away the sweat droplets, struggling for oxygen through the scorching mist that dries my throat.

"Thea!" Issac calls from somewhere behind, but I ignore him. My arms sink half a metre deep, and on unsteady legs, I step forward. The wall can't be as thick as I fear, or I'll not only roast myself alive but drain every drop of magic from my veins.

I walk and walk and walk for what feels like forever when mere seconds pass, but with the heat becoming unbearable, my mind grows too clouded. Especially when I must focus on moving forward and keeping my magic steady rather than simply staying alive.

A sudden wave of coldness travels through my body, and I blink to find myself inside the wall. Not much farther left, surely not much more...

"Thea, get out! We'll try again later, just leave it!" Issac's voice sounds distant, alarmed and though I can hear it I don't stop. I want to tell him we can't wait, that if we're to do this properly, we must do it now, and I'll sacrifice anything to ensure our success.

"Even your life?" Jino mocks, and I jolt. *"Can't do much when you're dead, can you?"* She giggles, and I grit my teeth, my flames suddenly blazing hotter until the entire space becomes foggy.

"I won't die," I reassure myself more than her, pushing harder.

"Keep telling yourself that, but it seems you always try risking your life as though it will somehow save your friends. Trust me girl, our death won't achieve that." Jino mocks, clearly amused by how foolish I can be.

"Shut up!" A sharp crack sounds ahead, and I freeze, eyes fixed forward. A moment passes before I stumble onto a

snowy path, clouds of steam filling the large entrance before fading. Finally, the air tastes wet rather than parched, and I choke as I inhale it. My skin burns so fiercely that the snow feels like blessed relief. I glance slowly around into the darkness, hoping no creatures heard my disturbance.

The cave stretches before me, quiet and intimidating. For a moment, I let myself wonder how life flourished here before it became buried beneath mountains of snow and ice.

"Thea!" Issac's arms wrap around my shoulders, pulling me against his chest. The hood slips from my head, and my body shivers from the sudden cold. "Are you mad? You could've been seriously hurt." He shakes me gently, but I smile watching our group file through the entrance I've carved.

"I'm fine, and we're in." I try to lighten the mood, but Issac refuses as his palm presses against my forehead.

"You're far from fine. You're burning up." He hisses, calling for Myra since she serves as our healer whilst Desily recovers.

My jacket is quickly stripped away, and only then do I realise I'm nowhere near as warm as the others. Perhaps I pushed myself too much. Myra kneels before me, summoning water from her satchel. I remain silent as the cool liquid covers my skin, beginning to glow. This is the first time I've felt Myra's power so closely. Surprisingly, it causes no pain. In all honesty, it feels similar to Desily's touch, though it vibrates through me rather than simply sinking in.

"You've done yourself proper, Starbane, but be more careful next time. Don't want to waste my powers just on you." Myra whispers, and I chuckle.

"Oh please, I know you'd rather see me dead." The girl

meets my gaze, mischief flickering in her eyes, the hatred I once saw weeks ago has vanished. We've grown closer, and whatever bitter feelings existed between us dissolved for the time being. Still, I can't pretend to be happy about her feelings for Issac, even so I refuse to hate her simply because she loves someone out of gratitude.

Ryo, Jassin, and Venali light torches as the rest of our group takes in the view. With Issac's reluctant help, I struggle to my feet, avoiding his scolding gaze and abandoning my jacket entirely. Now that I've spent my magic, it serves no purpose, my body temperature fighting to find balance between hot and cold.

"Thea, if you're feeling better, would you mind…" Ella gestures towards the dark tunnel, and I nod. The torches barely light what lies ahead; the only way to discover potential dangers is to send a fireball into that passage.

With a flicker of my fingers, a small sphere of flame appears in my palm. Using minimal strength to avoid damage, I hurl it forward. The dark tunnel bathes in blue light from the ice walls, but to my disappointment, no signs of civilisation emerge.

"Well, that's not promising," Myra mutters, and I sigh.

"Let's keep moving."

***

The darkness is unbearable. I blink twice opening my eyes as wide as possible to try and see something, anything. A statue, a roof, a sign of a monster, but the light from the torches barely wraps around our group. We've been at it for what seems like hours, keeping our conversations hushed and our footsteps void of noise. I knew the journey to the buried castle would be tiresome but this, this is torture.

As we venture deeper, I remain alert. Nobody can tell if monsters lurk in shadows, whether openings or dead ends await, or if we're even heading in the right direction. Besides that, the temperature makes everyone except me shiver. I think about warming them, but one warning glance from Issac has me dropping my hands. I know I should save energy, but watching my friends struggle lights every protective instinct.

"What's troubling you now?" Issac nudges my shoulder, and I shoot him an annoyed look, though it's difficult when he looks at me with such care.

"You know perfectly well what is," I mutter, and he chuckles.

"Forgive me for not letting you kill yourself." I cross my arms, half grateful I've lost the jacket and can move more freely than the others. If danger strikes, I'll respond first. Issac tugs my elbow, I nudge him away, but soon he pulls me closer, draping his arm across my shoulders.

No amount of warmth my magic produces could replace what I feel from his touch. It's softer than any flame, gentler than summer rays, kinder than anything that's ever graced my skin. Once, I'd have hated someone this close, letting them carve themselves into my very being, but now, everything has changed.

"Don't be angry. Just like you, I refuse to lose the person I love." I look up at him, but Issac quickly presses a kiss to my forehead, gazing into the darkness. "Light it up, red."

I crack my fingers and create a small orb of light.

"Finally! I was tired of seeing... well, nothing." Ryo groans, throwing himself between Issac and me. I smile at him just as our group halts behind us.

"Gods, at this point I'd welcome even a glimpse of natural light," Myra mutters whilst I think about directions. The cave stretches too wide and tall for our torches to reach the walls. Perhaps if I make the fireball slightly larger...

"I find it rather peaceful, the quiet I mean." Ella brushes her white fur coat whilst John peers around as though he can see past shadows.

I step forward, hoping nobody notices as the sphere in my palms grows an inch larger. Trusting my instincts, I hurl it into the distance. The path brightens, revealing more ice until...

My heart clenches as I spot a pillar in the distance, carved from thick ice. On each side stands a cave entrance, possibly leading towards the castle. With one glance at Issac, I sprint towards it, hearing footsteps thundering behind. Finally, after hours of wandering, we've found something.

"Wait!" someone screams behind, but I don't stop, not until I reach the entrance. "Guys, wait!"

Another fireball glows in my palm as the previous one begins dying. Just as I release it, someone lunges for my shoulder and the sphere slips towards the pillar. I watch it tremble, ice slowly cracking. I'm prepared to scream at whoever disturbed me, but when I turn, it's Theo standing there drenched in cold sweat, and right behind him, I see them. Monsters.

Issac halts before the left entrance with Jassin and Venali beside him. Ryo drags Ella towards us whilst John and Myra already use their powers against the approaching creatures.

"What are those?" Myra turns to me, and I swallow the

ball of anxiety.

Her water is slipping out of the waterskin attached to her waist, swaying from side to side like a serpent ready to strike. To her left, John is wrapped by something resembling dark mist, shadows perhaps.

My heart wedges in my throat as one of the monsters lowers itself, head the size of a three storey house moving around, listening for a noise. The creature is blind. Suddenly, its mouth falls open revealing a set of sharp teeth that span in circles all the way to the back of its throat. No, surely it can't be.

John is first to strike, the darkness around him moving without verbal command and racing towards the creature with incredible speed. I wonder for a moment just what he's about to do, but when the darkness twists into a sharp spike, my face drains of colour.

"Wait!" I shout jolting forward but it's too late. The monster shrieks, making the whole tunnel vibrate with the force. "Myra, run!" I scream, summoning my fire whip and lashing it towards the creature. Its maw gapes open, ready to consume anything in its path. The beast stretches at least ten metres long, if it reared up, it would tower over us. Its width rivals the thickest trees I've come across. Worse still, this isn't even fully grown. This is merely a baby.

"Thea, what the hell are those?!" Alea screams as I dash to get Myra and John before they're crushed.

Think Thea, think. You know this, you know what monsters are those and the best way to fight them. My heart pounds with every thought, with every second before a memory pushes past all the chaos.

Hard-bodied creatures with long, round forms in soft gray.

Limbless, eyeless monsters living in darkness, responding only to warmth.

Warmth.

My fire drew them out, but from where? No caves were visible, nowhere to emerge from. We hadn't heard them unless... I glance upward, sending a tiny fireball towards the ceiling. It takes mere seconds to reveal the first opening, and three more to realise we'd been searching for monster activity on the ground whilst they lurked above us the entire time.

"Everyone run! They're snow worms!" I crack the fire whip, trying to frighten them, but the creatures back away only inches. Shit, I need to redirect their attention.

"Snow worms?" Ryo squeaks whilst handing Ella over to Theo, who guides her to safety deeper into the left tunnel. In the distance, I see Issac charging towards us, and a plan forms. "What in hell's name is that?"

"Something we believed extinct for centuries," Ella whispers, backing away further.

"Clearly not!" Myra swirls her water, creating an ice barrier before fleeing, but this only angers one of the creature as it launches towards her, making the entire cave shudder.

I look at Issac, watching him pour blood past Myra, forming a wall that turns into sharp spikes. My eyes scan the area, spotting John on the ground clutching his arm. When did he get injured?

"Issac! Hold that wall as long as possible, I have a plan." I sprint forward after seeing him nod. Fire, I need to lead them away with warmth. That's our only solution. If I can get everyone into the same cave entrance whilst distracting the worms, we might escape. Otherwise, killing them here could be impossible with all this ice ready to crush us, not to mention these creatures mother waiting to be called.

I create a fireball large enough to light the tunnel. The worm before me trembles, and I make sure the heat won't melt the ice as I hurl it past their heads. One creature, the slightly smaller one, takes the bait and chases the light back towards where we came from, whilst the larger beast remains too focused on Issac to notice me standing beneath it.

My feet carry me towards John, who groans in pain while clutching his hand.

"Can you walk?" He looks at me suspiciously but nods, struggling to his feet and wobbling towards Issac. Flames spread over my fists as I consider my next move. The only way to drive it back is through fear and pain, but first—

"Everyone! Head for the caves and wait, it might become shaky in a moment." I cast one final glance at Issac, who appears worried yet holds his position. With his free hand, I see him forming larger spikes, ready to launch, but I halt him with my palm. Not yet. If we're going to succeed, timing must be perfect.

I try to circle the worm so its head and body face me directly, but the closer I get, the more unstable the ground becomes. I spot my friends in the distance, positioned by the cave entrances. Right, time to act.

I create another whip to wrap around the creature, this one longer and hotter. Once satisfied with its length, I lock eyes with Issac and give the signal. The spikes pierce the beast's flesh, making the floor shake violently. Just as its head whips around, I crack my whip and pray I've measured its length correctly.

My palms burn from trying to hold myself in place as

the flames loop around, but I refuse to let go, watching in suspense as the tip of the whip finally settles. With every ounce of strength, I drag the worm towards me, letting Issac escape.

The creature shrieks, and walls tremble as it crashes against the cavern sides. A few more seconds, just enough to anger it further. I yank once more, and the monster turns its fury towards me. Quickly, I drop the flames and leap aside as its gaping maw smashes into where I'd stood. A fireball, I need another fireball.

My heart pounds as I sprint, struggling to focus on creating twin spheres. One strikes the creature's face, leaving it dazed, whilst I prepare to hurl the second into the distance.

"Thea! Run!" Someone screams, but I'm too focused on the beast that refuses to follow the light. This one needs something bigger, something brighter.

I halt metres from the caves, pressing my palms together and drawing a breath. Focus, Thea. You can do this. My fingers twitch from exhaustion, palms aching from heat, but I pour everything into creating something I rarely use, the blue flames.

The worm rears upward, and I crane my neck as it looks down at me, or perhaps at the light I struggle to hold. I must make it larger.

"Hurry!" Not yet.

"Quick, before it—" The voice cuts off as something crashes to the ground, throwing me off balance. The impact shakes through walls and my bones before stopping, then I hear it, the cracking.

"The entrance—"

"Get inside!" I scream without turning. They must stay

safe. They have to.

"Thea!"

Now. I hurl the blazing sphere past the creature, making the cavern glow with light I've never seen, sparkling as it streaks beyond the worm, making the monster turn. I begin racing towards my friends, noticing Myra and Ryo positioned on the right whilst the rest of our group stands to the left. What are they doing—

I glance above them as ice slowly cracks, preparing to scream for them to move when the worm's tail strikes the ceiling. The world freezes as ground begins shaking, and with it, the pillar holding the entrance ceiling. I stare above Myra and Ryo, where ice chunks crumble downward, but neither notices, they're too busy making sure I return safely.

"Move back!" I shriek as time slows. The pillar finally gives up, and I launch myself towards them, throwing us all into the cave.

Everything blurs as a crash echoes behind us. We tumble before finally stopping, clouds of snow swirling around us. I cough, rising to my feet to check the damage, and colour drains from my face. The entrance has vanished.

"What—what are we going to do now?" Ryo stares at me, but all I can think about isn't our safety, but everyone else on the other side.

Chapter 34

The snow settles, and with it my mind begins to unravel. Hundreds of questions, thousands of possibilities, yet none helpful. I replay that very moment over and over, when I threw myself into a different entrance. An unknown path that might lead nowhere. Or somewhere, and it's not what lays ahead that worries me but my friends. The worms could attack them; they might be defenceless.

"Starbane?" Myra stands inches away, but her voice seems so distant I question whether I've hit my head. We don't know what happened to them, what awaits us, and worse, I'm almost at my limit. Without proper rest I can't break through the thick walls, but time seems to be sprinting away and I can't seem to catch up. With only Myra's power and Ryo's limited crystals, we stand no chance. But if it comes to choosing between them and myself, I'll always pick them. No matter what.

I look at the ice around us and reach towards the door that connects me to Issac, but it won't open. I pull and pull but it won't budge as if something is preventing me from doing so. Is he too far? Is he alive? I stare at my hands, wondering if I can access the black flames to melt the ice. If the roof will crumble down. If my friends are alive.

"Starbane!" Myra's hands grasp my shoulders, shaking me into the present. I blink at her, her blue eyes reflecting worry, something I haven't expected from a soldier like her. "I know what you're thinking, and no, you will not use your power. They'll be fine. We know Issac, and he won't let anything happen to them. He's strong, stronger than you think, so get a grip. We need your brain."

Ryo paces behind us, his hand tightly wrapped around his sword's hilt. I can tell he's trying to listen for something, anything that might show we're in danger.

She's right, of course. I need to get a grip because if I don't then this mission will be an utter disaster. Issac will be fine, the rest of the group will survive. It's been already established that he's far better at protecting people he cares about, now it's my turn to prove the same. I can't let them down.

"Did you just call me clever in your own way?" I quirk a brow at her, and she chuckles.

"I never called you stupid. Now come on. Let's follow the tunnel and pray to the gods we meet up with them later." I nod in agreement and let her help me up.

The cave walls glow bright blue, strangely letting in light. There's no darkness to pass through, but a lit corridor leading somewhere. I scan the area, looking up to notice tiny circles deep within the ice.

"The tunnels," I whisper, catching Ryo's and Myra's attention. "the light comes from tunnels made by the worms. Centuries ago, now frozen over but still there to let in light." I explain whilst continuing forward. If light filters through, that means we're either reaching nightfall or the day has started. If it's the former, that would mean we've been gone for hours.

I thank the gods for making the right choice in leaving Desily behind. Who knows what could've happened if she were here with us? I wouldn't dare imagine it. I'm not even sure if any of us have been hurt, but given Myra's confident strides and Ryo's curious eyes, I think nothing too serious happened to them.

We stumble upon a narrower path and agree to go single file. Myra positions herself at the rear with Ryo in the middle and me at the front, since I'm still the leader, though the majority of our group is lost somewhere. I slide my fingertips against the frozen walls and peer into the distance.

"Do you think they're all right?" Ryo whispers, and I tense, though I don't let them see it.

"They have to be. Their group is larger than ours, with the deadliest soldier by their side." Myra hums, and I let myself smirk. Issac won't let anything happen to them, and with John, Theo, Alea, Jassin, Venali, and Ella, they're much stronger than us.

"Right, I'm just worried." He adds, and I twist to look at his face.

"About what?" Myra grunts before locking eyes with me in a knowing look. She shares his concerns but won't let him see it. Ryo is just a child, no need to frighten him when his heart remains so pure.

"I don't know… that they could've gotten separated or hurt or—" He cuts himself off before looking at me, as if thinking about whether he should continue. Whether what he's about to say will add to my burden, though we're way past that. My plate has been full for over a century. "Or taken somewhere."

"By whom?" The girl scoffs, and I return to looking ahead.

"By things we haven't seen yet." I draw my brows together in confusion. Why would Ryo ever think something like that might happen? He's never been here and knows nothing of the ancient creatures that live in Sebraycia, so why would he suggest that?

I'm about to open my mouth when suddenly I lose my footing and feel my body tilt. I throw my arms out, sliding down before finally coming to a halt.

"Thea!" Ryo's voice echoes around, and I grunt in pain, massaging my tailbone. What the—

I blink once, twice. My mouth empty of words. I have landed in a strange cave and before me stands a work of art. Every surface tells a story carved in ice. Delicate carved snowflakes spiral across the walls, each one unique. Carved stars burst forth in patterns, their points catching and reflecting light. Crescent moons carved in relief wax and wane along the ceiling, creating an eternal night sky trapped in ice. In some places, I recognise chiselled plants native to Sebraycia, arctic roses with petals like glass, silver ferns that seem to sway, towering pines that once covered frozen forests, all long extinct yet preserved here in this very cave.

The entrance is here, we finally found it. Most miraculously of all, the corridor remains mostly unharmed despite the castle's fall. Only a few hairline scratches mark the surfaces. Otherwise, one could believe this palace was crafted yesterday.

"Thea!" I jump as someone's hand lands on my shoulder and turn to spot Ryo breathing heavily, his eyes wide as he takes in the scene. "Wow."

Myra stands right behind, and surprisingly doesn't utter a word as she takes in the beauty I too can't stop admiring. Her usually stern expression has softened. This is more than a relic, this is a place hidden from mortal greed, an artwork of the giants never meant to be recovered.

"We found it."

The three of us enter what's left of the castle with utmost caution. No one has walked these halls in centuries, and only the ghosts of the past know what lurks within these walls. I pass by enormous doors, spending no less than a minute checking the inside of each room. Broken beds, shattered wardrobes and chandeliers lay scattered around. I gaze up at the ceiling so tall you would need 10 people standing on each other's shoulders to reach the top. If the ritual is hidden somewhere here, it'll be in a place of significance. Not a library, not a bedchamber, no, something far grander.

Giants are peaceful creatures, quiet and reserved. They don't share the qualities the rest of us possess, greed. They care nothing for jewels or magic; they admire beauty. Especially the beauty of their land, hence why the castle was built from ice, why the walls depict their natural habitat. If they possessed something precious, something irreplaceable, it would be housed in a hidden, heavily guarded chamber.

By the time we reach the corridor's end, we're met with another passage to the left. If our group were together, perhaps this could go much quicker, but because we were torn apart, our search takes twice as long.

I let my hand slide over the ice, wondering for a moment how life looked within such a structure. I wonder if everyone made it out alive, and if those who didn't met some terrible fate. My eyes drift to Myra, who seems lost in thought as she gazes around the castle, and behind her, Ryo walks with his mouth slightly agape. He's never seen anything like this, he hasn't seen much in all honesty, being a soldier born in such times, so walking through a place like this must mean a great deal to him. It does to me, seeing them happy.

We wander some more, checking room after room, but still nothing except for a few oversized bones here and there. A thought that this place might be too vast for us to explore properly grows in my mind, and I purse my lip looking at the last set of doors that Ryo is about to push.

"Where is this bloody ritual?" Myra grunts as the heavy door creaks open. I peer inside and huff in annoyance when a large, empty hall stands before us. I imagine there used to be something here before, a meeting hall perhaps? We walk further in, our eyes scanning the surfaces, and I draw my brows together.

Why is it so empty?

"Something about this room feels different." I whisper and reach for my weapon, my gut telling me to prepare.

Myra and Ryo notice my unease and reach for their sides when suddenly the room begins to shake. I sway sideways, trying to catch my balance, and open the flow of my magic. The connection seems faint, given I've used too much of it recently, but if I must draw more than I should, I'll do it.

The ceiling above us makes a noise, and I look around. There are no adjoining rooms, and the vibrations aren't coming from behind. Could it be a worm? No, it would feel different, be quieter. I take a step towards what looks like blocks of ice stacked atop each other. I take what time remains to assess them. It's the only odd object in this empty space. What is it? Why there? Wait.

I run towards them, and the closer I get, the more I see it. The wall behind the blocks is separated from the rest of the room, and it's not just any wall. It must lead to where we need to go, to where the noise comes from, and those blocks of ice...

"A throne room." Just as the words leave my mouth, a hand the size of a small house emerges from behind the wall. Pale and worn with time, dressed in a glove that only wraps around the index finger.

My body freezes in place, but I fight through it because whatever is about to meet us might be our answer or our end. Surely, a moment later, a cane comes into view, followed by a robe torn in various places yet not dirty.

I curl my fingers into fists and swallow hard as the rest of the creature comes into view. Their long, white beard and thinned hair. Milky eyes scanning the area but ultimately landing on us, as though even blinded, it can see. This is no monster, it's a giant, and from what it looks like, it's the last one who survived the fall and stayed behind.

"H-How is he alive?" Ryo whispers, his voice trembling.

"They can survive years without food, though I think he didn't have to struggle given there are monsters everywhere here." I explain and proceed to spread my arms to get the two of them behind me.

"As if that's going to do something, Starbane," Myra scoffs, but her expression changes when the giant emerges fully. He's taller than any we've met so far, and without much struggle, he could crush us beneath his thumb. He takes two more steps and stops right in the room's centre, leaning most of his weight against the wooden cane.

"Who is here? Who dares to intrude upon the castle?" His voice rumbles deep. I feel my legs weaken, fear crawling from behind and telling me to run for my life, but there's no possibility I could ever do that. If I must use force to enter that cursed room, so be it.

"Althea Starbane. I came looking for something." I keep my voice steady against him. The giant growls but makes no move.

"So many before you, and yet they left empty-handed, if they ever did leave." He remarks, and I try to relax my body. Myra reaches for her water flask, but I stop her. Before we resort to violence, we need to use logic. Giants aren't aggressive by nature, but who knows what this one might be like.

"An artefact was brought here many years ago by the soldiers of Lord Graham. I need to get it, or the world will be in danger." I explain, and the giant's expression changes from unbothered to curious.

He shifts on his feet and moves towards the broken throne, picking up the remaining pieces before settling into the broken seat. As I thought, he won't attack. I gesture towards Ryo and Myra to stand down before taking a cautious step forward. The giant remains silent as I draw closer, his silhouette towering over mine. He's been here alone all these years. Why?

"Who are you?" I ask just as I stop a few metres from his enormous feet.

He tilts his head, ancient joints creaking, and groans. "I am Mirym, keeper of the chamber, the last one remaining."

My brows draw together as I realise the reason he stayed behind. "You're guarding the stored objects."

"I am, and that is why they still remain here, hidden, safe, and not in the wrong hands." His pale eyes scan me, and I purse my lips. If he's been here for more than a century making sure that the artefacts brought to Yalan stay untouched, it's safe to assume it won't be easy to simply walk into the chamber and retrive the ritual text.

"The object we need to get, you know what it is." I begin speaking, and the giant nods slowly. "So you know if we don't take it, Aagon will come looking for it too? You know he's evil."

"And what makes you better than him, Althea Starbane?" He interrupts, and I keep my lips sealed, slightly taken aback. If he's been around for years, he must know the awful things Aagon has done, yet he thinks I might somehow be worse?

"I haven't done anything bad." I try defending myself, but the giant laughs.

"Is that so? Is this why your heart beats so fiercely? Why your mind is so twisted?" I glance sideways at Ryo and Myra, and for a moment I fear they'll hear the truth about who I really am. That the sounds my body make betrays what the giant can't see. I'm not evil, I haven't done evil acts, yet part of me lives in shame for what has happened over the century. For my family, for humans I couldn't save, for lives I've stolen, for Issac and the manor. I might not be as evil, but I'm not pure, not since I died.

The room falls silent, and I feel my throat tighten at the sound of my heart pounding inside my chest. Does it betray what I really feel? What I try to hide? Is this what the giant means?

"Thea is not who you think she is." Ryo steps out of line, and my throat tightens. "She's also not the person she thinks she is, and will never be who people think she could become."

"Mmm, then what is she?" The giant suddenly intrigued leans back in his makeshift throne, and I remain still, shocked by the words coming from Ryo's mouth.

The boy tightens his grip on his sword and looks back at me with a smile that speaks only kindness. "She's intelligent and wonderful to be around. She's caring and compassionate like no other person I've ever met."

"Yeah." Myra moves forward, and my eyes widen because she's the last person I imagined would stand up for me. "She's a pain in the arse, and most of the time annoys the hell out of me, but I've never met anyone more selfless, someone willing to do anything for the people around her, even if it means death."

I blink at their confession, unable to find any words that could equal how grateful I feel for their support. How much it means to hear this after constant self-doubt. It seems what I thought was never true, and to the people around me, I'm never a burden but something better, something more precious.

"She's our hope. Our only hope at staying alive, so if you would be so kind as to take us to the chamber, I would be grateful." Ryo turns to face the giant, and I stifle a giggle hearing the shakiness in his voice. Only seconds ago he stood proud whilst speaking about me, where did that courage go?

Myra locks eyes with me and nods, words passing between us without uttering a single sound. *We've got you.*

The giant thinks for a moment before slamming his cane against the ice floor and rising from his seat. I wobble sideways, nearly falling to the ground, and watch as he shuffles towards us, close enough that I can smell the damp scent from his weathered robes. He then crouches, his massive frame folding, and looks at me once again whilst my heart pounds wildly.

"Your friends hold you very high, Althea, and for that I'll consider letting you through." My face lights up, the flame of hope burning bright. "But before that, I want you to answer a riddle that will determine whether or not you're worthy."

"A riddle?" I whisper, and he nods seriously. It shouldn't be too difficult, right? I've read enough to work out many ancient texts, understand old languages, and see what lies hidden. Time to truly put my knowledge to the test.

"Fine."

"Very well then." His voice drops to a whisper that somehow fills the entire chamber. "I am love that wears the face of loss. The heart that breaks to heal another. I am the seed that dies to bloom. The gift that makes us discover. In my pain, purpose finds its voice. I am both ending and beginning. What am I?"

I can see the confusion on Ryo's and Myra's faces as they try to find the answer to the riddle. I hear my own heartbeat pounding in my skull as I rethink his words repeatedly. My lip is trapped between my teeth as I focus on the distant wall and begin breaking it down.

I am love that wears the face of loss. Could that be a hint about a person? No, something else, a God perhaps? Is there a deity I've never heard about? One that overlooks human affairs?

Suddenly, my mind panics as I remember just how many secrets could still be hidden from me. Names I don't know, magic I don't understand, and secrets I haven't been told. The giant could ask me about anything, even if it's something

I've never come across. Perhaps that's why he wants to test me, to see just how educated I am. Because if I get the ritual and my intentions aren't as pure as he thinks, then the world could be doomed. Someone who hasn't taken their time to learn about their world shouldn't be trusted with anything precious, and that's what I'm proving. That I know exactly what's at stake here.

I am love that wears the face of loss. The heart that breaks to heal another. I am the seed that dies to bloom. The gift that makes us discover. In my pain, purpose finds its voice. I am both ending and beginning. I repeat the words in my head. What thing in the world could possibly exist that could love but show loss? That could break their own heart just to heal another? Magic? No, not that, dig deeper.

A seed that dies, but in its place something else emerges, a new chapter, a new opportunity. It's something that is a gift you discover in the moment, not before, just at the right time. Something you don't know until it comes.

I look over at my friends, their worry visible through their encouraging smiles. They put all their trust in me, in what I'm going to say, and for that I can't let them down. We're not leaving empty-handed.

I rethink the last two lines. It's something that can be found in pain, a purpose born in a moment, a destiny perhaps? Ending and beginning...

Just then my mind drifts to Issac, just for a split second as I remember his smile. To Desily and Alea laughing in our room and to Theo sipping his tea in the stillness of his lost garden. I think of Lathai and the way he always held me when things went badly. To Lisa and her lover who lost their lives whilst trying to protect one another. To my parents who gave away so much just to see me live my life.

The image disappears as soon as it appears, and I glance at the giant patiently waiting. All these people did so many things for me, and I in return would do the same. I would move mountains for them, light up the dark sky, and make sure peace is found. Our bonds make sure that an invisible contract no one ever agrees upon is made, a pact that states that no matter what, we would do anything for one another. This riddle was never about knowledge, it is a test to see exactly what kind of person you are and what lies in your heart.

"Well?" The giant hums as if noticing the change in my expression.

"I know the answer."

"Are you certain?" He raises his brows, and I nod.

If what I'm about to say is incorrect, then everything I've ever thought of my life and the people in it is wrong as well, because the love I feel for them is greater than anything in this world, and with that love comes the answer. "Sacrifice."

Chapter 35

The silence falls between us, heavy and suffocating, and I count every second passing. My magic tickles underneath my fingertips, warm tendrils of power coiling beneath my skin as if to let me know it's there if I need to use it. The sensation pulses gently. Though I'm certain of my answer, gods know if this is truly what the giant meant. I know this is how I see it, the meaning of his riddle, because with every word, a glimpse of my friends living happily ever after flashed before my eyes, all because I let myself fall before any of them could get harmed.

"You seem to be correct, Althea, and as I promised, I'll take you and your friends to the object you seek." I nearly faint upon hearing his words, my knees threatening to buckle beneath me. Relief floods through my veins, washing away the tension that had coiled in my shoulders. I glance behind at Ryo and Myra, who try to crack smiles but stay wary as the giant rises from his makeshift throne, causing the ground to tremble beneath our feet.

I nod in their direction, and the three of us follow Mirym down a set of steep steps leading downward in a tight spiral. There are no torches on the walls, no light pouring from worm made tunnels, just our eyes and hope that we will see just enough in this growing darkness. It's not easy making it down.

"That's it?" Ryo asks out loud, his hands looking for purchase before he jumps down. I arch a brow at him, the corner of my lips lifting without meaning to.

"What?" Myra asks before sliding down.

"I mean, I thought it would've been much harder, but a riddle and an answer and that's it?" He huffs, and I shake my head. Of course he expected more, an epic battle for sure because everything we came across so far threw us into instant fight, but giants aren't like this. They don't test your courage but the purity of your heart.

In the distance, a low rumble is heard as Mirym chuckles to himself. "Would you rather I test your fighting skills young man?"

I cover my mouth to stop myself from laughing when Ryo's face turns ashen.

"I—no, I'm absolutely fine sir! Thank you for letting us through, forget what I said." His head hangs low, and Myra and I exchange looks trying not to tease him further.

"Your heart is pure boy, more than your companions." Mirym mumbles to himself, and I scrunch my brows in confusion. Yes, I've killed before, I also carry a demon inside my body that had committed unimaginable things but what exactly has Myra done? "Don't let it get tainted. Don't let the temptation of war and honour cloud your mind. Being kind is far more honourable than shoving your weapon through another being."

These steps are twice our sizes but we manage as we climb down. I have to keep myself steady against the walls, my palms pressed flat against the ice-cold surface as the staircase grows darker. My fingers shake with excitement, my skin raising with goosebumps that have nothing to do with the freezing air. This is it, this is where I've wanted to end up for the longest time. This is where I wished to be whilst in the manor, whilst arguing with Lathai, whilst on the boat and in the cold wilderness, in the castle in Issac's arms, and sat between my friends. Our journey is halfway finished.

Ryo curses behind me as he slips on the ice for the third time, his boots scraping against the frozen surface, and Myra rolls her eyes before hooking their arms together.

"I thought you were meant to be scary and rude," Ryo whispers, his breath forming small clouds in the freezing air, and I stifle a giggle. Myra shoots him a look before smirking and dragging him more firmly onto the next step.

The boy momentarily loses balance, his free arm windmilling, but stays upright. "I am scary and rude. I don't know what makes you think otherwise."

Ryo thinks for a moment in silence, his brow furrowed, before opening his mouth again. "Because I've spent some time with you, and you're none of those things. You're rather nice actually, and if you stopped glaring at me like I've personally offended your ancestors, I would really consider having you as a friend."

Myra's cheeks flush a delicate shade of pink, and I look away, wanting to give her some privacy. I'm sure she hasn't allowed many people into her life, not since Issac, and although Ryo is younger than her, in elven years he's a bit older. He might act foolish sometimes, but that boy is a soldier, hardened by the world around us, mature to some extent. He's one of the only people I've met who still have hope, who still see the world in much better colours than me.

Ryo's heart is pure, foolish perhaps, but maybe that's what makes Myra's eyes sparkle just a little bit. The fact that someone doesn't recognise her for her reserved personality but the hidden motives behind her actions showing the person she truly is. Someone beside Issac has finally seen her.

"We're here." Mirym's voice rumbles through the narrow stairwell, and the three of us bunch together before his enormous figure. The space feels impossibly small with his towering presence filling it. We watch in fascination as he lifts his weathered cane and knocks on the massive door in three different places, once at the bottom, once in the middle, and once near the top, each knock producing a deep sound that echoes through the icy corridor.

Immediately, a soft glow begins to shine from within the ice itself, pulsing gently. Patterns of frost, delicate as spider silk and intricate as the ones you'd spot on your window on an early winter morning, start weaving themselves across the frozen surface. Snowflakes in shapes I've never seen, some resembling tiny stars, others like miniature flowers with countless petals, begin connecting at their tips with threads of bright blue light before expanding further into increasingly complex patterns. I watch, mesmerised, as they carve themselves into the hard surface without anybody's help, the ice seeming to flow like water under their influence. Magic, this door has been enchanted with ancient power that makes the very air around us hum with energy.

With a loud crack that echoes through the walls, something clicks into place, and the intricate patterns vanish as suddenly as they appeared, leaving only smooth ice. The door creaks open with a deep groaning sound that speaks of centuries undisturbed, the massive slab of ice shifting and sliding aside as though moved by invisible hands. I step forward, my eyes widening until they feel ready to burst from their sockets as the oldest treasury in existence is revealed before me.

The chamber beyond takes my breath away completely. Golden light spills forth from enchanted sources within, casting dancing shadows that seem to tell stories of their own. Mirym steps aside with surprising grace for his massive frame, and I venture into the cave, no, the sanctuary, filled with treasures that make my heart race with wonder.

Piles of gold coins shimmer, their surfaces worn smooth by countless hands over millennia. Timeless books bound in leather so old it appears almost black rest on ice shelves carved directly from the frozen walls, their spines marked with symbols in languages I've never come across. Weapons and armour crafted from materials I couldn't begin to name gleam with an otherworldly sheen, some appear to be forged from moonlight turned solid, others from what looks like solidified shadow.

Yellowing scrolls are scattered in careful piles in one corner, their edges brittle with age, and right beside them sit several wooden chests overflowing with clothes that shimmer like liquid silk, leather-bound notebooks with covers adorned in precious stones, and goblets made from metals that seem to shift colour in the flickering light. This place is history itself, a tomb of knowledge and wonder. It might hold answers as to who we truly are, how the gods came into existence, how we began existing, and it pains me that I don't have even a moment to spare to examine these treasures. To learn, to discover, to understand. I'm merely here for one thing and one thing only: the ritual.

"I sense it. The magic coming from the ritual. It's right behind that statue in a box." Jino's voice cuts through my awe, a sudden surprise given she hasn't spoken much in the past few hours. Her presence feels stronger here, as though the ancient magic in this place recognises her somehow. I don't bother questioning her as my feet drag across the smooth ice floor towards a statue that dominates the chamber's centre.

The carved figure depicts a woman of ethereal beauty, her face serene and timeless, cradling a baby in her arms with such tenderness that it makes my chest ache. The craftsmanship is beyond anything I've ever seen, every fold of her robes, every strand of hair, every delicate finger appears so lifelike I half-expect her to breathe. Surely enough, nestled at the statue's base, sits a ornate box made from wood so dark it seems to absorb light.

I reach for it slowly, my hands trembling as if afraid it might crumble at my very touch. The wood feels warm beneath my fingertips, humming with contained power. Once the brass latches click open, I lift the lid with the reverence one might show a holy relic. Inside, nestled in silk so fine it feels like touching air itself, lies the rolled scroll adorned with a black ribbon that seems to drink in the surrounding light.

My fingers hover just above it, and I can feel the magic radiating from the parchment. I'm curious enough to read it now, impatient enough to know how the time-worn words might taste on my lips, and tired enough to want all of this torment to finally be over. But I can't, not yet. Not here, not now.

"Hey." Myra's hand landing on my shoulder startles me from my trance, her touch grounding me back to reality. "Let's get going. We've got what we needed, and it's best we look for the rest of our group."

"Yes, of course." I nod, carefully lifting the scroll and securing it within my leather satchel, making sure it sits protected against my side. The weight of it feels both insignificant and monumentally heavy at the same time.

We move towards the door, my eyes scanning the treasury one final time, trying to remember every detail before it'll be sealed once again for centuries. Perhaps one day I might have a chance to return, to study these wonders properly, but not right now. Now we have to find our friends and complete what we started.

"Thank you," I whisper to Mirym as we pass his towering form and begin climbing the treacherous steps back towards the surface. My voice echoes in the narrow stairwell, sincere and heavy with gratitude. "I'll make sure this doesn't fall into the wrong hands."

"I trust you, Althea Starbane." His deep voice follows us up the spiral staircase, and those were the last words I heard from him before we left. The last time I thought to myself confidently that nothing could get in our way.

Chapter 36

The castle is bigger than I expected. We might have underestimated just how many corridors and doors we left unexplored and how lucky we got by finding the throne room so quickly. Now, however, we're lost inside a maze as we turn yet another corner, finding more doors.

"I can't do this anymore! I'm sick of seeing doors!" Ryo throws his arms in protest before moving to the first set.

"Better this than running into a monster," Myra adds as she pushes another door only to close it with a bang. "Could've asked for directions to the exit, Starbane."

"Yeah, I could've." I sigh as the door I open leads to yet another bedchamber. "But I've got a feeling we're close."

"I hope your feeling proves to be right," Myra murmurs before continuing her search.

I sigh and follow their lead. I have no clue just how long we've been stuck here, and what worries me is the fact that the more time we spend here, the less our chances of finding the others grow. We've been separated for hours at best, gods know where the wind took them. Perhaps they already made it to the surface.

"Issac?" A foolish attempt at cutting our search short. I know damn well these walls are too thick for the man to

hear me, yet I try.

"You wish he could answer you, do you not?" Jino laughs mockingly, and I roll my eyes. I've said it so many times, but I'll say it again. I hate having her inside my head and her being able to hear every thought and see every image when I don't keep my boundaries up. It's annoying beyond any reasonable explanation, and the only useful thing this connection proved to be is the fact I can speak to Issac—

"Wait, but he can answer you." A flicker of hope flashes through my eyes as I stop in place, letting Myra and Ryo explore the remaining rooms.

"And what makes you think I would help?" I can almost see her playing with the silken lengths of her black hair, bored expression on her face as she toys with my emotions.

"Because you want us out. I've got the ritual, and I won't make any progress if I don't find my friends, so tell me where he is." I demand, knowing too well how to play her games. She won't give anything up freely. You always have to bargain.

"Dear mortals, you are ever so tiring." The shuffling of her robes scratches against my brain in an oddly pleasant way, and then a click of the door. Silence. She's gone to check up on Issac.

I look back to Ryo and Myra, who are now standing at the end of the corridor. Both of them ready to give up. I share their feelings, we're wasting time here, and it's too late to go back to Mirym.

"I don't care. I can't do this again! It's always the same thing. A bed, a wardrobe, and that damn chandelier. If I see it one more ti—"

"What?" I cut Ryo off, my brows drawing together in confusion.

"Are you with us, Starbane? Have you looked into any of those rooms? They're exact replicas of one another." Myra sighs and crouches to drink water from her satchel. "I understand that the giants are very modest, but this is too much."

"No, that's not right." I spin around and run towards the first door, opening it wide and surely enough spotting what Ryo had said. A bed, wardrobe, and crystal chandelier. I run to the opposite side and notice the exact same thing. How have I missed it? Perhaps I was too focused on thinking ahead that I forgot to focus on the present.

These rooms aren't built to be the same, and even if they were, they're too perfectly matched. The same ripped bedding, scratches in identical spots, a missing crystal from the left side of the chandelier.

"What are you doing?" Myra calls out to me, but I'm too consumed by finding the culprit, the fault in this. It has to be something.

"Thea? These rooms have nothing that you might need. Well, besides the one at the very beginning. It has that creepy painting inside." Ryo scratches his head, and I turn to face him.

"Which room?" He points to one of the rooms we passed once we entered the corridor. This is it. This is where it's hiding. "Get ready; it might get nasty."

"What?" The two of them ask at the same time but don't hesitate when I call forth my magic, lighting my fists with pure, raw fire. Myra's water slides beside her, and Ryo's sword is raised high, his other hand resting inside the satchel with crystals.

I push the door open carefully, my eyes scanning the room

for things out of place, and quickly spotting the painting Ryo spoke about. It's a dark green canvas wrapped in a golden frame, with a creature sitting in the middle of it. At first glance, someone might mistake it for a monkey, but no, its tail is too long, its coat too dark and fluffy, almost resembling a lion's mane. A pair of leathery wings stick out of its back. Its long, taunting face bears yellow eyes and two crooked, pointy ears that twitch as though listening.

"Are you going to tell us what the hell is going on?" Myra barks, and I nod, raising my finger towards the painting.

"We've been tricked. This whole time we've been searching, we weren't looking at new places, we've been going in a loop."

"How?" Ryo swallows, crushing something in his palm I hope is a shield crystal.

"We've been put under illusion by this creature here. It's a Pooka." Right on cue, I fire a small shot at the painting, catching it ablaze, and whatever illusion held it in place begins to vanish. Smoke wraps around us, and I rush to catch my friends as the room transforms, perhaps the whole castle might.

"What the hell is a Pooka?!" Ryo shouts, waving his hand through the smoke. I fire up my fists more to bring some light as the darkness grows.

"A mischievous shape-shifting creature known for bringing both good and bad fortune. They can cast illusions as well." I explain, trying to stay focused. I've read about them before but never came across one. Gods know if they bite, but I hope not.

Suddenly, the darkness around us clears, and I let out a gasp because in that empty, neatly made bed lies a skeleton of a giant taken by time. The wardrobe that stood against the wall is now crushed into pieces on the floor, and the chandelier swings from left to right as the small black creature looks down on us with curiosity.

"So that was you." I acknowledge it, hoping it might bring us some of that good fortune the legends spoke about. The Pooka tilts its head, blinks twice, and then rips another jewel from the chandelier. "We don't want to hurt you, and we're not looking for trouble. We just want to find our friends." I explain, but the Pooka doesn't let its eyes wander too far.

I sigh and drop my fists, its head following my every movement. I draw my brows together in thought and look over at Myra and her water that is now standing taller than us, at Ryo who is wrapped in a crystal aura with his sword up. The Pooka doesn't listen because it's afraid. We're scaring it.

"Drop your weapons; get rid of your magic." I shake my flames away.

"What?" Myra lifts a brow at me, but one pleading look and her water goes back into her waterskin. Ryo swallows hard and with shaking hands puts his sword away.

"Will you help us now?" I ask again, and the Pooka blinks at me before slowly letting itself hang off the chandelier with one arm. Albris, please share your luck through this creature.

The Pooka begins to spin on the chandelier like it's a wheel, its other hand raising up, and suddenly stops, pointing behind me. "Thank you," I whisper and begin backing away.

"That's it?" Ryo questions, and I grab him by the collar, slowly pulling him with me. "Ow!"

"Are you that eager to fight it, little boy? Because if you want to, I'll be happy to leave you in the room with that creepy thing." Myra hisses, and once the three of us step out, she shuts the door closed.

Ryo wiggles out of my grasp and brushes his clothes clean as if invisible dirt clings to them. "You know what, I take it back. You are mean."

Myra giggles, and I join her shortly before my eyes look towards the end of the corridor where we stood not even ten minutes ago. There are no more corridors, no more doors, just a hole in the wall that seems to lead up. That's our exit.

"Come on."

We run straight into the staircase and begin slowly climbing. My heart beats faster with every step we take as my gut tells me our friends are somewhere close. They have to be.

"You might be right, or wrong," Jino interrupts.

"Where is he?" I ask and look down to avoid any cracked steps. Wouldn't want to fall now.

"It's hard to tell when both of you are stuck in an ice cave." She huffs, displeased. *"All I saw was water. Might be somewhere nearby, might not be. Who knows?"*

I roll my eyes, she's as helpful as ever, but still, that's a clue. But why water? Why would Issac and the rest of them jump into water that could freeze them all?

My stomach twists at the thought they could be hiding from danger. There's not a single healer with them, nobody who could warm them up, and if we don't show up soon enough, they'll freeze to death.

As soon as we step out of the staircase, I don't think where I'm going, I just let my feet carry me along the ice tunnels. There's no branching of the tunnel, no bright light seeping from above made by the worms. There's nothing here that could help me as I run and run ahead. My breaths unsteady, my heart beating too painfully, my head swarmed with worries.

Where are they? Where could they possibly be?

"Thea, slow down!" I hear someone call behind me, but my body moves faster than my thoughts can process. I don't want to waste any more time, we might have minutes, seconds even before something bad could happen.

Fuck, what do I do? What can I possibly do to find them here?

I come to a halt once the tunnel begins to split into two. Not again, gods please.

"What the hell, Starbane?" Myra is out of breath as she catches up to me, Ryo following shortly after. I clench my jaw, looking from left to right, trying to make the correct choice. "What's gotten into you?"

"We have to find them, now. We don't have time, and I can't explain." I look at her, and something in my eyes must terrify her because she quickly gets back up and looks around the walls.

"I've never tried this, so bear with me a moment." I watch as Myra's hand lands on the frozen wall, her fingers spreading across it and her eyes close. Something beneath her fingertips glows, her magic embedding itself into the ice, and suddenly—

"Bloody hell," Ryo whispers as the ice around us glows bright blue, tiny vein-like streaks spreading all over the surface. I look in awe as they travel beyond my sight. Right, Myra's power is water, and ice, after all, once was just that. She's far more aware of her abilities than I am and can do much greater things than I could ever imagine.

That makes me wonder just how much I have left to learn about my own power, just what exactly is my limit? Can Issac surpass himself, or has he already reached his potential? Will we ever have enough time to learn?

The light vanishes, and Myra pulls her hand away from the ice, her eyes shining deep blue before returning to their original colour. "I found them."

We follow the girl down the left corridor, our footsteps rushed, our breaths echoing against the walls.

"I didn't—know—you—can do—something—so—brilliant," Ryo speaks between stolen breaths.

Myra smirks before turning to face him. "You don't know a lot about me, kid."

"Hey! I'm not a kid; I'm older than you." The boy huffs and speeds up so that the three of us run beside each other. "And I wouldn't mind finding out what other impressive things you're hiding."

Myra looks at Ryo, something in her expression softening as she fights off a smile. I almost want to join her, almost want to be happy with them, when suddenly I feel my footing become unsteady. The surface beneath my foot shakes and crumbles away, the ice is gone.

Time slows as we stare at each other, my breath trapped inside my lungs, my hands reaching for Ryo and Myra. But not everything is how we want it, because if it were, I would turn back time. I would slow down and tread more carefully around the unknown surface. I would be more in charge of my head and less focused on following my heart. But I don't possess such powers, because life isn't fair, and now the only thing I can do is pray. Pray that we're going to be all right. Pray that I haven't made the wrong choices. Pray that this wasn't all for nothing, and pray that we weren't high enough to shatter our bones and die when we reach the bottom.

Chapter 37

W*ake up.* An angel, I think. An angel's calling to me. Her long hair brushes over my cheeks.

Wake up. Wake up. Wake up. She screams, and I reach my hand towards the bright light. Reach out towards this angel who's so desperate for me to awaken.

Wake up.

Why? Why can't I just stay here—

WAKE UP.

I gasp and my eyes snap open, consciousness hitting me. My body shivers, and my head throbs. Everything around me swims in thick fog. I cough violently. Harsh, wet sounds that scrape my throat. My lungs burn with liquid, my clothes clinging to me.

We fell.

The memory hits me hard. I blink, trying to clear my vision as I search for Ryo and Myra. Are they all right? Are they dead?

"Breathe." Someone says, rubbing circles on my back, but I'm too focused on finding my friends to care. I crawl away, my nails digging into the snow, my body fighting me, but I push through because I need to know they're safe.

My vision slowly returns. I'm inside a cave. A massive one

with light reflecting off the high ceiling from water below. I look up and spot the jagged hole we must have fallen through. Somehow, we survived.

I raise to my feet and look around, nearly losing self control when I spot Ryo and Myra. They sit on a rock, arms wrapped around themselves, shivering. Relief floods through me so hard I almost fall. I throw myself at them, wrapping my arms around their necks.

"Ouch! If the fall won't cripple me, you certainly will, Starbane," Myra grumbles, but she hugs me back tight.

"You're both alive." I whisper, my eyes shut. The relief is overwhelming. Knowing they're safe, that I haven't lost them. Nothing has ever felt this good.

"And so are we, if you care." A familiar voice makes me look up. There, stand Alea, Jassin, Venali, Ella, John, Theo, and—

My heart stops.

Issac.

I get up on shaky legs, looking at each of their faces to make sure they're well. Everyone smiles at me with relief. Everyone except him. Issac sits apart, distant and broken. His crimson eyes meet mine for just a moment before he looks away, terror and pain flashing through them before he hides it all behind forced concern.

Something sharp twists in my chest. He isn't standing with them, hasn't come to me, hasn't even said my name. The space between us feels huge, filled with things I don't understand. Every part of me wants to go to him, but I stop myself. We promised. No more games, no more lies.

I assess him quickly trying to figure out if he's hurt but Issac sits still, the only thing odd is his clothes being wet. Is this the water Jino mentioned? What happened?

My muscles squeeze as I fight against my body to walk towards him, to have him near me. But I can't, I can't do this again. I can't force myself at him, can't plead for answers. Issac isn't hurt, if he wanted to he would've been here by my side but something's different. Did he forget me once more? Did his urge to kill me reappear? Why isn't he saying anything? Why is he avoiding my eyes?

"Thea, the ritual. Did it get wet?" Myra calls for me, and I'm suddenly reminded of the piece of paper inside my satchel. I ignore the nagging thoughts about Issac and pull out the ritual. The paper slightly damp.

I look around at everyone. Some are wet from head to toe, others completely dry. Just what did they get up while we got separated?

"I hope nobody minds if I warm us up?"

"By all means, I'm freezing!" Ella shivers in her damp fur coat. Myra rushes to her immediately, pulling her into a hug whilst Ryo runs to Venali and Jassin, who ruffle his hair with fond smiles. I guess they've rested enough.

I hold out my palms and reach for my magic. The power flows through me as I carefully raise the temperature. Not too much. I can't risk burning the ritual. Warm air fills the space around us, and everyone sighs with relief as the bone-deep cold finally starts to fade. Theo is the first to approach, his lips curved into a smile, but his brows drawn together.

"What happened?" I sign, and he sighs.

"I think it's best if you ask Alea. Too many words." He rolls his eyes, and I smile. "You found it then?"

I nod and look behind the man to his sister, who reaches for me and pulls me into a tight embrace. I've never expected to get this close to Desily's girlfriend, to my former teacher, yet here we are, and I wouldn't change a single thing.

"I'm glad you're safe." She hugs me tighter, and I chuckle.

"Me too. What happened to you?" I bring my voice lower before speaking the next sentence. "What happened to Issac?"

Alea glances back at the man lost in his thoughts. It's almost as if he's not aware of sharing the space with us, almost as if his thoughts are far more important than anything else, and my worry begins to grow.

"When we got separated and the cave entrance collapsed, we had to keep moving forward," she explains. "We walked and walked, ran into a couple of monsters, but nothing special. It was about half an hour ago when we stumbled across this cave purely by accident. Ella slipped on some ice and pushed Venali, me, and Issac into the water. We wouldn't care much if not for—" She cuts herself off, and I dart my eyes between the man I love and the girl I acknowledge as my friend.

"What, Alea? What happened?"

"They fell into the purest water of Sebraycia." Ella joins us, and I stare at her, hoping she'd explain just exactly what the fuck I'm missing. "I thought it was a legend. I was sure of it, but it seems not to be."

"What does the water do?" I push, my fists shaking at my sides. I give myself exactly twenty seconds before I disregard all my previous thoughts about giving Issac space and let my legs take me to him. I need to make sure he's all right, that we are all right.

"It clears any enchantment put upon you. Any curse, any magic holding onto you from the past. It used to be told as a legend amongst giants. The magic water that you have to cross in order to meet the giant king, as only the ones with pure intentions and without any hidden motives could seek his audience."

I swallow hard, my eyes now locked on Issac, who seems to be going mad with each second passing. He sits on a rock with his head between his hands, rocking back and forth.

"Lord Graham's brainwashing—"

"Is gone. Issac's no longer bound to it. He no longer has to serve the Grahams." Ella explains, and the colour drains from my face. "Is that not good news?"

No, I want to tell her. No, it's not, because if Issac's no longer prisoner to his own mind and no longer has to unwillingly forget his past, that means everything that's ever happened to him came crashing at once. Issac is overwhelmed with memories.

I run to him, crossing the distance between us within seconds. I drop to my knees and reach for his ice-cold hands. He peeks at me from underneath his fringe, his crimson eyes full of unshed tears and devastation so raw it steals the breath from my lungs. My heart doesn't just break. It shatters into a thousand pieces, each shard cutting deeper than the last.

"Issac," I whisper his name.

"I remember."

I wrap my arms around his shoulders and pull him closer, and he crumbles. Completely, utterly crumbles. I feel his body shake under my touch, and feel my own heart squeeze when he doesn't return the gesture. When he just lets his body slump over mine with his hands gripping tightly onto his kneecaps.

I feel his shoulders shake with held-back sobs, his breath

coming in ragged gasps against my neck. My fingers run through his dark hair, tangling in the silken strands as my chin rests on his shoulder. I give him this moment of silence, this sanctuary of touch, because words feel too small, too fragile for the weight of his pain.

"I can't stand this, Thea. I can't. I remember it all, everything." His voice breaks on the words, raw and guttural, as if each memory is a physical wound being torn open. His grip tightens, his knuckles turning white and I know with certainty his knees will be bruised.

"It's all right, Issac. I'm here." I press my lips to his temple, tasting salt and desperation. "I'm here, and I'm not going anywhere."

"No, it's not all right." He pulls back just enough to look at me, and the anguish in his eyes nearly destroys me. Tears finally spill over, tracking down his pale cheeks. "I remember everything Thea."

"Issac, I know—"

"No. You don't understand. I remember everything. *Everything.*" He repeats as if that's meant to mean something to me, as if I should understand but I don't. The last word makes him choke. He coughs for a bit and then moves away just enough to put a space between us and dig the claws of uncertainty into my heart making it slowly bleed.

"I—" Words are desperately trying to form on my lips but nothing comes out. I don't know what to say. I have no clue how to comfort him and if there even is a way to do so. What could I possibly say? I'm sorry that your life was stolen from you? That you went through torture? That you became a slave? That they made you kill magical creatures and humans alike?

"I remember the torture, the hatred towards you, the way I spoke to you, the way I treated you, and things I can't even begin to explain. I can't stop seeing it. I can't stop replaying it in my head." His hands finally abandon his kneecaps and now find their purchase at his temples. Thumbs digging into the flesh as if Issac truly believes he can rid himself of those memories if he tries hard enough. "I did so many horrible things, so many lives lost. Gods you'll never forgive me. How could anyone ever forgive me. I wanted to hurt you, Thea. I did hurt you. The things I thought, the things I—" A broken sound escapes him, somewhere between a sob and a growl of self-loathing. I bite on my lip and chew at it hard enough to draw blood. Seeing Issac in his state is horrible. It's a torture because I can't comprehend what he's going through. All I can do to ease his mind is provide reassurance.

"Just talk to me Issac, tell me what's going on?" I plead, my hand reaching towards him only to have Issac jerk away.

"No, no, I can't. I can't tell you Thea. You won't forgive me, you won't believe me. You won't understand." He mumbles out, and I stare at him with eyes wide open and heart hammering inside my chest.

"But I've seen the worst of you. I've also seen the best and I haven't left so why won't you just say it? Why are you so adamant at keeping things I know a secret?" Issac stops shaking, and for a moment I truly believe he's going to look me in the eyes with understanding and say exactly what is crushing his soul at this very moment.

But instead I see fear. Raw fear taking control of Issac's mind as he stares at me. But fear isn't the only emotion I see flashing past his eyes. Regret, terror and the utter acceptance of helplessness before he speaks again. "Because if I do say those things aloud you'll never forgive me and the guilt will eat me away, but perhaps that's what I deserve. To rot away."

"No, we're not doing this again Issac. We forgave each other already. Don't you remember? Back in the manor we've spoken about this. I don't hate you, I could never so why—"

I yelp as he grasps my shoulders bringing me closer to his face. My heart aches to feel the warmth of his smile, the joy from his laughter, the love in his eyes but instead I get despair. He slowly lowers his forehead to mine, and that's the first time a sob pushes past my lips as if my body is telling me it's over. We're over.

"Those past few months," he begins and I can't stop the tears from rolling down my cheeks. "I've been the happiest since we were kids. I haven't remembered the past, and so I lived in the moment. I lived with you Thea."

"Then let's just continue living this way." Begging is my last resort to stop whatever's happening. Issac shakes his head, his eyes opening to meet mine.

"We can't, you don't understand Thea and I'd never forgive myself for letting you live this dream, this illusion masked by lies." His hand finally lands on my cheek, wiping the lost tears away.

"Just talk to me then. Just tell me Issac, please." My throat hurts as if I'd swallowed pins, scratching and burning every time I swallow.

"I can't. Not now, when I barely can understand any of this myself, when we're at war. I can't do this to you Thea, I could never after everything I—" His eyes close once again, his throat bobbing as he forces himself to finish speaking. "I already can't live with myself, and the idea of you hating me at this very moment scares the shit out of me. I'm a selfish coward, I'm so afraid of losing you that I'd rather hide the truth than let us face it."

"What? What truth? Issac I know everything, I understand it all—"

"You don't." He cuts me off, his voice serious. He places a kiss on my forehead before shuffling away. "I have no right to say this, but I hope when the time comes you'll try to understand."

With my mouth slightly agape I watch as Issac gets up from the rock, and deeply inhales as if his words were final, as if we came to some decision when I'm still lost and confused and my heart's beating too fast and my thoughts are too messy and my blood feels like fire and my tears are far too warm far too quick as they bounce off my palm.

"I think it's best if you leave me alone for a bit. I want to give you the best I can Thea, I want to be that person you dream of me becoming and to achieve that I need to collect my thoughts and make myself understand that even if I might lose you, the truth will set us both free. It's what's best for us, for you." I want to scream at him that he's wrong, that I don't understand, that we should do this together but the past few months made me into someone else. I'm no longer desperate for his feelings only, I understand now there's more besides us, there are people in my life I care about, and our personal matters can wait because I'm trying to save this entire world, not just Issac. I won't push for explanation and truth he so heavily guards anymore. If it's time he needs, then I'll give it to him because that won't run out anytime soon. We've survived worse, we'll survive this as well.

Issac glances at me, sadness taking over his features

twisting his lips into a pained grimace. "I don't want to lose you Thea but I'm done being a coward. I'm done living a lie and Gods help me if it isn't you who deserves peace the most. I'm done playing games so please can you do that for me, love? Can you wait for me to fix this fucked up head of mine and face you like a real man?"

I don't let my lips part afraid if they do I might beg him to stay. Heart contradicting my mind so instead I nod, watching him slowly make his way towards Theo no longer as Issac from the manor, or the cold blooded soldier, or the version of him I've had on Sebraycia but a cross between a stranger and someone familiar, someone who I knew once upon a time, someone who didn't get to live his life. The Issac that died trying to protect his home is back. *My* Issac is finally free but at what cost.

Chapter 38

I reach Ella, Myra, John and Alea, who seem to be deep in conversation. None of them dare to ask what happened between Issac and me. As soon as he started to freak out I noticed them moving behind a thick wall of ice, one by one, to give us privacy though I'm sure they still heard most of it in this small space. Theo and Issac had climbed up through the opening they fell from and disappeared from our eyes. Whatever it is they're discussing or not, I hope it'll somehow ease Issac's mind. Theo's his best friend. Perhaps he might help him more than I could.

I turn my head to spot Venali, Jassin, and Ryo approach, and I'm almost surprised to see them smiling. Ryo just does that to people. He cracks their shell no matter how hard they might seem.

"I think we should try going back up. The exit has to be somewhere." Alea throws out an idea just as I stop.

"Yeah, but I think you're forgetting about the worms, confusing tunnels, and the walk we did to get here." Myra scoffs, her arms crossed over her chest. Alea looks her over, words ready to roll off her tongue, and I know if I don't step in now, a fight might break out. We're all tired and hungry. We don't need to be divided as well.

"What if Myra uses her magic to find an exit? You did it earlier, right?" I suggest, and everyone turns to stare at me.

"What?" Ella blinks at her friend.

"She did! We saw her, and it was brilliant. The wall lit up and everything." Ryo gestures with his hands, trying to paint an invisible image, but only Myra and I seem to get his vision. The girl blushes before clearing her throat to speak.

"I could try, but as I said, it was my first attempt, and it nearly cost us our lives. I don't know where we're going to end up." She scratches her neck, but everyone awaits her approval. She's our only hope at getting out of this labyrinth quickly, and if any danger awaits outside this cave, we're all prepared to fight. "Fine, I'll have a look, but don't distract me!"

We watch as she walks away, and I turn to Alea, who stares over at the water, deep in thought. I tap her on the shoulder, trying to get her attention.

"Thea, you're all right?" She asks, and I put on a smile that doesn't reach my eyes. I can't bring myself to pretend my heart didn't just shatter, and my mind isn't racing with unanswered questions.

I part my lips but the same stubborn bulge shows up in my throat pushing tears to my eyes. "Oh Thea, come here." Alea wraps me in a tight hug and I let my head fall on her shoulder noticing just how gentle her hug is despite me knowing that under the pile of clothes hide hard muscles from years of tough training. "He'll come around, he always has."

"I know but it hurts." I whimper trying not to break down. It feels wrong to cry over him when our lives are in danger but at the same time it feels right after what I've just lost. Happiness was snatched away from me once again without warning and I am forced to pretend it's fine for the sake of others. Though I understand the unfairness of this all I have to wait until we reach the manor to let myself break completely. Can't do it now, not when they need me.

"I know, but at least I'm glad he's finally free." She rubs my back and I scoff. Free, whatever that means these days. Still I wipe the few stray tears with my sleeve and smile at her with gratitude.

"Me too." I reply back before reaching into my satchel. "Here, keep it. I trust you and your brother with it more than I trust myself."

I pass her the ritual, and her eyes grow three sizes bigger as she gently picks it from my palm.

"Are you sure, Thea?" She blinks at me shocked because Alea, always in the shadow of Theo could never imagine being trusted with something so important. Until now.

"You deserve it Alea, and I owe it to you and Theo after all so hold onto it until we're out." Alea nods her head in a kind manner, but I know to her it means a great deal. It's a way of me telling her she's just as important as her brother, that I trust her, and that nothing will change it.

"Right, I think I have an idea. Let's go." Myra shakes her hands to bring some warmth before moving to the only entrance the cave has. I look up and spot Issac and Theo standing in grim silence. Issac's face is paler than when he left me, covered in droplets of sweat, and not once does he look at me.

Ryo bumps his hip into my side, and I nearly stumble forward. "Come on, boss, we've got a lot to do."

"Oh, look who's not scared anymore." I push him jokingly before following the crowd. It's either laugh or cry, and I'm done crying for now. Ryo's company is exactly what I need at this moment.

Myra is leading our group out, and I watch as Ryo's eyes don't leave her even for a moment as she chats quietly with Ella.

"You'll burn holes into the poor girl." I tease, climbing up the small arch. "Just talk to her, Ryo, she won't bite."

The boy swallows hard, his eyes blinking at me as if I'd lost my mind. "No, I'm worried she'd do worse."

"Myra's not that scary. You said it yourself." I grab onto his hand as we reach the top and follow everyone into the tunnel they originally came from.

"Yeah, but she's too good for me. Too put together." He sighs and kicks an invisible rock, his shoulders slouching in defeat.

I ruffle his white locks before pulling him under my arm. "You don't know that, and you know why that is?" He arches a brow at me. "Because you don't know her, and she doesn't know you. This is all just a front, a mask put in front of others. We all wear them, let's be honest, but what's underneath. That's what matters."

"Do you wear one? When you're with me?" He asks suddenly, and I draw my brows together. What answer should I give him? Should I say I pretend to be strong and know everything when in reality I'm afraid I'll lose them? That I can't bear to think I'd be the reason for their death? It's so hard to be myself around them when all I see in their eyes is hope, and the only person who truly knows me can't even look me into mine.

"I do. Sometimes I have to, but not right now." I give him half a smile, and Ryo returns it.

"You don't have to hide around me. I'd like you even if you were a cave goblin." He whispers, and I elbow him to the side, laughing.

My head turns back to Venali and Jassin, who are smiling at each other, surely talking about their plans once we reach the castle. I'm happy to see they survived, that their bond wasn't damaged by some unimaginable evil, because losing someone, a sibling especially, is like losing half of your soul. Perhaps that's why I fought so hard at the manor to make sure Alea and Theo won't die. Why I made sure neither of them has to say goodbye.

The two of them are further in front of me, following after Myra in a hushed conversation. I catch the girl smiling as her brother signs something I can't quite see. Everyone's fine, well, to some extent.

Issac is walking in front of them, with Ella and Myra at the front of our group. His head's hung low, mind miles away. Part of me wishes to enter his thoughts, to use the connection between us to find out just what scared him so badly, what is it that he's hiding but I don't. He remembered beforehand about the torture, about the brainwashing and his horrible behaviour, so why, I keep asking myself, is he acting like this?

I remember he told me before that the nightmares of Lord Graham's torture won't leave him, so it can't be that. It must be something else, and I find it hard to believe that even after my reassurance, he's still scared he'll lose me. Whatever skeletons fell out of his closet, are worse than the ones I know of. Yet, I can't force time to heal this invisible wound. When Issac's ready, he'll talk, even if it's something we've already touched upon. I'm sure he'll reach out.

We turn a corner and come to a much more spacious cave, one with many holes drilled into the ice, and I'm glad Myra has the ability to find our route because this is too much. Hundreds of possibilities leading to gods know where and the darkness doesn't help, but at this point we're used to it and I'm far too exhausted to create a fire ball to make it brighter. Better save my energy for something worse.

I scan our group once again, counting nine of us when there were ten when we entered.

"What?" Ryo catches onto the confused look in my eyes as I count each person on my fingers stopping in my tracks.

"Where's John?"

Everything happens so quickly I barely have time to register as shadows explode from every direction, swarming us into a suffocating circle. A strange cloud of smoke releases before I have a chance to think of my next move and wraps around us. Terror claws up my throat as I feel my body tense, my magic prickling desperately under my fingers, but even as I push and beg for its release, nothing happens.

I crash to the ground, my body suddenly frozen, and look over at Ryo who's staring at me with the same look of pure, helpless terror in his eyes.

Then I hear footsteps. Slow, predatory. I force my eyes up to spot Venali and Jassin looking lost and confused. Their swords are raised, their backs pressed together, but nothing could prepare them for the sudden attack from above. A spike wrapped in shadows. One from the top, one from the right, one from the left.

Their bodies fall with sickening thuds that echo through my soul.

Their swords clang as they hit the ground. Crimson liquid

spilling everywhere, racing towards me as if I'm its vessel.

Lifeless eyes stare right at me. Asking, wondering. What happened? What happened, Thea? Why did you let us die?

I grunt, the first sound I manage to make before someone grabs me by the shoulders and begins dragging me into one of the tunnels. My heart's hammering against my ribs, my legs are made of cotton, and my blood turns to ice as I realise we're being taken away. We're being kidnapped.

"General will be so pleased we finally caught you, Althea Starbane." Someone whispers, their voice dripping with poison, and I look back to Ryo who's now being picked up by no one else but John. I feel myself shaking despite the paralysis, I feel my bones rattle, my jaw clench, my head ready to explode.

Traitor. Fucking traitor.

"Him? Oh, he was just a gift from our mutual friend." The person whispers into my ear, and bile rises in my throat when I note their pristine, white armour. Elven soldiers.

A shiver runs down my spine and I force myself not to vomit as fear wraps around my stomach, digs its claws into my abdomen and begins to feast on my insides. "Aagon was too kind."

I panic. Pure, white-hot panic floods through me. I forget how to breathe. I stare at my friends still walking, still too deep in conversation to notice the slaughter behind them. My eyes lock on Issac.

"Issac!" I scream through our connection, my voice breaking but the silence that greets me is deafening. *"Jino! Call him, tell him!"*

I scream and scream and scream so damn hard that even the voice inside my head goes dry. *"Issac! Turn around, please just turn around. PLEASE!"*

Tears stream down my face in rivers, and I hear the soldier laugh. A sound mocking my attempts because he knows my sheer will can't do anything. He knows I'm powerless, but I can't accept that reality. I can't accept the fact Venali and Jassin are dead, their blood still warm on the ground. That Ryo and I are in enemy hands being dragged away because of someone we thought we could trust. I can't accept the fact I might not see any of them ever again, and they'll never know where I am.

Desily.

Oh Desily. Forgive me.

"Anybody, please help." I force out one more time through the connection I share with Issac and Jino, pouring every fragment of my breaking heart into those words, but without any results. The cave entrance becomes more distant with each dragging step, their silhouettes shrinking until they're nothing but shadows, and all I can beg for right now is that they'll survive. They won't die. That Ryo won't pay for my mistakes, for my foolishness.

I believed them all for a second when they looked at me with hope that we could truly rebuild what we'd lost, but I let myself forget that we live in times of war. That not every person who looks your way is your friend. That even if you're immortal, your time can still run out. Because when you have someone dear in your life, that person becomes someone who determines your own time. Time you've spent with these people, and for me…

The time has run out.

Acknowledgments

I want to thank my boyfriend, once again, for helping my dreams come true. You are my biggest supporter, and I will never forget that. I hope you get invested in Book Two as much as you got into Book One.

I send the biggest thank you to Wendy, who once again spent hours editing my book and put a smile on my face with countless questions about what's to come next.

Thank you to Alex, for being my number one reader. It was you who truly made me want to get this story finished, and now I will do my best to complete the series faster so that you don't have to wait so long.

Thank you to my family for purchasing the book, though they can't read English. Your love and support mean more to me than anything.

To all my friends who were first in line to get their hands on Book One—you made me the happiest person ever, and I hope I won't disappoint you with what's to come!

To every other reader who decided to pick up Book One and stay, I want to thank you for your support and time. It means the world to me to have you discover this story and live the lives of these characters. I hope you stay here for the long ride ahead, because Book Three is about to be a roller coaster!

About the Author

D.E. Ciolak is a debut novelist whose passion for storytelling began in the small room she shared with her sister while living in Poland. What started as late-night writing sessions bringing her imagination to life has blossomed into her first novel, a testament to the power of persistent dreaming.

A graduate of creative writing course in Birkbeck, University of London, she has always been fascinated by the ways stories can transform our understanding of ourselves and the world around us. This novel represents years of careful writing, countless drafts, and the unwavering support of writing groups, beta readers, and her closest friends and family.

When not writing, she can be found hunting for new fantasy books that might inspire her own writing and reading unhealthy amount of fan fictions/manhwas.

Connect with her on Social Media!

TikTok:@d.e.ciolak

Instagram:@d.e.ciolak

Goodreads:D.E Ciolak

Also by D.E. Ciolak

Serenade of Shadows

In a world of brutal oppression, Thea's extraordinary journey begins with an impossible act of love. On her eighteenth birthday, she drowns while saving her best friend Issac—and then inexplicably returns to life, defying the very laws of nature.

Torn apart by violent elven attackers, Thea and Issac are separated with only a promise of reunion. For a hundred years, she searches relentlessly, her immortality transforming from a mysterious gift to an endless burden. Each decade becomes another step in a seemingly futile quest to find the one person who truly means everything to her.

Just as she prepares to surrender hope, a dangerous elven ex-general named Lathai reveals a shocking truth: her immortality threatens to unravel the world. Ancient forces are awakening, drawn by her unprecedented existence.

Now Thea must choose between reuniting with Issac or sacrificing him to prevent a catastrophic destruction that could annihilate countless lives.

www.ingramcontent.com/pod-product-compliance
Lightning Source LLC
LaVergne TN
LVHW050913080826
845145LV00001B/72

* 9 7 8 1 0 3 6 9 5 2 3 6 5 *